PRAISE FOR THE NOVELS
OF JOANN ROSS

One Summer

"Ross has a wonderful knack for creating a story so lovely that readers want to stay immersed in it forever. *One Summer* pulls readers into the wonderful world of Shelter Bay and holds them close, like family." —*Romantic Times*

The Homecoming

"Family and passion [are] Ms. Ross's trademark[s]. . . . Filled with captivating characters, humor, and an enduring love story." —Fresh Fiction

"Race to Shelter Bay as fast as possible. You won't be disappointed." —Once Upon a Romance

"A charming story of family, old friendships, and new love. . . . I eagerly await the next Shelter Bay novel." —Joyfully Reviewed

"One of the best books I've read this summer. . . . Ms. Ross penned such emotion into her story line and created characters that you easily fall in love with." —Night Owl Romance

"The Oregon coast has no better publicist than JoAnn Ross, and starting over can be as invigorating as a breeze coming off the ocean bringing the love of our life." —Bookreporter.com

"It isn't often readers find characters they're willing to spend a weekend with. However, that's exactly what Ross accomplishes . . . enveloping the reader in the lives of two endearing, albeit flawed, characters . . . an entertaining stay in Shelter Bay." —*Romantic Times*

Breakpoint

"This is probably the best book I've read this early summer. This hot novel has everything a reader might want in romantic suspense, from sexy, complex characters, to a fascinating setting and intense intimacy." —The Romance Readers Connection

continued . . .

"Richly drawn characters, a powerful story, and a heart-stopping ending." —Fresh Fiction

Blaze

"Seamlessly plotted. . . . Ross keeps the heat on right to the last page." —*Publishers Weekly*

"Dynamic . . . fast-paced, utterly engrossing." —Romance Reviews Today

Out of the Storm

"*Out of the Storm* sizzles! A captivating and entertaining blend of romance, mystery, and suspense." —Romance Reviews Today

Out of the Blue

"[An] adventurous, exhilarating story. Danger and intrigue are a constant presence. Highly passionate . . . outstanding." —Romance Junkies

"The best kind of romantic suspense: heart-stopping terror and a heart-tugging romance." —Romance Reviews Today

River Road

"Skillful and satisfying. . . . With its emotional depth, Ross's tale will appeal to Nora Roberts fans." —*Booklist*

"The romance . . . crackles and the verbal sparring keeps the narrative moving along at an energetic clip . . . delightful." —*Publishers Weekly*

Confessions

"[A] hot, steamy . . . page-turner." —A Little Romance

"Touches of humor nicely relieve the suspenseful nature of the intriguing and intricately plotted tale. Bravo!" —*The Paperback Forum*

Also by JoAnn Ross

Shelter Bay Novels
The Homecoming

One Summer

High Risk Novels
Freefall

Crossfire

Shattered

Breakpoint

ON LAVENDER LANE

A Shelter Bay Novel

JoAnn Ross

A SIGNET BOOK

SIGNET
Published by New American Library, a division of
Penguin Group (USA) Inc., 375 Hudson Street,
New York, New York 10014, USA
Penguin Group (Canada), 90 Eglinton Avenue East, Suite 700, Toronto,
Ontario M4P 2Y3, Canada (a division of Pearson Penguin Canada Inc.)
Penguin Books Ltd., 80 Strand, London WC2R 0RL, England
Penguin Ireland, 25 St. Stephen's Green, Dublin 2,
Ireland (a division of Penguin Books Ltd.)
Penguin Group (Australia), 250 Camberwell Road, Camberwell, Victoria 3124,
Australia (a division of Pearson Australia Group Pty. Ltd.)
Penguin Books India Pvt. Ltd., 11 Community Centre, Panchsheel Park,
New Delhi - 110 017, India
Penguin Group (NZ), 67 Apollo Drive, Rosedale, Auckland 0632,
New Zealand (a division of Pearson New Zealand Ltd.)
Penguin Books (South Africa) (Pty.) Ltd., 24 Sturdee Avenue,
Rosebank, Johannesburg 2196, South Africa

Penguin Books Ltd., Registered Offices:
80 Strand, London WC2R 0RL, England

First published by Signet, an imprint of New American Library,
a division of Penguin Group (USA) Inc.

ISBN 978-1-61793-397-4

Again, to all the men and women of the U.S. military—
and their families—for their service and sacrifice.

To the Ladies of Orcas Ridge, for the warm
welcome and fun lunches.

And, as always, to Jay—who once bought me a bag of
saltwater taffy at the Oregon coast, where Shelter Bay is
set, then proposed.
Here's to many more years of memorable
beach days together.

ACKNOWLEDGMENTS

As always, with heartfelt appreciation to my fabulous agent and cheerleader, Robin Rue. And her assistant, detail goddess Beth Miller.

Again, with thanks to the supersupportive team at NAL, who make writing such a joy. Between moving back to my beloved Pacific Northwest and coming home to my first publisher, my life is now pretty much perfect.

With gratitude to Paul Janovsky, for creating such beautiful watercolor art for *One Summer* and *On Lavender Lane*. And who (yay!) has signed on for future Shelter Bay covers.

And last but definitely not least, I was remiss in not acknowledging our own dear Shadow, eldest brother of our three current rescued dogs, and the model for Marine photojournalist Gabriel St. James' dog in *One Summer*. As Gabe learned, rescues rule!

1

Madeline Durand was braising short ribs in an Omaha department store when her husband's sex video went viral.

The day, which would go down as one of the worst in her life, hadn't exactly begun on a high note. Her early-morning flight from New York was delayed for three hours because of a late-spring storm that had barreled into Nebraska, bringing with it tree-bending winds, snow, and ice.

Lots and lots of ice.

On the plus side, when she finally did arrive in Omaha, she was greeted by a sixtysomething woman wearing a puffy down coat the same color as her weather-chapped cheeks, and a red knit hat pulled down over salt-and-pepper hair. Her down-to-earth midwestern friendliness gave Madeline hope that her luck may have taken a turn for the better.

"Hi, Chef Madeline! I'm Birdy Hinlemeir," she said enthusiastically, pulling off a red and white striped mitten and thrusting out her hand. "Head of the store's special events department. We're all so excited about hosting your cooking demonstration today."

"I'm happy to be here." Which was the absolute truth. After holding her breath while the pilot landed in what appeared to be near whiteout conditions, Madeline was infinitely grateful to be back on solid ground.

"Sorry about the weather," Birdy said as they walked

out into air thick with swirling white flakes. "We tend to have four seasons here: almost winter, winter, still winter, and wow, this has gotta be the hottest summer ever!"

"I take it we're in 'still winter.'" Madeline sucked in a breath as a freezing mix of snow and sleet pelted her face.

"Yep. We don't tend to get snow this late, but the weather's been really strange the past couple years. I guess Mother Nature had one more storm up her sleeve."

"You needn't apologize. Fortunately, I won't be cooking outdoors."

"Oh, the store will definitely be warm enough," the older woman assured her. "Your dish for the finished part of the demonstration arrived this morning, all packed in dry ice, so my assistant's heating it up for you."

"I appreciate that." Short ribs took three hours in the oven, so, following Julia Child's motto that a few simple steps ahead of time could make all the difference in the end, Madeline had preprepared a dish to serve to the audience.

"Good thinking, going with beef, since we're definitely a meat-and-potatoes crowd out here. It's not that often we get a celebrity at the store—usually it's just some local selling homemade jam or sausage—so we wanted to do it up right."

"I appreciate the effort. But I'm not a celebrity. I just cook."

"Well, to us you're certainly a TV star. I've never missed an episode of *Comfort Cooking*, but your new show, *Dinner at Home*, got my family sitting down at the table together again."

"That's always lovely to hear," Madeline said through teeth she'd clenched together to keep them from chattering.

"Of course, my own three kids have left the nest," Birdy confided. "But my daughter got laid off from her management job at ConAgra. The same week, her cheating husband left her for the woman who claimed to be her best friend. Yeah, right. That's a real good friend." She shook her head in disgust. "Anyway, with money tight right now, she and her kids have moved in with me until she gets back on her feet."

"I'm sorry about her marriage."

"Oh, in the long run, it's probably for the best. He was a no-good louse from the get-go. I tried to warn her, but what can you do?" She shrugged well-padded shoulders as she clicked a remote, causing a tomato red SUV a few cars away in the lot to chirp. "They never had anything in common. Nothing like you and that sexy French chef you married. Is it true one of his ancestors cooked for Napoleon?"

"So they say." Maxime had never been shy about mentioning that bit of family history.

"It's good to know your roots. One of my greats, going back several generations, came here to Nebraska on a covered wagon from Philadelphia. She had a baby along the way, and both mother and son lived to carry on the family line." She opened the hatch of the SUV, took Madeline's carry-on bag, and tossed it into the back.

Desperate for warmth, Madeline scrambled into the passenger's seat, only to find the inside of the car as cold as outside.

"We'll get the heat going right away," Birdy promised as she switched on the car, causing icy air to blast out of the dashboard vents. "Does your husband ever come with you on any of these trips?"

"Not so far. But running all his restaurants involves a lot of traveling of his own. He's currently in Las Vegas." And probably lounging by the pool while she was in danger of becoming a Popsicle.

"Small world. My Heather and Tom, her ex, got married there," she said as they headed out of the parking lot. "By one of those Elvis impersonators, which should've been Heather's first clue that they weren't exactly compatible.

Tom's into all the typical outdoors stuff. Hunting, ice-fishing, four-wheeling . . ."

"I imagine those would be popular activities here."

"True enough. But Heather prefers reading and going to museums and such. She volunteers at the library. I don't think they have a cookbook she hasn't read. She's the one who got me watching cooking shows. Two years ago, Hamburger Helper and a green-bean casserole were about as fancy as I got. Now I can whip up a three-course meal from what I find in the pantry."

"That's a useful skill to have." It was also something Madeline stressed on both her shows.

"You betcha. That's our *Dancing Cranes.*" Birdy pointed toward a huge statue that was barely visible through the horizontally blowing snow. "It's the largest bronze statue in North America."

"That's impressive."

"We like to think so. I realize that a lot of people on the coasts never think about us out here in the flyover heartland, but we're not all hicks in sticks. Kool-Aid and the Reuben sandwich were both invented right here in Nebraska."

"I didn't know that."

"It's true. Too bad you're not going to be here longer. There's even a Kool-Aid exhibit in the Hastings Museum, just a couple hours from here. Did you know that during the Depression, one of those little packages cost more than a loaf of bread?"

"I had no idea."

"It sure enough did. But people bought the stuff anyway. Imagine that. Hastings got an offer from some marketing folks to change the name of their town to Kool-Aid, Nebraska, but they declined the honor." Her dry tone suggested how ridiculous she'd found the suggestion.

"I think they made the right choice," Madeline said. "I haven't always lived in New York. I spent my childhood in an Italian village with my parents, and then, when I was thirteen, moved to an Oregon coastal town that's kept its small-town flavor."

Shelter Bay was also where she'd given her teenage heart to a rich "summer boy," only to have it shattered by Labor Day. But she'd tried, with not always successful results, to put that dark day in the past.

"I read all about that." The pom-pom on her hat bobbed as the woman nodded. "After your folks died in that plane crash, which was a crying shame, you went to live with your grandmother on her lavender farm.

"You can find anything on the Internet these days," she clarified at Madeline's surprised glance. "I even found your wedding photos. You sure were a picture in that white dress."

"My wedding photos are on the Internet?"

"The photographer has them in his gallery."

"I hadn't realized that." The idea of her personal photos out there on the World Wide Web was more than a little unsettling. Unlike her celebrity-chef husband, who thrived in the spotlight, Madeline had always been a private person. It had taken a lot for her to get comfortable in front of the TV cameras.

"Well, you needn't worry, because they're beautiful. Did you make that pretty flowered cake yourself?"

"No. I'm not much of a baker." Unlike the creative freedom and improvisation allowed by the comfort food she'd become known for, baking required precision, a strict attention to measurements, and much more patience than Madeline possessed. "My husband's pastry chef made it."

"I stick to cookies when it comes to baking," Birdy said cheerfully. "They're a lot harder to mess up than cakes or pies, and the grandkids love them." Her comfortable way with a total stranger reminded Madeline of her grandmother Sofia. "My mother-in-law's from South Dakota, so, now that she's passed, I get the job of cooking her kuchen for this year's Easter dinner."

As she launched into a lengthy explanation of the pressures of duplicating the recipe, which used raspberries atop a custard base, an oncoming car fishtailed on the icy road, then headed directly toward them.

Birdy twisted the wheel and braked at the same time. Although she managed to avoid impact, the SUV went into a skid.

As Madeline clutched the door handle, they skated on what felt like an ice rink beneath the tires, bumping over the rumble strip in the middle of the road.

"Hold on," Birdy advised with what Madeline found to be remarkable calm. "We're about to come to a stop."

Which they did as they plowed, hood first, into a frozen, exhaust-darkened snowbank.

"Don't you worry." After trying to back up only sent the rear wheels spinning, the woman, who seemed to have sturdy pioneer blood flowing in her veins, dug into her coat pocket and pulled out a phone. "We'll get you to the mall on time. Not that they can start without you."

She punched a single number on the keypad. "No point in calling for a tow truck since we're not all that stuck. The police will be here in a two shakes of a lamb's tail."

"You have the police department on speed dial?"

"My youngest boy, Jeb, is on the force, so I keep his number handy. He's the one who'll pull us out."

And, sure enough, before Madeline's feet could turn completely to ice cubes, a huge black SUV with white doors came up behind them, blue and red roof lights flashing.

The officer who climbed out of the driver's seat was large enough to have played linebacker on the Cornhuskers football team. He was wearing sensible snowpack boots, thick gloves, a parka, and a fur hat with earflaps. While his partner jumped out of the shotgun seat to set a flare and direct traffic, he crunched along the plowed snow at the edge of the roadway.

"Third time this week, Ma," he greeted her. Although his expression was resigned, his blue eyes revealed relief that the accident hadn't been worse.

"It wasn't my fault," she said. "The driver of the other car, who didn't even stick around to see the trouble he caused, went across the line first." She turned toward Madeline. "Tell him."

"Your mother did a lot better than I would have under the circumstances," Madeline said.

"Driven in a lot of snow, have you, ma'am?" he asked.

"No, but—"

"You must be the celebrity chef from New York City," he said, cutting her off.

Madeline was about to explain again that she wasn't a celebrity, but decided it wasn't germane to their situation.

"She is. And we need to get her to the mall on time." Birdy might be a good foot shorter than her son, but that didn't stop her from pulling out her mom voice. "Jebediah, meet Chef Madeline Durand. Chef Madeline, this is my baby boy. Who I'm usually super proud of." She drummed her mitten-clad fingers on the steering wheel. "Except for when he wastes time scolding his mother when she has important things to do."

"Nice to meet you, ma'am," he said politely to Madeline. "And I worry about you," he told his mother.

"Well, that makes us even for all the years I've worried about you," she shot back. "Now, if you don't mind, we're going to be late if we don't get this show on the road."

"That's very good," Madeline murmured after Officer Jebediah Hinlemeir trudged back to his Omaha Police SUV.

"One of the perks of being a mother," Birdy said cheerfully, as snowflakes began to pile up on the windshield.

"You get to boss around people bigger than you. Jeb's about to become a father himself in the next month or so, but he'll always be my baby. You and your husband planning to have kids anytime soon?"

"I do want children—someday—but we're both occupied with our careers right now."

Madeline wasn't prepared to share the fact that she and Maxime weren't exactly on the same page when it came to starting a family. Admittedly, the timing wasn't right now, when she was forced to give every waking moment to her work and supporting Maxime's far-flung enterprises. At twenty-eight, she had years left to convince her husband that she could, as her own mother had, successfully combine work and a career, despite Maxime's fear that a child would take her focus off her career. Or, more likely, as she often suspected, off him.

"Well, you're still young," Birdy pointed out. "Of course, your husband's quite a bit older, but age isn't such a big deal for men. They're not the ones with their eggs getting older by the day."

And wasn't that a fun thought?

It didn't take long for Jebediah and his partner to pull them out of the snowbank, and within fifteen minutes the SUV was crunching its way across the mall parking lot.

"Nice thing about winter," Birdy said, her optimism once again reminding Madeline of her grandmother. "The snow fills in all the potholes."

The kitchen setup in the store was as good as promised. As she entered the area to the enthusiastic applause of all the women—along with a few men—who'd braved the weather to show up today, Madeline felt almost like a rock star.

Birdy's assistant had warmed up the preprepared dish, sending the rich aroma of wine gravy and braised meat wafting throughout the store.

"That scrumptious smell's goin' to be drawing them in from all over the mall," Birdy predicted.

Which appeared to be true as the crowd grew while Madeline demonstrated how to caramelize meat in a sauté pan from ChefSteel, the company with whom her agent had negotiated an endorsement deal. Birdy had gone all out, setting up a video camera, which allowed those in the back of the crowd to watch on a large-screen television.

"Sizzling's good," Madeline said as the olive oil danced. "This part takes patience because you want the meat to be nicely colored on all sides. That's what elevates your dish to perfection."

She took the ribs out of the pan and put them on a plate. "Now we'll sauté our mirepoix—which is simply a fancy French name for a mixture of cut celery, carrots, and onions—in the drippings from the meat."

Again, the assistant had come through with the prep work.

"The fat in the pan is bringing up more meat flavors into the veggies," Madeline said as she stirred them. "We'll cook just until they're tender. An interesting little bit of trivia is that mirepoix is named for a duke who was a field marshal for King Louis the Fifteenth. According to the stories, despite being incompetent, he was given the post of ambassador because the king appreciated his wife's charms."

As always, that story raised eyebrows.

"Whatever Mirepoix's alleged failings, the man could definitely cook. He gave his name to lots of different sauces, but this one's become the standard."

As she went on to demonstrate how to deglaze with balsamic vinegar and red wine, Madeline thought the bit of eighteenth-century gossip was the cause of the murmurs humming through the crowd. Then she noticed a couple sharing an iPhone, while others around them were busily tapping into their own smart phones.

Curious, she glanced over at Birdy, who, after looking up from her own phone's screen, went as pale as the onions sautéing in the pan.

The older woman hurried over to Madeline. "Now that Chef Madeline's been good enough to share her wonderful culinary tips with us, Julie will be serving the final result," she announced. "And I know you'll all enjoy it." She took hold of Madeline's arm and dragged her behind a tall counter filled with shiny, upscale coffeemakers.

"What's wrong?" Madeline asked.

"I don't know how to tell you this, dear, but one of the women in the crowd apparently hit on a YouTube video while Googling your name. My guess is she's a shopper who didn't know about you being here today and went online to find out more about you."

"Which video?" The network kept several of her past episodes on their Web site.

Birdy winced. "It's hard to explain. Maybe I'd best just show you." She handed Madeline her phone.

The screen was small and a distracting glare from the store's bright overhead lights at first made it difficult for Madeline to make out what she was seeing.

It appeared to be a man and woman having sex. Energetic, hot, sweaty sex. Fortunately, the phone's sound had been muted.

Madeline was still wondering what this had to do with her when realization hit like a meat mallet to her head.

It wasn't just any man. The crescent-shaped birthmark on his butt gave him away.

It was Maxime.

Her husband.

Proving, Madeline thought as white spots like snowflakes began to dance in front of her eyes, that not everything that happened in Vegas *stayed* in Vegas.

2

The sky was high and as blue as a robin's egg the spring day Navy SEAL medic Lucas Chaffee buried his father at sea. The sea Duncan Chaffee had loved so well.

The *Kelli*, a gleaming white boat operated by Cole Douchett, brother of one of Lucas' former SEAL teammates, cut through the waves as they headed three miles away from the coast.

"How are you doing?" a quiet voice asked. Charity Tiernan had become his stepsister during the brief time his father had been married to her mother. She'd stayed his friend long after their parents' divorce.

"I'm okay. If he had to go, at least he went exactly the way he would've wanted. Having a great day on the water."

"That is something. Do you have any plans?"

He'd had one. One that he and his dad had been discussing in back-and-forth e-mail between Portland and Afghanistan for the past year.

Which was what made the timing of his father's death so ironic.

The plan, as carefully detailed as the opera house with its soaring wings that his dad had designed on Hong Kong's harbor, had been for Duncan to step down from the presidency of the architecture firm he'd founded; then the two of them would go into business restoring old homes up and down the West Coast.

Having grown up on construction sites, and mentally exhausted from struggling to save lives on battlefields, Lucas had jumped at the idea, which included taking the obligatory professional training and the exam covering business practices and laws. So, at the moment, he had an Oregon state contractor's license, but no work and no plans.

"I haven't a clue." He dragged a hand through his hair, which, while not nearly as short as a Marine's high-and-tight, was still shorter than he'd worn it during his days tracking down terrorists in the Afghan mountains. "I was thinking this morning Scout and I might hang out in Shelter Bay a while. In the house." His father had built the gray-shingled, oceanfront Cape Cod cottage as a place to escape after Lucas' mother had left them both. It was the same cottage where he and Charity had lived with their parents during what was, hands down, the second-best summer of his life.

The best had been that later summer when he'd discovered love with an impetuous, stunning girl with smoky eyes and a mass of dark, corkscrew curls that had danced in the sea breeze around a face that had, the first time he'd seen it, stopped his heart.

Even now, the memory of how that summer had ended pricked a heart that was already aching.

On hearing her name, Scout, the German shepherd seated beside him, happily thumped her tail. He absently reached down and patted the dog's head.

Charity's smile was brighter than the sun that was creating diamonds on the water. "Oh, I'd love that." She immediately sobered. "I'm sorry. I didn't mean it to sound as if I'm glad—"

"I know." He took hold of her hand, the one that wasn't holding the white rose she'd brought for the ceremony, as they stood side by side at the gleaming brass rail. Since turning his family's fishing boat into a tourists' charter boat, Cole had spiffed it up a lot. "I'd like a chance to catch up, too." It was his turn to smile. "And make sure that Marine you've hooked up with is good enough for you."

"It's a lot more than just a hookup. And Gabe is really, really good for me. You'll like him."

"He's a jarhead." Even after all these years apart, the easy verbal sparring felt familiar. And loosened the anchor chain that had been around his heart since he'd gotten the news of his father's heart attack from one of the associate partners in the firm.

"That's funny." Her eyes danced with teasing laughter. "Because although I wasn't going to mention it, especially given the circumstances, he called you a Frog Boy."

Lucas laughed. A deep, booming laugh that swelled his chest and broke the chain. "Your loyalties have shifted."

She immediately sobered again, reminding Lucas how much family meant to Charity. Which made sense, given her serial-marrying parents. "I was kidding," she said.

"I know. And I can't think of anyone who deserves a happily-ever-after more than you. So if you're happy, I'm happy."

"I'm beyond happy. What about you? Are you still involved with that decorator?"

"She's an interior designer." Brooke Kendall, who'd worked on developments with his father, was gorgeous, smart as a whip, talented, and ambitious. On the rebound from a divorce, she'd been available when he'd landed back in Portland two months ago after his separation from the Navy. "I suppose that depends on what your definition of *involved* is."

"But you're still dating?"

He cringed at the idea. "Geez, that sounds so high school."

After all he'd seen, all he'd been through, those days seemed to have taken place in another lifetime. He might not have come home with flaming PTSD like others he'd served with, but he wasn't the same person he'd been before his first deployment. Hell, he wasn't even the same guy who, despite his father's concerns, had turned his back on medical school and gone off to SEAL BUD/S training so he could do his part in the war against terrorism.

"You're right. I hated it when my mother kept referring to Gabe and me as dating. So, are you sleeping with her?"

"Dad taught me never to kiss and tell."

"Which pretty much answers the question. Is it serious?"

"No." What it was, he considered, was *convenient*.

"Exclusive?"

"I don't know." It had been for him. But now that Lucas thought about it, he'd never asked Brooke if she was seeing anyone else.

"Again, if you haven't even gotten to the point where you're discussing it, your relationship can't be that serious. Which, I suppose, is why you didn't bring her along today."

"She had an appointment." When Charity gave him a knowing look, he tacked on, "Hey, it's a big deal. A chance to handle all the interior design for Winfield Palace's new Paris hotel."

"When deluxe will no longer do," she quoted the chain's slogan. "That's impressive, and how exciting for her. . . . So, how do you feel about cupcakes?"

"I like them," he said, even as the non sequitur puzzled him. "Who doesn't? Why?"

"Because I have this friend . . . a baker in town—"

"No."

"You don't even know her. Yet."

"I'm sure, if she's your friend, she's wonderful. Better than wonderful. She's undoubtedly a paragon of womanhood. Who can bake, which is a plus. But since I don't even know what I'm going to be doing next week, this isn't a good time to meet anyone new."

"I'm not suggesting you give her your class ring and ask her to go steady, Lucas. I just thought you'd like her."

There were, Lucas knew, few individuals more determined than Charity. Which was why, according to Sax
Douchett, nearly every person in Shelter Bay had adopted
a cat or dog from the veterinarian's no-kill shelter. "And
since your designer might be going off to Paris—"

"She's not *my* designer."

"Well, then, why don't you at least keep the possibility
in mind?"

"I'll do that." It wasn't the entire truth. But he figured it
might put her off for at least a couple days.

It didn't.

"You have to eat," she pressed on, reminding Lucas how
stubborn his stepsister could be when she set her mind to
something. "What would you say to coming over to dinner
Wednesday night? Gabe will be back from his meeting
with his agent and publisher in New York. We can grill
some rib eyes and—"

"You, the jarhead, and steaks sounds great. But just because you're crazy in love doesn't mean that—"

He was about to tell her he'd really prefer she not invite
the cupcake baker when the boat reached the burial site.

Before he'd arrived at the dock, the cremains had already been transferred to a woven wicker basket lined with
biodegradable paper, then covered with flower petals.

His father had stated his wishes to be buried at sea. So
although Duncan Chaffee had never been specific about
the details, since he'd served in the Navy during Vietnam
and had continued to volunteer in various troop-support
groups, Lucas had decided to include some trappings of a
military funeral.

Sax came forward to present him with a folded flag.
Considering that his former teammate felt like the brother
he'd never had, Lucas knew the profound sympathy he saw
in Sax's eyes was genuine.

In contrast to the standing-room-only memorial service
his father's partners had insisted on in Portland, the one

that had Duncan's friends, peers, and clients flying in from all around the world, Lucas had purposefully kept this private service intimate.

On board along with Scout, who'd saved his team's lives while losing one of her legs to an IED, were Charity; Sax; and Sax's fiancée, Kara, who was Shelter Bay's sheriff—which was ironic, considering that Sax had at one time been the town bad boy. Charity's mother, Amanda Tiernan-Jacobs-Chaffee-Gillette-Rodzianko-Templeton, who may have divorced her third husband but had stayed a close friend, had flown down from Seattle.

Also in attendance was Sofia De Luca, who'd taken his father and him under her wing that first lonely summer Duncan and Lucas had arrived in Shelter Bay, after Lucas' sister's death and his parents' divorce.

Not only had she made sure they'd eaten, but she'd also offered compassion and a female friendship both man and boy had desperately needed. It was, unsurprisingly, Sofia who'd offered to cook this evening's funeral supper at her lavender farm.

Lucas also had a more personal connection to Sofia, since she just happened to be the grandmother of the girl he'd let get away.

He accepted the flag, handed it off to Charity, then took a deep breath before giving the eulogy he'd been awake all night writing.

"Thank you all for coming today. And a huge thanks to Cole, for providing the boat that's letting me fulfill my father's wishes."

Hell. It was even harder than he'd thought it would be. He cleared his throat to rid it of the word-blocking lump. Then put his hand on Scout's head, who, seeming to sense the tangle of his emotions, licked it with her huge tongue.

"My father had a profound impact on the life I live today. And the person I've become. When you spend a lot of time in war zones with other guys, you get to talking about family, and I've come to realize that the relationship between a father and son can often be complicated.

"Well, it was never that way with my father and me. Although our family had its challenges, I was fortunate to have a simple, powerful, loving relationship with Dad.

"Two days ago, I attended a memorial service for him in Portland. There wasn't an empty seat in the cathedral, which said something about both his ability to make friends and the respect so many held for him.

"It's typical at funerals and memorial services to remember only the good things. But I think it says something about my father that there was no bad. He was, hands down, the kindest, most optimistic person I've ever met.

"Duncan Chaffee loved people. In recent days, obituaries in newspapers all over the world have praised his artistic vision, the soaring beauty of the buildings he designed, his pro bono charity work. But you don't measure a man by his work and awards. You measure it by the lives he touched. The lessons he taught.

"To me, he'll always be the protector who chased monsters from beneath the bed when night fears kept me awake; the sportsman who taught me how to bait a fishhook and tack a sailboat; the booster who encouraged me to ask a girl, whose teenage beauty left me stutteringly tongue-tied, to dinner at the Crab Shack; and, most of all, the man who taught me to embrace whatever life threw my way."

Advice Lucas had held on to during his years as a SEAL medic in places most Americans couldn't name and none would ever want to visit.

"I've tried, over the past days, to make sense of my father's death. And the only thing I can figure out is that heaven must need an architect."

Navy SEALS were known for the rigid self-discipline drilled into them in training. But that didn't prevent Lucas' voice from cracking. As Amanda began to weep, he struggled for control, and, knowing his father would expect it of him, won.

"So"—he took another breath, gaining strength from the silent support he felt from those who'd always meant the most to him—"God, since I know he'd never ask for anything for himself, and I'm assuming you've already granted what would have been his sole request—to be reunited with my sister we lost years too soon—I'm asking that you provide him with his favorite simple pleasures.

"Please give him a worktable with a view of the outdoors. Although his favorite views were the Pacific Coast and the Cascade Mountains, he loved every inch of this magnificent planet you created, so changing vistas would be great.

"Please give him a sailboat so he can feel the salt breeze in his hair as he skims across the water, a TV so he can watch his beloved Oregon State Beaver football games, and a cold beer at the end of the workday.

"And please, God, give him all the love, laughter, and happiness he brought to so many others during his time on earth."

Although his heart was broken, Lucas managed to exchange a smile with Charity.

"That was lovely," she said, her eyes shimmering with tears.

"It was hard." *Really, really hard.*

"I know." She squeezed his fingers. "He'd started coming back here more the past year as he eased into retirement, and being with him was like that wonderful summer we spent together before he and Mom split up. He was probably, in many ways, more of a father figure than my own."

"He always thought of you as a daughter. I think losing you was the hardest thing about your mom's and his divorce. . . . Ready?"

"I suppose so." She didn't sound any happier about the

reason for this reunion than Lucas was. Together, hands entwined, they lowered the small, woven basket into the ocean Duncan had taught them both to love.

As it sank, flowers floated gently to the surface.

While Cole circled the boat twice around the floating flowers, allowing the others to toss their own blossoms into the water in a final good-bye, Sax, the musician of the group, played taps. The melancholy yet peaceful tones of the song lingered in Lucas' heart even after they'd ceased to vibrate in the sea air.

As the boat chugged through the waves back toward Shelter Bay, Sofia came over to Lucas.

"That was a very moving service," the older woman said. "I know your father's so proud of you."

"Thanks."

"That was Maddy, wasn't it? The girl you were afraid to ask out."

"Yeah." He managed a slight smile at the terrified twenty-year-old he'd once been. Then, because he was solely responsible for it having ended so badly, he said, "I'm sorry."

It was the truth.

"Oh, that's all water under the bridge." She waved his words away. "You were both young. Life moves on."

Madeline certainly had moved on. Just as he'd intended. And although heating up a military MRE was the height of his culinary skills, since arriving Stateside, Lucas had taken to watching her cooking shows. She was, impossibly, more beautiful than ever. And, he continually reminded himself, married.

"So," Sofia said, and then asked him the question he'd heard innumerable times in the last week. "What are your plans?"

"I'm not sure," he responded the same way he had innumerable times.

"I have a suggestion about that. And a favor to ask."

Although her smile was warm, Lucas could tell, from a life that had often depended upon his ability to read people's expressions, that Sofia De Luca was holding back a secret.

His curiosity piqued, as he suspected she'd intended, he merely arched a brow. And waited.

"I don't want to intrude on your thoughts right now," she said, avoiding answering his unspoken question. "We can talk after the supper."

"She's up to something," Lucas mused as he and Charity watched the older woman walk over to talk with Sax and Kara.

"Absolutely," Charity agreed. She went up on her toes and brushed a kiss against his cheek. "And if whatever it is will keep you in Shelter Bay longer, I'm all for it."

3

Somehow, although she couldn't quite get the image of her husband with another woman out of her mind, Madeline made it through the rest of the demonstration. And although she could tell that her audience was equally distracted, the short ribs proved to be a huge success. Afterward, not only did people line up to have her autograph her book, but there were more than a few sales of the pans she'd used to cook the ribs, which made the store manager, who'd come to watch the demonstration, happy.

Blessedly, not a single person mentioned the video she suspected they'd all seen by the time she plated the dish.

Although the original plan had been for her to stay in Omaha overnight, Madeline wanted to get back home. Especially after the operator at the Las Vegas hotel told her that Maxime had already checked out. This was not a conversation to be held over a cell phone. Madeline needed a face-to-face confrontation.

It was too soon to even begin to think about what she was going to do. Ever since viewing the video, her thoughts had been whirling like fresh basil leaves in a Cuisinart. She needed a clear head.

And a sharp fillet knife, a voice in some cold, angry corner of her mind suggested.

Not that she'd ever resort to violence. But for a fleeting moment, as Birdy, who was chauffering her back to the airport, pulled up to the departure curb, Madeline found the fantasy more than a little appealing.

"You take care now," Birdy said as she hugged Madeline good-bye. "And if that French husband of yours doesn't do the appropriate amount of groveling, you can tell him you know a very big cop who owns a gun. And knows how to use it."

Although she hadn't thought she'd ever find anything the least bit humorous about the situation Maxime had put her in, Madeline smiled, just a bit, at that. Again, the older woman reminded her of her grandmother Sofia, who'd managed to lighten her heart after her parents had died.

And who'd also held her and dried her tears during the second-most-painful period in her life, after that lying, cheating Lucas Chaffee had broken her heart.

As furious as she was at her husband, his betrayal caused memories of that fateful night with Lucas to flood into her mind in vivid, humiliating detail.

What was wrong with her? Did she simply have miserable taste in men? Or did she send out secret signals, like the ultrahigh pitch of dog whistles, that only men incapable of being faithful could hear?

The flight, which was just over two hours, seemed to take forever as her still-stunned mind struggled to make sense of a situation that had her feeling as if she'd suddenly fallen down a rabbit hole and ended up drinking Earl Grey with the Mad Hatter.

At least when she was in the air, she was unreachable by phone or e-mail.

Although she was tempted to take advantage of the free wine being poured in the first-class cabin, to numb her brain, Madeline wanted a clear head when she confronted Maxime, so she forced herself to stick to one Bloody Mary with her chilled black olive spaghetti salad. And managed not to pour the entire mini bottle of vodka into the mix.

When the plane finally landed at La Guardia, she was

not surprised to find her phone's voice mail filled with messages.

The first three were from Pepper McBain, her agent, assuring her that this unsavory publicity storm would blow over and it wouldn't hurt her relationship with either her new sponsor or the Cooking Network.

"After all," the brisk, savvy woman who represented some of the biggest food stars in the business said, "you're the injured party, darling. Everyone, from the network bigwigs to your audience, adores you. And, lucky us, not only are your shows on hiatus, but your contract's up for renewal."

"Lucky," Madeline murmured as she wheeled her carry-on up the jetway to the terminal. Apparently, Pepper had joined her down the rabbit hole and was now the one pouring the tea.

There were, unsurprisingly, more calls from the producer of her television shows. "Don't you worry about a thing, girlfriend," Janine Miller said, her staccato tone sounding even more New York rapid-fire than usual. "That video will probably send ratings skyrocketing. After all, other celebrities have rocketed to fame after a sex tape hit the Internet."

Although she knew Janine was trying to be supportive, such comparisons did nothing to boost Madeline's spirits.

Finally, she got down to a call from her grandmother, which was the most depressing of all, because if a seventy-something woman could hear about Maxime's video in a small, coastal town not known for being tuned in to celebrity gossip, it truly must have gone viral.

"Darling," Sofia said, "I'm so sorry about what happened and just wanted to remind you that if you do feel the need to get away, the farm will always be your home. I'm also starting a very exciting new venture I think you might just be interested in. Not that you don't already have a great deal on your plate these days. But call me when you get an opportunity. Meanwhile, take care. I love you."

For the first time since her life had come crumbling around her feet in that department store, Madeline's eyes stung with tears. After taking her in, Sofia had become more like a mother than a grandmother. Not only had she provided unconditional love, she'd also picked up her culinary training where her parents had left off and encouraged her lifelong dream of following in her parents' footsteps.

With her grandmother's blessing, after graduating from high school, Madeline spent the next years traveling throughout Europe, learning the ropes in restaurants that were often owned by chefs who'd been friends of her parents.

In her mid-twenties, she'd returned to the States, where she studied at the Culinary Institute of America. It was while working between semesters as a *stagiaire*—unpaid intern—at Chez Maxime, Maxime Durand's Manhattan restaurant on Columbus Circle, that she'd fallen in love.

It definitely wasn't love at first sight. In the beginning, she hadn't even been certain she'd last the summer. Within the first week working the line, she discovered that all the stories about Maxime Durand's infamous temper were not exaggerated. Making her wonder why he'd bothered to take her on in the first place, he didn't even try to hide the fact that he looked down his aristocratic Gallic nose at the country-style Italian and Greek food Madeline had grown up eating. Food she loved to cook: simple, but delicious meals revolving around sustainable, local food.

Their affair began predictably enough, with him giving her private tutorials after the restaurant had closed. While their cooking styles couldn't have been more disparate, there was no denying his genius, and she'd eagerly soaked up his vast knowledge of classic cuisine, like a rich tiramisu drenched in espresso and Marsala wine.

Although she'd grown used to being called Maddy during her years in Oregon, he'd insisted the name was too frivolous for a serious chef. Since the way he'd pronounced her name—*Mad-eh-Leen*—in his sexy French accent had practically made her melt like meringue topping a lemon pie in July, she willingly returned to her more formal birth name.

Two weeks after he'd first invited her to stay after hours at the restaurant, they had their first date in the kitchen of his Riverside Drive apartment, where they worked together on a meal of Coquilles St. Jacques, steak au poivre, garlic roasted potatoes, and chocolate crepes with fresh raspberries and Grand Marnier crème Chantilly.

Floating on air as she was, with a Jacques Brel CD crooning love songs in the background, the lit-up George Washington Bridge out the window could have just as easily been the Eiffel Tower.

They'd stayed up all night, drinking champagne, talking about how wonderful it would be to cook together all the time. To create a shared life around food. By the time the sun was rising over the river, Madeline had begun fantasizing about being married to this larger-than-life culinary genius.

Later, she realized she'd been naive not to pay more attention to the fact that every dish he'd made that night had been French. And whenever she'd tried to inject a bit of her own tastes into a meal, he'd brushed off her suggestions as "mere peasant food."

Now, three years after that memorable night, she decided that during the early days of their affair, she'd made a major mistake not to heed his continued insistence that having already failed at two marriages, he'd come to the conclusion that he didn't possess the "marriage gene."

Apparently, he doesn't possess the monogamy gene, either.

She was waiting on the sidewalk outside the terminal in the taxi line when a well-dressed woman strode up to her on an expensive pair of stiletto boots. "You're Madeline Durand."

Madeline hadn't become entirely accustomed to being

approached by strangers. She didn't think she ever would. But usually such encounters were positive, with viewers telling her how much they enjoyed her programs or book, or how, like Birdy, they'd started cooking because the recipes she created seemed so accessible.

That's what she was expecting now.

She was wrong.

Because, although she wouldn't have thought it possible, Madeline's already horrible day was about to get worse.

4

The French lavender lining the roadway leading to Sofia De Luca's Lavender Hill farm had burst into bloom, the grounds were bright with iris and rhododendron, fields of herbs were beginning to green up, and the rooms were perfumed with the quiet, soft scent of dried lavender potpourri. Lucas could not have thought of a better place to celebrate his father's amazing life with friends.

"Wow, what a crowd," Charity murmured as she found him alone in the octagon-shaped parlor. "Not that I'm surprised. Your dad was a popular guy."

"He touched a lot of lives." It seemed half the town had come to the supper, clasped Lucas' hand, and shared some personal story of Duncan Chafee. So many so that after a while he'd just needed to escape.

"That's how people live on," she said mildly. "In memories and stories. He truly did touch many lives. And was so proud of you," she added, making him wonder if she'd realized that as much as Lucas appreciated all those anecdotes, they'd left him realizing what a huge legacy his dad had left behind. A legacy that wouldn't be easy to live up to.

"He sailed into town a couple weeks ago and we had dinner. He told me all about what a hero you were. And how you'd saved so many of your teammate's lives."

"I'm no hero. I was just doing my job."

"Yeah. Kara told me that's what Sax always says when people bring it up. I don't believe him, either."

When he didn't respond, they went back to looking out the window, as comfortable with each other as if they'd been lifelong siblings, and not steps who only shared a summer together a very long time ago.

"I love wisteria," she murmured.

"Which would be?"

"Those." She pointed at the flowers that had climbed over the arbor. "The ones that look like a purple waterfall dropping from the sky."

It was a good description.

Another silence settled over them.

"It was nice of Sofia to hold this supper," he said after a time.

"Wild horses couldn't have stopped her. And . . ."

"What?" he asked when her voice trailed off.

She paused, as if carefully choosing her words. Then shook her head. "It's not any secret. You know her husband died."

"Yeah. Sax and Kara told me about that. I guess it was rough."

"Losing a life partner and your best friend can't be easy at any time. But yes, his cancer made it worse." She sighed. "Then Rosemary—that was her dog, who her husband had talked her into adopting—had to be put down last summer."

"That is tough."

"True. But I found her another—"

"Why am I not surprised at that?" The idea made him smile. His old teammate had also told him that Charity seemed determined to place a pet with everyone up and down the Oregon coast.

"It's an older bulldog who was abandoned pregnant. I was hoping Sofia and Winnie would fit. And they did." It was her turn to smile. "But although it's a cliché, she's not getting any younger, and I worry that this place might be becoming too much for her."

"She seemed distracted."

"She does, doesn't she?" Charity agreed. "I wonder if it has anything to do with that phone call she got after we got back to the pier?"

"I hope it wasn't bad news," they both said at once.

"Jinx." She hit him lightly on the arm. "You owe me a Coke."

They were laughing at the old schoolyard saying when the subject of their conversation joined them in the room.

"You've got quite a crowd out there," Sofia said. "Good thing I planned ahead and cooked for an army."

"I really appreciate you going to all this trouble." Lucas repeated what he'd been saying since she'd first approached him with the idea. "But I wish you'd let me pay."

"Don't be foolish. Your father was a dear friend. As are you. And friends certainly don't charge friends at a time like this. Although," she said, a little slyly, Lucas thought, "there is something you can help me out with."

"Anything."

"I've been rattling around in this house all by myself—well, myself and Winnie," she corrected as she smiled at Charity. "But as good company as the sweet dog is, she's not all that scintillating a conversationalist. Which is why I've been thinking of expanding to make room to bring more people here."

"Like a B and B?"

"Oh, gracious, no." She shook her head emphatically. "While I've always enjoyed cooking for people, I've never understood why anyone would want to spend their golden years making beds and cleaning bathrooms for constant houseguests. . . . No, I'm thinking of opening up a small restaurant."

"Would you be doing the cooking?" Charity, who was

clearly concerned about the older woman taking on such a project, asked.

"I'm not that ambitious, dear. No, I plan to start interviewing chefs in the next month or so. But I need a contractor willing to take on the job of turning my simple, admittedly outdated farm kitchen into a more commercial one."

It wasn't the lofty plan of restoring grand old Victorians from San Diego to Vancouver Island that Lucas' father had conceived. But, then again, the past years in a war zone had taught Lucas that life was what happened when you were busy making plans. And it would let him stay here long enough to reconnect with Charity. As well as Sax, who seemed to have settled comfortably into domestic bliss with his fiancée and her son while running his family's Cajun restaurant and dance hall.

"Sounds like an interesting challenge," he said.

He exchanged a look with Charity, whose expression shouted out, *Say yes!*

"How about I come over tomorrow?" he suggested. "You can tell me what you have in mind and we can start talking about plans."

The elderly woman's smile could have lit up all of Shelter Bay for a month of rainy Sundays. She reached up and patted his cheek with a weathered hand.

"You're such a good man, Lucas Chafee. And you remind me so much of your father at his age. I know you're going to have a wonderful future."

She paused. Just a heartbeat, but long enough to catch Lucas' full attention.

"That means a lot coming from you." Because he'd never been one to beat around the bush and knew Sofia was the same, he asked, "Is there something you're not telling me? Something about dad?"

"Oh no." She shook her head. "It's just that ... well ... something's come up, and although I'm not exactly sure how it's all going to shake out, would you have a problem working with my granddaughter?"

"Maddy? She's going to be your chef?"

"Oh, I didn't say that." Again Lucas had the feeling she was holding something back. "But she's currently on hiatus between seasons. She has two culinary shows on TV—"

"I've seen them," he said. That comment drew a surprised look from Charity.

"Have you?" Sofia's eyes lit up. "Well, then you know that she's developed into a wonderful chef. So I wouldn't be surprised if she decided to spend a bit of her hiatus here at home."

"I thought her home was in New York."

And didn't that draw another, more probing look from his stepsister?

"Well, of course it is," Sofia agreed. "But everyone needs a little R and R from time to time. And what better place than here at the farm? Besides," she tacked on, "although she'd deny it, I do think she worries about me getting older."

Lucas had known Sofia De Luca since he was a boy. He also knew she was not one to focus on age. Especially her own. Which could only mean she was playing the age card as an additional ploy to get him to agree to work on her project.

Possibly with Maddy.

Which could be really, really bad.

Or, on the other hand, fate could have just handed him a do-over.

Remembering what his dad had taught him about embracing whatever life tossed his way, Lucas said, "You've got yourself a contractor."

The warm, self-satisfied smile the elderly woman flashed at him suggested she'd never expected any other outcome.

5

Since the taxi line wasn't moving, Madeline put on her best public smile, dearly hoped the woman wasn't going to bring up that damn video, and said, "Yes, I'm Madeline Durand."

"Well!" The woman fisted her leather-gloved hands on her hips. "Let me tell you, I bought those pans you have on your show. And they're junk."

Do not argue with a viewer. Especially in public. If she hadn't already known that nothing was private these days, the past few hours would have hammered the point home.

"I'm sorry. What's the problem?"

"I was searing Parmesan-crusted pork chops in oil, just the way you said to, and they still burned so badly that they stuck to the bottom of the pan. Which, by the way, isn't nearly as easy to clean as you advertise when there's an inch of burned crud stuck to the bottom."

Madeline so didn't need this. "I'm sorry," she tried again as the line inched forward. "Did you heat the pan before adding the oil?"

"What does that have to do with anything?" Which gave Madeline her answer. "You shouldn't need a PhD to cook a damn pork chop."

Not only did she always, both on her show and in her cookbook, stress heating the pan first, but the booklet that came with the pans echoed that advice. But this was neither the time nor place to argue.

"They come with a lifetime warranty. If there's something wrong with the pan—"

"Didn't you hear me?" The woman's cheeks flamed. "The pork chops burned. Of course there's something wrong with the damn pan! Or maybe you had someone else ghostwrite that cookbook for you. Someone who's never been in a kitchen."

The woman's voice rose high enough to strip the yellow paint off the taxis that were pulling up to the curb. People were beginning to notice. And, oh, joy, they'd begun pulling out their smartphones. Probably to share that damn sex video with others in line.

"I tested every recipe in that book." Madeline tried for reason and prayed for the line to move more quickly. Why hadn't she just sprung for a limo or town car? Then at least she'd have a driver to run interference for her. Preferably a big one. With a pair of wraparound shades and a dangerous, don't-mess-with-the-chef vibe. "I also demonstrated most of the recipes, including the pork chops, on one of my shows."

She scrambled to remember which. "I think on *Dinner at Home*." Yes, that was it. "It'll be on the Web site if you'd like to—"

"I saw the damn show. And the dish looked real good when you cooked it. Which is why I decided to make the pork chops for my husband's birthday dinner. But, like I said, the pans are junk. You probably pulled some kind of bait and switch, making the finished chops in some decent brand. One you're not getting paid big bucks to endorse."

People now seemed torn between whether to check out the video or eavesdrop on this worsening conversation. Many, Madeline noted with a sinking heart, were managing to multitask.

No way was she going to discuss her contract, which wasn't, by the way, all that lucrative, in public, with a total stranger.

"Do you have a business card?" she asked.

"Why?" The woman seemed taken aback by the change in conversation.

"Because I'm very sorry for your problems, and if you give me your name and address, I'll see that a replacement pan is sent to you." She had no idea if ChefSteel would even do such a thing if there wasn't an actual flaw in the product. But if they wouldn't, she'd pay for one herself.

The woman crossed her arms over her chest. Given her body language, the idea, which certainly seemed generous to Madeline, apparently didn't impress.

"How's that going to help? Since the pan's obviously inferior to begin with."

"Fine." Now Madeline was losing patience. She dug into her purse and pulled out her billfold. "How much did you pay for the pan?"

"I don't have any idea. I bought them as a set. They're *your* pans. You should know they're only sold on the Shopping Channel as a set."

"Fine." Her dentist was going to love her. From the way she was grinding her teeth, he was probably going to make a fortune selling her a set of crowns. "What did you pay for the set?"

Her detractor paused just long enough to clue Madeline in to the fact that she was trying to decide how much she could get away with.

Surprise, surprise. She ended up naming an amount Madeline knew to be nearly double the actual price.

Wondering if she could write this off on her taxes as a promotional expense, or maybe goodwill, she began writing the check. "I'll need your name. Unless you want it made out to cash."

"Denise Walker." The woman snatched the piece of paper the second Madeline had finished writing. "How do I know this won't bounce?"

Bitch. "It won't. But I tape before a studio audience, so if it doesn't clear, you can show up and tell the world."

"Someone should tell the world that your pots are junk." The woman stuck the check in her bag. Then turned on a red suede heel and marched off.

"You're welcome," Madeline murmured.

"I would've decked her," a woman standing behind Madeline said. "But you handled it with amazing class."

"Thanks. I haven't had the best day. I really wouldn't want to cap it off by getting arrested for assault."

"Yeah. I heard about your day."

Of course you have.

"If my husband did that to me, they'd have to hide all the cleavers once I got home."

Madeline decided against mentioning she'd already considered that idea.

"But if it's any consolation, you're a lot better-looking than the woman in the video."

"Thanks." Not that it was any consolation.

"And a better cook than your weasel of a spouse. I've tried some of your recipes and they're great. But my husband took me to Maxime's in Miami for our twenty-fifth wedding anniversary, and I have to tell you, for such a big ticket dinner, we were not impressed.

"My eggplant-stuffed roasted salmon was surprisingly bland. Plus, my husband's scallops committed the cardinal culinary sin of being overcooked."

"I'm sorry." A word Madeline seemed to be saying a lot lately. Two more couples and she'd be in her taxi and, thank you, God, could escape.

"Well, it wasn't a total loss. I will say he's created the sexiest restaurant we've ever been to. Between the waterfall, the ocean view, and the cool South Beach vibe, not to mention the blindfolded Chocolate Seduction, we couldn't wait to get up to our room."

The Chocolate Seduction—which involved one diner

being blindfolded, then fed a sampling of exotic chocolates to guess the fillings—had been Maxime's idea.

Madeline had always suspected it was a dessert diners would order from room service, or take up to their rooms after dinner for fun and games later, but a surprising number of customers appeared to enjoy the exhibitionism of sampling while surrounded by strangers.

She was wondering if Maxime had re-created the Chocolate Seduction game with the woman in the video when the woman in the taxi line suddenly turned as scarlet as a boiled lobster.

"I'm sorry," she said. "I don't know what had me bringing up the sex thing. I mean . . . considering that he . . . You know."

Unfortunately, Madeline did know.

"Don't worry about it." *Finally!* She was being assigned the taxi that had pulled up to the curb. "It's good to hear that the dessert made up for a less-than-perfect meal."

"Oh, believe me," the woman assured Madeline as she escaped into the backseat. "It did."

The taxi had no sooner pulled into traffic when her phone rang again.

She debated not answering, but knowing her agent's tenacity, she'd just keep calling. And calling.

"Please tell me there's not another video out there," she said.

"No," Pepper said. "At least not that I know of, but considering all the rumors over the years, I need to warn you, Madeline, you should prepare yourself for yet more shoes to drop."

"What rumors?"

There was a pause on the other end of the line. For a moment Madeline thought that perhaps the call had been dropped, but then her agent, sounding uncharacteristically hesitant, asked, "Are you actually telling me that you've never heard the stories?"

"About Maxime? No." Apparently, the old saying was true: The wife really was the last to know.

"Oh. Well, don't worry about it. You know how rumors are; they probably don't mean a thing."

"What rumors?"

"Oh, Madeline." A huge sigh. "You've already had such a rotten day."

"It hasn't exactly been a picnic. But I did sell a bunch of pots and pans." Which was so not why she'd worked nearly her entire life to become a chef.

"Yay, you."

"Yay, me," Madeline echoed with a decided lack of enthusiasm. "You were telling me about rumors?"

"Oh, nothing specific. You know this city is basically just a small town. And people do gossip."

"People gossip about my marriage?"

There was another longer, deeper sigh. "We need to talk. Why don't you drop by my office on the way home?"

"Which one?"

There were two, including the "official" one in a beautiful landmark Victorian built by William Waldorf and John Jacob Astor III in the late 1800s. The other, which was usually saved for celebrations or serious career-planning sessions, was the Temple Bar in lower Manhattan's NoHo, located between the East and West Village.

"The one with alcohol." The bar. Which likely meant bad news. "I'm leaving now." The line went dead.

After giving the driver the new destination, Madeline leaned back against the seat, closed her eyes, and tried to tell herself not to borrow trouble. But that didn't stop her from worrying that perhaps ChefSteel had changed their mind about her being a proper spokesperson.

After all, there was a morality clause written into the twenty-six page contract. At the time she'd signed it, Madeline had assumed it referred to *her* behavior. But maybe any scandal would void the terms.

But would that really be such a bad thing?

In an attempt to bring in some much-needed additional income during the downturn of the economy, she'd started a part-time catering business. A chance meeting with a producer at a baby shower luncheon she'd prepared had led to a booking on *Today*.

Which, in turn, had led to a call from a vice president at the Cooking Network, who, after seeing Madeline cooking dolmades and pastitsio for Kathy Lee Gifford and Hoda Kotb, invited her to cook for a panel of network executives. Declaring her a natural, to her amazement, the executives offered her own show, *Comfort Cooking*.

She'd been inclined to turn down the offer. But, as Maxime, who'd always derided TV chefs in the past for prostituting their talent for the masses, had pointed out, it wasn't as if they could just pass up the money.

"Do you have any idea what it costs to open a five-star restaurant on the Vegas strip?" he asked. "One that can compete with Bobby Flay, Tom Colicchio, Wolfgang Puck, and Emeril?"

Which was how she had ended up on television.

And within six months had a second show, *Dinner at Home*, featuring quick and easy meals for busy families.

Forgoing anything resembling a normal life, she'd also published a cookbook, had a second in the publishing pipeline, and, on the advice of her newly acquired agent, had inked a deal with the company that made the cookware she used on her shows, which required yet more traveling, such as her trip to Omaha.

All to feed the ravenous alligator that Maxime's restaurant empire had become. After what he'd done, why should she care if the entire thing collapsed around him?

As it was, the career she'd looked forward to her entire life was looking more and more out of reach. Her parents had cooked for a living, true. But their goal, along with putting food on their own table, was to share their meals with others.

But now there were times when Madeline was forced to consider that professional cooking was becoming less about food and more about chef branding and ancillary marketing—pots, pans, spice rubs, television shows, books, even designer chef–labeled baby food.

More and more she felt as if she were running on a treadmill, or, to mix metaphors, the tail had begun wagging the dog.

Perhaps, before she confronted Maxime, she could give serious thought to her options. All of them.

6

Anyone just walking down the street might not even have known the Temple Bar existed, which Madeline had always thought was part of its charm and was what kept it from being packed with the *Sex and the City* crowd, who was more interested in seeing and being seen. The only eye-catching thing about the exterior was the white petroglyph-type lizard on the blue stone wall.

But the moment she entered the gorgeous deco room decorated in a 1950s-style dark mahogany, she felt her nerves, which had been tangled even before the video debacle, begin to loosen.

She passed the sweeping L-shaped bar and marble and mirrored walls to a comfortable lounge in the back, where Pepper was already waiting with an oversized dirty martini and a bowl of popcorn in front of her. Her lips curved in a welcoming smile, but even in the dim light, Madeline could view the concern in her agent's eyes.

"I love this place," Madeline said as she sat down at the table. The velvet drapes and backlighting added to the feel that the bar belonged to a different time. "I always expect to see *Mad Men*'s Don Draper drinking Manhattans."

Another cheating spouse, she considered as she took a bite of the popcorn, which was laced with sweet swirls of fried yam and beet strips. At least the advertising exec was fictional.

"Or Frank Sinatra," Pepper said as their server, a tall

redhead looking chic in Armani black, appeared to take their order. Both women were the picture of Manhattan elegance, making Madeline feel even more travel rumpled.

"I'll have the Black Crow." The vodka and Kahlúa would hopefully prepare her for whatever possible bad news Pepper was about to share, while, with any luck, the Vietnamese coffee in the cocktail would overcome the jet lag mixed with depression that was threatening to crash down on her.

"We'll also have an order of the salt-and-pepper cala-mari," Pepper told the server.

"What's up?" Madeline asked.

"Quite a bit, actually. But while we're waiting for your drink and our food, why don't you tell me about Omaha?"

"It was cold." Madeline plucked another bite of pop-corn from the bottomless bowl the bar specialized in. "Our car ran into a snowbank on the way to the department store, but the son of the woman who picked me up was a cop, so he got us on our way soon. And the store staff had everything set up and prepared."

"Well, I'm pleased to hear that something went well."

Although the bar was nearly empty, it took a while for their order to arrive. Despite being eager to hear Pepper's news, Madeline chatted a bit more about her experience in Nebraska. Leaving out the humiliating part about every-one racing to YouTube during her demonstration.

A little silence came over the table after she'd finished her story. The server showed up, placed their order on the table, and discreetly faded away.

"Well?" Madeline asked after taking a sip of the drink that was sinfully good.

"You have an offer."

"Good try, but you could have told me that over the phone. I'm not going to be distracted that easily. First things first. If you know something about Maxime, you need to tell me. If for no other reason than a friend wouldn't send another friend into what might be the most important conversation of her life unarmed."

"You're right." Pepper exhaled a long breath. Took a bite of the calamari. Madeline had never known her agent to be at a loss for words, as she seemed to be now.

"There's never been anything specific," she said finally. "I mean, not that I've heard, anyway, but you know how people talk. . . ."

"All too well." Especially today.

"Well, the word is that he was a player all during his other marriages. And you know what they say about leopards changing their spots."

"He's French. He flirts."

Even as she heard the excuse coming out of her mouth, she could hear Maxime's voice. How many times had he used that very excuse during the early days of their relationship, when she'd been admittedly insecure about his familiarity with the women who flocked to his restaurant?

Unlike so many upscale restaurants in the city, Maxime's had always been open during the noon hour.

"For all those ladies who lunch," he'd claimed when he'd first come up with the idea. "They're a valuable customer base too many chefs who refuse to lower themselves to serve food in the middle of the day are missing. Those rich socialites can't all eat at Bergdorf Goodman or Barneys."

At the time it had made sense. Now she wondered if he'd just been creating his own dating pool.

"Perhaps that's all it was." Pepper didn't even try to keep the skepticism from her tone. "But he was certainly doing a great deal more than flirting in the video."

"You've seen it?"

"Darling, everyone from Tulsa to Timbukutu has seen that video. Including, I suspect, Katrin Von Küenberg's husband."

Madeline recognized the name immediately. *Forbes* magazine had ranked her in the top twenty of the world's wealthiest women. A frivolous, global-party-trotting heiress in her younger years, after her father's death, she'd returned to Austria and taken the reins of her family's international fortune.

Among the Von Küenbergs' many holdings were factories that had provided tents and uniforms (and, rumors suggested, chemicals and munitions) to the German army in World War II and a brewing empire that had earned her nickname of Beer Baroness.

Madeline not only knew *of* her, but she also knew her personally. Along with having been dinner guests at her Upper East Side penthouse, she and Maxime had also spent a rare vacation week at her sprawling lake house in Bavaria, and another week cruising the Mediterranean in a yacht larger than the Shelter Bay farmhouse where Madeline had spent so many of her formative years.

"What does Katrin have to do with the video?"

"You obviously weren't looking all that closely."

"There was a glare from the overhead lights in the store. It was hard to make out details."

Which was only partly true. The fact was that her head had gone so light, she'd been afraid she might embarrass herself by fainting right there in store aisle. And, admittedly, practicing avoidance, she hadn't looked at it again. And hoped she'd never have to.

Also, her attention had been so drawn to Maxime, she hadn't paid any attention to whatever woman he was with. While suffering through that long plane flight, she'd decided it must be some Las Vegas call girl.

"You do know Katrin and her husband are involved in a nasty, take-no-prisoners divorce?"

"Of course. It's been in all the papers."

You couldn't check out of a market without seeing the tabloid headlines screaming the latest, so-called update. They'd been to dinner just two months ago when Katrin had mentioned that her husband—an American novelist of obscure, experimental literature—was causing her problems. Two days later, she leaked photos of him dressed in a bra, panties, black fishnet stockings, and high heels to the *National Enquirer*.

"I knew that he's challenging their prenup, but since when is adultery a valid reason to void a prenuptial agreement?"

"It's not. At least it's not typical." Diamonds flashed as Pepper waved away that idea. "After all, everyone cheats."

"I don't."

"Of course you don't, darling," the agent soothed expertly. "Apparently, he's trying to break it by claiming that he wasn't aware of the full extent of her fortune. Along with impaired judgment."

"I can identify with that one," Madeline muttered. Obviously her own judgment had been flawed when it came to her marriage. "How, exactly, was his judgment impaired?"

"He says he was high on cocaine when he signed it."

"Well, that's a novel excuse."

"Isn't it? I suspect he hired someone to make that horrid video to embarrass her."

"I don't know about Katrin, but it sure as hell has embarrassed me," Madeline admitted.

"You're the injured party. You should hold your head high. My guess is that if her husband can somehow prove that her and Maxime's relationship goes back to before the marriage, he might be able to argue that she didn't enter into the marriage in good faith."

"I can't believe this." Madeline rubbed her temples where the mother of all migraines was threatening to strike. Bad enough that she was publicly humiliated. Now her marriage was going to be dragged into the divorce of the century?

"It'll blow over," Pepper assured her quickly. "Things like this always do. Meanwhile, looking at the bright side: Not only is any publicity good publicity, but you're going to be perceived as the victim."

"Just what I wanted."

"Well, of course you don't. But better the victim than the slut home wrecker, darling. And think how many women out there will identify with you."

"I'd rather not." Publicly Cheated-on Wives wasn't exactly a club Madeline had ever imagined joining.

"Well, let's get on to the good news," her agent said.

"Let's," Madeline agreed. Anything to get off this topic.

"I received a call from a representative of OneWorld Airlines this morning. They want you to create a signature menu for their European flights."

"You're suggesting I cook airline meals?" Could this day get any worse?

"Well, you wouldn't be the one actually *cooking* them. But, yes, I think it would be a very positive opportunity. After Lufthansa started offering chef-driven meals for business and first class, the idea's proven hugely popular with flyers. Tommy Tang even inked a deal with Thai Airways."

"He told me. Quite honestly, I was a little surprised."

Madeline had run into the Godfather of Thai Cooking during a layover at LAX a few months ago, which was when he'd told her about the deal. Although their culinary styles couldn't be any more different, his tiger prawns topped with mango salsa were high on the list of top ten dishes she'd want for her last meal.

"People who can afford to spring for first class pay attention to chef's name on a menu when they get great food," Pepper pointed out. "Especially when the airline's spending big bucks to promote those meals. Which, in turn, builds name recognition and makes them more likely to frequent those chef's restaurants."

"Now you're talking about synergy," Madeline murmured. Which she'd been hearing as often as *ancillary marketing* these days.

"Exactly!" Either her agent didn't notice Madeline's decided lack of enthusiasm, or, more likely, merely chose to overlook it.

"Let me give it some thought. The timing isn't exactly the best right now."

"I totally understand." Pepper nodded sympathetically. Then polished off the rest of the martini. "Go home; talk things out with Maxime. Why don't I give you a call tomorrow afternoon?"

"So soon?" A betrayal as hurtful and public as what her husband had committed wasn't as easily dispensed with as a scorched béchamel sauce or a broken shrimp platter.

"I know." She reached across the small table and patted Madeline's hand. "But the offer is time sensitive. Although you're absolutely their first choice, they're also considering Rachael Ray. Or Sandra Lee." Her brow furrowed. Just a bit. "And, let's face it, darling. Although your food is superb, their public profile is a bit higher than yours."

How about a lot higher? And, since today's department-store challenge, along with her encounter in the taxi line, the idea of adding yet more "synergy" to her already-filled plate had Madeline back to picturing tails and dogs again.

"I'll call you," she countered. Pepper wasn't the only one at this table who could negotiate.

Although it obviously wasn't the answer she was hoping for, Pepper's red lips curved in a smile. "Wonderful." She glanced down at Madeline's glass. Which was, at this moment, closer to half-empty than half-full. Which, Madeline considered, could be taken as a metaphor for her life. "Would you like another?"

"I'd better not."

Although the idea of getting wasted was even more appealing than it had been on the plane, she needed to be firm and clearheaded when she confronted her husband. Although she may be swinging between wanting to go straight to bed and sob copious tears into her pillow, or screeching and throwing a well-aimed cleaver between his legs, neither would help this situation she'd landed in.

7

It was raining. A cold, hard rain that pounded against the windows like a shower of stones and blurred the lights from the traffic below the apartment and the bridge crossing the river.

Maxime, who'd arrived back home before Madeline, had already lit a fire and opened a bottle of cabernet.

She'd practiced all the things she was going to say. Questions she was going to ask, demands she was going to make, all the time staying coolly, calmly in control. Being the injured party, she was determined to hold the high ground and not allow him to weaken her resolve by setting a romantic atmosphere.

Amazingly, proving how deeply their relationship had sunk into the morass of avoidance, she and her husband first exchanged a bit of chitchat about their flights. They compared her in-flight spaghetti salad to his Philly steak, and decided she'd gotten the better meal.

Then they went on to discuss the weather. The weather!

And, yes, even how many damn pots she'd sold in Omaha.

Finally, unable to avoid the huge, rotting elephant carcass in the room another moment, Madeline stopped her pacing, stared unseeingly out the window at the cars making their way across the bridge, and said, "I don't understand."

"I never meant to hurt you, Madeline," he said with what sounded like sincerity. But then again, she'd believed him when he'd taken those marriage vows, which had included fidelity. "Although it's no excuse for what happened, I had no idea we were being videotaped. It was Katrin's bastard of a husband's doing."

"So the woman *is* Katrin Von Küenberg?" Despite the heat the crackling fire was sending out, Madeline was colder than she'd been in Nebraska.

"Oui." She'd noticed over the years that whenever he wanted to convince her of something she really didn't want to do, his French accent would thicken. "He's a greedy bastard who's after her money. He wants to break the prenuptial agreement and humiliate her while doing so."

His voice was hard. And coldly furious.

How strange that he'd be more concerned about his lover's feelings than those of his wife.

Strange and sad.

She turned around to face him. The anger in his voice was echoed in his deeply hooded eyes. She countered, "That may be. But unless he forced you both at gunpoint into that bed, I don't see how he's to blame for the situation."

"Touché." He tilted his glass toward her.

She didn't know this man. Didn't recognize him. Maxime Durand was known for never holding back his emotions. Arguments in his kitchens had ended up with him punching so many holes in the walls, he'd quit bothering to repair what his employees had taken to calling design features.

Her fingers tightened on the slender stem of her own glass. "Well." She felt tears sting her eyes and resolutely blinked them away. "Aren't we being ever so civilized?" Madeline was finding it difficult to work up the proper fury while feeling as if she'd been hollowed out with a dull melon baller. "Is this how your other marriages ended?"

"You knew I'd been married before," the stranger stated in a tone as cool and sterile as the décor of the room. "You knew those marriages had failed. I told you repeatedly that I don't believe I possess the marriage gene. But you refused to listen."

He had. And she had.

Her bad.

No, Madeline reminded herself firmly as an encouraging flare of anger flashed through her. *His.*

"I also warned you about the difference in our ages," he continued defending the indefensible. "I knew you were too young. But I couldn't resist your entreaties."

"It wasn't as if I got down on my knees and begged," she muttered. But, admittedly, she'd come damn close. "Besides, my father was seventeen years older than my mother."

"I'm well aware of that. Given that you pointed it out on a regular basis even before we began living together."

She hated that he was calm when she was not. Hated that he had the gall, after what he'd done, to use her own words against her.

She repeated what she'd always said. "They were totally compatible. In their marriage and in the kitchen. And my father never, *ever* strayed."

He shrugged as he refilled his glass from the decanter on the outrageously expensive ultramodern glass console table the designer had said would be perfect in the space. The table Maxime loved. The one Madeline found lacking in any warmth. Like the rest of the penthouse.

The kitchen was the only place she'd ever felt even the slightest bit comfortable. Unfortunately, it was also Maxime's realm, and she was basically relegated to saucier whenever they prepared the rare meal together.

After they'd returned from their honeymoon, Madeline discovered that instead of working side by side, as she'd imagined, her new husband was putting her at the front of the house at his restaurant, where she was expected to serve as both the dining room manager and hostess.

"Your beauty and charm bring my dining room to life, *darling*," he'd insisted. While admittedly flattered, she hadn't devoted all those years learning how to cook to end up spending each evening wearing Spanx beneath long black gowns, standing on foot-killing heels, greeting guests, and keeping service humming, all the while continuing to smile until her lips felt frozen.

He'd assured her it would only be temporary. But one month had turned into two. Then six. Then a year, then, before she knew it, although she was occasionally called in to help out on the kitchen line, most of her time was spent up front, and locked away in her office, running the financial side of the restaurant while her husband ruled supreme in the kitchen. On those increasingly rare occasions he was actually in the city. Most of the actual cooking had been taken over by his sous chef. Who was—no surprise, given the chauvinism of the business—male.

She'd believed him when he'd told her the trips were business. But now she was forced to wonder the same thing Katrin's husband was allegedly trying to discover for his own reasons. How long had the couple's affair been going on?

"Children don't always know what goes on in a marriage," he pointed out, dragging her mind back from that vexing thought to their conversation and her firm belief in her parents' fidelity.

"Spoken like a man who's never had, or even wanted, a child," she snapped. Then took a deep breath.

One thing at a time. And right now her bastard husband's unwillingness to have a family wasn't an issue on the table.

"My mother first brought me to spend days at my family's restaurant in Umbria when I was an infant," she said. Again repeating what she'd told him whenever the subject of children had come up. "I grew up there. I did my homework in the dining room before the restaurant opened for dinner. I spent most of my waking hours until I was thirteen years old at Trattoria Gabriella, and all I ever saw was love and respect. It was obvious to anyone who ever saw them together that they were soul mates."

Hadn't her mother always said that Nikos Galinas, Maddy's Greek father, had taught her mother to cook with passion, while her father, in turn, claimed that his dazzling Gabriella had taught him to cook with soul?

"Do you know the trouble with you, Madeline?"

"No. But I'm sure you're going to tell me."

"You're a romantic."

"Guilty as charged." Madeline was annoyed at how he made it sound like a flaw. "Which is why I cook from my heart instead of creating flashy, pretentious dishes designed to impress magazine critics and self-important foodie bloggers."

Bull's-eye.

His brows lowered above narrowed eyes. "Is that what you're accusing me of doing?" He splayed his hand across his chest. *"Moi?"*

"How long has it been since you've actually prepared a meal, or even a single dish, at any of your restaurants?"

He looked at her as if she'd gotten her degree not from the prestigious Culinary Institute of America, but from an online correspondence course. "We've been through this before, Madeline. I'm a visionary." There it was again. That condescension she'd grown accustomed to hearing in his tone. "I create the concept, then hire people to carry it out for me."

Madeline wasn't totally naive. She knew many chefs who'd built careers these days doing that same thing. But it was still so foreign to the way she'd grown up. The way she'd always thought she'd run her own restaurant. Someday. Marrying Maxime had sidetracked that dream.

"People always loved it when my parents greeted them when they arrived. Or at least came out of the kitchen at the end of the meal. It made their experience more personal." *And if there'd been a problem, like overcooked scallops, they would have damn well known it immediately and made things right.*

"So you've said. Time and time again. And as I've tried to explain it to you, time and time again, as impressive as their personalizing the diners' experience was, and as much as they undoubtedly enjoyed greeting their guests, their restaurant was much smaller. More intimate. And undoubtedly run at a slower pace."

"Italians enjoy savoring their food without having to feel they're being chased off so the chef can turn over tables faster."

He sighed. Heavily. As only the French could do. How was she suddenly the one defending her position?

"Times are different now," he insisted. "People who buy an Armani suit don't expect Giorgio Armani to be toiling away in some backroom sweatshop, personally sewing all the seams. Diners today are seeking a star-power experience in a fabulous environment that they can brag about to all their friends. They don't care who's actually preparing the food."

He was right about one thing: They'd had this conversation too many times to count. And it was more than obvious, even apart from his infidelity, that they'd never reach agreement.

He'd steamrolled over her, as he always did. By their second anniversary, which she'd spent alone, he'd opened restaurants in Miami, Washington, and Chicago.

Fortunately, there'd been the whales to keep the Durand restaurant empire afloat.

The little-known secret of the culinary world was that high-end restaurants such as Maxime's—with its enormous fresh floral arrangements, heavy silver cutlery, and white tablecloths—had relied on the "whale" customer, regulars who thought nothing of ordering a thousand-dollar bottle of wine to go with their hundred-dollar dinner, and putting the tab on their overblown expense accounts.

Then, seemingly overnight, the stock market plunged; 401(k)s turned into 201(k)s; the rich became if not poor, then a lot less rich; and the testosterone-driven whales, who for so long had seemed driven to outspend one another, stopped coming. In droves.

When television news cameras showed you getting called before Congress to explain your business practices, being seen eating at Chez Maxime's on Columbus Circle wasn't exactly in your best interest while you were trying to dodge indictment.

Nearly overnight, receipts at Maxime's New York and D.C. restaurants plummeted fifty percent. Along with a thirty-percent dive in Chicago.

While many chefs were forced to close their doors and others slashed their prices or offered two-for-one specials, free wine, and even early-bird specials, Maxime insisted gourmands who appreciated and understood great food would continue to pay for quality.

"Being a four-star chef is like being a shark," he said, adding Los Angeles, Dubai, and Miami to his empire. Since building the overpriced, money-devouring Maxime's Las Vegas, their bank account had begun bleeding so much red ink, it looked as if someone had spilled a barrel of pinot noir on the monthly statement. "If you don't keep moving forward, you die."

"Now you're moving on," Madeline said flatly.

He did not deny it. "It's for the best."

Tears she'd refused to shed stung her eyes. Looking at this man she'd thought she'd spend the rest of her life with was like looking through the rain-blurred window.

"Do you love her?"

He lifted his shoulders in that Gallic shrug she'd once found so sexy. "We suit each other."

"Meaning she's buying herself a stud to service her in bed and to show off at her society parties, and you hit the jackpot."

"We suit," he repeated evenly. Madeline knew it was truly over when he didn't rise to the bait. "She enjoys the spotlight, which being married to that so-called author didn't provide. Everyone longs for celebrity."

"I don't."

"You're an anomaly in the culinary world. Even your own network is turning more and more to reality programming."

Which wasn't her favorite topic of conversation, either. Even as much as they needed her income, she'd recently turned down a chance to host a reality program her producer had in development—*So You Think You Can Cook?*

"Why else do you think I came to America?" he asked.

"To cook."

"Darling, I could have cooked in France. Run a charming bistro somewhere in Provence like your parents' quaint little trattoria. But would Barbara Walters and Oprah invite me to appear on their programs? Would I be asked to collaborate with the White House chef on a state dinner? Would I—"

"I get it." Unfortunately, she did. Too late. "Without all those restaurants, you lose your celebrity status."

"Which is why I must keep them alive. Whatever the sacrifice."

"Wow. What you were doing with Katrin looked like one hell of a sacrifice." She welcome the renewed burst of anger that scorched away a bit of the pain.

"I may have overstated that," he admitted, looking slightly chagrined for the first time since she'd entered the apartment. "But do you have any idea how many young, talented chefs have put a target on my back? Also, Katrin's closer to my age. She's more experienced." He paused. "More open to adventure."

It took a minute for that innuendo to sink in. When it did, Madeline felt as if her head might explode.

"You're not talking about rafting down the Amazon. Or bungee jumping off some bridge in New Zealand, are you?" Could this get any worse? "You're talking about sex."

Oh, God, didn't New York get earthquakes? Couldn't the earth open up beneath the apartment and put an end to this conversation?

"And I don't?" she asked. "Satisfy you?"

Yes. It could get worse. Much worse.

He didn't respond for a long second that seemed like a lifetime.

"I love you, *Mad-eh-Leen*," he said finally. He'd gone all French on her again, but this time, she realized, trying too soothe rather than seduce. "Your youth, your enthusiasm for life, your love of cooking. But you and I"—another shrug—"we don't suit. Not for the long run."

"You don't know anything about love." Was that cold, flat tone coming out of her own mouth? Apparently it was, because it also matched the ice she could feel flowing over her broken heart. "And you never will."

She shook her head. "I'm leaving. I'll be back for my things later." She had to escape while she still had a shred of dignity left.

"You stay. You've had a long and difficult day. I didn't unpack. I'll be the one to spend the night somewhere else."

That somewhere else being Katrin Von Küenberg's bed.

"I don't give a damn where you spend the night. But here's a little news flash for you, Maxime. I loathe this apartment." Which had been—surprise, surprise—redecorated six months ago by the designer to the rich and Gotham-connected that Katrin had recommended. "You've no idea what a relief it's going to be to never have to look at this furniture again." Though she would, admittedly, miss the view.

Jet brows lifted. "You should have said something."

"I did. When you let the designer bring in all this Fortress of Solitude glass and steel, I told you it lacked warmth. And was uncomfortable. But, just like everything else about our life together, you refused to listen."

She stiffened her spine. Then her resolve. "Good-bye,

Maxime. My lawyer will contact you to work out the details."

She didn't have a lawyer—yet—but, fortunately, one of the things that made Pepper such a good agent was that she knew everyone.

"Fine. You should tell that lawyer I'm prepared to give you enough funds to start your own restaurant. As you've always dreamed of."

She'd been walking away, intending a grand exit, when his words stopped her dead in her tracks. She turned and stared, incredulous.

"You're offering to fund a restaurant for me?"

"It only seems reasonable."

"Reasonable."

Oddly, now that they were back to that, she felt herself deflating again, like a soufflé too long out of the oven. For a fleeting moment, she allowed herself a fantasy of opening up a restaurant right across the street from Chez Maxime's on Columbus Circle. Then beating the black-checked chef pants off her bastard, cheating, soon-to-be-ex husband.

"I would rather be deep-fried in a vat of hydrogenated fat than take a single, solitary penny from you." Her marriage might have dissolved before her eyes, but she still had her pride. "Especially since it would come from another woman. Thanks, but no, thanks."

It admittedly wasn't the best exit line. Nowhere near, "We'll always have Paris," or "Frankly, my dear, I don't give a damn," and maybe someday she'd wished she'd come up with something sharper. Wittier. But at this moment, at this horrible, very bad point in time, it was enough.

She walked out the door, head held high, and took the elevator back down to the lobby, where she had the spiffy-uniformed doorman call her a taxi.

"La Guardia," she said when she climbed into the backseat of the yellow cab. "Departures."

8

Denver, Colorado
One week earlier

Stephanie Fletcher had always believed in fairy tales. In her fantasies, someday, if she only believed hard enough and made herself perfect and deserving enough, a prince in shining armor would come riding up on a white horse to her family's small northern Arizona ranch, declare her the woman he'd been searching the entire world for, and carry her off to his castle, where white swans floated on mirrored blue lakes, bluebirds sang in flowering trees, unicorns walked in wildflower meadows beneath shimmering rainbows, and everyone lived happily ever after.

Even after she'd outgrown the unicorns, bluebirds, and rainbows, Stephanie never quite abandoned her dream.

She'd been waiting tables at the famed El Tovar Hotel on the south rim of the Grand Canyon between her sophomore and junior year of college to raise much-needed tuition money when Peter Fletcher sat down at her table. Heir to a Colorado oil-and-mining fortune, he'd seemed intelligent, witty, and devastatingly sophisticated.

And, if that wasn't enough, he was, quite honestly, the most handsome man she'd ever seen who wasn't up on a movie screen.

With the Arizona sunset turning his hair to molten gold, he'd personified a quote she'd torn from a magazine and pasted on her bulletin board back when she'd been in middle school: "Once in a while, right in the middle of an ordinary life, love gives us a fairy tale."

He'd swept her off her feet—which hadn't been all that difficult, since she'd been waiting for him for nearly her entire life—and into his bed. Unlike Cinderella, she didn't run away at the stroke of midnight, but stayed the night.

The next morning, he'd complained when she'd gotten up with the sun because her current schedule had her working breakfast and dinner.

"What am I supposed to do while you're gone?" he asked, looking unbelievably hot as he lay naked amid the tangled sheets when she came out of the bathroom, dressed in the uniform she'd been wearing last night when she'd left the dining room with him.

His chest was darkly tanned and ripped and, amazingly, after all the times they'd made love, he was blatantly, breathtakingly aroused.

She'd done that! The idea was enough to make her head spin. Stephanie was nothing like the women she suspected he was normally attracted to. The type of tall, sophisticated blondes from wealthy families whose engagement photos always showed up on the society pages of newspapers and glossy magazines. She was neither tall nor sophisticated. As for her family, like most ranchers, it was a constant struggle to stay afloat.

But instead of being tired of her that next morning, as she'd secretly feared, Peter was telling her he'd miss her and didn't know how he'd get through the lonely hours while she was delivering hash browns and fried eggs to the lodge's breakfast crowd.

"I want to stay," she said. "But I really need the job."

He waved the statement away with that beautiful, long-fingered hand that had created such havoc over every inch of her body. "You're too smart to be waiting tables."

Having been brought up to respect honest work and the people who did it, Stephanie had never felt embarrassed about her job. Until now.

"I need the money. For college."

She'd thought a career in hotel or restaurant management would be fulfilling, which is why she'd first begun working at the National Park lodge during her summer vacations back in high school, starting out washing dishes and eventually working her way up to server.

"Whatever they're paying you, I'll double it," he said without blinking an eye.

Her first thought was to wonder what it must be like to have so much money that you didn't even have to think about throwing it away. Her second thought was that his of-fer wasn't at all flattering.

She tossed up her chin. She might want to stay with him, more than she'd ever wanted anything in her life. But she was a rancher's daughter and had a strong streak of pride.

"I'm not some hooker you can buy to have sex with." She'd never been promiscuous. In fact, he was only her sec-ond lover, but she wasn't about to share that with him.

"I never, ever, thought that." He looked her straight in the eye. Which her father had always told her said a lot about a man's character. "Something happened last night, Steph."

His low, seductive tone was the one he'd used while they'd made love. Last night it had coaxed her into doing things she'd never done before. Now it had her going weak in the knees.

"It was something special. Something I've never felt be-fore. Surely you felt it, too."

"I did," she admitted.

"I think . . ." He paused and raked his hands through the gilt strands of his hair that had felt like corn silk against her breasts. "I think I might have fallen in love with you."

"It's too soon." Her voice wavered. She'd thought the same thing, but hadn't dared hope that they might be on the same wavelength.

"Logic would say so." Oh, God, she was drowning in his warm gaze. "But what I feel here"—he splayed his hand over his heart—"says otherwise."

Appearing totally at ease with being naked, he got out of bed, stood in front of her, and smoothed his palms over her bare shoulders.

"Spend the day with me, sweetheart. If we don't explore what's happening, if we let this moment pass, we could end up regretting it the rest of our lives."

Logic warred with emotion. "I can't think," she moaned as his mouth moved to her throat.

"Don't think." His lips burned a trail along her jawline. "Just feel."

He was everything Stephanie had waited for her entire life. Everything she'd dreamed of. So why was she hesitating?

"Yes." Her breath hitched as one of those wickedly clever hands cupped a breast. "Oh yes."

He responded by kissing her long and deep.

"Good girl," he murmured against her lips as he drew her back down to the bed.

They stayed there for the next four days, only calling out for room service. She resigned her job, but, as he'd assured her, waitress jobs were a dime a dozen. She could get another. If she wanted one.

Or, he suggested, they could get married.

Although she knew it cost him a great deal of pride, her father had allowed Peter's family to pay for the wedding, which, Stephanie's future mother-in-law insisted, must be held in Denver to accommodate all the family's friends and her husband's business associates.

Since Peter had insisted on a fall wedding, Stephanie dropped out of college—she could always transfer to UC Denver later, he'd assured her—and moved to Colorado.

A mere two months after he'd changed her life when he'd walked into that dining room, she was walking down a white satin runner in front of five hundred wedding guests at Denver's exclusive Coldwater Creek Country Club, where they spent the night before flying to his family's Maui home.

He'd taken advantage of the first-class perks, drinking the free liquor nearly the entire flight to Hawaii. When she'd tried, discreetly, to suggest he might want to slow down, he'd responded that he was only celebrating their marriage. Which, if true, a niggling little voice inside her had suggested, he wouldn't have been flirting with the blond, ever-so-attentive flight attendant.

She'd been Peter Fletcher's wife for less than forty-eight hours when she belatedly discovered that the problem with fairy tales was that they didn't warn impressionable young girls that the prince could turn out to be a frog once he took off that gleaming suit of armor.

And that when a man hit you, it hurt.

A lot.

The doorbell rang, sending a burst of adrenaline rushing through Stephanie's blood and dragging her mind from that honeymoon three years ago when her life had begun its downhill slide into hell.

With nerves tangled and anxiety gnawing at her gut, she crossed the massive foyer of the stone mansion that had become a prison, pausing in front of the heavy, gilt-framed mirror that had, according to the designer Peter had hired, once hung on the wall of a French palace.

The blond woman reflected back at her from that mirror, with her sleek, chin-length bob, was a stranger. The only recognizable things were the stress lines around her mouth and the fear in her hazel eyes. And the purple mark on the side of her face, which, if you looked carefully, wasn't as concealed beneath her makeup as she'd hoped. At least the turtleneck sweater covered up the fingerprint bruises on her throat.

Stephanie looked through the thick wooden door's judas hole and blew out a relieved breath when she saw the silver-haired woman standing on the other side of the door. A woman whose chic silk blouse and ladylike pearls looked totally appropriate in this gated community.

"All right," the "conductor" she knew only as Karen said as she entered the foyer. "Are you all packed?"

She'd been advised to travel light, which was exactly what she'd done. "My bag's upstairs. I hid it in the back of the guest-room closet. Just in case."

She didn't need to add that if Peter had arrived home from Cheyenne early, her carefully constructed escape plan would have had to be put on hold.

"Good thinking. Why don't you retrieve it; then we'll get going?"

Her bruised hip had her moving a bit gingerly up the Scarlett O'Hara staircase that she'd so often dreamed of someday having while growing up, when she'd been young, foolish, and romantic.

After pulling the cheap carry-on, which she'd bought specifically because it was at the opposite end of the spectrum from her matching Louis Vuitton luggage, from beneath a shelf of linens, and heading back down the hallway, she paused in the doorway of the overdone master bedroom, which looked as if it had been decorated by Marie Antoinette.

It was here, in that heavily carved Louis XVI bed, where she'd learned that a married woman, could, indeed, be raped.

Peter's escalating violence had contradicted everything she'd been taught about life, love, and the sanctity of marriage.

The day she'd walked down that aisle in Vera Wang purchased by her mother-in-law-to-be, wife beating had been beyond her imagination.

Even after he'd first hit her, she'd not fully been able to believe that it had happened. That Peter, her husband, could have done such a thing to her.

And even when the handprint on her cheek gave evidence to the contrary, she'd believed him when he'd assured her that it wouldn't happen again.

Because he was her *husband*.

The next time, desperately wanting—needing—to believe in him, Stephanie had accepted his excuse. It was an accident. A mistake.

When it happened yet again, then again, she blamed the stress of his life outside the home. Of course, she'd tearfully admitted to him, she didn't know the pressure that came with being the only son of a family of overachievers. No, she had no idea of the difficulties involved in international oil trading, where fortunes were made. And could be just as easily lost.

It was only these outside problems that explained his behavior.

Which meant that it was up to her to find a way to soothe. To ease his frustrations.

And when she failed, as she always seemed to do, Stephanie had only had herself to blame.

So she became quieter. More submissive. More of what Peter Fletcher wanted in a wife. Less of what he disliked. The map of her world narrowed, until it centered solely around her husband and her home as she slavishly conformed to every behavior that would demonstrate that she was a good wife.

And when she could no longer lie to herself, when she was forced to accept the painful truth that the devoted, sincere, loving man Stephanie had believed she'd married was, in fact, cold, calculating, manipulative, and violent, some last lingering scrap of pride had her lying to others to convince them that her life was, indeed, that fairy tale she'd dreamed of. Rather than the nightmare that more and more often had her waking up in a cold sweat.

"No more," she whispered, even as icy fingers of fear skimmed up her spine.

When she returned to the foyer, Karen reached into an

oversized tote bag and took out an envelope. "How are you doing?"

"I'm worried." And wasn't that an understatement? "Actually, I'm scared."

"You should be. What you're doing isn't going to be easy. And I'm not going to lie to you. It could be dangerous. But you're already facing danger every time you drive on a freeway. Or," she pointed out significantly, "remain in this house."

"I've never broken the law before." That was the absolute truth. As far as she could remember, Stephanie had never even jaywalked.

"Perhaps you've never had an important enough reason before." The woman gave her a long look that was laced with both sympathy and steel. "You're always free to change your mind."

"No." Stephanie shook her head. "I'm not going to."

After agonizing over the decision, she'd come to the conclusion she didn't have any choice. Hadn't the mothers of Moses and Jesus smuggled their sons to safety to protect them from infanticide? What she was doing was no different.

"I'll be fine," she said when Karen didn't immediately respond, but continued to study her. "I know what I'm doing."

"All right, then. Here's your new ID. You're now officially Phoebe Tyler."

Stephanie had chosen the name after a great deal of research, because not only had Phoebe been a Titan goddess in Greek myth, but it was also the name of an Amazon warrior. She knew, despite all the help she was receiving, that she was going to need all the strength she could muster. There was also the fact that Phoebe had been her favorite character on *Friends*.

"I like the sound of it." She'd tried out dozens of names in front of the mirror until this one had struck a chord. But this was the first time she'd heard anyone, other than herself, say it out loud.

"So do I, and I'm so glad you went with it. At first the engineer was leaning toward Sarah, which, being the fifth-most-popular name the year you were born, allows more anonymity, but one of the mistakes people make when choosing a new identity is to choose a name beginning with the same letter of the original one, which we didn't want to risk. Also, she and I agreed that Phoebe fits this new, strong woman you're becoming."

Stephanie—*No,* she thought, having been told that she'd have to embrace her new identity to make this work, *Phoebe*—smiled at that idea. When she felt the tug of unused muscles on either side of her mouth, she realized she couldn't remember the last time she'd smiled.

"Your first station will be San Diego. Christy will be your stationmaster there. I'm sorry I can't give you any information, but she'll be e-mailed your photo and will meet you at baggage claim.

"You'll stay with her overnight; then the next morning another conductor, whose name you'll learn right before you leave San Diego, will put you on a plane to Seattle, where you'll spend another night.

"Then you'll take the Amtrak Cascades down to Portland," Karen continued. Her brisk, matter-of-fact tone had Phoebe wondering how many travelers she'd dealt with. "You'll be booked in the train's business-class section because there are usually less travelers and they're more likely to be concentrating on their work than chatting with seatmates. I'm told the route has some gorgeous scenery, so that's a plus."

Although she found it ironic that she'd be taking an actual train on this underground railroad she'd entered, scenery was the last thing on Phoebe's mind right now.

"Your final conductor will meet your train and drive you down the coast to your final destination, which, depending on the traffic, could take another two hours. Perhaps a bit more if there's an accident tie-up on the coast road. But you should definitely be settled in Shelter Bay by that evening."

Three days and a few hours until freedom. The idea had, not that long ago, been incomprehensible.

"I don't know how to thank you." Phoebe brushed at the tears that had begun trailing down her cheeks.

"Just have a good life," Karen said, her tone softening a bit. "And, someday, if you're able, pay it forward."

"Oh, I totally intend to do that."

For victims of abuse, the shadowy network of volunteers and shelters were literally lifesavers. Stephanie also knew that every one of them understood that police and federal agents could show up on their doorstep any day due to the falsification of records they specialized in. Also, the very same dangerous abusers they were helping women to escape could find them.

These women weren't just saving *her* life.

As she pressed a hand against her still flat stomach, Phoebe vowed that whatever it took, whatever she'd have to do, she would keep her unborn child safe.

9

Lucas had already seen the sex video before showing up at Sofia's farm the afternoon after his father's burial. Although he'd never considered himself a masochist, Sofia's mention of Maddy possibly returning home to oversee the remodeling of the farmhouse had him Googling her name to see what was happening with her life, other than the TV shows he'd spent too much time watching like some lovesick teenager.

It did not take long. The first thing that came up was a mention of her husband's sex video. With another woman.

Wondering how widespread the video had become, he typed in the French celebrity chef's name. In a mere nineteen seconds, the search engine offered up 695,000 results.

Oh, hell.

After a hot night dreaming—in vivid, Technicolor detail—of the last time he and Maddy had made love, in the cave on the beach, with the moonlight streaming over her body, he'd awakened with the mother of all hard-ons and the crazy idea that just maybe, fate had decided to give him a second chance with the only female who'd ever gotten not only under his skin, but into his heart.

Not that he would ever hit on a married woman. Having lived through the pain of two of his father's divorces—first to his mother, and second to Charity's—there was no way

Lucas would ever try to get between a woman and her husband.

But whatever Sofia had not said had led him to believe that just maybe things were not all copacetic at Chez Durand. And if that was the case ...

It wouldn't be easy. He was fully prepared for bitterness. Anger. Accusations that he couldn't deny, and even if he tried to explain his reason for his boneheaded behavior, he'd undoubtedly only end up getting blasted even more for having been an ass. A stupid, ignorant ass who deserved to be skinned and parboiled.

Which, except for that skinning and boiling part, was pretty much true.

He'd screwed up big time ten years ago. But, dammit, it had been in her best interest, he'd reminded himself as he waited impatiently for the coffee to drip through the machine.

Yeah. Lucas rubbed his hand over his heart, which had begun to ache in that old, familiar way. *Try that line on her and see how it goes.*

Spending several weeks every summer at the coast, he'd seen her over the years. Watched her grow from a sad, slightly pudgy young teenager to a pretty girl whose curves had caused boys to follow her around like lovesick puppies. Boys she'd appeared not to notice, so intent had she been on her goal of becoming a chef like her late parents.

Then, the year he turned twenty, the day after he and his father had arrived in Shelter Bay for the summer, he'd gone to Lavender Hill Farm to buy some fresh basil for the spaghetti sauce his father had planned to make for dinner. The transition from girl to young woman, over mere months, had been staggering.

The moment he'd caught sight of her, with that amazing tumble of black, untamed hair blowing in the sea breeze around a sun-warmed face, her incredible eyes laughing, her wide, full lips stained and moist from the fresh raspberries she'd been eating right off the rambling bush, the world had tilted on its axis, sending him tumbling helplessly, impossibly, into love.

And although she'd been out of his life for more than a decade, he'd never been able to entirely banish her from his heart.

As he drove to the farm in a cold spring rain that blew in from the sea, splashed on the red hood of his pickup, drummed on the metal roof, and caused the windshield wipers to work overtime, Lucas realized that life had gotten a whole lot more complicated.

He'd already suspected, knowing Maddy's feelings about infidelity, that her marriage was probably on the rocks. When some tabloid entertainment Web site Google kicked up reported that Durand had moved in with his lover, an heiress involved in a messy divorce with her husband, Lucas knew that the Frenchman was toast.

And as bad as he felt for Maddy, as much as he wished she could have been spared that pain, the fact was that, at least for him, this was good news.

The bad news, he thought as he tightened his fingers on the steering wheel, was that the last time she'd seen him, he'd been tangled up on a couch with someone else.

To hell with trying to apologize. He definitely had his work cut out for him, since now, given that she was fresh off what sounded like much the same situation, he'd probably be forced to grovel. Big-time.

Which he'd be more than willing to do, if that's what it took to win Maddy back.

As he pulled up in front of the sprawling farmhouse, a familiar SEAL saying rang in his mind.

The only easy day was yesterday.

Squaring his shoulders, Lucas reminded himself that he'd always enjoyed a challenge.

10

Impossibly, things had gotten worse when Madeline had reached the airport ticket counter, only to discover that the last flight west from New York had left an hour earlier.

She could have called Pepper, whom she knew would let her crash at her Upper East Side apartment for the night. But the pitiful fact of the matter was that she felt so brittle, so cold, she was afraid that even the slightest bit of pity or sympathy would have her shattering into so many tiny shards, she'd never be able to put herself back together again.

No. Right now, she needed to lick her wounds in private. Which was how she ended up spending the night in the hotel across the street from the airport. Exhausted as she was, she nevertheless found sleep an impossible target as she lay on her back in one of the two double beds, rerunning not just her earlier conversation, but her entire marriage, like an unending loop she could not turn off. Or mute.

The scenes continued flashing through her mind as she made the flight to Portland, squeezed between a teenager who keep shaking his head in time to whatever music was pounding through his iPod and an elderly woman whose knitting needles never stopped flying as she worked on a sweater for, she'd informed Madeline proudly, her eighth grandchild.

She tried watching a movie, but wouldn't you know it? It

was a romantic comedy, which she definitely wasn't in the mood for. At. All.

She read the in-flight magazine but couldn't remember a single word.

So, in order to escape her chatty aisle neighbor, who, fortunately, hadn't recognized her, she closed her eyes and pretended to sleep while visions of that damn video danced in her head.

She was exhausted when she arrived in Portland. But not wanting to make her grandmother drive all the way into the city from Shelter Bay, she rented a car, and headed, like a homing pigeon, to Lavender Hill Farm.

It was a drizzly afternoon by the time she drove down the curving, lavender-lined roadway to the farm, and Madeline was feeling on the verge of collapse. The house, which had proven a haven after her parents' deaths, hadn't changed. It still gleamed as white as a surf-washed seashell. The double porches on both levels invited the inhabitants to sit, unwind, and enjoy the view of the gardens and the ocean beyond.

Her grandmother, whom she'd called when she'd reached the coast road, was waiting on the covered front porch and welcomed her home with a warm and comforting hug.

"Don't worry, darling," she said. "Everything always looks better after a good sleep." She held Madeline's upper arms and kissed both her cheeks. "I already have a nice pot of chamomile tea brewing. It's just what you need to soothe what hurts."

Sofia De Luca had always claimed that there wasn't a problem a stout cup of tea couldn't cure. So Madeline took a cup with her as she staggered upstairs to the bedroom that hadn't changed in the ten years she'd been away from home, stripped off her wet clothes, and put on the pair of pajamas that were lying on the end of the four-poster bed covered in the wedding-ring quilt Sofia had made for Madeline's parents for their wedding.

She'd taken the quilt to New York with her, but when she'd moved into Maxime's larger, more ornate apartment, he'd (surprise, surprise) declared it too rustic and home-made for his taste. So, rather than argue, she'd returned it to her grandmother, who'd put it back on the bed in the room where Madeline had spent her teenage years.

It was in this room where she'd sobbed into the feather pillow for her parents. Where she'd gossiped with girl-friends about boys, practiced kissing the back of her hand, and once had tried kissing her dressing-table mirror. It was here that she'd daydreamed about Heath Ledger, after watching him play outsider bad boy Patrick Verona in *10 Things I Hate about You.*

Knowing how much she loved the movie, Lucas had bought her a poster, which still hung on the wall opposite her bed, for her eighteenth birthday.

Although she'd torn Lucas' photo into pieces, then burned those pieces on hot charcoal in her grandmother's outdoor kitchen grill, she hadn't had the heart to take down the poster, which was proving even more bittersweet, con-sidering the talented actor's too-early death.

"How about ten things I loathe about you, Lucas Chaffee?" she muttered as she climbed into the same bed in which she'd wept over Lucas' betrayal.

Although Lucas' photo might be gone, there were others on her dresser. A photo of her parents in the courtyard of Trattoria Gabriella on the day of her baptism. Her mother, dressed in a flowing dress printed with red flowers, was holding her in her arms. While her father looked down at them, beaming with obvious paternal pride. Sofia, who'd made the white lace baptismal dress for her own daughter, Madeline's mother, was standing by her daughter's side, looking like a woman who'd been given a deed to her own diamond mine. Not that her grandmother had ever cared about jewelry. Her treasures had always been her plants, her friendships, and, most of all, her husband and her family.

As she'd always been about so many things, Sofia proved to be right about the tea. It did prove soothing. So much so that Madeline had no sooner returned the empty fragile china cup to its saucer and put her head on the down-filled pillow that smelled of the lavender her grandmother used in the rinse water when the events of the past twenty-four hours came crashing down on her.

Madeline had no idea how long she slept. It had apparently stopped raining, because light was filtering in through the white lace window curtain. Climbing out of bed, she went to the window and gazed out over the gardens and beyond, to where the sun had begun to set over the sea. The gilded, white-capped waves ebbed and flowed, as they had for eons, reminding Madeline what her grandmother, who'd certainly suffered her own troubles, always told her—that however grim things seemed to be at any given moment, life went on. And it was your choice how to live it.

Something to think about later, she decided as her stomach growled, reminding her that since she hadn't had any appetite after her confrontation with Maxime, the last time she'd eaten was yesterday afternoon, at the bar with Pepper.

She went downstairs and headed straight for the kitchen, where a note taped to the refrigerator with a photo magnet portraying a wicker basket of lavender informed her that her grandmother had gone into town.

Out for a bit to do some shopping, Maddy, darling, it read in the still-strong Palmer cursive handwriting Sofia had been taught by nuns so many decades earlier. *I have my cell on, so if there's anything special you'd like me to fix for dinner, just call. Meanwhile, help yourself to anything you need. xoxo, Gram.*

Given that her grandmother had been the one to continue Madeline's cooking education where her parents had left off, she opted to leave the menu up to her. Though she did feel guilty about causing her extra work.

Lavender Hill Farm's kitchen had always been the heart of the home. The rough-hewn beams and a native-stone fireplace were original to the house. As were the hickory floor and pine cabinets. It had been Madeline who'd taken the doors off the cabinets while she'd still been in high school, pointing out that not only did it make dishes more accessible, but it was also more modern.

Which now, thinking back on it, looking at the tattered cookbooks lining those shelves, modernity was probably the one thing her grandmother didn't want in a kitchen, but she'd never offered a single word of dissent.

The plank farm table and benches took up the center of the room. Madeline traced her mother's name, which had been carved in the top of the table decades before Madeline was born. When she'd first arrived after her parents' death, she'd touched that name several times a day, as if as long as it was still there, her mother wasn't entirely gone from her life. The various nicks and scratches, and even a few burns, spoke of all the years of meals served in this room.

A dog, who apparently had been snoozing on one of the hand-hooked rag rugs Sofia had created over a lifetime of rainy winters, looked up as Madeline entered the kitchen.

"Well, hello." She crouched down and patted the dog's wide head. From the graying muzzle, Madeline knew this must be the bulldog Sofia had adopted after losing her beloved golden retriever, Rosemary. "You must be Winnie."

The wiggle of the dog's rear end as it wagged its stumpy tail, along with a lap of the tongue on her face, confirmed the guess. It also confirmed that Winnie was no guard dog.

"I don't suppose you'd like to have breakfast with me?"

The clock might say nearly evening, but her stomach said breakfast. And apparently Winnie agreed, since her question earned an enthusiastic woof.

"I guess the answer's yes."

The Sub-Zero refrigerator and stove were two of the

few changes in the kitchen. Madeline had bought them for her grandmother when she'd signed her first contract with the Cooking Network. Maxime had complained that the expense was unnecessary, since Sofia wasn't a professional cook, and besides, she'd done just fine for years with her mismatched, outdated appliances.

Madeline had known at the time that it wasn't just the expense that annoyed him. Her husband had never taken to Sofia De Luca. And while her grandmother had never offered a negative word—other than to ask Madeline after the rehearsal dinner, and again right before she'd walked her down the aisle, if she was certain this was what she'd wanted.

"How about it was what I *thought* I wanted," she mused as she opened the stainless steel door to check out the fridge's contents.

Brown eggs rested in a blue ceramic bowl. There was milk, and in the produce drawer, she found button mushrooms, red bell peppers, and fresh spinach, which undoubtedly came from her grandmother's greenhouse.

"What would you say to an omelet?"

Another woof.

"And we might as well have some bacon." One of the ultimate comfort foods. It also got the dog up into a sitting position, looking as alert as Madeline figured an English bulldog could look. The little tail began thumping on the floor.

She opened the wooden bread box. "And English muffins." The breakup of a marriage was no time to worry about calories.

She cracked the eggs, saving the shells for her grandmother's compost bin, and washed the vegetables. As she was slicing them, which she'd done thousands of times over the years so automatically, her thoughts drifted back to New York.

Her phone battery had gone dead during the drive from

Portland to the coast. As she'd pulled up in front of the farmhouse, she'd decided that she wasn't going to recharge it. Not yet.

But she'd have to call Pepper and let her know what was happening. Also, since she'd walked out with only her carry-on bag, she'd need to arrange to have someone to go by the apartment and pick up some clothes for her.

Which brought up a staggering fact she hadn't even realized until now.

Before marrying Maxime, she'd had friends. True, most were involved in the food business in some way, but she'd had an active social life outside the kitchen. These past few years, all she'd done was work.

"And I wasn't even doing the work I wanted," she told Winnie, who cocked her head but didn't take her eyes off the bacon Madeline moved on to slicing. "How wrong is that?"

"Sounds wrong to me, all right." The deep voice behind her had her spinning around with the carving knife in her hand.

"Whoa!"

The man, wearing worn jeans, a denim shirt opened over a white T-shirt, and work boots, lifted both hands. One hand was holding a metal measuring tape, which went along with the tool belt worn low, gunslinger style, on his lean hips. In the other he had a metal clipboard. "Sorry if I surprised you."

"What makes you think that sneaking up behind someone's back—in their own kitchen—might be even the slightest bit startling?" She layered on the sarcasm as thick as the slab of country bacon she'd been slicing.

"I didn't know anyone was here." A yellow pencil was stuck behind his ear, drawing attention to the unruly sunstreaked hair she'd once loved to comb her fingers through. "Sofia said she was going shopping."

"She was." Madeline gestured toward the note on the fridge. "Is," she corrected.

"So I figured the house was unoccupied."

Did Lucas Chaffe have to look so damn good? Couldn't he have gotten fat? Okay, his work as a SEAL running around in the mountains of Afghanistan—the last she'd heard from Sofia, who insisted on updating her on everyone in town, even someone she had absolutely no interest in— undoubtedly kept him fit. But couldn't he have at least lost some of that thick hair?

"Obviously you figured wrong."

"It appears so. . . . Would you mind doing me a favor?"

"What?"

"Could you put that down?" He lowered his gaze from her face to the carving knife she'd forgotten she was still holding. "I've seen Taliban terrorists who don't have knives as big and sharp as that one."

"I suspect that's an exaggeration. Besides, I wouldn't think a big, bad SEAL would be afraid of a simple carving knife," she said even as she laid it on the butcher-block countertop. "What are you doing here?"

She couldn't imagine Lucas robbing anyone, let alone her grandmother. Then again, he was certainly still outra- geously handsome enough to play the movie role of a cat burglar. Though, she noticed, studying him more carefully, his face was leaner, more chiseled than it had been ten years ago. During the intervening years, he'd gone from a hot boy to a man.

Eyes, which had always reminded her of the melted chocolate in s'mores, narrowed. "Sofia didn't tell you?"

"I wouldn't have asked if she had." Though she had men- tioned an exciting adventure. *Omitting,* Madeline noted, *his name.*

"She wants to turn this place into a restaurant."

"You're kidding." Madeline looked around the cozy country kitchen she'd spent five wonderful years of her life in.

"I was kind of surprised, too. But that's what she says. And she hired me to help her make it happen."

"Since when do Navy SEALs cook?"

He laughed at that. The rich, deep, all-too-familiar sound sent waves of emotion flooding through her. Pain. Anger. And, dammit, an unbidden, knee-weakening burst of hormones so strong it had her reaching for the edge of the counter for balance.

"She said she's going to start interviewing cooks in the next month or so. As for me, other than heating up an MRE, which is military speak for meals ready to eat, more commonly referred to as Meals Rejected by the Enemy— and believe me, *you'd* never want to try them—I'm pretty much sunk.

"Jake, down at the Crab Shack, rubs his hands in glee when he sees me coming. I suspect he's got his eye on a new fishing boat. And I'll probably end up funding Kara and Sax's kid's college tuition with takeout from Bon Temps."

"Kara's pregnant?"

Her grandmother had caught her up on how Kara had come back to town with a son, and was now engaged to Shelter Bay's former bad boy, who just happened to be a former SEAL teammate of the man who'd invaded Sofia's kitchen. But she hadn't mentioned a pregnancy.

"Not that I know of. Though I wouldn't be surprised if she was. You pretty much risk pheromone overdose being anywhere in the proximity of those two lovebirds."

Although he'd broken her heart, then stomped on it, Madeline felt her lips threatening to curve. "That's sweet. They were such good friends in high school. It's nice they ended up together."

"Yeah. They're good people who've both been through a lot and deserve to be happy. Though it was a bitch Kara lost Jared. I guess Sofia told you about that?"

Madeline nodded. "It must have been awful for her."

And, she admitted, put her own failed relationships more in perspective. As bad as being cheated on was—and it felt like hell—she couldn't imagine losing her husband and the father of her child to murder.

"I'm sure it was about the worst thing that could happen," he agreed. "Which is why seeing the two of them together, with Sax playing dad to Jared and Kara's son, is so cool."

"I'm sorry about your father." Sofia had called her about Duncan Chaffee's unexpected death while she'd been packing for her trip to Omaha. As much as she still disliked Lucas for what he'd done to her, she never would have wished this pain on him.

He shrugged shoulders that appeared wider, more muscled than when she'd loved running her hands over them. Before continuing and moving them down the smooth, warm flesh of his back, and . . .

Madeline gave herself a stiff mental shake. Reminded herself that she was not the romantic girl she'd once been. The teenager who'd been forced to rebuild her life from the ashes of the pyre that had been what she'd honestly believed to be true, forever-after love.

Will you never learn?

"Yeah . . . well . . ." To the young girl she'd once been, the two-years-older Lucas had always seemed so confident. So sure of himself. It was strange to see him struggling now.

"Dad had a good life, you know. Actually, a pretty great life, with a few hard speed bumps along the way." He shook his head. And although it might have been a trick of the sunlight reflecting off the water outside the window, Madeline thought she saw a suspicious sheen in his eyes. "Damn."

He dumped the tape and clipboard on the table and thrust a hand through his hair. "It hurts, Maddy." The fingers of his other hand, which she could still remember exploring every inch of her body, splayed across his heart. "It hurts like hell."

Even as Madeline fought against it, she could feel that

lingering resentment she'd kept buried inside her starting to crumble, like a sand castle at high tide.

Please, no! She didn't want to care about any man right now. Not her cheating, lying, gold-digging husband. And definitely not Lucas.

But old habits, and, it appeared, old feelings, died hard.

"I'm sorry," she said again.

To keep from touching him, from putting her arms around him and trying to soothe, not as a former lover, but as the friend she'd once been, she jammed her hands into the pockets of the flannel pajamas she'd forgotten, until now, that she was wearing. "He was always so sweet to me. And I know how hard it is to lose a parent."

"It had to be worse for you. Hell, you lost both parents. When you were a lot younger than I am."

"I'm not sure comparisons matter when your heart feels broken."

"Good point. Thanks." His smile was a ghost of the one that had always warmed her from the inside out. The one that caused that sexily adorable crease in his cheek.

It was her turn to shrug. "So, if you're not going to be my grandmother's new cook, I take it you're doing the remodeling work?"

She remembered him puttering around the cottage with his dad. Remembered him telling her that while he enjoyed working with his hands and enjoyed the satisfaction of seeing something he'd helped build turn into a reality, he didn't want to follow Duncan Chaffee into architecture.

Architects spend way too much time in stuffy offices, he'd told her that long-ago summer. *Designing things other people end up getting to build. I admire my dad more than anyone I know, but his life wouldn't work for me. I might not have a handle on what I'm going to end up doing, Maddy. But I do know, whatever it is, it's gotta be something where I can be hands-on.*

"That's the plan," he said now. "My father retired a few

months ago. The idea was for the two of us to go into business together, restoring old houses."

"That sounds like a good plan."

"It was a great plan," he said. "And I might still consider it down the road. But, to be honest, my heart isn't into doing that right now. Not without him, since it was his idea in the first place. So I was sort of at loose ends yesterday when your grandmother offered me the job."

Suspicion stirred. "What time?"

"What time, what?"

"What time did she make the offer?"

"Oh." He rubbed his lightly stubbled jaw. "Let me think. She told me, while we were all on Cole's boat, scattering Dad's ashes at sea, that she wanted to talk to me about something. But she didn't actually tell me what she had in mind until the memorial supper, here last night."

Not that many hours after Madeline's world had exploded.

Surely her grandmother, who knew the story of that long-ago Labor Day breakup, wouldn't already be matchmaking? Not with the one man Madeline had sworn never to speak with again? Ever?

And yeah, so far you're sticking to that vow real well.

She had just determined that she was going to have to be tougher when she found herself drowning in chocolate brown eyes.

"I'm sorry as hell what happened between you and the Frenchman," he said. The sympathy in his gaze seemed genuine. It wasn't a gooey pity, but that of the friend he'd been before she'd admittedly pushed him into intimacy. "But I'm going to have to be honest here and tell you that it feels really, really good to see you again, Maddy."

11

"Don't do that." She held up a hand like a traffic cop and shot him a warning glare.

Lucas had thought he was making headway. Apparently, he'd been wrong.

"Do what?"

"You know."

He did. But damned if he was going to admit that after giving it some serious thought, he wouldn't mind starting over again. Doing things right this time.

Her hair was sleep tousled, which had Lucas imagining her in bed. Which wasn't the safest thought at the moment. But it was definitely one that had not only tortured his sleep last night, but had continued flitting through his mind on the drive from the cottage to the farm.

Her pink flannel pajamas definitely hadn't been designed with seduction in mind. But the ice-cream-sundae print only had him wanting to lick her. All over.

Her smoky eyes were almond shaped, and brought to mind tambourines and gypsies in colorful skirts dancing around a campfire. He remembered, one night, in their own special, secret cave, after they'd first made love on a burst of joyous, youthful romanticism, telling her exactly that.

And, oh yes, Lucas also remembered how the next night she'd actually shown up at the beach with a tambourine she'd bought at Moonstruck Music and danced for him.

Just for him.

As his hormones spiked, he wondered if she'd ever danced for the Frenchman.

Jealousy had teeth. And they were gnawing at his gut.

"What? I'm not allowed to say that I'm glad to see you? That you're looking damn fine on the eyes?"

She grimaced and brushed at her hair. "Liar. I look like roadkill."

"Not at all." Because he'd lied to her once, Lucas decided, now that fate—or perhaps that wily Sofia—had thrown them back together, he would tell the absolute truth. "You do look a little tired."

Because he could not be in the same room with her without touching, he skimmed a finger along the shadows beneath her remarkably expressive eyes.

Despite having grown up in Europe with parents who'd cooked not just for their neighbors, but for the rich and famous, she'd always been the most genuine person Lucas had ever known. Which is why her television stardom had come so quickly, he considered. Because the women who'd tuned in to every show, bought her book and pots and pans, and made her a household name could identify with her.

"And sad," he said. Also, despite the lush curves, which he was grateful to see she hadn't lost during her years living among the rich and chic in New York City, there was an air of fragility about her.

"I'm not sad." *Now who's the liar?* She batted at his hand and backed away from his touch. "I'm angry and disappointed and embarrassed."

He understood the first two. But the third?

"What the hell do you have to be embarrassed about?"

She held up a finger. Her unpainted nails were still short—better, she'd once told him, for working in the kitchen.

"How about the fact that if anyone Googles my name, a damn sex video is the first bazillion hits?"

"But you're not in it."

Color tinged her too-pale cheeks. "Of course I'm not. Just because I'm on TV doesn't mean I'm an exhibitionist."

"You don't have to convince me of that." Although she'd been the one pushing to take their relationship to the next level, she'd proven sweetly shy after that first burst of passion, afraid he'd find her soft, curvy body a turn-off. Which had so not been the case.

"I told you. Don't you dare go there."

"Where?" he asked with feigned innocence, remembering the first time he'd talked her out of her bra.

"You know where." He found her flare of heat encouraging. He'd rather have her angry at him than cool as a cucumber. Cool could mean indifference. Anger was an emotion he could work with. "Bad enough that, thanks to my grandmother, we're apparently going to be sharing this house for the next few weeks—"

"So, you're home for a while, then?" Things were definitely looking up.

"I don't know. Maybe. Probably." She threw her hands up, apparently forgetting whatever else she'd been about to list. There were very few things that could throw Maddy off track. Lucas decided he liked being one of them.

Unfortunately, she wasn't distracted for long.

"Getting back to my point, I'm embarrassed that people think I'm not good enough in bed to keep my husband from straying."

"O-kay. That one is so far off base, I don't even have words to respond." He leaned closer. "But you know what they say about actions being stronger than words."

Her back was against the counter. Even knowing that he was pushing, some voice of reason in the back of his mind cautioned that touching would be a major mistake.

At least at this point.

Instead, he put his hands on the counter, framing her between his arms.

"Lucas . . ."

The little hitch in her voice reminded him of the first time he'd kissed her.

They'd driven into town on some errand for her grandmother. What, exactly, he couldn't recall. But he did remember walking along the harbor as the old-fashioned gaslights flickered on, casting a fog-softened, warm yellow glow over the buildings that were not much different from the day they'd first been built during the 1800s.

They passed the bright and cheery shops, selling local crafts and gifts, and dropped into Coastal Candy, where he bought her a white bag of saltwater taffy.

They were sitting on the stone seawall, watching the fishing boats chugging back in with their day's catch of fish and Dungeness crab, when she held out a pink and white piece of peppermint taffy.

And suddenly, lightning struck from the crimson and gold, sunset-tinged sky, hitting his heart, which stumbled beneath his chest.

You're going to screw up a good thing, his head had told that unsteady heart.

You don't know that. And it's not like you're planning to do her right in front of all those tourists, another, more vital part of his body, argued.

It'll complicate things. She's leaving town. You're leaving town. You'll probably never see each other after this summer, his logical head had pointed out.

All the more reason to go for it, his traitorous body insisted. *Unless you want to spend the rest of your life wondering what it'd be like.*

Oh, hell . . .

He'd still been arguing with himself when she'd leaned forward just the slightest bit. And as he'd found himself drowning in her eyes, Lucas totally understood how ancient sailors had allowed themselves to be drawn beneath the sea by sirens.

Throwing caution, along with all his good intentions, to the wind, he'd made his decision.

It was only a whisper of a kiss. Just a brushing of lips, a touching of mouths. She'd tasted sweet. And tart. Lucas knew that he'd never again taste taffy or peppermint without thinking of this girl.

When her breath trembled, he imagined how it would be—lying with her on the beach as the waves washed the sands and the summer sun warmed her vanilla-scented skin. Her fluid body moving beneath his, the soft little cries she'd make as he tasted her. All over.

But for then, in that stolen, unexpected moment in time, when the tides seemed to have stopped their ebb and flow and the earth appeared to have stopped spinning, he'd forced himself to be satisfied with savoring her moist, luscious mouth.

"Do you remember," he asked now, "that day on the seawall? When I kissed you for the first time?"

From the way her pupils flared and her eyes darkened, he knew she did. "Vaguely."

She was lying.

He knew it.

And he knew that she knew that he knew.

"I've spent a lot of time thinking about it."

"Sure you have." Her brows drew together as her eyes focused like a laser on his. "I didn't just fall off the truffle truck, Lucas. If you actually expect me to believe that while you were traipsing all over the world fighting terrorists, you were thinking about kissing me, you've obviously mistaken me for that naive eighteen-year-old I used to be."

"I'm not saying that. But ever since I started watching those cooking shows of yours—"

"Coming from a man who's already stated that an MRE is the height of his culinary abilities, I'm finding the idea of you sitting in front of your TV, watching the Cooking Network instead of ESPN, a bit of a stretch."

"I caught a few episodes. While channel surfing," he lied. "And, hey, thanks to you, I now not only know how to double bake a potato, but I even have a handle on braising short ribs."

Lucas felt the change in her instantly. He could practically see the ice flowing over her.

"Back up." Both her hands pushed against his chest and her voice shook.

"Sure."

Lucas had gotten good at reading people's thoughts. Many times when it had just been his SEAL team and him alone up in the mountains of Afghanistan, his life had depended on it. A cold fury and what appeared to be pain had replaced the reluctant desire in her eyes.

"Although you're the last man on earth—other than my cheating rat of a husband—I'd want to spend time with, for my grandmother's sake, it appears we're going to be stuck with each other for a while," she said, her tone now as sharp as that lethal-looking carving knife she'd been holding. "However, I'm going to expect you to behave professionally. Which means, unless you want to lose them, keep your damn hands off me."

"Okay." He'd never been one to pressure a woman into bed (truthfully, he'd never needed to), and he damn well wasn't going to begin with Maddy. "But am I allowed to ask one question?"

"What?"

"Are you saying you've never thought about me?"

"Of course I have."

So he wasn't alone.

Her smile was as cold and sharp as an ice pick. "Whenever I'm pounding cutlets or making sausage."

"Ouch. That sound you heard was my ego deflating."

She tossed her head, morphing back into the self-assured TV chef who'd assured him that sizzling was good. Something he figured he'd better not mention.

"Don't ask a question if you're not prepared for the answer," she said. "Now, if you promise not to steal the silverware while you're alone in the house, I believe I'll change and go out for something to eat. I have a sudden craving for a Grateful Bread Belgian waffle."

With the deftness of moment he'd admired while watching her cook, she put the ingredients away, then left the kitchen with an amazing amount of dignity for a woman clad in peppermint pink, ice-cream-sundae pajamas and bare feet.

12

After getting her marketing done, Sofia dropped into the Dancing Deer Dress Shoppe Two for her weekly visit with Doris and Dottie Anderson, identical twins who owned the boutique. As usual, Adèle Douchett, Sax's grandmother, was there, though lately, due to what everyone hoped were temporary memory problems, her husband had taken to walking to the shop with her, then picking her up later.

Usually, Zelda Chmerkovskiy, who'd established Haven House, a shelter for abused women, and lived there as a sort of housemother, would join them. But according to Dottie, she'd called earlier to say she was helping a new resident settle in.

Sofia was grateful that whoever the woman was would have the former Ukrainian ballerina there for her. But she was also sad that such a place would be needed at all. The good news was that Maddy hadn't been in danger. At least she sincerely hoped that hadn't been the case.

"So," Dottie asked, with scandalized excitement, "is it true what people are saying about your granddaughter's French chef husband?"

"Dottie," Doris, the older by five minutes and the more sedate sister, chastened. "That's none of our business."

"I know." Beringed hands fluttered beneath the sleeves of the rainbow-colored blouse she was wearing over turquoise slacks. "But it's all over town."

"Unfortunately, I suspect it's all over the planet," Sofia said with a long sigh as she bit into a melt-in-the-mouth vanilla custard cupcake from Take the Cake. She always picked up a box before showing up at the shop, where the other women would have tea brewed with herbs from Lavender Hill Farm waiting. Today's blend was a refreshing lemongrass chai.

"And while the video appears to be genuine—"

"You've seen it?" Dottie's eyes widened.

"Sister," Doris warned cautiously.

"I felt I had no choice." Although Sofia and her husband had always shared a healthy sex life and she liked to think that she'd kept up with the times, she was still of a generation not that comfortable discussing intimate bedroom matters. Especially when they concerned family. "If only to know how bad things were."

"How bad are they?" Doris asked, proving even she wasn't immune to tabloid fare.

"Not good, I'm afraid." Sofia tried to close her mind to the images that seemed to have been burned into her memory as she took a long sip of the milky tea.

"Poor Maddy. My heart aches for her." Adèle Douchett shook her head with what Sofia knew was very real regret.

Adèle had been her dearest friend for fifty years, since they'd both arrived in Shelter Bay as young brides. Sofia from Livorno, Italy; Adèle from Louisiana's bayou country.

There'd even been a time when they'd both hoped that Madeline would marry one of Adèle's grandsons, giving them the great-grandchildren they both were yearning to spoil. Although Cole and Sax were both now taken, Sofia had been holding out hope for J.T., the youngest Douchett brother. She'd never believed Maddy's marriage to that Frenchman would last.

But now, with J.T. still traveling the world as a Marine and Lucas Chaffee back in town, her sights were shifting to a more eligible candidate.

After all, it had been obvious to anyone who'd taken the time to truly look—and she had—that what the two of them had shared ten years ago was much more than puppy love. And although what Lucas had done appeared on the surface to be unforgivable, Sofia had always suspected there was more to the story.

She'd been considering changes to Lavender Hill Farm for some time. But her life had been in flux after being widowed, and everything she'd read advised against making any major lifestyle changes after the loss of a spouse.

Still, while she had a great many friends, the unpalatable fact was that she'd slipped a bit into the doldrums. The new dog Charity had coaxed her into adopting—not that it had taken all that much coaxing, since Winnie was adorable, and needed her as much as she needed the dog—had brought sunshine back into her days.

But having always been active and involved in the community, Sofia needed more. She was ready to shake up her life a bit. And if she could do a little matchmaking while turning the Lavender Hill Farm's kitchen into a family restaurant serving fresh, sustainable food from local farms, why, all the better.

13

Of all the kitchens in all the world, Lucas Chaffee had to walk into hers? Well, it wasn't technically hers. But she certainly had more claim to it than he did.

Just the thought of his strolling into the house, as if he had every right to be there, caused myriad emotions to flood through Madeline.

Pain. Fury. Misery. Then, saving her just in time, before she'd done something really, really stupid, his comment about braising short ribs had brought back yesterday's humiliation and had her swinging back to fury. True, her anger had been directed much more toward Maxime than Lucas, but it had allowed her to escape the situation.

Even as she'd wanted to run away, to get as far away from him as fast as she could, she'd managed to wrap herself in a mantle of dignity and walked out of the kitchen just as she'd walked away from Maxime.

And while it took all her self-restraint, which was hanging by a single, tattered thread after the past two days, she didn't give in to the impulse to slam the door behind her.

She'd tried to convince herself that she'd gotten over Lucas Chaffee. That he'd been nothing more than a teenage romance gone bad. Besides, so much had changed in her life during their years apart.

Unfortunately, not everything.

She never could have expected that rush of emotion

when she'd turned around and saw him standing there, looking good enough to scoop up with a spoon.

"It's only because you're vulnerable right now," she assured herself as she went through the dresser drawer, coming up with a T-shirt and a pair of jeans she'd left here the last time she'd visited and had planned to return home soon.

That had been, what? Three years ago, for her grandfather's funeral.

Too long. Sofia was the only family she had left. And family deserved better. Oh, sure, she'd been insanely busy, trying to keep all her plates spinning. But that wasn't any excuse. Not when she considered that her grandmother hadn't exactly been living an idle life when she'd rushed off to Italy to comfort Madeline and bring her here to Shelter Bay.

A person didn't just decide to gut their kitchen and open a restaurant on a whim. So logic told Madeline that her grandmother had been thinking about this plan for some time.

"And I had to hear about it from Lucas Chaffee, of all people?"

She twisted on the shower with more force than necessary, then stood beneath the water, scrubbing away the travel grime. She was not nearly as successful at washing away the memory of the first time she and Lucas had made love.

She'd been a virgin, but not exactly by choice; she'd tried, with every teenage feminine wile she possessed, to seduce him for weeks.

"I don't understand," she'd complained as they lay together on a sleeping bag in their secret hidden cave beside the sea. He'd kissed her nearly to oblivion, and touched her in places that always tingled for hours after they'd been together this way, yet once again, he was somehow managing to pull back. "I turned eighteen today. So we're both adults. If you want me, and I want you—"

"It's not about want, *dammit," he'd said with what she remembered to be frustration. "*Want *is easy, Maddy. Too easy."*

"Perhaps it's easy for you." She'd lifted her chin as a tear escaped to trail down her cheek. "But not for me." She'd had her entire life planned. She was on her way to Europe to learn from the best. She certainly hadn't planned to fall in love. And definitely not with a summer boy, who was probably only interested in a vacation fling.

"No." He'd sighed as he'd cupped her face in his hand. "Not for you."

His expression, visible in the dark as the lighthouse flashed its warning to ships at sea, was as serious as she'd ever seen it.

"Oh, hell." His smile was a ghost of its usual laughing one. Later, when everything had gone so terribly wrong, she would remember that it hadn't reached his eyes. "I give up."

She'd flung her arms around his neck. Pressed her mouth to his and her body against his lean, muscled strength.

When she would have rushed to satisfy the hunger that had been building for days, he slowed the pace, kissing her gently, patiently. And even as he deepened the kiss, his lips remained as soft as sea mist.

Her thoughts, her body, her entire world had compressed to nothing but shimmering sensations. She was oh, so vividly aware of his sweep of his tongue against the seam of her lips, the hypnotizing touch of his hands stroking up and down her back, the glorious feel of his body responding to hers.

The heavenly kiss went on and on and on. Warmth flowed through her veins, causing her body to melt like dark chocolate left out in a hot summer sun.

"You're incredible."

"I'm not skinny enough." Although she'd already bared her breasts to him and was the one who'd been pushing for this moment, now that it had finally come, Madeline was worried that he'd find her body too round. Too soft.

"Who wants skinny? You have curves." His lips skimmed down her side, dipping in at her waist, then following the flare of her hip down to her thigh. "Which are much sexier." He nipped at the back of her knee, causing a jolt of heat. "And hot." He continued to leave a trail of sparks down to her ankle and back up again.

She couldn't believe his control. Whenever their lovemaking drifted too far from pleasure to passion, he denied his own hunger, as if determined, after all these weeks of waiting, to make their first time together—her first time ever—last.

"You're so incredible." His lips returned to linger at her earlobe. Her throat. "I've imagined you like this since I first walked into Sofia's kitchen for basil."

"I know."

And it had been driving her crazy.

The laugh that escaped against her shoulder was harsh and rough with need. "Sweetheart, you can't even begin *to know some of the things I've imagined."*

The dark, dangerous gleam in his eyes had the blood roaring in her head.

"Then show me." Breathless, no longer concerned about her weight or her nudity, she rolled over and straddled him. "Everything."

And he had. Because just the memory of that first time and all the summer days and nights that followed caused her blood to flow hotter in her veins, Madeline turned the faucet to cold.

"Thanks a bunch, Gram," she muttered between gritted teeth as the icy water streamed over her. "If I didn't need more complications in my life, you have to throw that man into the mix."

"Of course," she assured herself as she rubbed the lavender-scented towel over her body, "it's not as if I don't have a say in the matter."

Lucas couldn't become a complication unless she let him.

"Which so isn't going to happen," she vowed. He was part of her past, not the present.

By the time she'd dried her hair and dressed, Madeline had managed to convince herself that she was no longer that love-struck teenager she'd once been.

She was, after all, a grown woman who many people would consider a success.

"Some might say I'm even a celebrity," she said to Winnie, who'd come up to the bedroom.

She could handle one former Navy SEAL–turned–remodeling contractor.

"Piece of cake."

Her resolve strengthened, she went back downstairs, only to find the kitchen empty and the red pickup that had been parked in the driveway gone.

14

During his summers in Shelter Bay, Lucas had spent a lot of time hanging out at Bon Temps, the Douchett family's Cajun restaurant and dance hall.

From what Sax had told him, the place had been hit hard by a vicious winter ice storm a few years ago, then given a knockout blow when hurricane-force winds triggered by a Pacific typhoon had come blowing through.

Which was when Maureen and Lucien, Sax's parents, decided to retire. A plan that had lasted about six months. Now they were happily running a bait shop on the harbor, while his old teammate had restored the place, giving, as Sax had told Lucas, "a chance for people to eat themselves a good meal, kick up their heels, and pass a good time."

The place had changed during the time Lucas been away. The rough wood tables and benches that had brought to mind an old Cajun cabin had been replaced with gold, purple, and green Mardi Gras masks hanging on walls the color of Tabasco sauce. Beads in those same colors had been strung from the light fixtures.

He arrived during a lull between the lunch and dinner crowds, and caught Sax taking inventory at the bar.

"I'll have a Doryman's Dark Ale, barkeep," Lucas said as he sat down at the bar.

"Good choice." Sax reached into a cooler beneath the bar and pulled out the dark brown bottle with the blue pelican outline on the front. "You want your dinner to go or to eat here?"

"I'm getting too damn predictable," Lucas muttered.

"You're not going to hear any complaints from me." Sax pushed a bowl of spiced nuts in front of him. "Kara and I figure that now that you're going to be sticking around to remodel Sofia De Luca's farmhouse, Trey's college is pretty much paid for."

"Ha-ha." Lucas took a long pull on the bottle. After all they'd been through together, he and Sax tended to think a lot alike. "Coincidentally, I told Maddy the same thing less than thirty minutes ago."

"How's she doing?"

"She looked tired. But I think she's hanging in there."

"She was always a trooper. Even when she first came to town after her parents died in that plane crash. So, you want a menu? Or do you have it memorized by now?"

"I'll have the fish and chips. With your grandmother's comeback sauce."

"Yet another good choice. You're on a roll. Cole came in this afternoon with some black rockfish so fresh it practically jumped from his boat into my kitchen. Want me to put the order in now?"

"Sounds good."

He went back through the swinging doors into the kitchen. He'd told Lucas that when he'd first opened the place, he'd done all the cooking himself. But business had taken off, allowing him to hire a former line cook from a seafood place in the Willamette Valley. So now he mostly handled the bar menu.

It was strange thinking of Sax settled down with a fiancée, a son he was in the process of adopting, and a thriving business. Strange, but Lucas was happy for him. After all he'd been through, he deserved the good life. Which he seemed to have made for himself.

"Funny that you'd come back here," he said when Sax returned. "I seem to remember you always saying how much you wanted to escape."

"Yeah." His former teammate shrugged and began wiping the bar with a white towel. "Sometimes when you're a kid, you're too stupid to appreciate stuff the way you do when you get older." He looked up at Lucas. "Speaking of stupid, are you planning to tell Maddy the truth? About what happened back then?"

"I don't have a clue." Lucas traced a trail of moisture down the side of the bottle with a fingertip. "I suppose I'm going to have to."

"I guess that depends on whether you want her to continue to think you're the worst guy on the planet."

"There's a complication."

"Yeah. I heard about the video. Bad timing for you, bro."

"Maybe. But if the Frenchman hadn't gotten caught with his pants down, she wouldn't be back here."

"Which you're happy about?"

"I'm not happy she's hurt." He took another long drink of the ale. "But I can't deny that having a second chance is appealing."

Since the situation was complicated and he needed time to come up with a battle plan, Lucas didn't add that all it had taken was one look for him to realize that while many things had changed, he was still as crazy in love with Maddy as he'd been when he was twenty.

"You talked about her that night," Sax remembered. "Up on the mountain."

When so many of them had died. And it looked as if Sax, Lucas, and the other team members were going to be joining them. When you're staring death in the face, you tend to open up about things you'd never talk about otherwise.

"Yeah." It was when he'd admitted what he'd done.

When everyone in that bunker had called him an idiot. Something he'd already figured out for himself.

"Anything about your feelings change since then?"

"I can't believe it." He dodged the question. "The Saxman talking about feelings?"

"Hey." Sax shrugged. "What can I say? When you fall off the deep end into love, you tend to discover your inner feminine side."

"God help us all." Sax Douchett was probably the least of all the SEALs and Marines Lucas had teamed up with over the years he would have suspected to even *have* a feminine side. "If you're turning all Dr. Phil, there's no hope for the rest of us."

Sax's answering grin was quick and wicked and reassuringly familiar. "Don't worry. I was just pulling your chain. And you didn't answer my question."

While Lucas would never claim to be an expert on the subject of women, having screwed up so royally the first time, he decided to err on the side of caution this time and keep his feelings to himself. For now.

"We're men," he said. "Hell, not just ordinary civilian types. We're SEALs. The effing alpha dogs of the military. Are we even supposed to be talking about this touchy-feely stuff?"

"Former SEALs," Sax pointed out. "I've put all that behind me. And, believe me, there's a lot to be said for civilian life. Including having hot sex with a willing woman on a regular basis."

"It's not like Maddy's the only woman on the planet." And, although she had seemed tempted, he knew she was probably not all that willing. Lucas had been on missions that seemed easier to accomplish than winning her back.

"True enough. There's this cupcake baker— "

"Not you, too." Lucas' mood lifted enough to laugh at that. "Charity invited me to dinner with her and her jarhead. She was planning to fix me up with that baker."

"Sedona's hot. And smart as a whip." Sax looked around the restaurant with obvious pride. "She helped me get financing for this place."

"You got financing from a woman who bakes cupcakes?"

"No. I got financial advice from a former CPA–turned-baker, who hooked me up with some money guys. But she's definitely easy on the eyes. And damn nice, to boot."

"Doesn't exactly sound like the type of woman a guy just hooks up with for a quick, uncomplicated roll in the rack."

It was Sax's turn to laugh. "That's the same thing I said when Cole suggested I take her out."

He put the towel down, went into the kitchen, and brought out a platter piled high with deep-fried fish, beer fries, coleslaw, and two small bowls. One bowl held a tartar sauce; the other, Bon Temps' signature comeback sauce, which Lucas had learned the hard way should carry a label warning about the dangers of setting your mouth on fire. It was also addictive—thus, he figured, its name.

"You know," Sax said as Lucas bit into a fry. "I'm certainly not going to claim to be an expert on the female species—"

"This from a guy who had to use a spreadsheet to keep his women straight."

Lucas took a longer pull on the beer bottle in an attempt to quench the flames from the sauce he'd dipped the French fry into. The smile teasing at the corners of Sax's mouth told him that he was just waiting for Lucas to show any sign of weakness. Which, even as moisture welled behind his eyes, he refused to do.

"My reputation was highly exaggerated in those days. . . . My point is, I have learned women will forgive a lot. But they won't forgive a lie." Sax filled a glass of water from the bar hose and stuck it on the counter. "So, if you're considering starting things up with Maddy again, my advice would be to come clean. As soon as possible."

"I'll consider it." Even as he suspected Sax was right, Lucas also decided that he'd better make sure Maddy wasn't holding one of those deadly looking knives when he did confess.

15

As Madeline took a sunset walk through town, past the colorful wind socks flying above the storefronts, the tourists strolling along the seawall with their white bags of taffy and their ice cream cones, she could feel the stress of the past two days beginning to be blown away by the salt-tinged sea breeze.

She'd spent her first thirteen years in Italy and the next five here; then, after traveling the world learning her craft, she'd thought she'd settled down for good in New York City. But as she'd learned so many years ago, life could change in a heartbeat.

And now, as she watched the Shelter Bay lighthouse flashing its beacon to ships at sea, she realized that after leaving Umbria, Shelter Bay had always felt the most like home.

A feeling that intensified as she entered the farmhouse and smelled the familiar aroma of soup cooking on the stove.

"Maddy, darling," her grandmother called from the kitchen. "Is that you?"

"If it isn't, you could be in deep trouble," Madeline chided her grandmother. "You really shouldn't leave your door open to just anyone who might walk in."

"Oh, no one ever locks their doors in Shelter Bay, darling. I've lived more than fifty years in this town and never worried about anyone breaking in."

"Times change." True, the coastal town wasn't New York. But it also wasn't the same as it was when Sofia had first arrived.

"Besides, I knew it was you," she said as Madeline entered the kitchen. She was standing at the counter rolling out a pâte brisée dough. "I saw your rental car coming up the lane. How are you feeling?"

"Better. You were right about getting some sleep. And I took a long walk along the seawall."

"Nothing like a nice nap followed by some fresh air to clear the mind," Sofia agreed.

She turned the dough into a pie pan, then blended her premeasured marionberries, brown sugar, lemon juice, tapioca, flour, salt, and cinnamon together in a blue ceramic bowl that she'd had seemingly forever.

"Hopefully, you worked up an appetite."

"I'm starved." Before she'd reached the Grateful Bread restaurant, she'd been drawn in by the amazing aromas coming out of Take the Cake, a bakery that hadn't existed the last time she'd been home.

The owner, a lean blonde who looked as if she'd never sampled her own product, had been friendly and, although she mentioned being a fan, either she somehow hadn't heard about the video, which was unlikely, or had the grace not to mention it.

Deciding that there weren't many problems chocolate couldn't make better, Madeline had ordered the Baileys Irish cream cupcake. Both the chocolate cake and the espresso buttercream frosting had been made with Baileys, then dipped in chocolate and topped with a chocolate-covered espresso bean.

"It is," she'd told Sedona Sullivan on something close to a moan, "like sex in a fluted paper wrapper."

The baker had laughed at that. "That's exactly what I was going for."

"Well, you've definitely succeeded."

And she had. In fact, although Madeline hadn't been prepared to share that fact, the sinfully rich cupcake was better than any sex she'd had in a very long time. Still, as incredible as it was, it hadn't made up for her lack of any real food for over twenty-four hours, and she could already feel the impending sugar crash.

"I've started some zuppa di fagioli," Sofia said.

"I was hoping that's what was in the pot." It was one of her favorite recipes, handed down from Sofia's own mother. The first time she'd proudly prepared the Tuscan white bean soup for Maxime, he'd taken one spoonful, then haughtily dismissed it as peasant food.

"I remembered how much you enjoyed it. Also, I found some fabulous bocconcini mozzarella at Blue Heron farm that would make a fabulous spaghetti caprese."

"That sounds fabulous." Enough to make her stomach growl. "And the farm must be new."

"About a year," Sofia said, after a moment's thought. "Ethan Concannon bought the old Hardin place—you remember it, darling—and turned it organic, raising cattle, dairy cows, hogs, and chickens on pasture grass. Wait until you taste this cheese. It's heaven. I've already spoken with him about supplying my new restaurant."

"Ah yes, the restaurant. Lucas told me about that." And it still grated that her grandmother had chosen to confide in him before her.

"Did he, now?" Sofia poured the berries into the crust and turned her attention to rolling out the lattice top. "I also know how you love marionberry pie."

"You don't have to go to all that bother."

"Oh, it's no bother at all. I so loved cooking for family before you left home and your grandfather passed. It's not nearly as much fun cooking for one."

Good try. And, obviously, like the change in conversation, a ploy to dodge the questions Sofia had to expect.

"Well, I appreciate it. As for the restaurant—"

"I was getting bored," Sofia said, forestalling the argument she clearly saw coming. "Since I don't want to take up cruising, like so many other women seem to do after being widowed, I decided I needed a new challenge to help fill all the empty hours in my life. And fill the place with people so I won't feel so lonely."

Talk about ladling on the guilt. "Why didn't you tell me about it before now?"

"Oh, darling." She placed the lattice crust on top of the berries, sprinkled it with sugar, then moved the tin to a baking sheet, which she then put on the rack in the oven. "You already had so much on your plate, I didn't want to bother you."

"It wouldn't have been any bother. I never have so much to do that I don't want to hear about your life."

Damn. It was working. Madeline could feel the guilt settling over her shoulders like a wet, gray wool blanket.

"Well, things weren't settled yet. There were so many details to figure out. Although I'm terribly sad about poor Duncan, when Lucas came home for the memorial service and seemed a little bit adrift, the last little piece of the puzzle just clicked into place."

"You don't know anything about Lucas."

"Darling, I've known him most of his life."

"You've known him during the summers. People aren't necessarily the same when they're on vacation as they are in their real lives." And hadn't she discovered that the hard way? She'd thought she'd known the boy she'd given her heart to. She'd been so wrong. "And he's been away for a very long time. At war."

"All the more reason he's come home, I suspect. No doubt he's due for some well-earned peace and quiet."

"I'm not going to argue that."

Damn. Madeline had been so surprised and unnerved to find him back in her grandmother's kitchen, not to mention thrown back into her life, that although she'd felt truly sorry for him and empathized with his losing his father, she hadn't stopped to consider what he'd undoubtedly been going through all these past years.

"Which brings up another point," she said. "How do you know he isn't suffering from PTSD?" She hadn't seen any signs, but she certainly wasn't an expert on the topic.

"Well, I suppose it would probably be a bit surprising if the war hadn't affected him in some way."

Madeline had never known a more caring, empathetic person than her grandmother. But caring was one thing. An elderly woman possibly putting her life at risk with a man who could well be unstable was quite another.

"Do you think it's wise to just give him free run of the house?"

"If I didn't think that, dear, I wouldn't do it," her grandmother said reasonably. "He's obviously at loose ends, with his father's death having destroyed his plans for the two of them to work together. The plan that I suspect helped keep his morale up during the last year he was deployed. Since he obviously needed something to focus on, and I needed a contractor, it just seemed like a win-win situation."

When Madeline didn't answer, Sofia, who'd always been one to speak her mind, got down to brass tacks. "Do you believe there's a possibility that the reason you're not at all happy about my idea is because it involves Lucas Chaffee?"

"I don't trust him. I'm not sure you should, either."

Sofia sighed. "What happened between the two of you was a very long time ago. You were both young—"

"And he was wrong."

"I can't deny that." Her grandmother took off her white chef's apron. "But if you're comparing him to your husband—"

"I can't see any difference."

"Can't you?"

Madeline jammed her hands into her pockets. "No."

Which wasn't entirely the truth. Maxime was a conniving rat bastard who'd betrayed her in the worst way possible for money. Lucas had betrayed her for, as for as she could tell, no other reason than it had felt good at the time.

And, dammit, although maybe she should be all adult and let bygones be bygones, it still hurt. A lot.

"I need to ask a question," Sofia said. "It's not easy to ask. And it might not be easy to answer. But something occurred to me this afternoon that's been bothering me."

"Okay." Her grandmother did not often look uncomfortable. She did now. "Shoot."

"Did Maxime ever abuse you? I know he disrespected you. Terribly. But did he ever strike you?"

"No. My husband has many faults, one of which is a flash temper, but he never hit me. And I was never afraid that he might." If he'd so much as raised a hand to her, she would have been out the door on the spot.

"Well. That's a relief. And getting back to Lucas, I didn't hire him to be your boyfriend, darling. I hired him to remodel the kitchen."

"That's another thing." Madeline looked around the cozy room where she'd spent so many hours. The one in which she'd learned to roll out dough and julienne a carrot. "Do either of you even know what you'll need for a commercial kitchen?"

"Not really." The older woman seemed unperturbed by the magnitude of the project she was taking on. "But I've taken out some books from the library. And looked online. I've also gotten a list of what the state requires. Plus, I'm hoping that whomever I hire will be able to offer some suggestions."

"Do you have a list of candidates?"

"I was planning to set up interviews. Until the perfect candidate just fell into my lap."

"Who?"

Her sun-weathered face wreathed in a smile. "Why, you, of course."

Madeline almost choked. *Oh no!*

"Me? In case you haven't noticed, Gram, I have a job." She may be between TV seasons and contracts right now. But it wasn't as if she was on the verge of being unemployed and homeless.

Okay. Maybe she was currently without her own place to live. But that was only temporary.

"Well, of course you do, darling." Sofia immediately backpedaled. "And I didn't mean that I'd expect you to take on the job as chef. But since as long as I've known you, you've never been able to chill, as you young people say. I thought, perhaps, while you're back home, you could help Lucas and me design the restaurant. And maybe interview chefs."

"Oh, Gram . . ."

Her grandmother had taken her in when she'd had no one else. And although becoming a surrogate parent had curtailed hers and Madeline's grandfather's world travel to seek out native plants, not once had she heard Sofia utter a single word of complaint.

The fact was, she owed her.

"Just think about it," Sofia said mildly. "If you'd rather just relax and lick your wounds, which you're certainly entitled to do, I'll find someone else. After all, until that unfortunate incident, I hadn't thought of asking you for help."

Despite how much Madeline dreaded the idea of working with Lucas Chaffee, her grandmother's response nearly made her smile. Passive-aggressive had never been Sofia's style. The older woman had always been direct to the point of blunt.

So why this sudden change in tactics?

"If you're planning to get Lucas and me together again, it's not going to work."

"Why, I had no such idea." She splayed a hand across her heart, as if taking an oath. "Truly, darling, it's merely a coincidence you're both back in town at the same time."

While she still didn't exactly buy her grandmother's innocent act, Madeline couldn't argue that. No way could Sofia have planned the sequence of events that had led to both Lucas and her winding up in Lavender Hill Farm's kitchen.

"As it happens, I have some ideas," she admitted. Ideas for restaurant design that Maxime had never been willing to even listen to, let alone consider. He'd had his own vision, and, like everything else in their marriage, what Maxime wanted, Maxime got.

Sofia beamed with a delight she didn't even try to hide. "This is going to be so exciting," she said. "Do you know, I read that elderly people live longer if they have goals and projects?"

Madeline laughed and threw her hands up. Both metaphorically and literally. "You can stop, Gram. I surrender."

"It'll be just like old times," Sofia promised. "You and me working in the kitchen together again."

It did not escape Madeline's notice that she'd left out mentioning the third person involved.

Madeline and Lucas had shared old times, too. Times she'd tried, with varying degrees of success, to forget.

It's stupid, she chided herself. Stupid to let any man get under her skin this way. Especially one who'd probably hadn't given her a thought since she'd run away. As fast and as far as she could.

It wasn't until he'd shown up in her grandmother's kitchen, all windblown hair, chocolate eyes, and gunslinger tool belt, that Madeline realized that her husband's public betrayal had mainly hurt her pride. And although she'd refused to admit it, even to herself, Pepper's words about Maxime's being with other women hadn't been a total surprise.

The suspicions had flittered through her head from time to time. When she watched a jeweled hand linger a bit too long on top of his at the dinner table. When his eyes would follow an admirer across a banquet room with a bit too much speculation. When air kisses would miss the mark and land instead on his lips.

But she'd ignored them. Locked them away in a steel box with other memories and events that were too painful to be taken out into the bright light of day. Because if they were in the dark, she wouldn't have to face them.

Like her parents' death.

And Maxime's flirtations, which, at least in one case, were full-blow adultery.

And earning his very own special lockbox: Lucas Chaffee.

The same man who'd sauntered into her grandmother's kitchen as if he had every right to be there.

She'd work with him. But they'd be on her turf. And this time around their relationship would be strictly business.

Just because she had no choice but to let him back into her life—for a very brief, very impersonal time—there was no way she'd be foolish enough to let him back into her heart.

16

Proving that you can, indeed, make a silk purse out of a sow's ear, Portland's Pearl District, which had once been a decaying, downtown warehouse area, had, over the years, been gentrified into a chic, urban neighborhood. Many of the aging warehouses had been turned into luxury lofts and condos, stylish boutiques, specialty retailers, bookstores, and galleries featuring local artists. Trendy restaurants had sprung up to serve the residents.

Brooke Kendall's building boasted a fabulous view of the Cascade Mountains. Reflecting the owner's personality, the apartment exuded cool control. Glass and silver predominated, giving what Lucas privately considered an almost operating room–like sterility to a space decorated in shades of gray.

Tasteful modern graphics hung on pale gray walls, illuminated by track lighting along the twelve-foot ceiling.

The furniture, like the art, was contemporary. Italian black leather and molded, modular pieces covered in black and gray striped upholstery blended perfectly with black lacquer bookshelves and glass tables that seemed to float atop the gray and white marble floor.

The kitchen, with its Sub-Zero refrigerator and eight-burner, two-oven stove could turn any professional chef green with envy. Not that Lucas had ever seen Brooke even nuke a frozen dinner. Why should she, when the building's concierge was more than willing to call in her order to any of the hot, trendy restaurants in the neighborhood?

"So," she said, as she plated tonight's dinner from the foam cartons onto square white plates, "tell me about this job you've taken on. It's not exactly what you'd planned to do, is it?"

"No." Lucas opened the bottle he'd picked up before driving to Portland from the coast and poured the golden wine into two glasses with matchstick-thin stems that he always worried about snapping. "But Sofia De Luca rescued Dad and me when we were drifting after my parents' divorce, so I figure I owe her."

"That's very nice of you," she said as she carried the plates over to a glass-topped table set on a black lacquer base. "But if she's as wonderful a woman as you described on the phone, I'm sure she wouldn't expect you to pay her back after all these years."

"I don't think of it as payback. She's got work she needs done. I could use the job."

"Surely your father left you enough funds to take more time off."

"I don't know all the details yet. But even if he did, I want to work." He needed to work, but since returning from Afghanistan, he'd noticed so many people acting on edge around him, as if expecting him to go Rambo on them at any moment, that Lucas was working on at least looking more laid-back than he often felt.

"When do you start?" She picked a bit of stir-fried tofu from the plate of carrots, peas, baby bok choy and shiitake mushrooms in oyster sauce.

"I began taking measurements today."

Brooke was a vegetarian. Lucas was not.

His own pad talay, a stir-fry of prawns, mussels, scallops, calamari, and salmon with vegetables in a chili sauce was good. Maybe even great. But, if he was to be perfectly honest, he'd rather have those beef short ribs he'd watched Maddy braising on her TV show.

"Oh." She frowned as she took a sip of wine. "So soon?"

"What's wrong?"

"Well, I was thinking that perhaps now that your plans to work with Duncan have fallen through, you might be up for a trip to Paris."

Although France had much more to offer than the sandbox of Iraq or the desolation of Afghanistan, having felt the tension of years living in war zones begin to be blown away by Shelter Bay's sea breezes, the idea of traveling anywhere proved unappealing.

He put down his fork. "I take it that means you decided to accept that hotel offer."

"I did."

Lucas guessed that answered Charity's question about whether he and Brooke were "exclusive." He was also honestly relieved, having driven two hours to Portland this evening to find out how she viewed their relationship. Because if she considered them a couple, he would have had to break things off before life became more complicated.

Although he knew it was going to be a challenge, the moment he'd seen Maddy in her grandmother's kitchen, Lucas had wanted her. And not just for a night. Forever.

"My sister—you remember; I mentioned her. . . . Charity?"

"Of course I remember. You were children when your parents were married."

"That's her. Well, she asked me something during the burial," he said. "About us."

"Us?" A perfectly shaped blond brow lifted.

"Yeah. You and me. She wanted to know if we were exclusive."

She laughed. "You're kidding."

"Actually, I didn't know what to tell her."

"Really?" She suddenly looked like a woman who'd just had a live grenade dropped in her lap. "You didn't believe . . . I mean, I thought I made it clear that I was coming off a divorce."

"You did, but—"

"Lucas." She sighed. "I realize that making the transition to civilian life must be difficult—"

"Actually that part's not proving so hard. It's my father dying that sucks."

"Well, of course it does." She took another, longer drink of wine. "My parents and I aren't nearly as close as you and Duncan seemed to be, but I'll be very sad when I lose them. . . . But if you were looking for anything permanent—"

"I wasn't." It was the absolute truth.

"Well, then." He watched as cooling relief flooded into her Nordic blue eyes. "It sounds as if we're in total agreement." Putting her black linen napkin on the table, she reached across the glass table and touched his hand. "We've had fun," she said. "But you were my rebound lover, Lucas. The way I was your transitioning-back-to-civilian-life lover."

The relief he'd seen earlier in her eyes flooded through him. "Well, sounds as if we were on the same page."

"Totally," she agreed. Then licked her bottom lip in a way he'd come to know well. "We do have that khao neow dam piag," she reminded him of the black sticky-rice desert she'd ordered along with their entrees. "Unless you'd like something else for dessert?"

Her throaty tone offered a gilt-edged invitation.

"You know," he said. "As great as that sounds, I really do need to get back. I promised Sofia I'd show her some initial sketches."

"All right." She tilted her head. "You're sure you're not annoyed with me for going to Paris?"

"Not at all. It's a super opportunity and you deserve it."

Deciding that saying that she'd just solved what he'd feared could be a problem might not be what she wanted to hear, Lucas instead said, "Paris in the spring is also a huge plus."

"That's exactly what I was thinking." From her smile and the anticipation on her face, he realized that mentally she'd already moved on.

Feeling uncomfortable just eating and running, he offered to stay and help her clean up, but she'd assured him that the maid would take care of everything in the morning.

Then walked him to the door and gave him a quick, final kiss good-bye.

As he took the elevator down to the lobby, Lucas' mind turned, as it so often had over the years, to Maddy.

And for the first time in a very long while, he felt as if he was getting his life back on track.

17

The trip had gone like clockwork, leading Phoebe to believe that the volunteers who'd shepherded her from Colorado to this small, quaint town on the Oregon coast had a great deal of experience.

Even as organized as they'd been, even as much as all the women at the various stations along the way had reassured her, she'd felt as if she hadn't let out a full breath until she entered the stained-glass door of Haven House.

The Queen Anne Victorian was high on a hill, overlooking the town of Shelter Bay and the harbor. The door was answered by a willowy woman who appeared to be in her seventies. She wore skinny jeans, a red sweatshirt that read *You don't stop dancing because you grow old. . . . You grow old because you stop dancing*, and gold sequined sneakers.

"Welcome to Haven House," she said, holding out a slender hand tipped in a French manicure. "I'm Zelda Chmerkovskiy. But since that's admittedly a mouthful, everyone just calls me Zelda."

"I'm Phoebe."

"I know. I've been expecting you." Her smile was warm, her accent tinged with what sounded like a trace of Russian. "We have your room all ready."

"It's a beautiful house," Phoebe said.

"Isn't it?" Zelda said. "Let me give you a quick tour on the way to your room. The original owners were the Stuarts, and Mrs. Stuart had grown up in Boston and was accustomed to a full Victorian household staff. So when they moved west for her husband to establish a timber business, Angus, her husband, built this home to accommodate their family, which grew to eight children, along with their servants.

"Unlike many homes, where servants were stuck up in some tiny garret, the Stuart servants were fortunate to live on the first floor. There were originally four bedrooms on this floor, along with a bathroom, a kitchen, and a work area. But a more recent owner established it as a bed-and-breakfast and altered the floor plan, so now there are two bedrooms and two baths. They also turned the work area into this lovely sunroom."

She paused in the doorway of a room that featured a tile floor, floor-to-ceiling windows, white wicker furniture, and a lush jungle of green plants and vases of cut flowers.

"It's lovely," Phoebe said.

"Isn't it? Do you enjoy gardening?"

"I'm afraid I have a black thumb." Concerned that she was being asked about any skills she could bring to this community of women, she said, "But I am comfortable in the kitchen." Restaurant work had been her favorite of her hospitality training.

"Oh, good. We lost the only one of us who can really cook last month, and—"

"Lost?" Phoebe's blood chilled at the possibilities that flooded into her mind. Each more unappealing than the last.

"Oh, not really *lost*," Zelda assured her quickly. "She got a job making pies at a local bakery and moved into an apartment. While we were all happy for her, I have to admit that we've also been getting a bit tired of scrambled eggs, cereal, and sandwiches."

"I'm not a professional," Phoebe said quickly, on what even she realized was a knee-jerk lack of confidence. "But at least I could grill the sandwiches."

"Oh, that would be a wonderful start. Our security system is set to notify the fire department if the smoke detector goes off. I've burned so many things, including last night's grilled cheese, the department has begun calling before they leave the station to make sure it's not another false alarm."

Phoebe smiled, as she knew she was supposed to, even as she felt another knot untie in her stomach at the mention of the house's security alarm. Then again, given its residents, she supposed that was to be expected.

"Mr. and Mrs. Stuart lived on the second floor." Zelda continued up the staircase lined with oil and watercolor paintings of what Phoebe took to be local scenery, including a lighthouse perched on a cliff. The mahogany newel post and banister had been polished to a satin sheen. This was obviously a house well loved by it residents. "We have a total of fifteen rooms, each with its own bath. Many have a private deck."

"This isn't anything like what I was expecting," Phoebe admitted. She'd been picturing, at best, dorm living. At worst, something like what she'd seen in documentaries about women's prisons. But even that would have been welcome after the gilded prison she'd been living in. "It's like a resort."

"It is, isn't it?" Zelda smiled. "I love watching our new residents' faces when they first see it. The gardens aren't quite up to snuff yet—spring came a bit late this year—but they're glorious when they're in full bloom. Which is why I asked if you were a gardener."

"I'd probably kill the plants. But I can weed."

"Great. We all take turns here. It's more like a commune than a shelter." She put an arm around Phoebe as she led her down a long hallway on the third floor. "I have a feeling you'll fit right in."

Two days later, assuring her that she was now safe, Zelda sent Phoebe off to explore the town and bring back an order of cupcakes from the local bakery, where the shelter's previous cook now worked.

Although she hadn't wanted to admit it, once she'd found sanctuary, Phoebe would have been more than willing to stay in the house forever.

Which would have been a mistake.

The air was tinged with the scent of salt as light mist fell from a quilted pewter sky. She walked along the harbor, where boats carrying whale-watching tourists chugged away from the dock. Sailboats, their stiff white sails billowing in the wind, skimmed across the blue-gray water, while huge sea lions lounged lazily on docks, barking to one another.

Forsythias were shedding the last of the yellow bell blossoms, which were strewn on the cobblestone sidewalk like gold coins. After passing the tidy shops with their colorful wind socks blowing in the sea breeze, and homes with well-kept yards that smelled of flowers and freshly cut grass, she climbed a hill where a bronze statue of a young woman, looking out to sea, supposedly waiting for her fisherman husband's return, stood in the center of a spring green expanse of grass surrounded by late-blooming daffodils and crayon-bright tulips.

In the distance, a white lighthouse speared upward from a cliff at the edge of the ocean.

Not far from the waiting-woman statue was a playground, where a woman, clad in a turquoise parka, pushed a small child on a swing. Watching them laugh together, although she knew intellectually that it was too early, Phoebe imagined she felt her baby stir. And knew that she'd done exactly the right thing.

She also thought, as she headed back down the hill, following Zelda's hand-drawn map to the bakery, that although everything she'd read about running away from an abusive situation advised never staying in one place for very long, she could easily picture herself being happy here, in this small town where everyone seemed to know everyone and people waved to one another and stopped to chat.

Of course, the downside was that it would be difficult keeping a secret in such a place. And she definitely had more than her share of secrets.

The amazing aromas drifting out onto the sidewalk from Take the Cake helped unclench her stomach, which had tightened in its too-familiar way. Having planned her escape for months, Phoebe decided that she owed herself some time to relax. She'd escaped Peter physically. Now, the trick, as Zelda had told her over a pot of freshly brewed Earl Grey tea in the pretty sunroom, was to put him out of her mind.

Although the older woman didn't know all the facts that had brought Phoebe to Shelter Bay, obviously women didn't arrive there at all times of the day or night, from all over the country, to enjoy a spa day.

She wove her way through the white wrought iron chairs on the front patio and into the store, where the pretty blonde wearing a pink apron and standing behind the counter greeted her with a smile.

"Hi. You must be Phoebe."

Her nerves balled up and frayed at the recognition. Then, reminding herself that Zelda had called ahead, Phoebe forced herself to relax.

"That's me." Did her smile feel as forced as it felt?

"It's nice to meet you. I'm Sedona Sullivan."

"The owner." Zelda had mentioned her.

"Again, that would be me. So, what can I get you?"

"Didn't Zelda tell you when she called her order in?" As her hands grew wet, Phoebe had to resist rubbing them on her linen slacks.

"She said you were coming, but didn't mention anything specific, which makes sense, because I tend to bake whatever I feel like when I get up in the morning." The easy smile lit up the baker's blue eyes. "Which, as a recovering CPA, I know isn't exactly the best way to run a business. But hey"—she shrugged shoulders clad in a T-shirt the same color as the apron—"if I'd wanted to worry about numbers all day, I'd have stayed behind a desk."

The little bell on the door jingled as someone else entered the bakery. "Hi, Kara," Sedona Sullivan looked past Phoebe to greet the new customer. "I've been waiting for you to show up."

"Some cops need a doughnut fix. I prefer cupcakes," the female voice behind Phoebe said.

Cop? Dizzy with panic, she struggled not to give in to the fear that had her knees threatening to buckle as the woman wearing a starched khaki uniform came to stand in front of the display case beside her.

"Hi," she said. Her tone was friendly, but her quick, sweeping look made Phoebe feel as if she were cataloging her vital statistics in order to check them out on some police Most Wanted list. "Are you visiting?"

"In a way." Phoebe had to push the words past the lump in her throat. "I'm between places and was considering settling down here."

"It's a great town," the sheriff said. "Of course, I'm admittedly prejudiced, having grown up here, but I can tell you that our crime rate definitely is lower than most places." Her smile was quick and warm. But her eyes, while friendly enough, also asked questions Phoebe was not prepared to answer.

"That's good to know." She turned her attention toward the glass case. "What would you recommend?" she asked the other woman.

"Oh, gee, that's like asking a mom which child she likes best. But I do know that Zelda's personal favorite is lemon coconut." She glanced out the door where a couple clad in baseball caps and matching blue rain parkas had settled down at a table. "Why don't you decide what looks good while I run out and get their order?" she suggested.

And didn't that sound so easy? But just looking at the vast choices of pretty, decorated cakes was enough to make Phoebe's head spin. Other than the decision to call that underground-railroad hotline she'd found on the Internet, she couldn't remember the last time she'd made any of her own decisions.

Peter had chosen their wedding venue. Their honeymoon location. Their home. Their decorator. Her clothes. He'd hired the maid, the pool boy (though, in his case, it was a pool girl, which Phoebe had figured out was because he didn't want to risk her being alone with any other male), and the landscaper, who was seventy, if a day. And therefore safe.

He chose where they'd eat when they went out, which had happened less and less frequently, and all their friends from the beginning of their marriage had been his.

His behavior, she'd been assured by her rescuers, had been classic abuser. But even knowing that didn't help her when it came to choosing a damn cupcake.

"The red velvet's delicious," the sheriff volunteered as Phoebe stood frozen, staring blindly into the case. "My son, Trey, is crazy about the banana." She pointed toward a cupcake in yellow fluted paper, topped with what the calligraphied sign in front described as a caramel buttercream frosting. "My fiancé usually goes for the carrot cake." That one was easy to spot because of the small marzipan carrot on top of the cream cheese frosting. "He claims it counts as health food since Sedona also puts apples in it. It's both a vegetable and a fruit serving."

Her laugh was warm and rich and had Phoebe thinking that were it not for that badge she was wearing, they might even someday become friends if she stayed in Shelter Bay.

As it was, she couldn't risk the friendly sheriff with the strawberry-blond hair getting suspicious.

"Thanks," she said. "They all look delicious."

"They're to die for. You can't go wrong whichever you choose."

The baker was back. "I'll just be another minute," she assured both women as she poured two mugs of coffee that smelled a bit of cinnamon, and plated two devil's food cupcakes, which she delivered to the couple at the table.

"Sorry about that," she said when she returned behind the counter. "But they only had a few minutes before they have to get back on their tour bus for the trip up to Cannon Beach." She input the credit card information in the computerized register. "So, can I help you with any explanations?"

"The sheriff assures me they're all great," Phoebe said.

"I like to think so," Sedona replied mildly.

Realizing they were both watching her and wanting to escape as quickly as she could, after ordering two lemon coconuts, two carrot cakes, a red velvet, and a banana, Phoebe just randomly named assorted others until she had the dozen Zelda had sent her for.

"And one extra makes a baker's dozen," Sedona said, as she added a chocolate cupcake with buttercream frosting, topped with perky sugar pansies to the others in the pink box.

"Thanks." Phoebe reached into her purse and pulled out the bills Zelda had given her.

"Thank you," Sedona said as she rang up the order and made change. "Come again."

"I will."

Oh, God. She was on the verge of hyperventilating. Desperate to get out into the fresh air before she humiliated herself with a full-blown anxiety attack, Phoebe hugged the box tight and made her escape.

"Wow," Kara said as both women watched her practically run out of the store. "If she'd been wound any tighter, we would've been picking up pieces of her all over this bakery."

"She's staying at Haven House."

"Yeah, I got that. But I would've figured it out, anyway, from that deer-in-the-headlights look. When she actually dared to look at anything but the floor."

"It must be terrifying," Sedona said. "Having to run away to be safe."

"Probably less terrifying than living with a fucking wife abuser."

Kara's sharp tone and the fact that she'd dropped the F bomb, which Sedona had never heard her do, had realization dawning.

"Oh, hell." She closed her eyes and shook her head. "I'm sorry. I didn't think about Jared."

"That's okay." Kara exhaled a long breath and shook *her* head. "I overreacted."

"I don't believe that's possible. Given that your police officer husband was killed by a batterer."

"Still, I'm a cop." Kara squared her shoulders. Lifted her chin. "Professionally, I should be able to deal with it."

"Anyone ever tell you that you can be too hard on yourself? You may be a cop, but you're also a widow who lost her husband to a senseless act of violence."

"True. But you know what they say about what doesn't kill you. And I did end up with a happily-ever-after."

Kara's gaze drifted out the window again. "I hope she's as fortunate. Meanwhile, I think I'll do a check on her. Just in case whoever it is she's running from finds her and decides to show up in town to drag her back home."

18

Since he wasn't due at Sofia's until afternoon, Lucas took advantage of the free morning to go surf fishing.

Scout raced ahead of him, down the zigzag wooden steps from the cottage to the beach, where lacy white surf rolled across the sand, then ebbed back again.

The sky was burnished pewter, a few shades lighter than the steel gray sea. Every so often the sun would pierce through the clouds, causing diamonds to dance on the waves. Although he'd traveled the world for the past ten years, Lucas had continued to feel the same connection to the sea he'd experienced the first summer his father had brought him to Shelter Bay. The summer after his sister had died and his grieving mother had left the gray drizzle of the Pacific Northwest—and her equally devastated husband and son—for a new start beneath Colorado's blue skies.

He'd often thought that Magellan had gotten it wrong, because there was nothing peaceful about this part of the Pacific. It could be unpredictable. Wild. Even dangerous. Which he'd always thought mirrored his own life.

Out on the horizon, a fishing boat chummed the waters. Gulls trailed behind it, diving, screeching, and fighting over breakfast. Closer to shore, a pod of seals swam parallel to the beach, doing their own morning fishing. Sandpipers skittered along the edge of the surf as the German shepherd took off on her self-appointed yet ultimately impossible role of keeping the beach seagull free.

As the dog raced up and down the sand, her barks carried off by the breeze, Lucas cast his line into the white-capped breaker waves, then let the sinker dig into the sandy bottom, allowing the sand shrimp and clam-neck bait to sway enticingly back and forth with the movement of the water.

One of the things the military had taught him was patience. He kept casting and reeling the line back in until he felt the sharp, telltale tugs at the rod tip. Jerking sharply to set the hook, he reeled in a fat sea perch. While Scout kept the circling gulls at bay, he took out the hook, put the fish into his creel, rebaited, and cast again.

He'd caught his limit in less than thirty minutes, and killed time throwing a piece of driftwood into the surf for Scout, who'd race into the waves, retrieve it, and come racing back to drop it at his feet, her wet tail wagging merrily as she waited for another throw. The same way she'd walk with his SEAL team for miles over rocks and desolation in Afghanistan, she appeared indefatigable when it came to ocean fetching. And although there was a vague threat of a riptide, sneaker wave, or even a shark, at least Lucas no longer had to worry about her stepping on a booby trap and losing another leg. Or worse yet, her life.

He'd just thrown the stick for what felt like the umpteenth time when, out of the swirling mist and fog he viewed a woman clad in a bright yellow slicker and tall black boots, clamming in the shallow water.

Intent as she was on her harvest, she didn't notice that she was no longer alone until Scout, sighting a new playmate, went racing toward her and dropped the driftwood right next to her shovel.

He watched as she laughed, patted the dog's head, threw the stick into the water, then looked around for its owner.

Although she was far enough away to keep him from

seeing her face, Lucas knew Maddy had recognized him when her shoulders stiffened.

She half turned as if to walk away; then, as he watched, she appeared to make the decision to stand her ground.

As he walked toward her across the damp sand, Lucas had a very good idea how those perch had felt when they'd found themselves hooked.

"Are you following me?"

"Not to quibble the point, but since the beach was deserted when Scout and I came down, I could ask the same question of you."

"To which the answer would be a definitive no." She glanced down at the dog, who was standing over the driftwood, furry tale wagging like a metronome, looking back and forth between them, eyes pleading for someone just to throw the stick, please.

"Is this your dog?"

"Yeah. I brought her back with me from Afghanistan." Because *the gaze* was working as it always did, he gave in, picked the stick up, and threw it into the surf. She ran after it, pausing only to bark a warning to a pod of pelicans flying by in fighter-jet formation.

"Is that where ... ?" Her voice drifted off as if the question was too difficult to ask out loud.

"She lost her leg to an IED on a booby-trapped house door," he supplied. "Which gave a whole new meaning to 'taking one for the team.'"

"I'm sorry."

"Yeah. So was I." He'd spent years treating guys wounded in battle, including a really bad copter crash in the Hindu Kush. He'd saved more men than he'd lost, but every life he hadn't saved still haunted him. But never had he felt ice-cold panic as he had when amputating the loyal shepherd's leg while under fire.

They both watched the dog happily bounding through the surf. Apparently realizing her humans were otherwise occupied, she began tossing the stick into the air herself. Then racing after it.

"She seems to have adjusted remarkably."

"Physically, her recovery was amazing." Lucas rubbed his jaw and wished he'd taken time to shave before leaving the cottage. "She did, unfortunately, return home with a rough case of PTSD, but Charity—that's my half sister, but since she was only here one summer, you might not have met her—"

"She's the vet Gram adopted Winnie from."

"That would be her. I don't think she's going to be able to rest until every abandoned or abused animal on the planet has a home. . . . Anyway, she's had animal behavioral training and says that Scout's about ninety-percent back to her old self, which isn't always the case. You should've seen the dog a few months ago. She spent most of the time with her tail between her legs, hiding under tables and trying to avoid people."

"That's so sad."

"War's a long way from playing fetch. But to her, sniffing out bombs was just another game in the beginning, and she was probably one of the best ever born to it. She also was great on house-to-house searches in some of the more remote villages we were sent to."

"Damn." Her brow furrowed and her midnight eyes darkened.

"What?"

"I'm really trying to hate you." A thin white line circled unpainted lips he could still taste. Lips he was aching to taste again.

The definitive words, Lucas told himself, were *trying to*. "You hold a grudge a long time."

"Yes." He was tempted to rub at the furrow between her brows, then decided not to push his luck. So far she hadn't slugged him with that clam shovel, which was encouraging. "It appears I do."

"What happened between us was a long time ago." Surely the statue of limitations on stupidity would have run out by now. "Would it matter if I had a reason?"

"No." She lifted her chin. "As you said, it was a long time ago. There's no point in rehashing old memories." Her curt tone declared the topic closed.

He should just let it go. Count himself lucky that she didn't intend to drag him over the coals.

They were no longer those two crazy kids they'd once been. They'd grown up. He'd changed more than he ever could have foreseen that stolen summer. She'd obviously changed, too.

Let it go.

Too late.

During all those summers he and his dad had come to Shelter Bay, the community had seemed frozen in time. From what he'd seen so far, except for the new names on the storefronts, and more tourist boats than fishing boats in the harbor, that hadn't changed.

It had also been the very trait, which, when he'd found his postwar plans in shambles, had drawn him back.

One thing he hadn't counted on was that Maddy would be returning home, too.

It's true, Lucas thought on a burst of optimism. *Timing really is everything.*

19

"Look," he said, "I understand you're still hurting—"

"Don't flatter yourself." A gust of wind blew her hood back. Frustrated at this situation she'd landed in, Madeline ignored it.

After a night spent tossing and turning as images of that damn video of Maxime flashed through her mind, chased by other images of this man with a cocktail waitress from the Stewed Clam, she'd finally crawled out of bed, dressed quietly while Sofia was still sleeping, and come down to the beach. She'd hoped that the brisk, fresh air would clear her head and the endless surf would soothe, as it had when she'd first started coming here after her parents' deaths.

Which it had. Until she'd looked up and seen Lucas standing there. Wondering how long he'd been watching her instead of running away, as she'd been tempted to do, she'd stood her ground and made him come to her.

"What I am is annoyed that you've managed to insinuate yourself into my grandmother's life. And for some reason, which totally escapes me, she seems to like you. Which means that by default, I'm stuck with you, too."

"You've gotten tougher."

"I've had to," she said with a tone a great deal drier than the weather. There were, however, limits. Deciding it was time to cut this conversation short before it got more personal than she was prepared to handle, Madeline picked up her red clam bucket. "I suppose I'll see you at the farm."

When she turned to walk back to the wooden steps, he caught her arm. "This isn't going to work."

"On that we can agree." She pried his long fingers from her sleeve. "So, why don't you just tell my grandmother that your plans have changed and you won't be able to do her remodel after all?"

"I gave my word."

"Then break it."

"It's not that easy. Sofia's like the grandmother I never knew. I wouldn't begin to know how to say no to her."

"Oh, really?" Damn the man; he had her trembling. Not as he'd once done, but with anger and, worse, remembered pain. "Give it a try," she advised. "I'm sure it'll come back to you."

"Okay." His tone was short and far more harsh than she'd ever heard it. Suddenly, he looked and sounded like the warrior she knew him to be. "That's it. I'm already sick and tired of dancing around the damn topic. We need to straighten this out."

Although she didn't believe he'd actually hurt her, the hard look in his eyes had her backing up a step. "What we need is to get out of the rain." The mist, which had turned to a drizzle while they were talking, was becoming a drenching rain. And getting colder by the moment.

"Okay. Come up to the cottage. We can talk there. Unless you want to dump our problem on your grandmother."

"No." She hated that he was right. "And, for Gram's sake, I'm willing to work with you on planning her remodel. But that's it. There's nothing you can say that'll change anything about what happened back then."

"Yeah, that's what Sax said you'd say."

She'd been reluctantly walking back toward the stairs, but that muttered comment had her stopping in her tracks.

"You discussed our personal business with Sax Douchett?"

"Guys might not share as much as women, but, yeah, we've been known to talk about regrets. You were mine. . . .

"Not you," he tacked on quickly, "but how things ended between us. So, yesterday, when I stopped by Bon Temps for something to eat and told him I'd run into you in Sofia's kitchen, he told me to man up and tell you the truth."

Madeline couldn't believe this. Was there nothing about her damn life that was private? "I *saw* the truth."

"You saw what you thought was the truth," he corrected. "It was what I wanted you to see."

"Right." Rain streamed from her hair and face. She put down the pail long enough to drag a handful of wet curls out of her eyes. "You actually expect me to buy the story that you *wanted* me to see you sprawled on your father's couch, making out with a cocktail waitress?"

"Who are you going to believe?" he asked. "Me or your lying eyes?"

"Excuse me if I don't find betrayal a joking matter." She picked up the pail and began walking again.

"Okay." He blew out a long breath. "That was inappropriate. I apologize. Now, do you want to discuss it out here in the rain? Or indoors over some coffee and heated-up bread pudding?"

"I thought you didn't cook." Even as she asked the question, Madeline assured herself that the only reason he was able to throw her off track was that the debacle with Maxime had gotten her off her game.

"I don't. It's leftovers. Sax always serves me twice as much as I need. I suspect it's Kara's doing, so I won't starve."

"You could always learn to cook."

"Or maybe once we get the restaurant up and going, you could cook for me."

"Why, what a good idea." She flashed him a sweet, feigned smile. "I'd love nothing more than to make you a pesto and hemlock pizza with a big piece of arsenic pie à la mode for dessert."

His answering laugh was too rich. Too warm.

And too, too familiar.

As she climbed the steps up the cliff, Madeline sternly reminded herself that a strong, sensible, responsible woman who'd already been burned once by this man could not allow herself to be so easily turned into Silly Putty by a look. A touch. A laugh.

She was going to have to work on that.

Really, she was.

Beginning now.

20

The Chaffee summerhouse was just as Madeline remembered it. When visitors approached from the road, the house looked like a cozy Cape Cod cottage, with weathered gray shingles, white trim, and clapboard shutters.

But when you walked in the front door, you found yourself facing a wall of glass that framed the beach and the ocean all the way out to the horizon.

"This view still takes my breath away," she admitted as she shrugged out of her wet slicker.

"Dad appreciated designs from the past." Lucas hung the jacket next to his own on a pegged rack by the door. When he put his sandy boots in the boot box, Madeline followed suit and tried not to think how oddly right it looked to have her things next to his.

"Which is why, instead of building some stark, modern box that might've landed this place on the cover of *Architectural Digest*, he wanted the exterior of the house people viewed to fit into the rest of the town. But since he was also a form-follows-function guy, he thought it would be criminal to block this million-dollar view with traditional cottage windows."

"Probably a lot more than a million dollars these days," she said as she crossed the wide-plank wood floor to the window. Fortunately, the slipcovered couch where he'd betrayed her had been replaced sometime over the years.

"I've missed this," she admitted. "Not this view, specifically. But the town. And the ocean."

"The East Coast has an ocean." He crossed the room to stand behind her.

"True. But it's not the same thing." Instead of pale sands strewn with pretty pink and cream shells, a huge pile of driftwood logs had washed ashore. Green kelp covered everything, like nets left behind by careless fishermen. "Eastern beaches tend to be much tidier."

"And crowded, I'll bet."

"You'd win that bet." She sighed. "Until this morning, when I went clamming, I couldn't remember the last time I'd been outside without anyone within sight."

"We're definitely off the beaten track here."

She looked up at him. "It sounds as if you plan to stay."

"I got a call last night from this guy. He's a retired stock-broker from Seattle who bought the old cannery down on the harbor and is looking for someone to fix it up."

"From the high-flying world of stocks and bonds to canned fish is a huge jump for a second career."

"He's not going to use the building for canning. He's an artisan furniture maker who reclaims wounded urban trees that are going to be destroyed, which apparently is becoming the 'in' thing among wealthy collectors. That counter"—he pointed at the kitchen counter that hadn't been there ten years ago—"is from a red maple that came down in a storm up in Astoria."

"It's stunning." And all the more appealing because of the crack, which was evidence that the life of a tree wasn't nearly as easy as it looked when it was just standing in a park or forest.

"Isn't it? Dad bought it about six months ago. He e-mailed me photos because he thought we could see about maybe incorporating some of the guy's work into the mill-work of the houses we were going to restore."

He paused and dragged a hand through his hair. Madeline knew firsthand the hurt he was feeling. She also knew that he'd never quite overcome it.

"Anyway, he decided that he'd rather set up his own shop, now that he's escaped the daily office grind. He was about to lease space on Pioneer Square in Seattle, but then he came down here on a fishing trip, started talking with Dad, who was at the marina that day, spotted the cannery, and decided to turn it into a workshop and lease out gallery space."

"There are a lot of local artists who'd probably sign on right away." Shelter Bay had, from its early days, drawn artists and musicians who enjoyed the solitude and creative inspiration of the sea and mountains. "And the location's a draw, being right next to the farmers' market. And down Harborview from the marina."

"That was his thinking. He's already got commitments for seventy-five percent of the planned space. Now he just needs someone who can turn the plans into reality."

"It sounds like quite a challenge." And made her wonder how Lucas also planned to remodel her grandmother's kitchen.

"A lot easier than humping up a mountain with a hundred-pound pack on your back while bad guys are shooting at you."

Again, she was forced to realize that whatever else he'd done, specifically to her, the man standing so close that she could feel the heat of his body was also a hero.

She was trying to morph the two disparate men into one in her mind when something out in the silvery mist caught her attention.

"Oh, look!" She drew in a short breath. "The whales!"

Several decades ago, a pod of whales had been making their annual migration from Alaska down to Mexico when, for some reason no one knew, they'd decided to settle on this part of the coast. Not only had they added to the local color, but they'd also proven an important part of Shelter Bay's economy, drawing visitors from around the world.

"Aren't they incredible?" she breathed.

"Incredible." The rough, deep tone drew her attention. and when she glanced up at him, he wasn't looking out at the huge sea mammals cutting a determined swath through the waves, but down at her.

"This isn't what I came here for."

He arched a brow. "Did I say anything?"

"You didn't have to." The way his eyes had darkened told her exactly what he was thinking. And, as remembered awareness hummed between them, he was not alone.

"But you can't blame me for finding them incredible," he said.

Her foolish, rebellious heart had begun fluttering like a wild bird. "The whales?"

"They're cool. But I was referring to your eyes." He cupped her check. "I'd almost managed to convince myself over the years that I'd imagined how remarkable they are. But I didn't. They're never the same color."

"Of course they are." She swallowed. Licked her lips and realized her mistake when hunger flashed in his watchful, espresso-hued gaze. "They're gray." Which, unlike both her mother and grandmother, who had flashing, dark eyes, she'd always considered a boring, indistinct hue.

"Technically, perhaps." His enticing touch trailed down her cheek and brushed over lips that had turned as dry as a boxed mix pound cake. "But they're as changeable as the sea. Yesterday, in Sofia's kitchen, they looked like storm clouds.

"Then earlier, on the beach, I decided they were more pewter." His mouth was a whisper from hers. "And now they've turned the hue of polished silver."

"Good try." Because his touch was leaving sparks on her lips, she backed away. "But if you brought me up here because you had the crazy idea that you could just sweet-talk me into forgiving you, Lucas, you'd be wrong."

She'd loved him, dammit. Blindly, with every fiber of

her foolish, eighteen-year-old being. He'd been the first man to whom she'd ever given her heart so fully. *Correction,* she realized now, as she fought a temper she hadn't felt toward her cheating, lying husband. *Not the first,* but *the only one.*

Maxime had been right about her having loved the idea of being married to him. Of sharing a culinary life together, the same way her parents had for so many years. But dazzled by his charisma and talent, she'd mistaken awe for love.

Which was undoubtedly why she was feeling more regret than remorse over the crumbling of a marriage that probably should have been declared DOA at the altar.

"Although the idea of making up in bed is, admittedly, appealing," Lucas said, "I brought you up here to tell you that I never slept with Ashleigh."

"If that's true, and I have only your word for it, then it's only because I interrupted things by showing up unannounced."

Since his father had been spending the night in Portland, she'd taken advantage of Lucas having the cottage to himself and had brought the ingredients to cook him dinner. Along with flowers from Sofia's cutting garden and candles to set a romantic mood.

"She didn't come here for sex. She was a friend who was doing me a favor."

"I might have been stupid, but I wasn't blind. I could tell that much for myself." Admittedly, although they'd been twined up like a pair of octopi on the couch, they'd both been fully dressed. But that was undoubtedly only because she'd arrived before things had had a chance to really heat up.

"I needed you to think I was cheating."

"What?" A temper she'd never known bubbled up inside her. A hot, poisonous stew of emotions. "Why?"

"It was for your own good."

"How was breaking my heart for my own good?" A heart that was currently lodged in her throat.

"You went to Europe," he reminded her.

"Because you broke my heart," she repeated furiously. It still stung.

"Do you have any idea what it did to me to hear you announce that you'd decided to stay here in Shelter Bay instead of following your dream? That you didn't need to travel the world to learn how to cook? That Sofia could teach you everything you needed? I couldn't let you pass up that opportunity. Not for me."

Surely he couldn't have . . .

Baffled, and needing a moment before she could trust her voice, Madeline stared up at him.

The room was suddenly dead silent. There was only the sound of the wind moaning in the top of the Douglas fir trees that surrounded the cottage on three sides, and the rain, which had turned into a full-fledged storm, hitting the glass wall.

She finally found her voice. "Are you actually saying that you staged that whole horrid scene so I'd get upset and storm off to Europe?"

But she hadn't stormed. She'd fled. With her bleeding heart in tatters.

"You'd been planning that trip for years," he reminded her. "You had your passport, you'd hooked up with some of your parents' chef friends, you were on your way to becoming the person you are today. The gorgeous celebrity chef on my TV."

"Liar. I'm not gorgeous."

At this point she undoubtedly looked like a drenched, dark-haired Little Orphan Annie. She could feel her hair springing into a mass of wild, frizzy, wet curls; she wasn't wearing a smidgen of makeup; she was wearing jeans and an oversized sweatshirt with embossed puffins on the front that she'd borrowed from Sofia; and she needed to lose ten—okay, make that fifteen—pounds. Which didn't help when the television cameras added even more.

"If you actually believe that, then you need to get a new mirror," he said.

It was ridiculous to receive pleasure from a glib compliment that undoubtedly worked with females from eight to eighty. Ridiculous, foolish, and dangerous. She'd also let him distract her from her point.

"I'm also not a celebrity."

It was the same thing she'd told Birdy. But now Madeline was forced to wonder exactly how far her life had gone off track. And which of them she was trying to convince. She'd never wanted to be a celebrity. All she'd ever wanted to do was to cook. To share her food with others for love. Not fame or fortune.

"Try telling that to your fans. And those groups that get together around the country every Thursday night to cook dinner along with your show."

She moved closer. Until they were toe-to-toe, which forced her to tilt her head back to look up at him. "How did you know about that?"

"I Googled you. Because," he said, holding up a hand to forestall whatever she'd been about to say, "although I never realized it until I heard you were coming back to town, I guess I'm a glutton for punishment."

"Then you should absolutely love this."

Although she knew it was a cliché, and although she'd never, ever hit anyone in her life before, she slapped him. Hard.

The sound, as sharp and loud as a rifle retort, had Scout, who'd been happily curled up on an overstuffed sofa, diving beneath the table.

"Oh, hell," Lucas muttered. He did not, she noticed, even touch his reddening cheek. "Could we just take a time-out for a minute?"

21

Knowing pretty much what the dog was going through, Lucas crouched down and stuck his hand, palm up, beneath the table.

"That's okay, pretty girl," he soothed, in much the same way he might talk to a woman he was trying to seduce. "There's no shooting, darlin'. And no one's going to hurt you."

The dog was cowering as if a horde of terrorists were about to storm down on her.

"Oh, God. I'm so sorry." Maddy dropped to her knees beside him.

"She'll be okay." He glanced back over his shoulder toward the kitchen on the other side of the large room. "There's a carton of jambalaya in the fridge. Maybe you could get her a piece of shrimp. That usually works."

"I feel like the worst person in the world," she muttered as she got to her feet and retrieved the snack.

"It's no big deal. You should've seen her the other day when a car backfired while we were driving into town. I had to stop by the Cracked Crab and order a fried-fish sandwich from the drive-through to coax her out from beneath the seat."

"That's so sad." She was back on her knees again, so close he could smell the vague scent of coconut shampoo in her hair.

"Like I said, she's making progress. Why don't you try giving it to her? Not with your fingers. Put it on your palm. It's less threatening that way."

"Shouldn't you do it? I'm the one who terrified her."

"Don't worry. If we're going to be working together, it's good that she gets to know you. Besides, unlike people, dogs don't hold grudges."

"That's all your fault." Her tone, probably in deference to the dog, was softer than her accusation. "What was I supposed to think when I saw you tangled up with another woman?"

"Like I said. Exactly what I wanted you to."

"Good doggy," she soothed when the dog whimpered, seeming, despite them speaking quietly, to sense their argument. "Good, Scout . . . And you"—she shot him a blistering look—"were an idiot."

"On that we can agree. My only defense," Lucas said, as Scout snatched the pink shrimp from her hand, then licked Maddy's palm with a swipe of her long pink tongue, "is that I was twenty years old, with not a single clue about what I was going to do with my life, while you, despite being two years younger, already had everything all figured out."

She slanted him a hard look. "So you decided to take any decisions regarding my own life away from me." A black nose inched its way from beneath the wood planks.

"Not any decision. Just the important one you were about to blow. Dammit, I was trying to do the right thing. I just went about it the wrong way."

Hell. His rough, frustrated tone sent the nose back beneath the table again. Lucas dragged both hands down his face and struggled for control. How was it that he could keep his head in the middle of a violent battle, but he couldn't get through a conversation with this woman without wanting to bang his head against the rocky cliff?

"Look. I loved you, okay?" he said through gritted teeth,

struggling against a teeming flood of guilt and frustration. "Enough to know that someday down the line, if I let you give up your dream for me, you'd end up resenting me. And I wasn't willing to risk that. For your sake or for mine. Because it never would've worked out."

"Well, we'll never know, will we?" She kept her tone quiet, in deference to the dog. But her voice wavered, either from a need to weep or shout. Lucas couldn't tell which, but neither one was good.

The dog's dark nose came out again, followed by the rest of her head. When Madeline patted it, Lucas covered her hand with his.

He felt her tense, but she didn't pull away. Lucas decided that once Scout did come out, he was going to get the dog the biggest, juiciest bone in town.

"If you told me this to get on my good side, thinking I'd consider you some sort of noble, self-sacrificing, romance-novel hero—"

"No."

As ridiculous as it was, Lucas was suddenly feeling twenty again. He was not inexperienced with women. On the contrary, he'd always liked them. And respected them. And when things ended, as they invariably did, he and the women would stay friends.

Except for the one time it had really mattered.

"I told you, and not in the way I'd planned, because I wanted you to know why I did what I did back then. Even if you hate me for it."

"That's a bit strong." Scout was scooting forward on her belly, inch by inch, reminding Lucas of how he and his team had often been forced to make their way down to a Taliban stronghold under the cover of darkness. "I tend to save hate for really bad things. Like child abusers and people who drown puppies and kittens."

Encouraged since he'd come this far, Lucas decided just

to go for it and tell the truth, the whole truth, and nothing but the truth. "I also told you what I'd done because I'm still crazy about you and have every intention of marrying you."

"I see." Her cool tone was not encouraging, but Lucas had overcome tougher challenges. "Interesting how you've maintained the same bad habits. Once again, you're leaving me nothing to say about my own life."

Damn. When she was right, she was right. But still . . .

Apparently sensing the lessening of hostilities, Scout wiggled the rest of her way from beneath the table. Then immediately rolled over, offering her stomach to be rubbed.

Apparently still trying to make amends, which was so not necessary, since, as he'd told her, the dog didn't hold grudges, Maddy obliged.

"I understand you need time to process all this." Lucas cupped her too-stubborn chin in his fingers and turned her face to his. "But while you're thinking about it, know this: Whatever you've thought of me over the years, whatever you think about me now, the fact is that I love you, Maddy. And although I tried like hell to forget you these past ten years, I always will."

"In case it's slipped your mind, I'm a married woman."

"Are you going back to your husband?"

"No." He saw the truth of that declaration in her eyes, which had turned from the stormy gray of temper to a calmer, more deliberative hue. Yep. Although Lucas wished he could have protected her from the pain she must have suffered, he didn't mind that that Frenchy was toast. "Not in this lifetime."

"Well, then." He leaned forward and brushed his lips against hers before she could read his intention and pull back. "I'm willing to wait for you to realize you still love me back."

"What if I don't believe in love anymore?"

"I'll just have to change your mind."

She stiffened. He could feel the chill. "You think it's going to be that easy?"

"We SEALs have a saying: 'The only easy day was yesterday.'"

"Just because I'm divorcing Maxime doesn't mean I'm going to jump out of the sauté pan into the fire and marry you."

"Okay." He linked their fingers together. "I'll settle for a series of one-night stands."

"That's an oxymoron. A *series* signifies more than a single encounter."

When she went to pull her hand away, he lifted it to his lips and brushed a kiss over her knuckles. "Not if you take it one night at a time. Then a next night, and a next—"

"Then it's still no longer a one-night stand. It's an affair."

"Which I'll take."

"Why am I not surprised?" She lifted a brow. "Whatever happened to marriage?"

"Oh, that's still on the drawing board. I just figured with all you have on your plate right now, it might be less threatening to you to think of using me merely for sex."

"I don't want you to love me."

"Too bad." He wanted—intended—to have this woman back not only in his bed, but in his life. Whatever it took. "And too late, because that ship sailed a long time ago. . . . Look, you don't have to say anything now, Maddy. But since I admittedly screwed up by lying to you ten years ago, I decided to be up front about my feelings and my intentions this time around."

"Read my lips. Not only am I am not going to marry you, but this partnership, or whatever it is that we've been forced into for Gram's sake, is going to remain strictly business. No way I'm allowing it to get personal."

"Again, too late. Because it got personal a long time ago, Maddy." Concentrating on the positive, Lucas decided that this was an improvement over her looking as if she wanted to fillet him, tie him to a cedar plank, then grill him over hot coals.

"You've just made my point. That *was* a very long time ago. We're both different people. And I've no intention of going back."

"That's what you say now. But here's the deal: We were friends before we were lovers, so I'm willing to start with that. Plus, you're right. We've both changed. I'm a lot more patient than I was back then." While impulsive, over-the-top behavior made for some really nifty war movies, Lucas had learned as early as BUD/S training that in real life it could land you in hot water. Really fast. "I'm willing to give you time to get used to the idea."

"That's not going to happen." Now that Scout was out from under the table and back to happily chewing on a plush octopus Charity had sent home with the dog, Maddy scrambled to her feet.

"Never say never," he replied mildly, as he stood up, as well.

"We're never going to be able to work together if you insist on making things personal."

He lifted his hands, palms out. "Okay." He hissed out a breath. Patience, he reminded himself yet again, was reputed to be a virtue. "Since I agree we're going to need to be grown-ups this time around, I'm willing to keep things totally professional while we're working together."

"Good."

"However, if you decide to change things up after hours, I won't complain."

"Don't hold your breath." Her eyes locked on his. "As for your crazy marriage idea, for the last time, that's not going to happen. No way. No how."

Because he was in a really good mood for the first time since getting the call about his father, Lucas laughed. Then, because it had been too long since he'd touched her, he skimmed a finger down the slope of her nose.

"One word of advice," he said. "I wouldn't bet your grandmother's farm on that, darlin'."

22

Sofia was bustling around in the kitchen when Maddy returned to the farmhouse.

"How was your time at the beach?" she asked, greeting Maddy with a hug.

"Wet. But successful." She put the bucket of clams she'd dug onto the counter by the sink. "I'd forgotten how good being on the beach is for clearing your mind. I came up with a recipe for clams Kokkinisto I want to try."

"Oh, that sounds fabulous. And if it works, I can serve it in the restaurant."

"Speaking of the restaurant, I ran into Lucas on the beach."

"Oh?" Her grandmother took a stack of Tupperware containers filled with what looked like lasagna from the refrigerator. "How did that go?"

"Okay, I guess." Madeline wasn't about to tell her grandmother about his ridiculous claim that he was going to marry her. As if she didn't have anything to say about it. Which she most certainly did. "He mentioned taking a job to restore the old cannery."

"Oh, how wonderful!" Sofia clapped her hands. "I've been so hoping someone would come along and do something with that old building, but with the recession, I feared we'd have to wait a very long time."

"Some stockbroker from Seattle bought it. He's retiring

and looking to turn his woodworking business into a second career, and thought that building would make a good workshop. Then he'll lease out the rest of it for shops."

"That's a marvelous idea. Why, I know several people right off the top of my head who'd probably be interested."

"It might work," Madeline allowed as she began rinsing the sand off the closed shells of the clams in the sink. "But, you know, I'm a little concerned about Lucas being able to handle such a big job and still have time for your kitchen remodel."

"Oh, I'm sure he'll manage. He is, after all, a former SEAL. I suspect they're very good at multitasking."

"Well, it's your restaurant," she allowed, thinking that for someone who'd always dreamed of her own place, she was certainly spending a lot of time helping others create theirs. Not that she begrudged her grandmother this change in lifestyle.

She glanced over at the stack of containers as she put the clams in salted water in the fridge. "Whose army do you intend to feed with all those?"

"I'm taking them over to Haven House," Sofia said. "It's a shelter for women escaping domestic abuse."

Just the idea was so sobering that Madeline decided, on the spot, to stop feeling sorry for herself. It also explained why her grandmother had asked her if Maxime had ever been violent.

"They don't have anyone there who can cook?"

"Apparently not. At least not proper meals. Zelda, who runs the home, says that the only resident who did know how to operate the oven got a job at Take the Cake and moved out, so they've pretty much been living on frozen microwave dinners. Which, of course, is a very expensive way to eat."

"Not to mention unhealthy," Madeline said.

"Which is why I've been helping out." Sofia pointed toward a covered five-gallon bucket. "Those are scraps from the garden. I'm dropping by the farm to pick up some eggs and give them to Ethan for feed."

"From garden to chicken and back to the garden," Madeline murmured.

"The perfect food recycling," Sofia said. "Nothing gets wasted because I also use the shells in the compost that goes on those vegetables."

"I love it. I'd also like to come meet your farmer." A thought suddenly occurred to her. "If you promise not to try to fix me up with him."

"I wouldn't think of it, dear." Sofia's tone was innocent. *Too innocent,* Madeline thought suspiciously.

"I don't understand how people can reach adulthood without knowing how to cook a few basic dishes," she complained to her grandmother as they drove the short distance to the shelter.

"They teach sex education in schools. Why can't they teach culinary basics, which are equally important?

"At the very least, everyone—men and women—should know how to properly roast a chicken or make mashed potatoes that don't come out of a box. And breakfast. Not only is it the most important meal of a day, but if a man's going to sleep with a woman, it seems the least he can do is make her a decent omelet and brew her a cup of coffee the next morning."

"Your grandfather brought me a cup of coffee in bed each morning, made with freshly ground beans."

"See? That's what I'm talking about. What woman wouldn't love a man who'd do that? Even if they're willing to live on take-out pizza and fast-food burgers, they need to realize that food is also seduction."

She shook her head, getting fired up on a topic very close to her heart. "And, excuse me, but is it asking too much that any meat shot up with hormones and chemicals and treated with ammonia should not be shipped to the market for human consumption?"

"You're preaching to the choir, darling."

Madeline folded her arms and looked out the window as they drove past the harbor, then up the hill. An idea was forming in her mind. It was as filmy and amorphous as fog skimming in from the ocean, but she decided to share it.

"How wedded are you to the idea of the restaurant?"

Her grandmother shot her a curious look. "I've been considering it for some time. Since your grandfather passed. I need something more to do with my days, and, to be perfectly honest, I could use the additional money. Taxes on the farm have gone up, while revenue has dipped. Not as badly as many businesses, but too many people view fresh herbs, and especially flowers, as an indulgence."

"Flowers, perhaps," Madeline agreed reluctantly. "But growing your own herbs actually saves money over buying dried, and good seasoning can make less-expensive cuts taste better."

"Agreed. But it's often a difficult message to get across."

"Well, it shouldn't be." The idea was beginning to establish clarity. "What if you opened a cooking school?"

"Me?"

"Well, you wouldn't have to be the one doing the cooking. Although you certainly could," she said quickly. Her grandmother, after all, had had a major hand in developing Madeline's own culinary skills. "You were going to hire a chef. Why not hire someone who can also teach? People will pay for lessons, but we could also teach the women at that shelter—"

"Haven House."

"Haven House," Madeline said. "After all, the entire idea of a shelter is to get women back on their feet and out into the world, right?"

"That's Zelda's goal. Apparently, she had a ballerina friend who was killed by an abusive husband. Which is why she established the home in the first place."

"That's tragic. But learning to cook is a basic skill, so

even if they don't get a job working in some restaurant, it will give them self-confidence. I mean, it's just too sad not to be able to feed yourself."

"You do have a point," Sofia mused. "But even if Lucas gives me his best price, which he's already told me he'd do, the construction isn't going to be inexpensive. I'm not sure there's enough people in town to support such a project."

"Lavender Hill Farm is well-known because of all the special herbs you and Grandpa have brought in from all over the world," Madeline argued.

Damn. Too late, she was wishing she'd taken Maxime up on his offer. Not to fund a restaurant for her, but if she'd taken the money the beer baroness had offered, she could just hand it over to this woman who meant more to her than anyone in the world.

"I know if the word got out, you'd have people—even chefs—coming in from all over. But here's another idea. Why not have the students cook for the restaurant? You could keep the costs down because you wouldn't be paying them. They'd learn basic dishes, you'd build a customer base in town, plus among tourists, and it would be a win-win all around."

"It is an interesting idea," Sofia murmured as she pulled up in front of a Victorian at the top of one of Shelter Bay's many hills, which often inspired descriptions of the coastal town as a little San Francisco. "Though a bit ambitious."

Madeline was not used to hearing any hesitation in Sofia's voice. Usually her grandmother was the empress of self-confidence. Now, for the first time, she was forced to acknowledge that the woman who'd put her own life, traveling around the globe, on hold to raise her granddaughter, was not as young nor as vigorous as she'd been when Madeline had left home ten years earlier.

The unpalatable realization that Sofia wouldn't always be in her life had just hit when Madeline's phone rang.

The caller ID showed a New York area code. But it

wasn't Maxime. Unable to make up her mind whether she was unhappy or glad about that, she answered. "Hi, Pepper. Can you wait just a minute?"

She turned toward her grandmother. "Would you mind if I take this?"

"Of course not, dear. I see Ethan's truck, which means he's already here. I'll just go in and have him come out and help me with the food and scraps."

Madeline watched her grandmother climb the steps to the house's front porch. Was she moving slower? Did she actually seem a bit shorter than the last time Madeline had been home? Frailer?

Putting that concern on a back burner for now, she returned to the phone call. "What's up?"

"What's up?" Her agent didn't bother to hide her frustration. "I've been calling for hours."

"Sorry. I hadn't noticed my phone's battery had died."

"Was that before or after the dog ate your recipes?" Pepper asked dryly. One thing that made her one of the best agents in the business was her excellent bullshit detector.

"Okay. You caught me. It really did die. But mostly I just needed some time to absorb all that's happened in the past couple days."

"I totally understand. Especially after what I read on Page Six this morning."

"What now?" The *Post*'s celebrity gossip column was the city's guilty pleasure. Even people who swore they subscribed to the more sedate *New York Times* couldn't resist at least checking it out online.

"You haven't seen it?"

Why am I always the last to know? "I wouldn't have asked if I had. Also, I'm not in New York."

"Which brings up another question. Where the hell are you? When I couldn't get hold of you, I called Maxime's cell. He said you hadn't returned to the apartment for your things."

"I haven't returned because I'm back home."

"Home? Surely you didn't go running back to Sunny-brook Harbor?"

"I didn't go *running* anywhere. And it's not Sunnybrook Harbor; it's Shelter Bay. Given that it's west of the Hudson River, I can understand why you might have trouble remembering its name."

"Ha. I happen to know that it's in Oregon."

"Wow, and you did that without even having to call a friend."

New Yorkers were, by nature, some of the most provincial people Maddy had ever met. Pepper, except for summering at her house in the Hamptons, behaved as if venturing anywhere off the island of Manhattan required a passport.

"Don't be snarky, darling. If you remember, I helped write your Cooking Network bio. Getting back to my reason for calling—which, by the way, how are you?"

"Surviving. Better than that. I'm actually planning the next stage of my life."

"Then my timing is once again perfection. I bring news. Business news."

"Which I want to hear." Not really, but Maddy didn't think Pepper would want to hear that her career wasn't exactly at the top of her concern list right now. "After you tell me about Page Six."

The other woman's sigh was audible. "Maxime and Katrin were out last night at a fund-raiser."

"Good for them."

Madeline wasn't surprised that her husband had already moved on with his life. But if she were Katrin, she wouldn't exactly be comfortable out in public when most of that public had seen her not only naked, but in the throes of passion with another woman's husband.

"She was flashing a ring the size of Alaska. On her left hand. I'm guessing ten carats at the very least."

Okay. That was annoying. "I hope she bought it herself."

Bad enough she'd been working her tail off to keep Maxime's damn restaurants afloat. The idea of any of her money having gone to buy his mistress an engagement ring had her risking her molars again.

"I suspect she's had it waiting in the wings," Pepper said. "There are also some rumors floating around that didn't make it into the paper. Though the writer did hint at the idea that Katrin, not her husband, is the one who arranged for the video to be secretly taped. And that she's the one who released it."

"Why would she do that?" Madeline had no sooner asked the question than she guessed the answer. "Maxime was stalling about leaving me."

Not because of any loyalty to his wife. But because of what Sofia had once told her when she'd started dating. Men were less likely to buy the cow if they could get the milk for free. If he'd thought he could get Katrin to put money into his business without having to enter into any type of monogamous personal commitment, so much the better.

"And she needed to get me out of the picture," Madeline guessed. "So she could move in for the kill."

"That would be my guess."

"They deserve each other." Once again Madeline was more annoyed at how naive she'd been. "He did explain that it wasn't personal. But she had the deep pockets necessary to fund his empire."

"Better her than you." Pepper had always been outspoken about where the majority of Madeline's earnings had ended up. "I received a call from ChefSteel yesterday."

"They want to drop the endorsement deal." She'd been worried about that. In the beginning. Now, with her entire life in flux, she was almost relieved.

"Didn't anyone tell you that jumping to conclusions can land you in hot water? No. Just the opposite. They're so happy with how the sales have jumped in the past month, they want to renegotiate the contract. To give you your own line." She paused dramatically. "How does the Madeline Durand Professional Chef Collection sound?"

"I don't know."

"What's not to know? Did you not hear me? They want to *renegotiate*. That means more money, Madeline. Especially since we'll hold out for a much larger percentage of sales this time."

"The money would be nice." Especially since she could use some of it to help her grandmother with her new business venture. "But—"

"I know. You don't want to use the bastard's last name. I can totally understand that reasoning. Which is why I suggested they just go with the Madeline Collection. In many ways, what Maxime did is going to help with your brand. We can start shifting you to a single name. Like Madonna. Beyoncé. Oprah."

"Lassie," Madeline added to the list.

"Why do I get the feeling you're not doing cartwheels?"

"Because I'm not as limber as I was when I was eight years old. Plus, I'm not sure I want to do it."

"What?" It was not often Pepper was caught by surprise. This was obviously one of those times. "Why on earth not?"

"Because I woke up this morning thinking that life's become a treadmill. I'm totally in the weeds right now, Pepper." And had been for longer than she'd realized. "In fact, I was going to call and ask you what you thought it would cost me to get out of that original contract."

"Bite your tongue!" Now she was not only surprised, but poleaxed, as Sofia would say.

Even as Madeline braced herself for a long, forceful, and undoubtedly practical, business-minded argument about why she needed to get back to New York City now, Pepper pulled out a surprise of her own.

"We need to talk. I'm coming out there."

It was Madeline's turn to be stunned. "Here? To Shelter Bay?"

"Well, apparently, if I showed up in Sunnybrook Harbor, you wouldn't be there. So, I suppose I'll be flying to Shelter Bay." There was another brief pause. "Your little village does have an airport, right?"

"Actually, there is a regional airport about twenty-five miles away. But you'd have to change planes in Portland."

"Oh, I won't fly in those little puddle jumpers. They're like sardine cans with wings. And they don't even have a first-class section."

"Horrors. But it's only a forty-minute flight from Portland. And they do serve cupcakes and muffins." Sofia had told her that Sedona, who ran the Take the Cake bakery, had recently signed a contract to supply the small, regional airline. "Though, granted, then you'd have to drive up the coast from there."

"In a Conestoga wagon, no doubt."

Madeline laughed. "If you're determined to come—"

"Not if you'd just come back to the city. Where you belong."

"I can't do that right now." Madeline wasn't sure where she belonged. Which was what this trip home was all about.

"Fine. Then I'm coming."

"You've always loved negotiating."

"That's like saying, 'I enjoy breathing.'"

"Great. So, here's a counteroffer for you from me. Get back to ChefSteel and buy me a month to let all this stuff sink in. Then we'll talk."

"A week."

"Two. And that's my final offer."

"You drive a hard bargain."

"I had a good teacher."

"All right. Two weeks. Then either you're coming back to New York, where you belong, or I'm coming out there to drag you back." She let out a long breath. "That works, since I have meetings for the next few days I can't get out of. And speaking of negotiations, I'm in ongoing talks regarding a mouthwateringly handsome astronaut client, who, if things work out, will be the next Bachelor handing out a red rose to some lucky girl on national TV."

There was another signature pause. "I could introduce you."

"Thanks. But I think I'll pass."

Having already lost her husband to another woman, Madeline wasn't the least bit interested in meeting a man who was actually going to go on live TV to find his soul mate. As if that was going to happen. Worse yet, he was going to possibly break the hearts of other women while America tuned in week after week. Was nothing private anymore?

"It's probably just as well. If he does get on the show, he'd have to keep you a secret, and that's no way to begin a relationship. . . . You know, the more I think about it, the more appealing I find the idea of my coming to you. Where better to talk than some quaint, seaside town with surfers as eye candy?"

"It's not exactly Malibu," Madeline warned, wondering exactly how much Pepper actually knew about life outside the boroughs.

"Well, I know that. I've been to Malibu. I have a client who has the most amazing beach house there. My entire apartment could fit into his master bathroom. . . . But I digress. Stay calm. Don't let the bastard get you down. And whatever you do, don't answer the phone for any reporters."

Reporters. Madeline hadn't even thought of that possibility. Fortunately, her cell phone was not only unlisted, she was on a do-not-call list.

Like that was going to stop the people who wrote for those tacky tabloid rags.

Deciding to jump off that bridge when she came to it, she got out of the SUV and was headed up the front steps when the idea that had been simmering in her mind earlier came back to her.

It was, she decided, brilliant. And it would not only keep Pepper happy, but also solve her grandmother's financial problems.

She thought about calling her agent back. Then, as the door was opened by a tall, whip-slender woman with a long, silver slide of hair falling over her shoulders, Madeline decided that the topic could wait two weeks until her agent arrived.

Just through thought of Pepper showing up in Shelter Bay in her black Armani suit and Prada pumps made Madeline smile.

23

Phoebe was alone in the kitchen, kneading bread and humming to herself. She couldn't remember the last time she'd sung, and while humming wasn't exactly going to get her on *American Idol* anytime soon, she was the closest thing she'd felt to relaxed since . . . well, probably before her marriage.

She was kneading bread. There was something very relaxing about the repetitive, rhythmic motion. She found her concerns drifting away, like the sea foam on the beach, and she began to synchronize her breathing with the movement of her fingers.

In . . . Out . . . In . . . Out . . .

Her shoulders, which were always so tense that they felt like those expensive cedar hangers she'd left behind in her huge walk-in closet in the Colorado house, were actually relaxed. Peter had gotten so jealous at the idea of her going to the gym, he'd bought her enough equipment to open her own fitness business. It was then that she'd quit working out.

Now she could feel those neglected muscles in her arms and shoulders getting a good workout as she massaged the whole-wheat dough. And it felt good.

Centered in the moment as she was, undistracted by any wandering, distressing, negative thoughts, her life, which had been a roller coaster built on eggshells, began to feel full. Almost effortless.

Happy.

"Blackbird singing in the dead of night," she transitioned from humming to actual words, "take these broken wings and learn to fly."

Which was exactly what she was doing. She hadn't cooked since she'd left the ranch to go to college. Summers had been spent working at the Canyon, where she ate her meals in the employee kitchen. Then, after she'd gotten married, the housekeeper Peter had hired barely allowed her into the kitchen long enough to scramble an egg or make a sandwich.

She turned the elastic brown dough and put her hands in deep, nearly to her elbows, wondering why she'd never noticed how sensual bread making could be.

Her mind began to drift as she looked out the window at the white sails on the bay. *What would it feel like,* she wondered, *to go skimming over the glassy, smooth blue waters?* She imagined herself on the deck of one of those boats, her hair blowing in the breeze.

What it felt like, she imagined, would be pure freedom.

Growing up, long before Peter had insisted she join his mother's book club, where members always seemed to vote for depressing stories with tragic endings, Phoebe had loved to lose herself in romance novels, where couples, after overcoming obstacles, strolled into a metaphorical sunset to a place where happily-ever-afters were guaranteed.

Her mind wandered from the bay, beyond the bridge, to the sea. And instead of a sailboat, she found herself on a tall-masted ship, pulled close to a shirtless pirate as the ship, with its skull-and-crossbones flag filled with wind, plowed through the waves.

He was tall, his body tanned to the color of chestnuts. His arm, which he'd put around her waist, was strong, but in a good way. In a way that made her feel not threatened, but protected. In fact, he may have kidnapped her, as pirates in stories often did, but from an evil duke who'd kept her locked in a dungeon and only allowed her out when he wanted to use her for his own twisted pleasures.

Her rescuer was laughing, a bold, rich, masculine sound that slipped beneath her skin, warming Phoebe from the inside out. Making her tingle in places she'd forgotten she could tingle.

He was looking down at her. As if she were a hunk of freshly baked bread dripping with herb butter and he was a man who'd been starving all his life.

"Next port: paradise," he promised her.

Then his head swooped down and his mouth was hot and hungry, and because she would've melted right down to that wooden deck if he hadn't been holding her so tight, she clung to him as her knees turned to water. . . .

"Excuse me."

The deep voice crashed into her fantasy like an icy wave washing over her from a storm-tossed sea.

She froze. Gathered her scattered wits, then slowly, trembling, looked back over her shoulder. And came face-to-face with her pirate.

He was not conventionally handsome, like Peter. His face was too harshly chiseled; his shaggy hair, which brushed the collar of his denim shirt, was a far cry from her husband's five-hundred-dollar salon style. Rather than being sun gilded from hours spent on tennis courts and golf courses, his hair was black, as dark as a moonless night, while lake blue eyes smiled at her from that deeply tanned face.

"I'm sorry." His voice was smooth and rich and deep. And it strummed chords in Phoebe she was amazed to discover still existed. "I didn't mean to spook you."

The sunshine yellow kitchen was shrinking. He was large. Too large. Too male. But when he smiled, Phoebe sensed that despite his size, which overwhelmed the small kitchen, he was harmless.

The muscles in her stomach unclenched.

"I knocked on the door frame," he said when she still hadn't found the words to answer. Even being seen talking casually with another man had, on several occasions, earned her a painful punishment once she and Peter had gotten home behind closed doors. "But you were singing," he explained. "And you looked a million miles away."

"I was." She looked down at her hands, still buried in the dough. Which was a good thing, because otherwise they'd probably be shaking. It hadn't taken her long to realize that Peter enjoyed her fear. Which was why she was determined never to show it to anyone ever again. "I'm sorry. Can I help you?"

"I'm from Blue Heron farm. I've got Zelda's order out in the truck." He held out a large, dark hand. It was nicked and scarred, and looked as if it could wrap around her neck. "Ethan Concannon."

"I'm Phoebe." She lifted her hands out of the dough and wiped the flour off onto the front of her jeans. Because his hand was still out there, waiting, she gathered up her courage and extended her own. "Phoebe Tyler." The name, which had seemed so alien the first time she'd used it, had begun to feel right. As if she'd been born with it.

Her hand disappeared into his, which caused a moment of jittery panic. But she did not pull it away.

"Welcome to Shelter Bay, Phoebe Tyler." His tone was mild, but his eyes, as they held hers, reassured. Was she really that obvious? Could he feel her quick, instinctive tremor? Could he, heaven help her, read her mind?

Then she remembered where, exactly, she was. At a shelter for battered and abused women. If he came here often, and his ease in the kitchen suggested he did, he was probably used to dealing with women like her.

It wasn't personal. He was just being friendly. And trying, despite his size, not to frighten her. That momentary speculation she'd seen flash across his face hadn't truly been interest. She'd merely layered that fantasy of her pirate's lustful gaze onto him.

Which made her really grateful that he couldn't read her mind.

After what seemed like forever but was undoubtedly only a few seconds, he released her hand. "You must have replaced Julie."

"Julie?"

"She used to be the one who cooked here. She's now working at Take the Cake."

"Oh. Zelda told me about her." She'd even, for a fleeting instant, thought about asking to meet her, if only for proof that life did continue after escape. But then the sheriff had come into the bakery and all thoughts had fled her head.

"She was great to work with. She had very good ideas about what she liked." He slipped the hand that had held hers into the front pocket of well-worn jeans that were torn at the knee. "How about you?"

"Me?"

"What do you like?"

It took her a minute to realize that he wasn't being personal, but talking about recipe items.

"I don't know." Since that sounded stupid, she added, "It's been a while since I cooked."

"Yeah. Seems to be a lot of that going around," he said agreeably. "Why don't you come out to the truck, see if anything strikes your fancy? Then we can plan what you'd like me to bring. We do organic-only at the farm. Do you like beef?"

"I grew up on a ranch." *Oh no!* His easygoing friendliness had thrown her off guard enough to break one of the most important rules of escape. The one about not ever giving any clues to her past life.

"Ever taste grass-fed beef?"

"No." Another clue, but she couldn't exactly back away

from the ranch question now, and how many places raised grass-fed beef, anyway?

"You're in for a treat. There's nothing like it."

"If you do say so yourself." Where had that come from? Another rule from her marriage was that you *never* made fun of a man.

But instead of turning red with fury, he threw back his head and laughed. "It's not conceit if it's true. Maybe you can come out to the farm sometime. Look around, see what we have to offer. I'll even grill a steak."

"Oh, I don't think—"

"I'm not asking you out on a date or anything," he assured her. "Just thought, if you're going to be here a while and do the cooking, it'd be helpful to give you a demonstration of what we have to offer."

"I'll keep that in mind."

He nodded. "Great. For now, let's go see if anything on the truck appeals to you. This time of year, everything's greenhouse grown, but it's all organic."

Like most of the women at Haven House, she was nervous around a man, which made sense. Ethan also understood how his size could be particularly intimidating for a woman who'd suffered abuse. Which, if the fading yellowish brown bruise on her cheek and the way she'd trembled like a leaf when she'd seen him standing in the doorway were any indication, this one had.

She reminded him of one of the wild birds he'd rehabilitated at the farm after donating some of his marshy back acreage to a volunteer group to use as a preserve. She was fragile. But deep down, where it counted, there was a core of strength. Ethan recognized it when she'd allowed him to touch her. It was only hand-to-hand, but in that fleeting moment, he'd experienced an emotion he hadn't felt in a very long time. One he hadn't expected to ever feel again.

Like the broken-winged, red-tailed hawk he'd begun working with, she'd require patience to get close to.

Fortunately, he thought, as he watched her ooh and aah over the bright red, yellow, and green peppers; leafy lettuce; ripe tomatoes; and cartons of speckled, organic eggs, like a woman exploring jewels at Tiffany, he wasn't going anywhere. And, it appeared, at least for now, that neither was she.

24

Lucas had just arrived at the farm when Sofia and Maddy drove up. He'd done a lot of thinking about the restaurant while he'd been fishing, and had a few ideas he would have discussed with Maddy if they hadn't gotten so sidetracked on the past.

But now he was in full work mode. Though, he admitted as he watched those long legs climb out of the passenger's seat, while he'd assured her he could keep his mind on business, there hadn't been any prohibition mentioned against enjoying the scenery.

"The plan's changed," she announced before he could even say hello.

"Okay."

He wondered if she'd talked Sofia out of working with him. Maybe she'd pushed for her grandmother to bring in a contractor from the Willamette Valley. Or Portland.

"Maddy had the most wonderful idea," Sofia said. "Along with a restaurant, we're going to start a cooking school."

He glanced over at Maddy, whose set face suggested she expected an argument. "Okay," he repeated. "How many students are you thinking of?"

"We talked about it on the drive home from Haven House," Sofia said. "And ten to a dozen seems like a workable number."

"That'll take an additional room." He ran a few numbers through his head. "And a lot more money."

Maddy folded her arms. "Afraid you won't get paid?"

"No. I was merely thinking that if Sofia's doing this to shore up her finances, pouring more money into the place might not be the best idea. Since it would probably take a while to turn a profit during the best of times."

Which these were not.

"Maddy had an idea about that, too. She wants to make it a reality show."

Whoa. "A reality show?"

Apparently, his skepticism and lack of enthusiasm for that idea showed on his face, because the creator of what, in his opinion, was a cockamamie idea squared shoulders clad in a crisp white blouse.

"Nothing's set yet," she admitted. "I'm going to have to discuss it with my agent, and obviously we wouldn't want to show any students from Haven House, since their anonymity's so important. The network's been after me to do another show, and none that they've suggested have sounded at all appealing. But everyone loves to live vicariously through other people's remodeling projects, so I figured we could begin by taping some of the renovation to use on the opening episode of the show, then switch to the school. We'd pitch it as a before and after, along the lines of the Cooking Network meets HGTV."

Since he didn't want to get into another argument with her, Lucas didn't share his feelings that the appeal of those reality remodeling shows was in viewers being able to enjoy other peoples' remodeling horror stories.

"So I'd be part of this project?"

The upside of the deal was that he'd be working with Maddy every day and she wouldn't be able to yell at him because it would ruin her friendly, accessible, on-air image. The downside was that he'd be on television. And not in any manly hunting, fishing, or gun show. But on the freak-

ing Cooking Network. And wouldn't his former SEAL
teammates rag on him about that? He could just hear them
asking him to whip up a soufflé over a campfire.

"You could be," she responded. "If your price is right."

"And you'd have to be willing to appear on television,"
Sofia said, jumping in to act as peacemaker, revealing that
he wasn't the only one feeling all those confrontation vibes
emanating from the originator of this supposed plan.
"Which I can understand might prove a problem for you."

"It would've back in my SEAL days, since we needed to
stay under the radar, but it wouldn't be any big deal now.
I've already said I'd keep the cost down. Hell, since it would
essentially be free advertising for me, I'll throw in my labor
for free."

"Oh, that would be wonderful, dear." Sofia beamed.
Then turned toward her granddaughter. "Wouldn't it?"

"Every little bit helps," Maddy said mildly. But he could
sense a slight softening in her stance. "I also happen to have
a ring burning a hole in my purse that I could sell to add to
the coffers."

He had a suspicion he knew what ring that might just be,
since her left hand was bare.

"Okay, here's the thing," he said. "I've already given
some thought to this before you expanded the idea from a
restaurant to a school, and I came up with some ideas I'd
like to share with you."

"And we'd love to hear them," the older woman said.
"Wouldn't we, darling?"

"Why not?" Maddy agreed with a decided lack of enthusiasm.

"Let's start in the kitchen," he said, as they entered the
house.

"Well, there's an idea," Maddy said dryly. "Since that's
where the cooking takes place."

She wasn't going to give him so much as an inch. Which

was only going to make victory, when he won her over, even sweeter.

The minute he walked into the kitchen, the same thought occurred to him as the last time he'd visited and seen the familiar, scarred table. The idea of gutting it to turn it into a commercial restaurant had been bothering him from the beginning. He knew he could design a space that would work. But it would never be the same.

"If these walls could talk," he murmured. "Right there"—he pointed at the table—"you fed Dad and me the best spaghetti and meatballs I'd ever eaten."

"You were both a little lost at the time and needed love."

Lost was putting it mildly. His baby sister had died after a valiant battle with leukemia, and his mom, battling her own pain, had taken off to Colorado, leaving his father and him devastated and drifting. Sofia De Luca had provided the anchor they'd both so needed.

"And that's what made them the best," he said. "I've never eaten anything as good as that meal. Even though I was just a kid, I could tell that you'd poured your heart into that meal. I suspect Dad felt the same way. Every time I walk in here, I remember that was the moment I thought we just might make it after all the bad stuff that had happened to our family."

"If you don't cook with love, there's no point," Sofia said. "That's always what's made Maddy such a good chef."

"That comes through on the programs."

"Oh, please." Maddy rolled her expressive eyes.

"It's the truth. And I'll bet the network people told you the same thing, so if they and your viewers can recognize it, why would you think I wouldn't?"

"You're just trying to win me over."

"Guilty as charged." The fact was, they were both back where they'd begun, and she was just going to have to get used to being thrown together again. The same way she was going to have to get used to the idea that they belonged together. And always had. "But that doesn't mean it's not the truth. . . ."

"So"—he moved the conversation back to his reason for coming to the farm today—"I hate the idea of gutting all the memories this place holds. Not just for me, but for everyone else who's ever been privileged to eat here."

"The entire point was to tie the restaurant into the farm," Maddy countered. "To emphasize fresh ingredients. If we leased some vacant building downtown, it might get us more walk-in tourist business, but it wouldn't be the same."

"She has a point," Sofia agreed.

"Which is why I'm not suggesting that," Lucas said. "Especially since whatever place you found would probably require a complete redo. And starting over, just the way you want it, is always preferable to a remodel, which would require new wiring, plumbing, sheet-metal work, and a bunch of other stuff to bring it up to code. That's why I was thinking that an addition would make the most sense."

"An addition?"

"You could build onto the left front." He pointed toward the exterior kitchen wall.

"And ruin the integrity of the farmhouse style," Maddy pointed out with a distinct lack of enthusiasm.

"Good point, and one we wouldn't want to do. After Dad and I decided to work together, I did a lot of research, since I didn't have his architectural background and wanted to get up to speed."

He took out an iPad with the sketches he'd done after Maddy had left the cottage.

"Since it's important to maintain proportion when adding on substantial square footage to a farmhouse of this era, we'll want to pay particular attention to scale and have the addition contribute to the appeal while being subordinate to the original."

"That's very good," Maddy allowed as she studied the

first drawing, which was the farmhouse as it looked now. But he'd also drawn in the lavender fields, since they were an important part of the vision he'd come up with.

"Thanks. I don't have Dad's talent for architectural design, but I can draw enough to get by. . . . What I'd suggest is locating the addition ten or twelve feet back from the facade. Also, since the most expensive parts of a house are the roof and the foundation, a two-story building would give you half the roofing costs and half the foundation costs. You also save money in plumbing and heating with two stories."

"Lots of restaurants in New York have the kitchen and restaurant on different floors, but I was thinking more of an open-kitchen concept," Maddy said.

"Do you think that's wise, dear?" Sofia asked. "Given that students will be doing the cooking? They might get more nervous with an audience."

"Good point." Once again, she was thinking of what her parents had done. But what worked for them in their small Umbrian town wasn't necessarily right in this instance. "And one we'll have to think about."

"If you did build up, you could always use the space above the restaurant for an apartment if you ever wanted to take on a boarder."

"Or have someone move in to help around the place," Maddy suggested, getting into the spirit of the idea.

Which didn't seem to thrill her grandmother. "I may be old, dear," she said with typical Sofia spunk. "But I'm not decrepit. At least not yet."

"Of course you aren't," Lucas and Maddy said at the same time. They exchanged a look. "But one of the concepts Dad was really into was working on projects dealing with aging in place. Having an available apartment might come in handy down the road. If not, there are a lot of things you could do with the space."

"I'll consider it," Sofia said. "Though it's not as if I don't already have guest rooms in the main portion of the house."

"Here's another idea I was playing with." Lucas scrolled over to the next page. "To keep from having this house in a state of construction chaos, I'm suggesting you might want to go for a traditional carriage house, which Victorians often put in their side yards.

"It would connect to the main structure by this enclosed breezeway attached to what's now the kitchen's outer wall." He used the touch pad to draw an enclosed walkway.

"Oh, I like the windows," Sofia said.

"Although guests won't be using it to go back and forth, you still don't want it to seem like a tunnel. Or bunker. The windows let in light and continue the look of the house's facade.

"Then, since you don't sound as if you need the space from a second story, how about using half of it for your training kitchen? It's bound to take up more space than an actual one. You'd leave the other half open, which would give you a soaring ceiling to open up the dining room. Especially if you add skylights here. And here."

He quickly sketched what he was seeing in his mind. He'd begun using the electronic tablet while in Afghanistan, exchanging ideas and Victorian design features with his father by e-mail.

"Oh." Sofia literally drew in a breath. "I love that!" She turned toward Maddy. "What do you think, dear?"

"I think it could work really well. The interior wouldn't be traditional, like people would expect from a farmhouse, so it would add an element of surprise. And since the food is all about being fresh and simple, the design should reflect that. Though"—she looked up at Lucas—"it should also be homey. Nothing too stark and modern."

"I totally agree," he said, thinking of the sterility of Brooke's Portland apartment. "We can bring warmth in with paint and by putting in some exposed ceiling beams. I also thought it would be nice to duplicate this house's front porch."

More quick sketching. All those years of drawing with

his own pencils and pad while sitting next to his dad as he'd worked at home had paid off. Lucas would never have any of his work hanging in a gallery, but he could get an idea across.

"It'd give diners a nice place to sit out and have drinks and watch the sunset over the water," he said. "Even on drizzly days, since it's covered."

"That is so perfect!" Sofia said.

"That's a good idea," Maddy allowed. He may still be in the doghouse, but she was beginning to warm to the idea. "It beats people standing around the hostess's table or sitting on a bench inside," she said.

"You'll probably want the bench, but we can make it work. We can also mix things up with lighting and interior design, which I'm totally leaving up to you. Since you're the expert on restaurants.

"You'll want a lot of windows, which will not only bring in light, but give diners a view of the lavender fields and the ocean." He took some tall, double-paned windows from the computer program's library and moved them into place.

"Maybe some atrium doors here leading out onto a patio." He added a set of French doors. "Nothing too big or commercial-looking, but it'd probably be a popular spot on sunny days."

"I love it," Sofia said on a long, happy sigh as she viewed the result. "What do you think, Maddy?"

"Although I really hate to admit it, I think you've nailed it," she told Lucas. "I also like that if we needed to, with a few upgrades and that breezeway, which would involve knocking through the exterior wall of the house, although we're keeping this kitchen intact, we could utilize it if we needed it for larger groups. Say, a banquet or wedding."

"Along with the fact it's the most logical place to add on to the original house, that was also my thought."

"But how are you going to heat the new section with that breezeway? Isn't that a long way to push air?"

"You're right. The main house's heating system isn't capable of pushing hot air through the fifty feet of breezeway into the new addition, so my plan was to install a stand-alone gas heater and hot water system. We'll also insulate the walls and ceiling to keep the warm air from escaping through the high ceiling."

"It seems you've thought of everything."

"It's just a start," he warned. "Since it's new construction instead of a remodel, I'll want to run it by one of the architect's in Dad's firm."

"What's that going to cost?" Maddy asked.

She'd changed from the naive young girl he'd fallen in love with. He supposed it wasn't a surprise that she'd grown much more skeptical. "Nothing."

"Why would he do that?"

Yep. Definitely skeptical.

"Number one, he was close friends with Dad." He ticked the reasons off on his fingers. "Two, his wife's a huge fan of your shows. And three, he happens to be my godfather. I was even ring bearer at his wedding."

Sofia beamed at that idea. "And I'll bet you were just darling."

"I've no idea. I just vaguely remember being irked because when we went to the tux store, I didn't get to wear a bear costume."

"A bear costume?" Maddy asked. Then he watched as understanding dawned. "You thought you were going to be a ring *bear*?"

"Hey," he said a little defensively, "I was five years old."

"Makes sense to me." Her smile, the first full one he'd seen, lit up her face. "Okay, as much as I hate to admit it, that really is cute. I'd also pay to see you in a bear suit. . . . You said his wife's a fan?"

"Apparently, their TiVo is loaded up with your shows. Which she refuses to erase."

"I'm flattered. Do you think she'd like an autographed cookbook?"

"I know she'd love one. As for the design, since I want to give him some ideas to run with, we should probably get a head start," he suggested.

"As if you haven't already," she said beneath her breath, but loud enough for him to hear.

"I was referring to layouts for your kitchen, the dining room, and such," he said mildly. "Where you want the appliances, the storage, your students' mise en place, that sort of thing."

"How do you know about mise en place?"

"I told you: I've been getting up to speed on restaurant design. It's French. Meaning 'to put in place.'"

"That's it. But it's more than having a physical place for ingredients and prep; it's also a state of mind. In order to work in a professional kitchen, you have to be able to multi-task while you weigh and assign each task its proper value and priority. Along with always anticipating and preparing for every possible situation."

"Sounds a lot like being a Navy SEAL," he said.

When she angled her head, a slice of sun streaming through the window lit on her hair, bringing out reddish highlights. When he imagined those wild curls draped over his chest, then lower, his mouth went as dry as sawdust.

"I suppose it does," she decided. He could tell she was surprised by the idea that they'd have anything but a rocky romantic history and shared chemistry in common.

25

One of the things Madeline had once loved about Lucas was the way they could talk about everything and anything. At first, when she was thirteen, somehow understanding that her grandmother had suffered her own horrible loss—that of a daughter—she'd tried not to dump too much of her own hurt and sorrow on the older woman.

But Lucas, who'd not only lost a sister to leukemia but also his mother to divorce, had understood what she'd been going through, and had spent many hours with her, walking on the beach, sitting on the rocks, letting her spill out her pain and her anger at the unfairness of it all.

"Life isn't always fair," she remembered him telling her. At fifteen to her thirteen, he'd seemed so much wiser. More experienced. "If it was, Elvis would still be alive and all those impersonators would be dead."

She remembered it being the first time she'd laughed since being told about that plane going down.

He'd been a friend before he'd become a lover. Perhaps, she thought now, they might find their way back there again.

"Although I'm not an architect like my dad, I did build my share of Lincoln Log and LEGO buildings," he said now. "And I've read a lot about architecture, because while I might not have wanted it for my own life, there's nothing like being part of a building coming to life. And while I was reading about the culinary business, I realized it has a lot in common with building."

"How?"

"Both cooking and building came into being to fulfill necessary human needs."

"Eating and shelter," Sofia said.

"Exactly. Both involve a merging of science and art. Both, if they're done right, depend more on taste than on any current fashion, and both serve patrons."

"That's very insightful."

That line, more crease than dimple that Madeline had always loved, winked in his cheek when he smiled. "Thank you."

"And carrying that analogy further," she mused aloud, "construction involves building elements, which could be seen as ingredients, plus, as you pointed out on the placement of the new wing, there are dimensional rules for proportion and size—"

"Which would be your measurements," he agreed. "And then once you have those, an architect or builder has to combine them in the most harmonious way."

"Which would be the same as a recipe giving the best taste," she said.

Another quick grin warmed his eyes. "Bingo. Give the lady a Kewpie doll."

She wished he hadn't put it that way. It reminded her of the time their last summer together when he'd taken her to the county fair, spent ten dollars winning her a stuffed dog at the shooting arcade, then kissed her dizzy on the Tilt-A-Whirl.

"I'm impressed," she said. It was the truth. He'd really done his homework and gotten up to speed fast.

"Thanks. I try."

"So, now that we seem to have a basic plan, why don't you stay for dinner?" Sofia suggested. "Maddy dug some clams this morning."

"He knows," Madeline said. "We ran into each other on the beach."

"Isn't that nice?" Sofia smiled. "Well, she's planning to make Kokkinisto, and I already have a marionberry pie, which I remember being your favorite."

"With ice cream?"

"Vanilla bean," she confirmed. "I made it myself. Afterward, you and Maddy can start discussing details."

"I appreciate the invitation," he said. Then turned toward Maddy. "And I've love a chance to taste those clams, since you've never cooked for me."

Madeline folded her arms. "Which isn't my fault," she reminded him of that fateful night.

"Touché. But here's the deal. I've already accepted an invitation from Charity to have dinner with her, her jarhead, and Sax and Kara."

"By *jarhead*, you would be referring to a U.S. Marine."

"That's it. But, apparently, he calls me a frog boy, so I figure we're square. She also said something about a cupcake baker."

"From Take the Cake?" *Blonde, blue-eyed, and lean as a whip?*

"That's her. Which, thinking of it, maybe we can talk to her about financing."

"What would a baker know about financing?"

"That's the same thing I asked Sax when he told me she was responsible for him getting the money to fix up Bon Temps when the bank wouldn't give him a loan. Apparently, she's a former CPA who knows a lot of finance people."

"Oh. That's quite a career change."

"Sedona's smart as they come," Sofia said. "And so nice. She actually grew up on a commune in Arizona."

Where she undoubtedly picked up the concept of free love, Madeline thought as something stirred. Something that felt too much like jealousy for comfort.

She realized that somehow Lucas had picked up on her train of thought when a too-sexy sparkle lit up his eyes. But, thankfully, he didn't comment.

"Then I've got to run up to Portland tomorrow morning to handle some stuff left from Dad's estate," he said. "How about we meet here around three?"

"Fine."

She shouldn't be piqued that he'd turned down an invitation to dinner. After all, Sax was his closest friend and former teammate, and Charity, being his stepsister, was the only family he had left other than his mother, whom he didn't appear to be all that close to. And no wonder, given the circumstances of her having left her husband and son to fend for themselves in such a sorrowful time.

Plus, despite his ridiculous earlier claim he was going to marry her, she'd already insisted their relationship was only business.

Which, suddenly, perhaps because of the sexy cupcake baker, he appeared willing to accept.

It was what she wanted. What she'd insisted on.

So why did she feel like a teenage girl stood up on prom night? For the head cheerleader?

She might not have a CPA. She might not look like a quintessential California girl with that smooth slide of blond hair and big Barbie blue eyes. But she was an intelligent woman. A talented, successful chef. A celebrity. Of sorts.

She could multitask with the best of them, was level-headed, and, unlike so many in her profession, was not given to temper or wild swings of emotion.

So, she wondered as she stood at the kitchen window and watched him walk back to his truck, with all that she had going for her, how had she managed to make such a mess of her life?

26

"So," Charity said as she handed Lucas an icy bottle of beer. "Kara tells me that you're planning to stay in town a while."

"Which she undoubtedly heard from Sax."

She shrugged shoulders bared by a filmy top that reminded him of Monet's water lilies. Lucas had been surprised when he'd returned home and seen the woman, who'd always worn jeans and T-shirts, dressing softer. Her style, if that's what you could call it, had always been basic Gap, though she had told him about all those designer suits she'd worn during her engagement to a rich, weasely lawyer.

That Chicago Junior League woman was now long gone. And although she still hadn't embraced her fashionista mother's style, she looked and dressed in a more feminine way. And seemed happier than he'd ever seen her.

Which, he had to figure, had a lot to do with the jarhead grilling thick, marbled rib-eye steaks and ears of corn. Not to mention the two former foster children—a little blond girl and freckled-face, red-haired teenage boy—they'd taken in and were planning to adopt. Being a nurturer at heart, Lucas knew she'd made a super mom.

"Sax is going to be Kara's husband," Charity said. "Which means they share stuff. So, is it true?"

"Yeah. I took another job along with the one Sofia offered."

"So Sax said. The cannery sounds ambitious. And it'll be great for the town. My receptionist's an artist. I'm sure she'd love another outlet. Sax's grandmother volunteers teaching some of the women at Haven House to knit. If they could sell some of the things they made, they'd earn much-needed income, as well. Have you come up with a plan for the restaurant yet?"

"I did some preliminary modeling sketches. But now it seems to have expanded into a cooking school."

She laughed. "I learned while remodeling this place into a clinic that construction plans multiply like tribbles."

The Victorian in question that served as both a clinic for her veterinary practice and living quarters had begun as a bordello for seamen who'd stopped in port, and later spent several incarnations as a B and B. In fact, Lucas and his father had stayed there for a few weeks while building the cottage.

"That tends to be true." He glanced over at the Marine, who'd cut off a couple pieces of one of the steaks and tossed the first one to a little black dog who'd been sitting patiently waiting, and then another to Charity's huge white Great Pyrenees, who snatched it out of the air and immediately gulped it down. Then one to Scout, who thumped her thick tail with canine happiness. Which wasn't surprising, since rib eye was a helluva improvement over the MRE leftovers she'd grown used to eating. "I like your Marine."

"Thanks." Her face softened and her eyes warmed. "I like him, too."

Which was more than obvious. Given that the two of them were as lovey-dovey as Kara and Sax, Lucas was wondering if the town had put something in the water.

"Thanks for not inviting the baker."

"I still think you would've liked her. But Kara tells me

that Sax says you have other plans." Her voice went up a little on the end, turning it into a question.

"Word gets around fast."

"It's a small town. And your friends care about you."

"Well, since you brought it up, he's right. I do."

She eyed him over the salted rim of her margarita glass. "That was certainly quick."

"Not so quick at all. I'd say it's about ten years too late."

"He also told me what happened." She scooped some guacamole onto a chip. "Back then. And why."

"Terrific." He took a long pull on the bottle of beer and thought that a tequila shot might be more appropriate for this conversation. That's what he got for spilling his guts that day on the mountain. Which was easier to do when you didn't believe you were going to make it out alive. "Now it's your turn to tell me I'm an idiot."

"Well, that's your word, but I'm not going to argue it. However, I have to qualify the description to admit that you are a sweet idiot. And well-meaning."

"Try telling that to Maddy."

"Have you told her yet? Your motive for letting her believe you were unfaithful to her that summer?"

"Yeah. Today."

"And how did that go?"

He shrugged. Took another drink. "Let's just say she didn't give me the humanitarian of the year award."

"It's been a horribly rough week for her. She's bound to have conflicting emotions."

"Yeah. I may be an idiot, but even I could figure that out. Which is why maybe I ought not to have told her I intend to marry her."

"What?" The chip, which had been headed toward her mouth, dropped to the patio. "Tell me you're kidding."

"Since it's obvious to everyone that I screwed up by lying to her back then, I figured I ought to be up front about my intentions this time."

"That's admirable, though perhaps unwise. Didn't it occur to you that you're rushing things? Three days ago, she believed she was in a stable marriage."

"You might be right about my timing not being the best. But I don't buy that part about her marriage." Lucas scooped up another chip and handed it to her to replace the one the little black mutt, proving himself a speedy opportunist, had immediately scarfed up. "If her relationship with the Frenchman wasn't already on the skids, she wouldn't have come back here. She'd have stayed in New York and tried to work things out. She's not someone to cut and run."

"Yet, according to Kara, that's exactly what she did ten years ago."

"Only because I didn't give her any choice. And she didn't exactly run, but just continue on with the plan she'd already mapped out. I just gave her a push."

"Over the edge."

That hurt. Unfortunately it was true. "Believe me, she's not that same girl. She's an adult. One who knows her own mind."

Charity raised a brow as she crunched the chip. "Are you saying she's already agreed to your master plan?"

"Well, not yet," he admitted. "I'm working on it."

She considered that for a moment as she took another sip of margarita. "Kara and I were talking about inviting her out to lunch to catch up and hopefully cheer her up. . . . I suppose, just possibly, if your name happened to come up during the conversation, we could put in a good word for you."

"You do that, and you'll have a slave for life."

"Sorry, frog boy," Gabe, who'd come over to put his arm around Charity, said. "That job's already taken."

As if to prove his point, he tunneled his hand beneath the hair Charity had begun wearing loose, lowered his head, and took her smiling mouth.

The kiss was short, but from the way her hands tightened on the stem of the margarita glass and the glazed look in her eyes when they came up for air, it had obviously been potent.

And, although as a SEAL, Lucas had never imagined ever being envious of a jarhead, at this moment, watching the two of them together, he damn well was.

27

Frustrated when thoughts and dreams of Lucas had caused another fitful night, Madeline finally gave up on sleep and decided to take a long walk on the beach. This time, however, although Lucas was in Portland, so odds of accidentally running into him again were slim, she chose a beach south of the one his cottage overlooked. Unfortunately, it was also painfully close to the cave that held so many bittersweet memories.

Still, the walk did clear the cobwebs from her head. Enough that she could begin to view Lucas' behavior that night in a less harsh light. He'd hurt her. Horribly. But remembering back to how she'd sprung her romantic plan to stay with him, she realized that he must have felt boxed in. Especially when she'd refused to listen to him when he'd tried to convince her that she should go through with her European food tour. That they had the rest of their lives to be together.

Unfortunately, teenage insecurities had her afraid he'd meet someone else while she was away. A fear he'd obviously not only sensed, but played on when he'd set up that scene that had made him look so guilty.

Looking back on it now, she realized that she hadn't been the only one hurting. Because not only had he been her best friend, but she also now realized that he had truly loved her. Which meant that even though he'd gotten the reaction he'd intended, he'd had to suffer his own heartache at the way things ended between them.

She'd just gotten back to her car when Kara Conway, who'd been Kara Blanchard when they'd all gone to school together, called and invited Madeline to lunch with her and Charity Tiernan.

She assumed the women intended to lobby on Lucas' behalf, but since it had been too long since she'd seen her friend or even indulged in any girl talk, she immediately agreed.

Three hours later, she was on her way to lunch at the Sea Mist, when, as she passed the Dancing Deer Two boutique, a display in the store's window caught her eye. The spring dresses were bright, flirty, and nothing like she normally wore on her show or in the city.

"Which is precisely the point."

If she was going to move on with her life, she wanted it to be a *new* life. Wrapped up in a pretty box with a shiny ribbon as a gift to herself.

Which is how she ended up leaving the store with the suit she'd worn to Omaha (which was what she'd planned to wear to lunch, given that her choices were limited at the moment) in a shopping bag and wearing a sleeveless, full-skirted dress covered with red, purple, and orange roses, a purple cardigan, and a pair of strappy red sandals. She'd also bought underwear and three casual outfits to tide her over until she could retrieve the clothes she'd left back in New York.

Thanks to the speedy help from the elderly twin sisters who owned the store, she managed to be in and out in under fifteen minutes, making it to lunch with two minutes to spare.

The Sea Mist restaurant hadn't changed since the last time Madeline had eaten here. The paneled walls were still stained a light blue-gray designed to appear weathered by decades of wind and coastal storms. A mural of the Shelter Bay lighthouse covered one wall, while old black-and-white photos harking back to the town's seafaring days had been hung on the others.

The female figurehead of Rubenesque proportions, salvaged from the prow of some ancient ship and now arching over the doorway, had Madeline feeling downright svelte. Although the patio, right on the water, had always been a favorite of locals and tourists alike, because it had begun to sprinkle and the clouds had caused a drop in temperature, the three women decided to eat inside next to the glass wall that offered a spectacular view of the boats coming into and out of the harbor.

"This is lovely," Madeline said. "I'm so glad you invited me."

"We're glad you're back home," Kara said. "Although I'm so horribly sorry for the circumstances."

"It hasn't exactly been a stellar week," she admitted as the waiter deposited a basket of sourdough bread and herbed butter in the center of the wooden table that gleamed with the patina of years of lemon oil.

"The bastard Frenchman is lucky he lives on the other side of the country," Kara said. "If he showed up here, I'd have to shoot him."

"You're kidding." True, it had been years since she'd seen Shelter Bay's sheriff, but surely Kara hadn't changed that much?

"Unfortunately, since I take my serve-and-protect duty seriously, I am." She sighed. "But the fantasy is definitely appealing."

"I'm really good at neutering," Charity said. "Granted, I've only ever done dogs and cats, and turned one calf into a steer during my large-animal course during vet school, but the process shouldn't be all that different on a human male."

They both had Madeline laughing. She'd been afraid the

lunch would prove uncomfortable, but she had already begun to relax. She was also remembering how nice it had been to have girlfriends before her career had taken over every moment of her life.

"I considered that," she admitted. "After all, I do have a cleaver. And know how to use it."

"Oh, I would so love to witness that," Kara said as she tore off a piece of the fragrant bread. "The rat doesn't deserve you."

"Thanks. On that I can agree. Although it's embarrassing as hell."

"I don't know why," Kara said. "He's the one with his tattooed, bare butt all over YouTube."

Madeline wasn't surprised her former classmate had seen it. Truth be told, she'd have looked, too.

"That's pretty much what Lucas said."

"He's right. You're the injured party. And the way you've been handling it, not taking the two of them on in the tabloids, is really classy."

"It helps that the tabloids haven't found me yet." Though, since even Birdy had known she grew up in a small town on the Oregon coast, it wouldn't take long for the vultures to locate her.

"I realized this morning that not only do Maxime and his beer baroness deserve each other, but I have only one regret about walking out."

"What's that?" Charity tore off her own piece of bread and slathered it with butter.

Since Charity Tiernan's mother had divorced Lucas Chaffee's father before Madeline had come to live in Shelter Bay, they'd never met.

But although Madeline had been worried that the veterinarian might feel protective of her stepbrother, Charity proved warm and open, and she didn't pry for information about his and Madeline's relationship.

Which had Madeline liking her right away, although it

was a little odd thinking that if Lucas hadn't pulled that stupid trick to get her to leave town and they'd eventually gotten married, there was a possibility that she and Charity could be somehow related. Was there even such a thing as a stepsister-in-law?

"When I was walking out of our apartment, he offered me money for my own restaurant," she said.

"Which, of course, you took," both women said.

"Actually, I turned it down. I know," she said, holding up her hands. "I was all caught up in pride and, as Gram would say, I cut off my nose to spite my face."

"I can understand pride," Charity said, "having caused a huge scandal by running away from my wedding ten minutes before I was supposed to walk down the aisle."

"You didn't!" Madeline was pleased to have the conversation turn to someone else's personal scandal.

"I did. Which shocked everyone who'd shown up to attend what was being billed as Chicago's wedding of the year. But if I hadn't dared to do that, I never would have ended up back here and fallen in love with Gabe." She bit into the bread. "God, this butter is good."

"The chives give a nice bite to the flat-leaf parsley, thyme, and basil," Madeline agreed. "But it's the virgin olive oil that makes it so creamy and brings it to the next level." She also decided to drop in sometime during a lull in service and meet the chef who'd obviously had serious training, along with having an excellent palate.

"That's so cool you know that," Kara said. "I know what tastes good, but I have no idea why. Sax does most of the cooking for us."

"Remembering some of the meals at Bon Temps growing up, I suspect that isn't exactly a hardship," Madeline said.

"Not at all. There's something so sexy about a man in the kitchen." Kara sighed happily, reminding Madeline what Lucas had said about she and Sax being so crazy about each other. Then, realizing what she'd said, she winced and said, "Oops."

"Don't worry about it. I know exactly what you mean. And you're right. I remember my mother saying much the same thing. Which is one of the reasons, I think, I allowed myself to believe I was in love with Maxime. Because I believed we had the love of food in common."

"And you didn't?" Charity asked.

"No. He loved fame. The cooking, I realized, was always secondary."

"Which for you is the other way around," Kara guessed. "I remember loving slumber parties at the farm because you always had us making our own pizzas. Which were so much better than takeout."

"They always are. And any fame, such as it is, I've managed to achieve was merely a way of funding my husband's restaurant empire. I could walk away tomorrow, if it weren't for Gram's idea of opening a restaurant and cooking school."

"I was there when she brought up the restaurant idea to Lucas," Charity said. "Then he told me last night about the idea of expanding to a school."

"I'd sign up for a class," Kara said.

"So would I," Charity agreed. "But getting it off the ground is bound to be pricey."

"That's putting it mildly. All the more reason I wish I'd taken the money." She shared her idea of the reality show, which both women thought would be fun to watch.

But Kara was more cautious. "Yet there you'd be again," she pointed out, "putting aside your own dream of a restaurant for someone else."

"I owe Gram."

"She's family. And you know she'd hate for you to think of it as an obligation."

"I know. But that doesn't stop me from wanting to help her out."

"You always talked about opening your own restaurant," Kara remembered. "Especially after visiting that place in California."

"Alice Waters' Chez Panisse. She pioneered the philosophy of cooking with the freshest seasonal ingredients that are produced sustainably and locally, and a food economy that's good, clean, and fair. I also visited Darina Allen of the Ballymaloe Cookery School in Ireland for one of my programs. She's doing much the same thing."

"Sounds as if you've got all the ingredients for that right here," Charity said. "I've heard Lavender Hill Farm is world famous for its variety of herbs."

"Gram was invited to the White House for the launch of the vegetable garden," Madeline said. "The arugula and celery they grow there are from her seeds. Which continue to be harvested year after year."

"So, you have the veggies and herbs. And Ethan Concannon's grass-fed beef is not to be believed. We grilled steaks last night, and not only do they have fewer calories, but they tasted so much richer and, well . . . "

"Fuller," Madeline supplied. "More what beef should taste like."

"Exactly. He also has free-range chickens that lay the coolest different-colored eggs."

"I've met him," Madeline said. "I was at Haven House yesterday when he delivered vegetables."

"He is so hot," Charity said on a long sigh.

"You're engaged."

"True. But that doesn't mean I'm dead. And you have to admit, he's gorgeous. With all that dark hair and his neon blue eyes, he reminds me a bit of a hunky artist farmer."

It wasn't a bad description, Madeline thought. "His vegetables certainly looked as if they could have washed off a Renaissance painting."

"As much of a foodie place as New York City is, it sounds

as if Charity's right about your having everything you need right here," Kara said mildly.

Surprisingly, even when her first thought had been to come winging back here like a homing pigeon, the idea had never occurred to Madeline. As much she loved Shelter Bay, her life had always been focused on learning her craft from the best chefs across Europe, then polishing her classical skills at one of the premier culinary schools in the world. After which she'd work her way up through the ranks in New York City, where, as the song went, if she could make it there, she could make it anywhere.

The dream, nourished first by her parents, then by her grandmother, had never seemed impossible. After all, the first thing she'd learned at the institute was that attitude determined altitude. And she'd come to learn with a lot of attitude.

Which, little by little, had been chipped away.

Now, although she still believed that she could beat the chef's pants off Maxime in the culinary crucible of Manhattan, she wondered if somehow she'd gotten so focused on her youthful vision that even after having lost that focus for a while chasing after money, perhaps she'd also failed to take time to rethink her original dream.

What she wanted, what she'd always wanted, was to cook great food with integrity. To respect the land, the food, and the family farmer, the way her parents had always cooked. Undoubtedly, she could move to some rural village in Umbria or France or Greece, and do exactly that.

But, as Kara and Charity had just pointed out, the possibilities also existed here, as well. The seafood coming in every day from the rivers, streams, and Pacific Ocean was second to none. Oregon was abound with native mushrooms and berries and fruits.

And then there were more and more organic farmers embracing the farm-to-table movement. Farmers like Ethan Concannon.

"Maddy?" Kara asked, breaking into her thoughts. "Are you ready to order?"

She glanced up, surprised to see the waiter who'd arrived while her mind had been spinning with possibilities.

"Ready." For possibly more than lunch. Perhaps, she thought, it was time not just for fine-tuning her life, but for an entirely new start.

28

Since he arrived back at Shelter Bay after the meeting with his dad's lawyers in Portland, Lucas followed what was beginning to become a habit and dropped into Bon Temps.

"How did things go in the city?" Sax asked as Lucas climbed onto what he'd begun to think of as his stool.

"Okay. Although my head's spinning from the numbers. I knew my dad was well-off, but I had no idea how much money he'd made over the years."

Even with his father having been generous to various charities around the world, as the estate attorney had shown him, with judicious investing, Lucas could afford to never work another day in his life. All the way back to town, he'd been trying to figure out how to get Sofia and Maddy to let him help out with the project. Maybe if he offered to become an investor . . .

"So, I guess I'm going to have to start stocking more imported beer," Sax said. "Since it sounds as if you can afford it."

"Ha ha. Just give me something local." Given that Oregon seemed to have gone wild about microbrewing since he'd been away, there was a bunch to choose from.

"It's a little out of season, since it's a winter ale, but it is raining today, and given your circumstances, it fits." Sax reached into the cooler and pulled out a brown bottle.

Lucas laughed. "Mogul Madness Ale," he said, reading the green and white label.

"Beats the Double Dead Guy," Sax pointed out. "Especially since it appears you're now a mogul."

"Which is weird. But I guess it *is* better than being Double Dead. Though there were sure a lot of days I thought we might've been poster guys for that label."

"Ah, the good old days." Although he seldom drank when he was behind the bar, Sax opened a bottle for himself. "To old days. And better days yet to come."

"I'll drink to that," Lucas said as they tapped bottles.

The ale was strong and dark and went down smooth, leaving tastes of nuts, berries, and something like mocha. The fact that he was even learning to distinguish the different hops and flavors told him how far he'd left those days in the mountains, jungles, and deserts behind.

"Do you ever think about them?" he asked. "The old days?"

"Not as much as I used to. Only about every other day."

That wasn't all that encouraging. "Scout has PTSD." He'd left the dog with Charity while he'd gone to Portland.

"Yeah. I noticed that when Kara dropped a pan lid last night and the dog hit the flagstone patio like a Blackhawk was about to come flying over, guns blazing."

"We're working on the noise thing. Charity says it'll take time."

"I'd say she's right. I had ghosts for a long time after I got back home."

"Don't we all?" There were times that the faces of all the men Lucas couldn't save infiltrated his sleep.

"Mine were real. They actually talked with me. And rode in the car and razzed me. It freaked me out at first, then it started feeling kind of normal, like when we were a team."

The team where Sax had ended up the sole survivor. Lucas hadn't wanted to bring that up. But now that the man who was as close to him as any brother could have been had brought it up, he decided the topic wasn't off-limits.

"You used the past tense."

"Yeah. It was funny, but once I started getting more involved with Kara and Trey, and falling in love with both of them and moving on with my own life, the guys went to, well, wherever ghosts go when they get tired of sticking around."

"So you're okay now?"

Sax took a drink of ale and considered that. "I'm not the same guy I was back when I was a kid, raising hell, drag racing, and talking you into TPing old man Gardner's trees."

Lucas grinned at the memory. "And Kara's dad took us in, called our parents, then made us spend the next week picking up litter along the road."

"Yeah. But the upside was we made some bucks turning in all those bottles."

Which they'd used to rent some girly magazines from Jake Woods, who owned the bait shop Sax's parents had bought from Jake's kids after the grizzled old guy had passed on. At least half the guys in Shelter Bay's high school had, at least once in their lives, rented out *Playboy*, *Penthouse*, or the videos Jake had kept beneath the counter.

They were good memories, reminding Lucas that he'd managed to pack more living into summers in this small coastal town than he did the rest of the year living in Portland. Though, back then, since his dad was traveling so much, he spent a lot of time with housekeepers after the divorce.

"Then there was that summer you pretty much bailed on the rest of us for Maddy," Sax remembered.

"That was a great summer. Most of it, anyway." When just the memory was enough to make him hot, he tilted the bottle and enjoyed the cool slide of dark ale down his throat. "Until the end."

"Kara says Charity told her that you told Maddy you

intend to marry her." Sax pulled out a bowl of Tabasco-hot beer nuts. "We've got a bet going that the story got confused. Kara believes it. So, if she wins, she gets to load up our Netflix queue with sappy, romantic chick flicks from the fifties and sixties."

"Except for that high school romance *10 Things I Hate about You*, Maddy tended to be more into the old black-and-white forties flicks," Lucas said, remembering. He also remembered buying Maddy that movie poster to hang on her wall for her eighteenth birthday. "What happens if Kara loses?"

"This is the good part. When I turn out to be right about your stepsister getting it wrong, because no way would a former teammate of mine be such a numb nut, we're renting the entire first season of *The A-Team*."

His cocky grin was a twin of the one that had gotten them all through a lot of shit over the years. Even with a horde of Taliban screaming down on them, it was hard to believe you were going to die when Sax Douchett got that grin on. "All fourteen episodes."

"You'd better be prepared to buy Kleenex by the case, then. Because you lose."

Sax choked on his beer. "You are freaking kidding me."

"Nope. That's exactly what I told Charity." Lucas took a handful of the nuts and imagined flames coming out of his mouth.

"Okay, obviously one of those TBIs from getting blasted while not wearing your helmet all the time has boggled your brain. Because that's about the most dumb-ass idea I've ever heard of. Ever hear of subtlety, *cher*?"

"I've heard of it." He polished off the beer, hoping it would quench the flames. It didn't. "And I'm usually a fan of the concept. I just didn't feel it fit this situation."

"And you thought that why?"

Lucas shrugged. "I lied to her. Big time. She says I broke her heart."

"There's a news flash."

"Well, it also left a huge, gaping hole in mine, but I decided sharing that might be TMI. Under the circumstances."

"Gee. Think so? Want another?"

"I'd better not. I'm having a meeting with her in"—Lucas glanced down at his watch—"fifteen minutes, and I want to have all my wits about me."

"Too late. You obviously left them up in the Kush." Sax took away Lucas's empty bottle and filled a glass with water from the bar hose.

"That's pretty much what Charity said. But, like I told her, I lied to Maddy last time. So I figured it was only fair that I be totally up front this time."

"You haven't been back that long," Sax pointed out. "Playing devil's advocate here, I have to ask if you've considered that what you really need is to get laid."

"For your information, there's a woman in Portland I hooked up with right after I got back, and I was doing okay in that regard. So it's not as if I'm walking around Shelter Bay with blue balls."

He scooped up another handful of nuts. "Do I want Maddy in my bed? Hell, yes." And anywhere else he could have her. "But I also want her in my life."

"Maybe you're just tapping into old feelings."

"Like you did with Kara. Which appears to have worked out okay."

"Got me there," Sax said agreeably.

Although he'd tried not to show it, anyone with eyes could've seen that Sax had fallen hard for the girl he had promised her boyfriend—and first husband—who'd taken off and joined the Marines, that he'd watch out for her. From what Lucas had been able to tell, he'd kept his word. And his feelings to himself.

"As for tapping into old feelings, sure, Maddy and I share a history going back a lot of years. And I still have feelings for that summertime girl. But I want to marry the woman she's grown into."

"Well, then, good luck with that. But I have just one more piece of brotherly advice to give you."

"And that would be?"

"Kara wasn't around that last summer, since she'd gone off to San Diego to marry Jared, but she and Maddy were close friends once. And since they're out to lunch with Charity today, I assume they'll slide right back into where they were when they left off."

The way he and Sax had. "Yeah. I got that feeling last night when Kara came over at the barbecue and warned me not to hurt her."

"That's the deal. The woman I'm going to marry is now invested in the situation. Which means that if you screw up, she's going to be really, really pissed. . . .

"Now, I seriously doubt she'd use that Glock she looks so damn sexy wearing to shoot you. But, since she instructed me to warn you that you're toast if you hurt Maddy again, you've now dragged me into your damn drama.

"Which, in turn, means that if you fuck things up, it could come back on me."

He folded his arms and gave Lucas that same, don't-mess-with-the-big-bad-SEAL look Lucas had seen stop bad guys in their tracks. "If I end up sleeping on the couch because you make Maddy cry, *I* may shoot you."

Even knowing that Sax wouldn't risk that *Leave It to Beaver* life he seemed to have created with Kara and her son, Lucas wasn't fool enough to argue the point.

"Roger that."

29

Since it had been years since she'd had the local Dungeness crab, Madeline ordered the crab cakes served with a ginger plum sauce and a smooth beurre blanc. The French muscadet wine added a light and refreshing flavor to the buttery sauce, while the shallots added a tang, all of which paired perfectly with the crab.

Charity ordered a salad of char-grilled, citrus-glazed wild Alaskan salmon, romaine, field greens, and local hazelnuts finished with cranberry-lime relish and a citrus-shallot dressing. Kara went for the fish and chips, with the cod seasoned to perfection and fried in a light-as-air tempura batter.

Since they all shared bites, Madeline realized that if she was going to help Sofia open a restaurant in a town with food this great, she was definitely going to have to spend as much time on the menu as she would the building of the school and restaurant.

A scheduled afternoon spay had Charity rushing off and forgoing dessert, leaving Kara and Madeline alone at the table.

After a quick perusal of the dessert cart, which had Maddy thinking she'd probably gained ten pounds just looking at the display, they decided to split the white chocolate Grand Marnier cheesecake dipped in dark chocolate, with an Oreo crust.

"This is just like old times," Kara said happily. "Even if we usually hung out at the Crab Shack or your grandmother's house."

"Simpler tastes, simpler times," Maddy said.

"My tastes are still pretty simple, but I can recognize good food when I taste it." She took a bite of cheesecake and studied Madeline for a long time. "So, since I know you have a meeting with Lucas this afternoon and I've never been much for playing games, I'm going to cut straight to the chase. He told me what he told you. About what he did back then with that waitress from the Stewed Clam."

"Did you know about that then?"

"Not at the time. Since I was unmarried and pregnant, I was focused on my own problems. Plus, I left town right after graduation, so I missed all the fireworks. It must have been horrible, and I'm so sorry he hurt you. And that I wasn't here to help."

"As you said, you had your own problems to deal with. But yes, he hurt me. He broke my heart."

"But you got over it."

"Do you mean, did I allow myself to care for another man again? Yes, I did. And look how well that turned out."

"You wouldn't be the first woman to make a mistake and choose the wrong man."

"True. And, unfortunately, I won't be the last. But, although I did manage to move on with my life, whenever I've thought of Lucas over the years, I've always hated him with the heat of a thousand suns."

"And now?"

"I want to," Madeline admitted. "But not only does Gram seem to like him, and he's admittedly being a big help with her new plan, it's also proving hard to hate a guy whose dad just died. Especially since, other than those few holidays he'd spend with his mom in Colorado every year, his dad was essentially the only family he had left."

"I can't imagine how I'd react if anything happened to

Trey, so I'm trying not to judge Lucas' mother. But having
your mom desert what's left of the family, after all that happened to them, had to leave scars."

Kara sighed. "Anyway, I was thinking last night, watching Lucas behaving as if he'd just slid back into life here as
a laid-back summer guy, that perhaps you're not getting the
entire picture of what he's been through since you two
broke up. And what he's experienced that's made him
change."

"Does he know you're having this conversation?"

"I offered to speak to you," Kara allowed. "But I didn't
tell him what, particularly, I'm going to share, because like
so many vets, he's been closemouthed about his war days.
Which makes total sense, because SEAL missions are secret to begin with. But Sax had more problems than Lucas
is displaying, so he did tell me some things that he gave me
permission to share with you."

Her somber tone had Madeline digging back into the
cheesecake. "Are you sure we have enough chocolate for
this discussion?"

"It's not an easy one. But I've decided since Lucas seems
to be serious about winning you back, it's important. Because,
as much as I care for him, I also wouldn't want you entering
into a relationship without knowing some background."

"Which should be his to tell."

"True." It was Kara's turn to take a big piece of the cake.
"But put yourself in his place. If you were in love with
someone and trying to convince them to give you a chance
to show how right the two of you would be together, would
you start out by sharing some of the darkest moments of
your life with them?"

"Of course not. But eventually I would."

"When you felt safer."

"When I felt safer," Madeline agreed, finding it a little
surprising that for all his swagger, Lucas might not feel
comfortable around her.

"It's probably the smart thing to do. But here's the thing: I was watching him joking and playing around with the dogs and Trey, Angel, and Johnny last night, and I came to the conclusion that he's holding back because he doesn't want his friends to worry about him."

"Which you do."

"I worry because I know that he'd have to be superhuman not to have some unresolved issues, and I worry that ignoring them so he can concentrate on you might put him at more risk for PTSD-related problems."

"Surely not everyone who returns home from a war suffers from PTSD," Madeline said.

"No. Of course not. But Sax does a lot of advocacy work with veterans' groups, and a recent study suggests that twenty percent of Iraq and Afghanistan veterans have PTSD. Though even one would be too many."

"I suggested he might have problems to Gram. But she wasn't worried."

"Neither am I, really. Though I do suspect that part of the reason Duncan Chaffee decided to retire when he did was because he'd begun to get worried about Lucas. Sax said his e-mails were sounding more guarded. And the fact that he wasn't sharing stuff the way he always had suggested he was having more and more trouble dealing with it. Especially when you think about it, a SEAL medic isn't exactly called upon to do his work when things are going well. . . .

"But they're doing better testing on returning troops, and forcing them to take a decompression time before getting out, so that's encouraging. Plus, he has a great, close support base with Cole and Sax and now Gabe. And Sax's dad served in Vietnam, so he's another resource."

"And then there's Scout," Madeline suggested.

"Absolutely. That dog's proving to be a big help. Especially since she needs Lucas' help with her own problems. So I don't think you need to be concerned about him going off and doing anything dangerous.

"The reason I wanted to talk with you is that I suspect he's going to go overboard trying to prove to you how normal he is. Which means that you might not really get a handle on how much he's changed since that twenty-year-old college sophomore who broke your heart."

"I guess everyone knows about that?" Madeline was getting used to the idea that no one anywhere had a private life anymore.

"Not everyone. But you know how small towns are." Kara shrugged. "Everyone pretty much lives in everyone else's pockets. Which has both its good and negative points.

"Getting back to Lucas. Of course, I have no way of knowing most of what he's experienced. But Sax did tell me about a time when they were on a mission in the Afghan mountains. Apparently, it was a ridiculously risky operation. Since they'd gotten delayed for various reasons, if they'd landed in the planned location, they would have been climbing the mountain in the dark.

"So, rather than delay the mission—which was to take out an al-Qaeda stronghold—overnight, the command decided they'd land on the top of the mountain. In the dark."

"Which had to be riskier," Madeline suggested, shivering beneath her pretty new cardigan as she imagined a moonless sky and the wind wailing through the desolate mountaintops. She'd always thought she was tough. Not only had she survived her parents dying suddenly, but she'd had her heart broken, toured Europe while still a teenager, and then established a career in the testosterone-driven culinary world.

But she could not imagine doing what Kara had just described.

"Lucas was the medic on the Chinook. Which also included, along with the SEAL team, Marines, Rangers, and some CIA operatives. Oh, and an Air Force Special Forces guy and the Army SOAR pilot. SOAR's like special forces, so we're talking a very elite team.

"Sax told me that Lucas was the most amazing special-ops guy he'd ever teamed up with. If there was any army, anywhere in the world, that had better equipment or drugs than the U.S. Army did, Lucas would track it down and make sure he had it in his overloaded Mike bag."

Cooking had a language all his own. But hearing Kara use a military term for what she guessed must be a medical supply kit, had Madeline thinking, as she suspected the other woman wanted her to, what a different life he'd been living these past ten years.

"Anyway, the Chinook was shot down. And although the safer thing would've been to stay on board until a rescue copter could come in, there were terrorists on the ground shooting at it, plus it started to catch fire."

She briefly closed her eyes and shook her head in a way that had Madeline suspecting that Sax had given her more details. And that they were very, very bad.

"The first firefight, as they evacuated the Chinook, lasted nearly thirty minutes. The Rangers, because of some stupid 'Lead the way' creed, charged off the copter, blasting away, as Sax described to me, like they were reenacting the shoot-out at the OK Corral. Unfortunately, they ran straight into a barrage of bullets, grenades, and RPGs that were pouring in at them from a camouflaged bunker they hadn't been able to see from the air."

"Oh, my God." Madeline's blood chilled.

"It got worse when the Marines followed. Sax said that if they'd been on Omaha Beach instead of a snowy Afghan mountain, it would have looked like the opening scene of *Saving Private Ryan*."

"I hated that movie."

"You're not alone there. Naturally, they called for an evacuation, but since they were just a small cog in a larger wheel, the commanders decided that to try to get another copter into a hot zone would be unsafe and unsound."

"You're kidding." Madeline waved away that question.

"Never mind. It was rhetorical. So, they left the survivors up there? All alone?"

In the dark? And the cold? In one of the most dangerous places on the planet?

"They dragged the wounded into the bunker after clearing it out." Madeline knew that couldn't have been as simple as it sounded. She'd seen enough war movies to imagine the shouting, the shooting, the blood. "Then they hunkered down for the night.

"Of course, when the sun came up—and Sax said it was appropriately bloodred—they realized that they were sitting ducks if they stayed there. But they were also in the midst of a blizzard, and since the pilot was badly injured, taking him out of the bunker would risk him dying of hypothermia. Unfortunately, once again command wouldn't send another Chinook into that spot until nightfall, and Lucas determined the pilot wouldn't last the night."

"So what did they do?"

It was strange, Madeline thought. Like watching a movie or reading a novel. She found it nearly impossible to think that the young man who'd bought her taffy then kissed her at the seawall, who'd made love to her in a cave that sparkled like diamonds, and even had flirted with her in her grandmother's kitchen could have experienced anything like this. Not just the battle and the snow and the danger. But the immense responsibility he'd taken onto his shoulders.

Kara had mentioned wounded. Which meant more than merely the pilot. And it had been up to him and his Mike bag to keep them all alive. What were the odds of everyone surviving?

"A CIA guy who'd come along on the mission knew about a medical relief camp that had been set up after a recent earthquake. To get there would take four to five hours. Straight up."

"And straight into enemy territory," Madeline guessed.

When she realized she was holding her breath, she had to remind herself that Lucas had obviously survived the mission or he wouldn't be here in Shelter Bay. As had Sax.

"Worse yet, the camp was on the Pakistan side of the border."

"Were they even allowed to go there?"

"Not then. The rules of engagement were changed later, but at the time, if they crossed the border, they'd be risking headlines, congressional hearings, and court-martials. And if that wasn't bad enough, as you pointed out, the al-Qaeda and Taliban holed up all over the mountains weren't all that hospitable to outsiders."

"Especially ones wearing the uniform of the U.S. military." Madeline took another big bite of cheesecake.

"Especially. Sax said it was a classic military catch-22—that by trying to save the life of the pilot who'd saved theirs with what he said was a near-miraculous landing, they could end up getting him, along with the rest of the survivors, all beheaded on Arabic television."

"But they went for it." *Of course they did.*

"They didn't hesitate. Lucas triaged the guys who'd be okay to stay behind; then they got the few Rangers who remained behind to pull the wounded up the mountain on SKEDs—that's like a stretcher on skis. Lucas managed to keep the pilot alive the entire time, despite what Sax said involved many more firefights even worse than the first—though, blessedly, he didn't describe it in detail."

"Dammit." Madeline pressed her fingers against her temples. "Of course Lucas kept him alive. Because that's what he does. He takes care of people."

"Like he was trying to take care of you that summer," Kara guessed what had just dawned on Madeline. "I realize how you might think he was trying to control your behavior, and yes, he was. But he really was trying to do what he thought was best for you. In his stupid guy way."

"I hate this," Madeline muttered. "I hate that he's spent

the past ten years in war zones. And I also hate that now I'm going to have to apologize for hitting him."

Kara's brows rose. "You hit him?"

"Well, I didn't slug him. But I did slap him." She held up a hand, forestalling any comment. "And I know it's a cliché." She sighed. "But I was so damn mad that he thought he had any right to take away my choices back then. Then Scout got horribly scared because I guess the slap sounded like gunfire—"

"And she hit the floor."

"Actually, she hit the floor, then crawled beneath the table."

Despite the seriousness of the situation, Kara laughed. "For someone who probably came back to town for some much-needed R and R, you've certainly landed yourself in a lot of activity."

"Tell me about it." Madeline pressed the tines of her fork on the now nearly empty plate, picking up the last of the Oreo crumb crust.

30

After all Kara had shared, Madeline wasn't prepared to meet with Lucas this afternoon. Not until she had time to think about what he'd been through. Process the changes in the boy she'd known back then and the man he'd become. She called the cell number he'd given her, only to be put into voice mail. Which suited her fine, since, if she were to be perfectly honest with herself, she'd have to admit that he was a difficult man to say no to.

After leaving a message to put off the meeting until tomorrow, she called her grandmother so Sofia wouldn't worry, and told her that she was going to take a little drive along the coast road to clear her head.

"Your husband called looking for you," Sofia said, her voice dripping with vinegar. "I told him I had no idea where you were. Which just happened to be the truth, since I didn't know if you were still at the Sea Mist. Or perhaps with someone else."

Someone meaning Lucas.

"The meal part of lunch was cut short," Madeline said. "Charity had surgery. But Kara and I stayed and talked. Caught up on what's been happening since we last saw each other."

Which wasn't precisely what the conversation had revolved around. But close enough.

"How nice for you. Kara's such a lovely young woman.

And she seems to have settled into her father's sheriff's role as if it were created for her. She's also a wonderful mother. And, of course, you nearly have to wear sunglasses whenever you're around her and Sax Douchett. There's just the brightest aura around them."

"*Aura?* Since when did you get into that woo-woo stuff?"

"Oh, I've always been aware of spirits. Some of the places in the jungles Joe and I visited searching out our herbs are just alive with their presence. But I've definitely been more aware since Joe's death, because he still shows up to be with me."

"Really?" Madeline didn't exactly disbelieve in ghosts and spirits and things that went bump in the night, but neither had she experienced them. Her parents certainly hadn't shown up to help her through her grief over missing them.

"I never would have gone ahead with the restaurant idea without his encouragement," Sofia confessed. "It was just like old days again, walking through the garden, turning over the soil for spring planting, chatting with him about plans and dreams."

"That's nice." Even if her grandfather hadn't actually somehow managed to come back from beyond wherever death was, Madeline was glad her grandmother had found a source of comfort.

"I realize a great many people might just write it off to hopeful thinking or an overly active imagination, but he's as real as you or Winnie. Who, by the way, also seems to see him, because she wags her stubby little tail whenever he visits."

Okay. That got to her. Madeline felt her eyes beginning to moisten.

"I'm really happy for you, Gram," she said. "Oh, not that Grandpa died. But that he's still with you."

"To tell you the truth, darling," Sofia confided, "I wasn't

the least bit surprised, since we always had a wonderfully strong bond. Which is what I've always hoped for you."

"Which you didn't believe I'd found with Maxime. Which is why you asked me twice before the wedding if I was sure marrying him was what I wanted."

There was a pause. Long enough that for a moment Madeline thought her phone might have dropped the call.

"I understood the man's appeal," Sofia finally said carefully, obviously wanting to choose her words wisely. "He was older, powerful, forceful. I'm sure he could be a very strong mentor."

Another pause. "But, no, I didn't envision him as husband material. At least not for you. But"—Madeline heard the shrug in her grandmother's voice—"you were a grown woman, capable of making your own choices. And your own mistakes."

"Well, that one turned out to be a whopper."

"We all make mistakes, darling. Which is how we learn."

"You didn't make a mistake with Grandpa."

Sofia laughed softly. "Perhaps because I didn't have any time to think about all the pros and cons. The day I met Joe, he told me he was going to marry me. Oh, I was so sure I was going to spend the rest of my life being a culinary Margaret Mead. I had no need for a man. At least not on a permanent basis. Besides, I thought that was an obnoxiously brash way to treat a woman. Staking a claim on me, as if I were some Hereford he could brand."

Madeline laughed at that image. "I'd like to see anyone try."

Her grandmother had always been the most independent woman she'd ever met. Then again, she reconsidered, her grandfather had also been a force of nature, as that story she'd never heard demonstrated. Yet together somehow they'd worked out a balance that, at least from the outside, had always seemed perfect.

"So, obviously you said yes."

"I didn't have any choice." Sofia sighed. But it was a happy sigh obviously replete with memories. "He just wouldn't give up, and swept me off my feet. We were married less than a month after we met. Then I got pregnant on our honeymoon, and your mother was born early, eight months after our wedding, in a palm-wood house with a thatched roof in an Asurini do Tocantins village in the Brazilian jungle.

"Your poor grandfather was going crazy because he was forced to stay outside the house while I was giving birth, with the help of the other women and a midwife, because it was taboo for any male to come into any contact with the blood of a female giving birth. After your mother was born, the midwife painted her with genipap so she'd grow faster. And your grandfather was instructed to sing to her every day, for the same reason."

"That's a wonderful story." And one Madeline had heard from her mother, but once again it brought home how much those two adventurous individuals had given up when they'd settled down to raise their orphaned granddaughter. "I love you, Gram."

"I love you, too, darling. Now, don't worry about getting home in time for supper. There's always something we can warm up. You just enjoy your drive."

Which she did. She drove along the winding coast road, stopping for a bag of taffy in the same store where Lucas had bought her that special one on a day she'd never forget. She ate it sitting on the same seawall where he'd kissed her and watched the kayakers and beachcombers down below. Wildflowers covered the hills and cliffs, brightly colored kites flew high above the water, and sea lions lounged on the rocks with their newborn pups, making a racket.

It had been a good day, and as she walked on the long expanse of beach, the sand glistening with sea foam and crushed shells, she could feel the knots in her shoulders, which had locked up in that Omaha department store, begin to loosen.

She was just congratulating herself on turning a corner when her cell rang again.

Recognizing the number on the caller ID screen, she was tempted to throw the phone into the waves. But instead, knowing that there were details to attend to that weren't going to go away on their own, even as she damned the timing, she answered.

"Hello, Maxime."

"Hello, Mad-eh-Leen," he said in the heavy accent that had once had the power to melt her bones.

She so didn't need this. "Cut the French crap Maxime, and just tell me what you want. And if it's money, you're flat out of luck. Because all of mine seems to be tied up in your overpriced restaurants, where you never met a cow that wasn't corn-fed in a feedlot. Actually, I'll bet you've never met a cow up close and personal in your life. Because you have people to do that for you."

"I did not call to get into an argument about classic versus sustainable cooking," he said.

"Trust me, both can be done. So, why are you calling?"

"I need a divorce."

"Well, imagine that. We have something in common."

"I mean soon."

She could hear the stress in his tone. *Interesting.*

"Soon as in . . . ?"

"Yesterday."

"Sorry. Yesterday's already in my rearview mirror. Try again."

"If you would sign the papers, you could be a free woman within a week's time."

"And where would I have to go to pull off this quickie-divorce feat?"

"That's the beauty of the idea," he said, a bit of his former convincing tone creeping back into his voice. Whenever he pulled that out, she was in trouble. "You don't have to go anywhere. You can stay wherever you are. Which would be?"

"I'm in Oregon."

"Ah. I suspected that you would go home to the farm. If you give me your address, my attorney can FedEx the papers to you in the morning. If you send them right back, prepaid, of course, I'll handle the rest by flying down to the Dominican Republic."

"And will Katrin be traveling with you?"

There was a pause. "Yes."

"Well, then. You'll be able to pull off a divorce and a honeymoon in one easy trip. Now, that's frugality for you."

"I understand why you'd be upset—"

"No, Maxime," Madeline broke in. "You're wrong about that." As he'd been about so many things. Then again, hadn't she? Understanding what people meant when they suggested the breakup of a marriage was never entirely one-sided, she said, "What I am, actually, is grateful that Katrin is taking you off my hands. Since her pockets are ever so much deeper than mine could ever be."

Which, as he'd explained, was the point.

"But here's the deal. I have terms."

"Terms?"

"You know what you said about funding my restaurant?"

"Yes." He sounded hesitant. Wary. Making Madeline wonder how much of that earlier offer had been a bluff. Which, if it had, only went to show that he'd known *her* better than she'd known *him*.

"Well, I still don't want it."

"Ah." His relief was more than a little evident.

"What I want, and insist on having, is being paid back every penny I invested in your various restaurants. Which I was led to believe was an investment in our marriage."

There was a very long pause. Madeline thought she heard him cover the mouthpiece and speak to someone else.

"That sounds fair. But the problem is that I have no idea how much that would be."

Of course not. He'd been like a damn sponge, soaking up her hard-earned funds like a haphazardly breaded eggplant soaking up olive oil.

"Well, fortunately for both of us, I do. I've kept records. Detailed records. Of every dime invested and where it went."

Another pause. She could almost see the color blanching out of his face. "And how much would that be?"

She knew it to the penny, having studied the numbers she kept in an online file-storage site while stuck at the airport hotel.

"That much?" he asked, sounding honestly surprised when she told him.

"No one has ever accused you of not being high maintenance, Maxime."

He covered—not well—the mouthpiece again. She could hear him relating the numbers to someone. Obviously Katrin. And possibly her lawyer. And accountant. And whatever other people she had taking care of her beer bucks.

"You can supply these numbers?"

"I can get you the spreadsheet right away. And copies of records. But, of course," she added on her sweetest tone, "those might take several weeks to compile."

"Done," he said, apparently having been given the okay to accept that amount. "The papers will arrive tomorrow."

"I'm sorry. Were you thinking that was my final offer?"

"Of course." There were not many times she could remember Maxime Durand sounding anything but self-confident. This was one of the few times his veneer had slipped.

"Well, it's not." She took a breath. Then went for it. "I want double."

"Double what?"

"Double what I've paid you. Because, in case it hasn't occurred to you or your new wife-to-be, if I refuse to sign those papers you're so eager to send me, and instead hire my own attorney to attach claims to each and every one of your restaurants, you could be tied up in court for a very long time. New York, after all, despite now allowing no-fault divorce, is not the easiest state to actually accomplish that."

"The restaurants are teetering on bankruptcy, as you very well know." A bit of bluster had returned. She imagined his complexion going from rice white to beet red. "You would end up with nothing but lawyer fees to pay."

"Wrong again." Oddly, she was beginning to almost enjoy this conversation. "I'd end up with the satisfaction of watching an empire fall. Sort of like Rome, after Nero spent too much time fiddling and not enough time tending to business. *Double*, Maxime. And all my things boxed up from the apartment and FedExed to me so they arrive before Katrin's private jet clears New York airspace for the Caribbean."

"Un moment, s'il vous plaît."

Ha! She had him flustered. The only times he switched totally to French were when he lost his temper, was in full-out seduction mode, or seriously distressed.

So she gave him his moment.

Bet he chooses door number three.

She could hear the conversation in the background. The staccato female tones did not sound at all happy.

And then, finally, after she'd held for more than five minutes, he was back. "Madeline." The cajoling French accent was gone. "You have a deal. My attorney will contact yours in the morning."

"Make that afternoon." She still had to find a lawyer. "I'll e-mail you his name and phone number."

His answering curse was French and crude. "Afternoon it will be."

He did not bother with pleasantries, but merely cut off the call.

"Well. That's that."

And as she stood there at the edge of the continent, with the white-capped waves washing in and the sandpipers skittering along the edge of the surf and the gulls circling overhead, Madeline realized that it was, indeed, possible for a person to feel both relieved and sad at the same time.

31

Lucas was disappointed, but not surprised when Maddy canceled their afternoon meeting. Kara had already called to tell him that she thought their lunch had gone well. In fact, he'd been on the phone with her when Maddy's call had come in, which is the only reason he'd missed it.

"Timing," he told Scout, who was sprawled on the sofa, head on the arm, watching him pace the plank floor, "is everything."

He could just go over to the farm. It wasn't as if he didn't have an excuse. He'd given a lot of thought to the farmhouse remodel during the drives back and forth from Portland. Everyone always complained about contractors not showing up.

"So how could anyone complain about one who actually did?" he asked the dog, who barked in what seemed to be full agreement.

Lucas had never considered himself an impatient man. He'd been known to lie on his belly for hours, even days, if it need be, scoping out a valley, waiting for a target to appear. Patience had been drilled into him from the first day at BUD/S training. In fact, from what he'd been able to tell from his class, more guys rang out of training due to impatience than lack of guts or strength.

You learned to choose not just your target, but your time. And although he wanted to go over to the farm and drag her back here by her long black curls, like some Neanderthal cave guy, he'd gained enough knowledge of women to realize that would be the last thing she needed.

Then again, if he just sat back and bided his time, she could be back on a plane to New York before he'd gotten a fair chance.

Because he decided to give her this time to process whatever Kara had told her, he snagged an oyster po'boy Sax had sent home from Bon Temps and a bottle of beer from the fridge and went over to the window wall, where the telescope his father had bought him for his eighth birthday stood on a tripod.

A white, waxing moon was rising, lighting up the waves in a silvery trail that made it look as if you could just walk out to the horizon and over the edge of the earth. In the distance, the jagged pillars of sea stacks—land that had broken away from the continent—stood like ghostly sentinels, draped in shawls of fog.

He was looking through the telescope when, in the flash of the enormous prism of light from the Shelter Bay lighthouse, several hundred yards off shore, he spotted geysers of water—monumental clouds of spray and foamlike explosions. A moment later, a pod of whales breached in unison, leaping into the air and crashing back into the sea.

They were, he realized, literally playing in the waves. Several of them began sailing, enormous tails held aloft above the surface as they approached the shore. Just when Lucas feared they'd beach themselves on the treacherous rocks, they'd turn around, heading back to sea for another sail.

Although it was difficult to tell with the dimming light, most appeared to be California grays, on their annual six-thousand-mile migratory spring trek up the Pacific coast from their mating and birthing grounds off the Baja coast, back to the Bering Sea.

He sharpened the lens's focus, catching sight of a few

humpback whales, which were relatively rare in these waters, though a few pods were spotted every season. This was the first time in several years he'd been fortunate enough to see them himself.

As the whales moved on beneath the water, he idly scanned the beach while drinking his beer. Which was when he spotted Maddy. All alone, perched atop a huge driftwood log.

Drinking from what appeared to be a bottle of champagne.

Which, depending on what Kara told her, and how she'd taken it, could be good. Or bad. Whichever, it could definitely end up dangerous.

"Come on," he told Scout. "Looks like we've got another rescue mission on our hands."

32

As luck would have it, there was a market not far from the beach. Still wired on adrenaline from her conversation with her soon-to-be-ex-husband, Maddy bought a bottle of chilled champagne and six plastic glasses. Not that she was planning to invite anyone to her party, but they only came in a set.

Then she drove down the curving road to the beach not far from Lucas' cottage. Though she had no desire to see him, he just happened to live above one of the best stretches of coastline around.

She made her way down the wooden steps, belatedly realizing that she should have taken off the heels. Which she did, leaving them next to a pile of driftwood logs.

Then, barefoot, she walked across the sand, opened the small robin's-egg blue box she'd been carrying around in her purse since leaving for the airport from the apartment, took out her wedding ring, and flung it as far as she could into the water.

There was a flash; then, after it disappeared beneath the waves, she walked back up to the logs, brushed the blown sand off one of the lower ones, sat down, popped the cork, and poured the sparkling wine into one of the stemmed plastic glasses. As the past ten years of her life drifted through her mind, like a documentary on some mental video screen, she began making inroads on the champagne.

The moon rose as Madeline drank. And remembered.

"There comes a time in every woman's life," she quoted her favorite-ever movie actress, "when the only thing that helps is a glass of champagne."

She took another drink. When the bubbles didn't feel quite as sparkly, she wondered if her tongue was becoming a bit numb, and held the dark green bottle up to the moonlight to judge the level of champagne remaining.

"Bette Davis. In *Now, Voyager* . . . No. That's not right." She shook her head.

"*Old Acquaintance*. 1943. Davis said it to Miriam Hopkins. When at the end of the movie, after all those years of feuding, they're left with just each other."

She nodded her satisfaction at having remembered. Forties movies were not just her favorites; they were her forte, having spent so many late nights in her teens watching them on television with her grandmother.

Toasting the actress and herself for recalling the line, she tossed back the champagne. "It was probably for the best. Because it if has tires or a penis, it's just bound to cause you trouble."

"The tide's going to be coming in soon," a familiar deep voice warned.

Speaking of penises . . .

"That's what it does." She took another drink. "It comes in. Then goes back out again. . . . In. Out. In. Out. Which is probably one of the few things—hell—maybe the only predictable thing in life." She looked up at Lucas. "What are you doing here? And didn't your father ever teach you that stalking a woman isn't the best way to win her over?"

"I'm not stalking you. You're on my beach."

"Ha! Wrong answer." She held up an index finger. Or was it two? "I may have been away for a while, but I happen to know that beaches in Oregon are public. So you have no right to claim this one, Lucas Chaffee." Damn. Her tongue really was getting thick.

"You got me. But it's the beach below my house, which is how I spotted you. And did it ever occur to you that walking out on a public beach alone late at night can get you into trouble? Why don't you just send out an invitation to the Green River Killer while you're at it?"

"He's in prison. I saw him on one of those TV news-magazines a few years ago. He claimed his career was killing people. He may not be legally insane, but I gotta tell you, he's definitely crazy."

She shook her head. "Then again, maybe we're all crazy. In our own way."

She polished off another glass and reached for the bottle she'd stuck into the sand.

Lucas was quicker, scooping it up. "You're drunk."

"You think?" She considered that for a moment. "Maybe just a little." She held out her glass, inviting him to fill it again. "But not enough. Not yet."

"What happened?"

"Shelter Bay is not a war zone. And I'm not a terrorist. So it seems to me that I should be able to celebrate without being interrogated by a Navy SEAL."

"Former SEAL. And it was merely a question. So, what are we celebrating?"

"Independence Day."

"Sounds good to me. You're not talking about the Fourth of July kind of Independence Day with parades, flags, and fireworks, though, are you?"

"No. Though fireworks might be in order."

Then she thought of his poor, sweet, three-legged dog who'd followed him down and was now sitting alert at his feet, seeming to be watching for any seagulls that might dare try to land. "On the other hand, probably not . . . I'm getting a divorce."

"I thought we'd already determined that."

"True." She nodded. Slowly. Solemnly. "But today made it official."

"You don't waste any time." He sat down beside her.

"My husband and his lover are in a hurry. Enough so that he was willing to pay me back all I put into his restaurants."

"Good for you."

"It gets better. I held out for more."

She could see the smile tugging at the corners of his mouth. The mouth that she was suddenly wishing was on hers. That idea made her head spin. Or, more likely, it was the champagne.

"Even better."

"I've discovered lately that I'm a very good negotiator. Better than good. Excellent. Maybe even world-class . . .

"So, now that I have enough money for the restaurant and school, I decided to throw my wedding ring into the ocean so some poor, unsuspecting woman won't buy it on Craigslist and end up with bad-luck vibes and a lying, cheating husband."

She waved her hand toward the moon-gilded surf. "It was a combination engagement and wedding ring. Two carats. Marquis cut. Surrounded by another two carats of pavé diamonds. From Tiffany's." She pointed down at the blue box she'd dropped on the sand. "Though I never wore it on TV, so you wouldn't have ever seen it, being such a huge fan of the Cooking Network as you profess to be. It was, let me tell you, very, very flashy." She was having to concentrate not to slur her words. "Blindingly so."

"Which isn't at all you."

She bestowed her sweetest smile on him. "You know me so well, Lucas. Which, although I hate to admit it, is making it more and more difficult for me to hate you."

In fact, it was odd, she thought, through the cloud hazing her mind. Ever since she'd run into him in her grandmother's kitchen, Lucas had stirred her up, tangling her emotions. But for some reason, his sitting here beside her, while bringing back memories, also calmed her down. And felt surprisingly right.

"I'm glad to hear that. Thank you."

"You're welcome. Are you going to pour me some champagne or not?"

He shrugged. Seemed to give up.

"You're a grown woman. If you want to get trashed because some jerk's too stupid to realize that he had a gem far more precious than some overpriced hunk of crystallized carbon, far be it for me to stop you," he muttered, pouring a few more inches into the glass.

When she continued to hold it out, he cursed beneath his breath and filled it to the plastic rim.

"I'm *not* getting drunk because of Maxime. Not really. I'm getting drunk because . . . well, because I never have before."

"Ever?"

Although he'd known her for only five summers, from when she'd first arrived in Shelter Bay at thirteen to that summer after her high school graduation, she'd always been a straight arrow. Which is why, although he'd walked around with a near-perpetual hard-on, he'd been so hesitant to be the one who took the virginity she'd suddenly been so eager to give up. He'd known sex was a serious thing to her.

What he hadn't foreseen was that she'd been willing to toss away all her plans for her life once he'd given in.

"Never." Her mist-dampened curls fanned out as she shook her head. "Ever. So, it seemed like a good idea tonight." Her brow furrowed. "But thank you for saying that about me being a gem. That's sweet. Very, very sweet."

She smiled up at him, her eyes gleaming seductive silver. Although Lucas knew it was his imagination, he could've sworn he heard the sultry songs of sirens singing out beyond the breakers.

"It's true."

"It's still sweet. Why don't you have some champagne? I hate to drink alone." She frowned. "I left the other glasses up in the car."

"I'm not fussy." He tilted the bottle to his lips and allowed the champagne to slide down his throat. Although he preferred beer, the French bubbly wasn't half bad.

They sat there, side by side, in a surprisingly comfortable silence, watching the waves wash onto the shore.

"I saw the whales earlier," he said. "Right before I came down here."

"That's so special. I love the whales." She took another drink. "Love. Them. Remember that time one washed up on shore?"

It was the summer he'd been seventeen. She'd been fifteen, and he'd returned to town to discover that the last of her baby fat had turned into amazing curves. "Yeah."

"That was so sad."

The entire town had tried to keep the tragically misdirected, huge gray whale hydrated. He and Maddy had both been part of the bucket brigade. Oregon State had sent team of biologists, who, when the tide failed to wash it back out to sea and its breathing had become labored, had no choice but to euthanize it.

"So, so sad." He heard the choked sob on her voice.

"Yeah. It was." With his fingertip, he wiped away the tear that was trailing down her cheek.

They fell silent again. He hoped she was thinking of better summers.

The temperature began to drop.

"It's getting cold," he said when she shivered. "We'd better get you inside."

"Inside your place?"

"Well, I could take you home. But you're not driving yourself, because friends don't let friends drive drunk. You're also welcome to spend the night."

"Aha!" She turned toward him and lifted her glass to, apparently, make some sort of point. "We're back to that."

She really was on her way to being wasted. "To what?" He plucked the nearly empty glass from her hand, put it on the sand next to the bottle, and stood up.

"To you wanting me." Although he'd expected an argument, she took hold of the hand he extended, allowing him to help her to her feet. "And me wanting you."

He suspected it was the alcohol that had loosened her inhibitions enough to allow her to make that admission out loud.

"I always want you." He took hold of her shoulders, balancing her when she swayed. No way was he going to let her climb that wooden stairway to the cliff on her own. "But you're safe tonight, Chef Madeline."

"Oh." Those full lips he was aching to taste turned down in a pout. "Isn't that just like a man? You've already changed your mind and undoubtedly moved on to some other woman."

"I haven't changed my mind. In fact, if the tide wasn't about to start coming in and the temperature wasn't dropping like a stone, I'd be temped to reenact the beach scene in *From Here to Eternity*."

"Like we haven't already."

Now, there was a summer memory. He could recall that night in the cave in vivid detail. Hadn't he relived it in dreams over the years? Which wasn't helping his control any.

She was doing that swaying thing again. Catching her before she toppled into the tide, which was getting closer, Lucas scooped her up and threw her over his shoulder.

33

"I'm perfectly capable of walking myself."

Like hell. "Shut up," he said mildly.

"Excuse me?"

"I said, shut up. You've had a rotten few days."

"They haven't exactly been a picnic," she agreed.

"Which is why I don't think you'd want to top them off by falling down the steps, breaking your neck on the rocks, being washed out to sea, and ending up some shark's entrée."

"Well, that's an appealing scenario. Don't forget my shoes," she said. "They're new."

He bent down and scooped up the flimsy little red sandals that had been a ridiculous choice for the beach.

"I know why you came down here," she claimed.

"You canceled our meeting. I figured this was as good a chance as any to talk with you."

"Liar." He heard her deep sigh. "It's because you can't stop being a hero, isn't it?"

He stopped walking. "Where did that come from?"

"Kara told me about what happened in Afghanistan. When the helicopter crashed."

There was no way his best friend's wife could even begin to know what happened that night. No guy in his right mind would ever share the details of those hours of horror with anyone, let alone a woman he loved. But apparently Sax had given her the PG version.

Probably because it would've been a little hard to hide those ghosts he'd talked about. Even if he'd been the only one to see them, they would've had to have affected his and Kara's relationship.

"Trust me. I'm no hero." He started up the stairs again, reached the top, and headed into the cottage.

"That's what Kara always says Sax claims. But I don't believe it."

"We were just doing our jobs. Same as anyone else. End of story." He hoped.

"God, I've always loved this house," she said, as he carried her into the cottage, seeming to give him his wish. "When you stand at the window, it's as if you can see forever. Or spread your wings and fly."

Isn't that what she'd done? But as clueless as he'd been about women back then, and he'd been as dumb as a stump, at least he'd understood that Maddy had to leave Shelter Bay to truly soar.

"My grandpa Joe swept Gram off her feet," she said as he carried her down the hall.

"Good for him. They always seemed to have a great thing going."

"They were madly in love," she continued as they reached his old bedroom. He hadn't yet felt comfortable moving into his father's master. "And my point was that although every woman fantasizes about being swept off her feet by a hero in shining armor, being hauled off over a man's shoulder like a sack of potatoes—which, I'd like to point out, is not the way Rhett carried Scarlett up that staircase—isn't turning out the slightest bit romantic."

Amused, annoyed, and, dammit, aroused, especially since her skirt had tumbled nearly over her head when he'd hefted her up and his hand was splayed on the smooth, pale skin

at the back of her thigh, he dumped her on the bed he
hadn't bothered to make this morning. She bounced. Twice.

"You want romance?"

He leaned down, took her chin in his tensed fingers, and
closed his mouth over hers.

And—*pow!*—felt as if he'd just been hit with a cluster
bomb.

Her taste, headier than the champagne she'd drunk, exploded inside him.

It would've been easier if she'd pulled away. Resisted
even a little bit. But no. Instead she grabbed hold of the
front of the blue dress shirt he'd worn to the meeting with
his father's lawyer, pulled him down onto the bed, and
threw herself into the kiss. Heat scorched through him. Images of smoke and flames sparked in his mind.

He could have her, he thought, as she tugged his shirt
from his jeans with fevered hands. She twined around him,
her short, neat fingernails digging into his back, her legs
holding him in a vise, her breasts flattened against his
chest.

Lucas had fantasized about this moment more times
than he could count over the years. There'd even been
times when he'd been sleeping on the hard Afghan ground,
with his pack as a pillow, that he'd wake up hard as a pike
because of dreams of this woman. He'd always wanted a
second chance with her.

"Do you have any idea," he asked against her ravenous
mouth, "how hard you're making it for me to do the right
thing?"

"I'll help." Her hand moved to the fly of his jeans. "And
speaking of hard . . ."

Oh, sweet Jesus. "Dammit, Maddy!" He caught her wrist
and pulled her hand away before her stroking touch had
him going off. "There are rules."

"Forget about rules," she said recklessly. "Everyone else
does."

"I'm not everyone else." He touched a hand to her cheek, holding her gaze to his. "And, more important, neither are you."

"I wanted you to kiss me. To touch me." He watched her throat as she swallowed. Took in her smoke gray eyes that were trying, unsuccessfully, to focus. "I want you to make love to me. I need you to make love to me. To prove . . ."

Oh, hell. She didn't need to finish that sentence. Damn, that Frenchman had done a number on her.

He groaned. Could she make this any more difficult? The last time she'd begged him to make love to her, he had, even knowing the timing was all wrong. And look where that had gotten them.

"I want you, Madeline." Although he knew he was playing with fire, taking a risk, he took hold of her wrist and pressed her palm against the front of his jeans again. "I've been walking around stiff as a damn pike since you came back to town."

"That's just physical. You could've taken care of it yourself."

"True." And hadn't he been tempted? "But I've been waiting. For you."

"Well, then." She smiled up at him, teasing, tempting. "What are we waiting for?"

Rational thoughts fled. The good Lord had given him both a brain and a penis. Unfortunately, when it came to Maddy, Lucas only seemed to have blood enough to run one or the other.

His head swooped down again, his kiss hot, hungry, and rough with built-up sexual frustration. Images rushed through his mind—hot, tempestuous images as dangerous as a storm-tossed sea.

It would be so easy. It was so damn tempting.

It was also wrong.

He abruptly tore his mouth from hers and buried it against her neck. After a long, aching moment, he drew back, shaken by the intensity of the visceral need for this woman that still had parts of his body in a vise grip.

"Lucas?" Her heavy eyes slowly fluttered open. They were wide and vague and confused. "I don't understand."

Desperate but determined not to show it, he stood up. "That makes two of us. But here's the deal. You're drunk. Which is totally understandable under the circumstances. But when we make love, and we will, I want you stone-cold sober. So that, when I'm finished with you, even years—hell, decades—from now, when we're old and gray and walking on the beach with our great-grandkids, all I'll have to do is look at you and you'll remember every single thing I did to you." He slipped off her sweater and skimmed a hand down her arm. "With you."

"I don't remember you being so arrogant."

Although he could still feel her pressed against him, still taste her on his lips, he laughed. "Determined," he corrected. "Which is why you're going to marry me."

"Ha." She tossed her head. And from the way her eyes nearly crossed, he suspected just that gesture had made her dizzy. "I told you, that is not going to happen. I'm not going to marry anyone. Ever again." She batted her eyelashes at him in a very un-Maddy-like way. "Though, if you get back on this bed, I'm willing to let you be my rebound boy toy."

It took an effort not to laugh.

"Why don't we discuss that idea in the morning?"

"I'm not sure I'll even be speaking to you in the morning."

Her haughty-empress-of-the-realm tone, a vivid contrast to her tousled, warm, and sensual appearance, did make him smile. "I'll take my chances. And a rain check." He skimmed a hand down her hair. "Good night."

"A rain check," she muttered. "Good idea. Since if we did make love right now, I have this sudden fear I'd humiliate myself by falling asleep before we got to the really good parts."

That said, she rolled over, and like a stone, dropped straight into sleep.

From her steady breathing, he decided she hadn't passed out. Just collapsed from having run on fumes these past few days.

He considered taking her out of that dress; then, deciding there was only so much temptation he could handle, Lucas got a quilt out of the hall closet, covered her with it, and left her to sleep off her independence indulgence.

He stripped off his jeans and shirt and sprawled on the couch. As Scout blissfully snored on the rug beside him, Lucas felt as if he were about to explode, his aching body rock hard and frustrated.

An hour later, unable to sleep, he made his way painfully across to the kitchen, where he poured a glass of ice water. As he chugged it down, he willed it to cool his lingering hunger.

It didn't.

Five hours later, after checking in to make sure Maddy was still okay, he pulled on a pair of sweats and a ragged gray hoodie and went down to run on the beach.

The fog had blown in during the night, cloaking the beach in a cold mist that should have cleared Lucas' mind and body, but didn't. Nor did the rain falling from the dark sky.

He was too tangled up with thoughts of Maddy. As he'd been so many times over the years, but his mind had gone to her seemingly nonstop since she'd suddenly shown up in Sofia's kitchen. It only made sense that he'd think of her while planning her grandmother's addition, but she'd also infiltrated his mind during his drive to Portland and back.

The past few nights he'd gone to sleep wanting her. Dreaming of her. Hot, vivid dreams that had him waking up frustrated.

And even as Scout ran on the sand beside him, seemingly unhindered by the loss of her leg, Maddy's scent, the feel of her silken skin, the taste of her, lingered in his mind.

He ran all the way to the lighthouse and back, around a bend in the coast, past the cave that held so many memories. By the time he returned to the cottage, his heart was pounding against his ribs, his blood was flowing, he was drenched with rain and sweat. Unfortunately, the enforced PT had failed to drive Maddy from his mind.

He had been up front about wanting her. And although she'd admittedly been wasted, he believed that she'd been telling the absolute truth about wanting him.

But something Brooke had told him about him being her rebound had echoed in Maddy's claim that while she had no intention of marrying him, she was more than willing to let him be her lover.

Which, while appealing, wasn't enough. While he'd never thought of himself as a greedy man, Lucas wanted more than just a hot night. Or even a sizzling affair. He'd done those and knew that passion always flared out quickly.

He also understood that she was still technically married. They'd be working together for the next few months. Giving her time to get used to him in her life, to come to trust him, to realize that he was nothing like her cheating, lying, ex-husband, was the logical conclusion.

The only problem was, there was nothing remotely logical about his overwhelming feelings for the woman currently sleeping in his bed.

34

It was the sound of the rain on the roof that woke her. Feeling as if her head was filled with rocks, Maddy moaned and pulled the pillow over her head when she saw Lucas sitting in a chair across the room.

"Rise and shine," he said so cheerfully, Maddy thought there wasn't a jury in the world who'd convict her if she took a meat mallet to his head.

"Go away," she muttered from beneath the goose-down pillow.

"I would. But having been where you are right now, I can tell you that you'll feel better with something in your stomach."

"Oh, God." Just the idea was enough to make her moan. "Why didn't you stop me last night?"

"I suggested you might want to go easy. But you seemed to have a different goal in mind."

"I was celebrating."

"That's what you said at the time. But given that you threw four carats of diamonds into the ocean makes me think you were more likely trying to drown the Frenchman."

"That, too," she admitted.

"If you'd asked, which you didn't, I could've told you it wouldn't work."

She pushed the pillow aside and opened eyes that felt as

if the entire beach full of sand had ended up beneath her lids. "Tried to drown a lot of Frenchmen with champagne, have you?"

"Whiskey was more my adult beverage choice. And it wasn't a Frenchman. It was a woman."

That got her attention enough to make her push herself into a sitting position. Her stomach roiled as the boulders in her head tumbled. Surely he couldn't mean . . .

He leaned down and pushed what had to be a rat's nest of hair off her face. "And, yeah, if you're thinking that woman in question was you, you're right. It always left me with a hangover about like the one you're suffering now. And you know what?"

"What?"

"Ten years later, I still haven't found a way to get you out of my mind."

"That's a low blow. To play on my emotions while I'm at a distinct disadvantage." She slapped his hand away. "Given that I'm dying."

"You're not going to die. Though you'll probably wish you could." He held out the glass in his other hand. "Here. Drink this. It'll help."

She looked with open suspicion at the rust-colored liquid. "What is it?"

"It's an old Cajun recipe for hangovers."

"You're not Cajun."

"True. But Sax is. And he's the one who taught me how to make it."

She studied it more closely. "I hope you had a hazmat suit on while you prepared it, because it looks like toxic waste."

"Tastes like it, too," he said agreeably, with a coaxing smile. "Trust me."

She did, she realized. Which just went to show how much her life had changed in a mere few days.

She took a tentative sip. And had to put her hand over her mouth to keep from spitting it all over the bed.

"Ugh." The taste was enough to keep anyone from drinking ever again. "What the hell is in it?" She could detect the Tabasco, but with her tongue coated with whatever beach sand hadn't ended up in her eyes, her palate was in worse shape than she was.

"You don't want to know." He actually had the nerve to grin at her. "Drink up. I've got coffee waiting."

"Anyone ever tell you that you're a sadist?"

"Nope." Another grin. Damned if he didn't seem to be enjoying this. "And you'll thank me later."

"If I don't kill you first," she muttered. Then swallowed the unsavory sludge and felt her stomach rebel. "I really think I'm going to die." Was that a whimper she heard coming out of her Sahara-dry mouth? She *never* whimpered. Of course, she'd never suffered a morning-after hangover, either.

After handing him the glass, she flopped back against the pillow and flung a hand over her eyes. "Then again, I'm even more afraid that I won't."

"Poor baby." She felt the mattress sag as he sat down on the bed beside her. "He wasn't worth it."

"I know." His fingers had begun massaging her temples, where maniacs were pounding away with jackhammers. "But I was just so mad."

"But you won." He pressed his lips to her hair. "You beat the bastard. At his own game."

She'd thought, at first in shock, and later, on the plane flying back to New York from Nebraska, that she'd never feel whole again. That she'd never be happy again. But now, although she still felt as if she hadn't managed to put all the pieces back together, she realized that when Lucas was right, he was really, really right.

"I really did," she agreed. "I took the bastard down."

"And his beer baroness, too."

"Her, too," Madeline agreed. Then, despite the pain, she smiled.

35

Phoebe was in the kitchen of Harbor House, whisking eggs for omelets, when there was a knock at the kitchen door. Her nerves immediately tangled; then she reminded herself that Zelda had warned her that Ethan Concannon would be coming by this morning with a load of fresh vegetables and more eggs.

Which wasn't why she'd put on a bit of blush and mascara, then spritzed on scent from the display of sample bottles she'd found on a little tray on the top the dresser of her room.

Liar. The cologne in the small bottle with the daisies on top had smelled light and happy.

She brushed the flour from her apron and opened the door, then drew in a sharp breath as she viewed him taking up nearly the entire doorway, a crate of vegetables in his hands and a smile in his eyes.

"Good morning." His voice was as dark and warm as hot chocolate.

"Hi." She sounded breathless. Which she was. She dropped her gaze to the crate of colorful vegetables he held in his arms.

"Oh, those are beautiful."

"Thanks." He glanced past her. "Mind if I come in and put them down?"

Color flooded into her cheeks. "Of course not." She

moved aside and began making room on the counter next to the vegetable sink. "They really are fabulous!" She dove into them, pulling out a box of white button mushrooms. "They look like photographs in a cookbook. Or from a painting."

"We aim to please."

She'd just taken out a bunch of leafy green spinach when she froze at what she feared might be a sexual innuendo. Goose bumps rose on her arms.

"I was talking about the vegetables, Phoebe," he said gently.

"I know." Her laugh, meant to toss her fears off, revealed her nerves.

"So." He stuck his hands into the pocket of his jeans, rocked back on the heels of his work boots, and glanced over at the Pyrex bowl next to the stove. "What are you making?"

"Scones and spinach omelets. With fresh fruit."

"Sounds great. You looked happy."

"Happy?"

"I saw you through the window," he revealed. "I was just passing by," he tacked on quickly.

"I know."

She'd reacted instinctively, and now she realized that *he* was the one afraid. Afraid of frightening her. She didn't want to be treated like some nervous-Nellie victim. What she wanted, she'd realized as she'd brushed on that color in her too-thin cheeks this morning, was for him to look at her like a woman.

"I made this uncomfortable," she said as she began to whisk the brown-shelled eggs. "I'm sorry."

She wasn't looking up at him, but heard the sigh.

Then she heard him approach slowly before she felt a soft hand on her arm. "Don't," he said gently.

"Don't what?" It was little more than a whisper. Not from fear. But because, heaven help her, his touch felt so good.

"You didn't do anything you have to apologize for. If anything, I'm the one who's making it uncomfortable. I like you, Phoebe."

"You don't know me." And hadn't she been in this situation before? With disastrous results.

"That's true enough." He dropped his hand. Stepped back to put some space between them. "But it's something I'd like to remedy." He glanced down at the bowl. "After you're done taking out your anger on those poor eggs."

Despite her words and his acknowledgment, he'd nailed that. She had been taking out her repressed fury toward Peter on the eggs she'd begun whisking too hard. And too fast.

"I'm sor—"

She stopped in midapology when he touched his fingers to his own mouth, suggesting she not finish that apology.

"It's complicated," she said instead.

"Life often is." He squared broad shoulders that strained at the seams of his denim shirt, as if declaring that topic closed. "So, how would you like to come out to the farm after you're finished making breakfast?"

"To *your* farm?" *Alone? With him?*

"Well, I could take you around to some of my competitors. Not that I'm blowing my own horn, but none of them have as good produce or stock as Blue Heron does."

"He said modestly." As the words came out of her mouth, Phoebe inwardly flinched.

Instead of being annoyed at her teasing, he laughed. "It's not bragging if it's true. Lily used to come visit from time to time. She liked choosing her own produce. And getting out in the fresh air."

And had he looked at her predecessor the way he'd looked, just momentarily, at her? Had they had an affair? Was this merely a fresh market where he could pick up women desperate for a kind word? A gentle touch?

"Phoebe." Her name, spoken in that low, solemn tone,

drew her mind away from an image of the sexy farmer entwined on some quilt with a willing, faceless woman who'd worked in this kitchen before her.

"What?"

"I'm not him."

"Who?" Ice froze in her veins. Surely he couldn't know.

"Whoever it was who hurt you. Who put that bruise on your face. And if I'm proving damn clumsy at knowing how to talk to a woman I'm attracted to, it's because I'm out of practice."

"Well." She put down the whisk. Folded her arms and looked at him. "That's something I'll need to think about, Mr. Concannon."

"Ethan."

"Ethan." She tilted her head and studied him. His rugged cheeks were dark, revealing that the words had not come easily for him. Which is why, although her entire life was a lie, she decided to find out a bit more truth about him.

"You said you're out of practice."

"I haven't even thought about how to ask a girl out since I was fifteen." This time his smile was filled with rue.

Well, that was telling. Either he was gay, which, from the vibes she'd picked up, he most definitely wasn't, or he'd married his high school sweetheart.

"Are you married?"

"No."

"But you were?"

"Yes."

"What happened?" Had Mrs. Concannon gotten tired of the hard work and lack of the excitement rural living required?

The light left his blue eyes, like a candle snuffed out by a stiff sea breeze. "She died."

36

After three Motrin tablets, which Lucas referred to as vitamin M, the glass of toxic gunk he'd forced her to drink, and two mugs of coffee, Madeline was beginning to feel like a new woman. Enough that she thought, just maybe, she might be able to keep some food down.

"Pop-Tarts?" she repeated back to Lucas when he suggested putting two in the toaster for her. "That's what you eat for breakfast?"

"You already turned down the Cocoa Puffs. And if I were here by myself, I'd eat the crab étouffée that's in the refrigerator. But you're probably not ready for that yet."

"Crab étouffée isn't usually a breakfast food."

"Perhaps not for you. Though I'll bet you wouldn't blink an eye at a crab omelet."

"True. But you'd need eggs to make an omelet." The entire contents of his refrigerator had turned out to be a half quart of milk, a six-pack of beer with one bottle missing, and various foam and plastic take-out cartons from Bon Temps and the Crab Shack.

"I like étouffée. Especially since Sax uses his grandmother Adèle's recipe, which beats anything you'd get in New Orleans. Besides, I've kind of gotten out of the routine of eating proper meals at designated times."

That declaration brought her mind back to what Kara had told her over that sinfully rich, chocolate-coated cheesecake. Madeline couldn't remember everything she and Lucas had talked about last night, but she recalled that lunch discussion in stark detail.

"How about this?" he suggested. "We'll go into town to the Grateful Bread. Then we can discuss the plans I came up with over a proper breakfast."

She glanced down at the rumpled dress she'd had no choice but to put on after her shower. "I look a mess."

"You never look anything but gorgeous." He leaned down to refill her coffee mug. "But we can stop by the house for you to change."

Something suddenly occurred to her. "I need to pick up my car."

"That's already taken care of."

"Oh?"

He either didn't hear or chose to ignore the sudden chill in her voice. Madeline decided the latter. "Kara sent a deputy to drive it back to the farm this morning. You did, by the way, conveniently leave the key in the ignition. She told me to tell you that while Shelter Bay might not have big-city crime, she wouldn't advise doing that on a regular basis."

Leaving the keys in the ignition—something she'd never do—was, admittedly, yet more proof of how upset she'd been after her conversation with Maxime. But she still wasn't happy about Lucas once again leaping in to take charge.

"And you thought calling the sheriff to have my car driven home was your business why?"

"Because I figured you'd probably wake up with the mother of all headaches, and driving back on that curving coast road might not be the best thing for your stomach."

"You don't get carsick if you're the one driving," she muttered.

She took a drink of the coffee, which was rich and strong and actually very good for a guy who said opening an MRE was the height of his culinary talents. Which the Pop-Tarts and Cocoa Puffs seemed to confirm.

"Since we have to go back to the house, I might as well have breakfast there." Okay, maybe she wasn't feeling quite up to whipping up a gourmet brunch, but she could scramble an egg. Not that she'd have to. There were very few things her grandmother enjoyed more than feeding people.

"We could. But we're going to be spending a lot of time at the farm. Besides, I like the idea of taking you out."

"It wouldn't be a date," she warned.

He shrugged, reached into the box of cereal on the counter, grabbed a handful, and popped the chocolate cereal bits, which had to taste like brown Styrofoam, into his mouth. Which made her shudder. "You can call it whatever you like," he said agreeably after he'd crunched the cereal pieces down. "But I'm going to think of it as our first date."

"Our first date was the Fourth of July Crabfest." And she'd never forgotten it.

"On the beach. I'd already kissed you at the seawall the day we were eating taffy. But that night at Crabfest was the first time I really put everything into it."

While the rockets went off and the sky lit up with red, white, and blue fireworks. And when the crush she'd had on Lucas since that first summer, when she'd been a lonely, chubby, thirteen-year-old girl, had exploded into knee-weakening, heart-swelling love.

"And I put everything I had right back into it." Every atom in her body had come alive, and if he'd taken her there, on that quilt Sofia had sent along, right in front of the entire town, she wasn't sure she would've had the presence of mind to stop him.

He grinned at the memory. "You did indeed." Then sobered. "There were times when the RPGs were flying and the planes were bombing targets in the mountains, that the blasts, which looked kind of like fireworks, reminded me of that night. And, although I know it's going to sound like a cheesy line, I'd remember kissing you, and know that if I died at that moment, at least I'd have understood what fighter pilots experience when they do Gs in a dive. If that kiss had lasted another few seconds, I probably would've embarrassed myself from passing out."

It was an exaggeration. And, yes, maybe a little cheesy. But it worked.

"I felt the same way," she admitted. "Like I was on a roller coaster."

His grin widened, making her think that it was unfair that any man should have teeth that straight and that white. "Exactly. And since you've already told me you're an excellent negotiator—"

"When did I say that?"

"Last night. When you told me about getting all those bucks for Sofia from the Frenchman and the beer baroness."

"That was a great feeling." She remembered it now.

"And well it should be. So, how about we negotiate ourselves a compromise?"

"And your initial offer would be?"

"I take you to breakfast at the Grateful Bread. And promise not to kiss you silly in front of everyone there."

She had been craving one of their waffles since she got back to town. And they did need to talk about the kitchen. And the truth was, even though a headache was still lurking behind her eyes, she was having the most enjoyable time she'd had in a very long while.

She got up, put her mug in the dishwasher, and said, "You've got yourself a deal, sailor."

37

"Madeline spent the night at the cottage with Lucas," Sofia divulged as she, Adèle Douchett, and Zelda sat in the sun-room at the farm and knitted colorful blankets for Project Linus, a charity that provided "comfort" blankets to needy children. Adèle had gotten the two women involved, and Sofia had found it an enjoyable hobby to fill those hours when she couldn't work in the gardens.

"Well, there goes any hope I had for her and J. T. getting together once he gets out of the Marines," Adèle said with a slight sigh. "Though I'm happy for her. She and Lucas did seem so much in love that summer they were together, but"—she shrugged—"teenage romances don't always end up in marriage."

"Oh, I don't think she's ready to be talking about marriage," Sofia said. "Since she's still legally married."

"I read on the front page of that tabloid at the market this morning that her husband is marrying *that woman*," Zelda said, needles clicking rapidly.

"The woman from the video?" Adèle asked with raised brows.

"The very one. Mary Chapman had the tacky paper displayed front and center, in the rack next to the cash register, which I personally thought was in poor taste given that Sofia's granddaughter just happens to be the injured party."

"Did you know about this?" Adèle asked her longtime friend.

"No." The very idea of Maddy being treated so poorly had Sofia dropping a stitch. She was also going to have a little chat with Mary. Although the owner of Harbor Market liked to consider herself the town crier, there were limits.

"But he did call here yesterday wanting to talk to her. I told her about it when she called to tell me she was taking a drive along the coast after her lunch with Charity and Kara."

"Well, the coast road does conveniently lead to the Chaffee cottage," Adèle said.

"True enough."

Sofia didn't share what else Lucas had told her. That her granddaughter had indulged in a bit too much champagne and he hadn't wanted to let her drive home. He'd assured her that everything was fine, but she'd been worried ever since that the horrid husband had done something to further upset Maddy.

If he'd been calling to ask for a quickie divorce, surely that would have been good news. Because the idea of her granddaughter still harboring feelings for a man who obviously had none for her was disheartening.

"So," she said, belatedly wishing she hadn't brought it up, "speaking of teenage love and marriages, are Sax and Kara doing any wedding planning?"

"No." Adèle sighed. "Not that the entire family, including Cole and Kelli, haven't been nudging them toward marriage. They've come close a couple times, then Kara has called it off."

"Well," Zelda said, "if the girl isn't entirely sure, it's probably for the best."

"Oh, she's absolutely sure. It's just that, apparently, she made this promise to her mother that they'd have a double ceremony. But with all the troubles in the world, Faith hasn't been able to get away."

Kara's mother, Dr. Faith Blanchard, was a neurosurgeon who had, for several years, worked at Shelter Bay's hospital. Then she'd fallen in love with her late husband's former deputy, who, it had turned out, had been secretly in love with her for some time, and together they'd joined the Worldwide Medical Relief and had been traveling the world. From what Adèle had reported back, the two seemed determined to work in every dangerous hot spot on the planet.

Remembering the thrill of extreme travel, there were times Sofia envied Faith Blanchard and John O'Roarke. Though, if she were to be entirely honest, she'd have to admit that while the fantasy of adventure was appealing, these days she was much more content to be knitting and drinking tea from a pretty cup on a rainy day than slogging through some hostile Amazonian jungle.

"I'm sure Faith wouldn't hold her to such an agreement," Sofia said.

The two women had appeared to have had a rocky relationship during Kara's teens and when Kara had first returned home with her young son after her father's death, but by the time Faith and John had left Shelter Bay, it was obvious that mother and daughter had grown as close as Sofia had always felt with her own Gabriella. And with Madeline.

"I know she wouldn't. But I suspect it's because of their earlier problems that Kara's sticking to her guns." Adèle put down her needles long enough to select a lemon shortbread cookie from the plate of tea treats Sofia had baked this morning for their knitting group meeting.

"That's probably the case," Zelda agreed. "Since I was very young when I was taken from my family to be trained for the Bolshoi, I barely remember my own mother. Then my career kept me from having any children of my own."

"But you do have children in some way," Adèle pointed out. "Your students adore you."

"I enjoy teaching." Zelda, who was as reed thin as when she was a principal dancer for the famed Bolshoi Ballet, opted for a chocolate-dipped brownie. "But it's not the same."

"No," Sofia agreed. While motherhood wasn't for everyone, her heart ached a little at Zelda's loss. The former ballerina would have been a very good and loving parent. "But you've made up for that a bit with Haven House."

Although the reason for the shelter's existence was a serious one, Zelda smiled at that idea. "I care for them as if they're my own daughters. And I'm always so proud when one of my little birds flies the nest.

"And speaking of romances," she said, returning to their earlier topic, "I have reason to believe Ethan Concannon has feelings for one my girls."

"Really?" Sofia perked up at that idea. Although he never talked about it, he'd been widowed under horrible circumstances, and she'd always thought that although he was warm and sweet and friendly whenever they talked, an air of tragedy hung over him. "Which one?"

"Our newest resident. Which, of course, is a problem," Zelda admitted. "Because it's too soon for her to be interested in any man."

"Does she seem interested?"

"She put on cheek color after I told her he'd be delivering vegetables today. Which, by the way, is not a normal delivery day. But Ethan seemed taken with Phoebe when they first met. And here he is, back so soon."

"That's probably a good sign." Sofia refilled their cups with a bright, robust orange-cinnamon spiced tea she'd purposefully chosen for this gloomy day. "Wanting to pretty herself up a bit."

The young woman had looked pale and a little lost when she and Maddy had taken over the packaged dinners. And, of course, there'd been that shadow of a bruise that her makeup hadn't entirely been able to cover.

"True. I just hope she doesn't get hurt. But she's a grown woman. And she managed to get herself out of an abusive situation, so I have to accept that she's undoubtedly stronger than she looks."

"I suspect you're right," Sofia said. "As Eleanor Roosevelt said so famously, we women are like tea bags. We don't know our true strength until we're in hot water."

"And isn't that the truth," Adèle agreed.

All three women in the room, who'd each faced their own individual challenges over the years, were proof of that. As she saw the red pickup turn up the lane, Sofia decided that her own granddaughter was yet another example of the former first lady's axiom.

38

Although the Grateful Bread's name was a not-very-subtle riff on the '60s band, the restaurant itself was not as flamboyantly psychedelic as its name suggested. Granted, there was the required peace sign painted on the wall, a poster of multicolored dancing bears, two green and white street signs—one reading DEAD HEAD WAY and the other saying SHAKEDOWN STREET, the title of one of the Grateful Dead's albums—on the wall opposite the peace sign. The most popular place to sit had always been the booth at the back of the restaurant created from a cut-in-half VW bus. But the rest of the interior had been warmed up with wood counters, tables, and booths, their cushions covered not in floral patterns or tie-dye, but a subtle moss green.

And the aroma that greeted Madeline when she walked in the door with Lucas was not incense but the incredible bread that gave the restaurant its name.

"There's no lack of restaurants in New York, but I really missed this place," she said, sliding into one of the booths by the front window.

The bus was already taken by a group of teenagers whose Goth makeup and piercings seemed as out of place in bucolic Shelter Bay as the daisy-painted bus. That was one of the things she'd always enjoyed about the town. While it might look as if it had washed off a Grandma Moses or Charles Wysocki painting, like so many beach communities, its residents not only welcomed and embraced individuality, but they also encouraged it.

"There were more than a few times when I fantasized about the cinnamon buns from this place," Lucas said.

The waitress, wearing a floaty calf-length skirt, a tunic printed with butterflies, and a necklace of tiny seashells strung on silver wire, approached with a carafe of coffee.

"Well, look at you two," she said. "If this isn't just like old times."

"Look at *you*," Madeline told the woman, at whose birthday party she'd met Lucas fifteen years ago. "You're pregnant!"

Vanessa had already been dating Jimmy Roy Lovell, a newly arrived boy with blond hair like Brad Pitt's in *Legends of the Fall* and a Southern accent that had more than a few girls jealous of Van for nabbing him first.

"Number three." Vanessa Lovell, née Martindale, rubbed her baby bump with obvious pride.

"Oh, wow." Madeline felt a little ping that was too close to jealousy for comfort. "That's so cool." She hadn't made it home for either of the shower invitations she'd received. But she had sent a selection of organic onesies for both of Van's sons, including one with the saying *Party at My Crib*, which had made her laugh. "Boy or girl?"

Her friend grinned. "Girl. So you're finally going to be able to buy that pink stuff you complained about not being able to get last time."

"I didn't complain," she said, not quite honestly; all the ruffled dresses had been so tempting. "When are you due?"

"Not for another six weeks. But it seems like forever. I swear, I now know how a pregnant elephant feels. Coffee?" She held up the carafe, reminding Madeline that this wasn't a social visit.

"Thanks. I'd love some." The caffeine buzz was beginning to wear off. "I didn't realize you were working here." She wondered if Van and her husband needed the money.

The last time they'd talked—which was too long ago—he'd been working as a crab fisherman in the icy waters off the coast of Alaska. Maddy had watched *Deadliest Catch* once, mostly because she was curious what her best friend's husband did for a living, then found it too stressful to tune in a second time. She wondered at the time how Van could have handled the separation and the worry.

"I don't just work here." She poured the coffee first into Madeline's and then into Lucas' mug. "Jimmy and I own it."

"You're kidding!" When that sounded condescending, Madeline quickly backed up. "I mean, of course you're not, but I didn't realize you even wanted to own a restaurant."

"Well, I never had the lofty big-city dreams you did," she said. "Although Jimmy was making good enough money that I could stay home with our boys, I was going crazy with him being gone so many months of the year. So I started working here part-time. Then when Roberta and Roxie— You remember them?"

"Of course."

The women had arrived from San Francisco sometime in the seventies and opened the restaurant, which quickly became a popular breakfast location for tourists and locals alike. The Sea Mist, Bon Temps, and the Crab Shack might be the places to go for lunch or dinner, but the Grateful Bread had always claimed the breakfast crowd.

"Well, they took a trip up to Vancouver a few months ago. And came back married."

"Oh, that's sweet."

"Isn't it? They've been together forty years." Van sighed a bit at that, and when her eyes moistened, Madeline hoped it was hormones and not any hint of a problem with her marriage. "We had a big party here for them to celebrate. Then they shocked me by asking if I wanted to buy the place.

"Of course, with two kids and one on the way—I'd

just found out I was pregnant—that seemed like a crazy thing to do, but Jimmy and I talked it over, and since he'd decided that his Southern blood wasn't meant for Alaska, and they were willing to stay for a while to help teach us the ropes before retiring to Hawaii, we decided to go for it."

"I'm so impressed." Which was true. Especially since Madeline couldn't remember Van ever making anything more complicated than a grilled cheese sandwich.

Then again, Madeline considered, she'd always done the cooking whenever her friends slept over at the farm.

"Wait until you taste your breakfast before saying that," Van said, placing a hand-written menu down in front of them. "I have to admit that I'm a little nervous about cooking for a celebrity."

"We're old friends. And I'm not a celebrity." Madeline considered getting one of those little button recorders that fit into greeting cards, carrying it in her pocket and hitting PLAY whenever the subject came up so she wouldn't have to keep saying that.

"Well, you can deny it all you want, but you are to everyone here in Shelter Bay. And apparently the Cooking Network thinks so, too, because I just heard this morning that you're being offered a million dollars a season with a three-year deal."

Madeline almost spit out her coffee. "Where did you hear that?"

"From Mary at the market. She heard it on the radio."

"Well, I don't know what she was listening to, but it's totally false."

"Really?"

"I'd know. I'm between contracts and we haven't even discussed another season."

"Well." She smiled at that idea. "I guess that means that you're going to be sticking around a while. To help your gram with her restaurant."

"It's going to be a school, too." Madeline decided she might as well get the facts out there before the biggest gossip in town got the message wrong. Again.

"Oh, that's great. I'd love to take a class after the baby's born. I took a few culinary courses at the community college, to get up to speed, but to be perfectly honest, I learned more from Roberta and Roxie."

"That makes sense since they were better chefs that most instructors I've met." Which was true. Every so often one would apply to work at Maxime's, proving that sometimes, the old adage "Those who can, do. Those who can't, teach" was actually true.

"We're closed on Mondays," Van said. "Maybe you can drop by the house. Meet the kids and we can catch up."

"I'd like that."

"Me, too. And maybe I can learn some of your trade secrets." She laughed. "Just kidding. It'll be just girl talk. Like the old days. I promise.

"Well, I'd best let you two look over the menu while I get back to work," she said, as she noticed a couple across the room finishing their meal. "Take your time, we're not that big on turning over tables here. Oh, the eggs are organic. We get them from Blue Heron farm. I don't know if your grandmother told you," she said to Madeline, "but there's a new owner who's doing some fabulous things. I'd definitely suggest either his smoked salmon or the smoked bacon. Both are to die for."

She hustled off, and as Madeline watched her laughing and chatting with the couple, she said, "She seems happy."

"Yeah. She does. You two used to be really tight."

Although Lucas didn't ask, she could hear the unspoken question in his tone. "I know. The funny thing was, we wrote back and forth all the time while I was in Europe. It was after I got back to the States that things got crazy."

"Sounds as if you've had a lot on your plate the past few years."

"Haven't we all? That's still no excuse to lose track of friends."

"Van seems willing to pick up where she left off."

"Yes." Madeline studied the menu for a moment, and found even more enticing items than Rebecca and Roxie's waffles she'd been craving. "Do you think that's possible?"

"Why not? If both people want it. Are you and I different people than we were ten or fifteen years ago? Sure. Do we still have that connection? I'd say yes. At least on my part."

She took a drink of coffee and eyed him over the thick white rim of her mug. "Mine, too," she admitted. "But remember, that doesn't mean I'm going to marry you."

He flashed her his most encouraging grin. "Sure you are. You're just not ready to admit it yet. Meanwhile, we'll take things one step at a time. Like deciding what to eat."

39

Because he was enjoying her company, Lucas decided to table any discussion about the restaurant until after they'd eaten. So as they worked their way through tall glasses of fresh-squeezed orange juice, three fried eggs, perfectly fried strips of bacon, buttermilk biscuits, and sweet potato hash for him; along with organic, steel-cut oats topped with fresh berries, and an egg scramble with smoked salmon and goat cheese for her, he caught her up with what was happening with Sax and Kara, and Kara's mother, whom Madeline admitted had always intimidated her.

"I think everyone in town felt that way," he said. "The one time I went to her, after I hit my head on a rock surfing, she wasn't all that warm and fuzzy. But she was a damn good doctor. Remember Danny Sullivan?"

"It's hard to forget someone who was a dead ringer for Donny Osmond."

"Funny. That's what all the girls used to say. I never saw it, but maybe I was just jealous."

"That's hard to believe, since you never seemed to have any problems getting girls."

"Since we're getting along so well, I'm not going there," he said. "Anyway, Danny got shot in the head and Kara's mom operated on his brain and saved his life. According to Sax, it was touch and go for a while."

"That's horrible. What's he doing now?"

"Oh, he's back to teaching. And just married a nurse who has a kid from a previous marriage. They've got another on the way."

"Seems to be a lot of that going on," Maddy murmured, glancing over at Van, who was seating what appeared to be a group of tourists at a four-top next to the window, which looked out at the seawall and the harbor beyond.

"Cole married Kelli. They've been working on getting pregnant, which isn't proving as easy as they were afraid it would be back when they were in high school and had that scare. But personally, from what Sax said and the way Cole described it, I think they might be trying too hard."

"I've heard that stress can make a difference. One of the producers on my show went through what sounded like hormone hell trying all sorts of expensive, painful, and unsuccessful medical methods before she and her husband finally gave up and adopted. Two months after they brought their daughter home from China, she got pregnant. The old-fashioned way."

"Lucky them. How about you?" he asked. "You ever think of having kids?"

He could tell by the way her hand, which had been reaching for a piece of the whole-wheat toast, froze above the plate that she hadn't been expecting the question. And the fact that she didn't just answer with a yes or no had him suspecting the topic might not be the best one for a first date. Or even an outing she refused to consider a date.

"Yes." She picked up the quartered toast and took a bite. "I have," she said. "Although there's this feeling in the culinary world that women have to sacrifice their lives to the kitchen god, to give up any idea of a family if they want to be successful, that's not my ultimate goal. I've put off starting a family because I wouldn't want my children raised by a nanny or a housekeeper, and so far I haven't figured out how to be in two places at the same time."

"Having a housekeeper as a mother model isn't the

worst thing in the world," Lucas volunteered. "After my mom left, ours filled in the best she could while Dad was spending so much time working all over the world."

"But it's not the same as having two parents who are there to do homework or talk about everyone's day over dinner," she said.

"No," he agreed. "It's not."

"I've given it a lot of thought and talked with a lot of other women chefs. Some have chosen to concentrate on their careers. Some went the nanny route. Others have stay-at-home husbands."

"I work from home."

She frowned. Looked down into her coffee as if she was searching for some answer in the black depths. "You're pushing again," she said finally.

"No. I was just pointing out a fact."

She shook her head, but he thought he saw a hint of a smile teasing at the corner of her luscious lips.

"I spent my first thirteen years in my parent's restaurant, but I know women who've tried taking their children to work and found it scary because kitchens can, on a good day, be a madhouse. I know others who've given up restaurant work for a while to teach. Which they say keeps their passion for cooking alive."

He wondered if she might consider teaching at Sofia's school, but decided that was definitely a decision she was going to have to make by herself.

"I think what I'd want to do, in a perfect world, if I had my own place, would be to separate family and work," she said slowly. She was pushing her scrambled eggs around on the flowered plate. "Which would mean hiring a young sous chef I could trust to take over for me during the times I wasn't there."

She took a bite of smoked salmon and seemed to be thinking it out in more depth. "I wouldn't want to be gone all the time, like my husband is from his restaurants, but I suppose I could learn to give up some control. To the right person."

He thought it was odd that she specifically wanted a young chef.

"I'm approaching thirty," she told him when he asked her about it. "Which is actually getting up there in this business. Culinary life is like dog years. But I have hopes that things will change because they can't keep going the way they are or we're going to have more and more people either burning out or dropping out."

She sighed. "More and more chefs are coming into culinary schools from other occupations, which I partly blame on all the TV shows, although I've admittedly contributed to the problem. Doctors, lawyers, cops, Wall Street traders . . . They're all making up a huge percentage of wannabe chefs. Did you know there are one hundred and fifty hot new chefs every year?"

"I don't think I could name one," he admitted. "Except maybe that Puck guy, because I used to buy his frozen pizzas at the grocery store whenever I was back for training in San Diego. Oh, and your soon-to-be-ex-husband, but that's mostly because of the video."

Great move, Chaffee. "Excuse me while I ask Van for a butcher knife," he said. "To cut out my tongue."

She shrugged. "Don't worry about it. I'm beginning to accept that it really doesn't have anything to do with me. . . . And yes, Wolfgang Puck also contributed to the celebrity culture everyone seems to get caught in. You only know two names. With very few exceptions, most people couldn't name one of each year's stars.

"Which is why no one should get into this business just to get on television or see their name in lights or have a cookware line named after them."

"I saw the commercial for your pans on your show."

"I needed the money. Simple as that," she said. "I don't

think I'm going to be renewing because it involves too much travel, and it's not what I got into the business for."

She shook her head. "I'm sorry. I tend to get carried away. As you can see, I'm a lot more passionate about cooking than I am the business stuff."

"Never complain about being passionate. It was one of the things that attracted me to you. That and your eyes. Which are remarkable."

"When they're not looking like road maps, you mean."

"So you're human. Deal with it."

"Is that tough love?"

"Yeah. I guess so."

"Well, thank you. I much prefer it to people treading on eggshells around me. And, to get back to your original question, yes, although I realize it's going to take a lot of juggling, I do want a child. I'd settle for one. But having been an only myself, I'd prefer at least two."

Bingo. "That's pretty much the same thing I was thinking. I wasn't an only child all my life. But for most of it. And I've always regretted losing my sister. Though I suppose it kept me from getting sent to juvie for punching out any guy who might someday have made her cry."

"Well, then." She took another bite of toast. "You're fortunate *I* didn't have a big brother."

"Sweetheart, you've no idea how many times I've told myself that over the years."

Van, who'd left them to their conversation, returning only to refill their coffee cups and make sure they didn't need anything, arrived at the table with the check.

"No hurry," she said again. "How were your meals?"

"Fantastic," Maddy said.

"Roberta and Roxie couldn't have done any better," Lucas said. "I like the way you've added the sweet potato hash instead of just the plain white potato ones."

"That was Jimmy's idea. It was his mama's recipe while

he was growing up in South Carolina." She laughed. "You know what they say: You can take the boy out of the South, but you can't take the South out of the boy."

"I took a bite of Lucas' hash," Maddy said. "It was fantastic. The cumin was a nice surprise, and the cayenne and paprika added just the right amount of heat."

Pleased color bloomed in Van's cheeks. "I'll have to tell him you said that. It'll make his day."

"It's true." Watching Maddy, which was easily becoming his favorite thing to do, Lucas could practically see the lightbulb flashing on over her head. "Do you think he'd be willing to teach it at Sofia's school?"

"Willing?" Van laughed her surprise. "I'd like to see you try to keep him away. He'd be so honored."

"We wouldn't be able to pay much," she warned. Lucas found the *we* an interesting choice of words. Although, as if perhaps though she might not realize it yet herself, she was already considering staying here in Shelter Bay.

"But"—she lowered her voice—"if you promise not to tell Mary, there's a chance that the Cooking Network might be willing to put the school on the air. And if so, then we could negotiate. Especially if he has any more of those Southern breakfasts up his sleeve."

"Oh. My. God." This time the heat coloring her cheeks had her fanning her face. "I swear, he'd just die."

"It's just an idea," Maddy warned.

"Oh, I've never been one to count chickens," Van assured her. "But it sure is a fun thing to think about. Not so much for the money, but the thought of Jimmy bein' on TV. I've always thought he was handsome enough to be on TV. The first time I saw him, I thought he looked just like Brad Pitt."

She sighed as she picked up the AmEx card Lucas had put down. "And I still think so, though I'm sure no Angelina Jolie."

"He got lucky with you," Lucas said. "And obviously is smart enough to realize it."

"You always were a sweet-talker, Lucas Chaffee," she said with a sassy toss of her chestnut hair. "Now you just need to turn that talent to keeping Maddy here in Shelter Bay, where she belongs. We could always use another restaurant, and since we don't serve dinner, so we can spend evenings home with the kids, we wouldn't have to worry about competition."

"That's sweet," Maddy said, as they watched her head back to the cash register with more of a spring in her step. "That she's still so crazy about her husband."

"I think that's the way it's supposed to be. What did you think of her idea?"

"The one about me staying here?"

"Yeah." He studied her, wondering when she'd gotten so good at hiding her thoughts. Perhaps, he considered, when she'd realized that her marriage wasn't turning out to be all she'd hoped. "I guess this place would be a big letdown after New York."

"Not a letdown. Just different. There are a lot of chefs who've decided to work outside cities. Lee Skawinski's Cinque Terre, where he specializes in small-town Italian cooking, was voted one of the top-ten best farm-to-table restaurants in America. It's in Portland. Maine, not Oregon," she clarified. "And Lisa Nakamura, who was chef de cuisine at a restaurant *National Geographic* called the number-one restaurant destination in the world, opened up a restaurant on Orcas Island, in Puget Sound, where she's blending classic French technique with simple, Pacific Northwest flavors and ingredients.

"It's a fallacy that people have to live in big urban areas to get good food. If nothing else, it makes sustainable cooking much easier if you go where the food actually is. . . .

"What?" she asked, when she stopped to take a breath and noticed he was grinning at her. "You're laughing at me."

"No. I'm just enjoying your enthusiasm. And how sexy you are when you talk about food."

Pleasure lit her eyes. "Food is sexy," she said. "Well, except maybe Pop-Tarts."

Displaying less-than-ideal timing, Vanessa chose that moment to arrive back with his credit card. Lucas signed the check, adding a hefty tip, and he and Maddy both agreed that they'd be returning soon. If nothing else, the food really was great, and it gave him an alternative to Cajun and the seafood at the Crab Shack.

"Maybe you should cook me dinner one of these nights," he suggested once they were alone again. "Educate my palate. Teach me all about the sex of food."

"There's this quirky Japanese movie, *Tampopo*, about a mysterious truck driver coming to town and helping a widow rescue her noodle restaurant, which has a gangster as a secondary character. It's mostly only known among chefs and foodies for its soft-core food porn."

Her seductive smile reminded him that food had been used as temptation ever since Eve had polished up that shiny red apple. "If you ever saw it, you'd never look at an egg the same way again."

"Now you realize I'm going to have to go looking for it." He reached across the table, took her hand, and pressed his mouth to the center of her palm, then folded her fingers over the flesh he'd warmed. "Our second date could be dinner and a movie."

She laughed, as he'd meant her to, even though, holding her wrist as he was, he felt her pulse pick up.

"I'll think about it."

She stood up. Since she'd insisted on taking the time to stop by the house long enough for her to shower and change, she was wearing a pair of light blue jeans and a sunshine yellow pullover sweater. Although he'd really liked that sexy dress, Lucas found her just as appealing in the casual clothes.

"While you're at it, think about this," he suggested.

As they left the restaurant, his hand on her back, he bent

down and murmured just a few of the things he'd spent a sleepless night imagining doing to her. With her.

"Sorry," she said. Although she'd kept her tone brisk and matter-of-fact, he knew his suggestions had gotten to her by the color that had risen in her cheeks. "I'm busy to-night. It's Gram's night to host her book club. She roped me into joining the group."

"Who said anything about night? As it happens, I'm free this afternoon."

"No, you're not." She moved away from him as they reached the truck, but he beat her to the door. "You're working on Gram's restaurant."

"You're the boss."

"Yes." She smiled at that idea. "It appears I am."

She smelled like spring. And temptation.

A temptation he found impossible to resist.

He cupped her chin in his fingers. Moved closer.

"Lucas," she warned.

He lowered his head. "Just one minute."

Then leaned down.

And did what he'd been wanting to do since he stood in the doorway that morning, watching her sleep, forcing him-self to resist the urge to join her in his bed.

40

His mouth was softer than it had been when she'd attacked him after killing off nearly an entire bottle of champagne. Rather than plundering, as they had in her too-hot dreams last night, his lips gently touched hers. Lightly, tantalizingly, retreating before she could respond. Or reject.

Then, when she didn't reject, he took the kiss deeper, savoring, enticing.

Madeline had never been one for public displays of affection. She found them embarrassing to watch, and even more so to participate in.

But as she clung to his shoulders, the reality of being parked in front of the restaurant faded, time gradually ebbed, and she imagined the asphalt beneath her feet giving way, like sands under a retreating tide.

When her mouth opened in a soft sigh of acceptance and wonder, Lucas slipped his tongue between her lips, kissing her with the slow and easy confidence of a man who'd kissed more women than he could count.

Don't think about that. Not now.

His lips continued to linger, tasting at their leisure in a lengthy exploration that had her trapped in misty layers of sensation.

When she linked her fingers behind his tanned neck, arched against him, and clung, he murmured something against her mouth—it could have been her name, a curse, or a prayer—then pulled her even closer, allowing her to feel his heart beat against hers.

His teeth nipped at her lower lip. On a throaty moan, she poured herself into a kiss that went on and on, going deeper. Darker.

His wonderfully wicked hands grabbed her hips, pressing her back against the truck as he moved between her thighs. He was rock hard. Solid. And huge.

And then he was gone.

He'd dropped his hands and pulled away.

"Damn." He was winded, his chest heaving as if he'd just run a marathon. "I apologize." He sucked in a breath. "I lost control."

Madeline drew in her gulp of air and licked her bottom lip. "You weren't the only one."

"Yeah, but I *never* lose control. Not ever."

"Well, that makes two of us. So it appears you're human, too. Deal with it." She threw his own words back at him.

"Bull's-eye," he said. He gave her a long look that made her heart—which had just started settling back down—stutter. "So, what do you want to do about it?"

"Forget it happened?"

"Not a chance. We could go to the cottage. I'll take you up on that rain check."

She couldn't remember any promise of a rain check. Then again, much of that champagne-fueled night was foggy. Madeline didn't even want to consider how many brain cells that pricey bubbly had killed.

"It's not raining."

"Not now." He winked, then opened the door, giving her a boost up into the high seat. "But this is the Oregon coast. I figure I won't have to wait that long."

She bucked her seat belt. "Arrogant."

He grinned, his momentary annoyance about having lost control disintegrating like morning fog. "Patient."

*   *   *

An idea had sparked while Madeline had been talking with Van about having Jimmy teach the students at the new school how to cook his sweet potato hash. An idea that the more she thought about it, the more she thought it would not only work, but it would also help fund the school and restaurant, as well as spreading her message of sustainable, healthy, good-tasting food.

And keep everyone, including herself, happy. But she needed to come up with a more concrete plan. Then make a few phone calls.

"How long," she asked Lucas as they drove back to the farmhouse, "will it take build the addition?"

"That depends on how much you want done," he said. "Obviously longer than just taking a sledgehammer, gutting Sofia's kitchen, and putting in new appliances, countertops, cabinets, and floor, like we would if it were a straightforward residential remodel. The house has good bones."

"It does," she agreed. Like so many of the homes in Shelter Bay, it had been built to last.

"If everything falls into place, we could probably get it done in four months. If we have permit or weather delays, etcetera, six months."

"That's doable. Especially since the garden goes into fall and winter root vegetables that can be used in the recipes."

"You've given this some thought."

"I've fantasized having my own restaurant since I was a little girl."

"I remember you talking about that. Which you sort of have done. Since the Frenchman's built a bunch of them."

"Those are his restaurants. Not mine."

Yet she'd funded them. Could she have been any more foolish? Somehow she'd fallen into that male chef/female chef trap. The one that often had women in a kitchen prepping vegetables while the guys were on the hot line sautéing the salmon. One of the things that irked her most about her chosen profession was how many male chefs expected to be king. And how many women, such as she'd done, surrendered power so easily.

"And every single one of those restaurants reinforced my belief that I wanted something far more simple," she said.

She'd always found the indoor waterfalls in Miami over the top. And when one of Maxime's top competitors in Las Vegas had his designer create a four-story-high wall of all the wine bottles, with "wine angels" lifted on high wires for patrons to watch as they retrieved those bottles for their meals, Maxime had gone all out, creating a replica of the Palace of Versailles's Hall of Mirrors. She'd tried to suggest that all those glass and gilt, enormous chandeliers, and frescos painted on the massive domed ceiling were the height of ostentation, and it wasn't as if her husband had the treasury that had been available to France's Sun King. Even in the current culinary Gomorrah Vegas had become, it distracted from his food.

Despite what that complaining diner in the taxi line had told her about those dry scallops at his Miami restaurant, when he actually lowered himself to prepare a meal himself, his food was admittedly exquisite.

"Then that's what you should do," Lucas said. "Create your vision. Your way. You tell me what you want, and somehow we'll make it happen."

We. How strange to think of the two of them being a team. Especially factoring in their past. But it seemed that's what they were becoming. And, oddly, it was feeling more and more right.

"There was a time when I probably would've gone with something more Italian themed, in an attempt to replicate my parents' restaurant," she confessed.

"Stone walls, murals on the wall, grapevines on trellises."

She smiled at the memory. "It worked in its place," she said. "But move it to Shelter Bay, and it could come off looking like Italy at Epcot."

"Dad accidentally took all the fun out of Disneyland for me forever by pointing out that Walt Disney ruined Ludwig the Second's crazy operatic castle at Neuschwanstein by turning it into Sleeping Beauty's castle. One thing I learned growing up with him was that all good architecture belongs to its place. That buildings are always part of a context.

"The same way your parents' restaurant undoubtedly was a part of the fabric of Umbria, the iron grill work of New Orleans, which is perfect for there, would look foolish in New England because if you situate a building in different surroundings, its character changes.

"Another example, although they're both on oceans, are those stark white Mediterranean houses from your father's native Greek Islands. Originally whitewashed to reflect the heat of the sun, they'd stick out like sore thumbs here in the cloudy Pacific Northwest.

"Exactly." Madeline was pleased he so quickly understood something that Maxime either could not or, more likely, would not grasp. She could also tell that while Lucas might not have wanted to follow his father into architecture, he was as passionate about what he'd chosen as a second career as she was about her own.

"What I want is to accentuate the farm-to-table profile of the restaurant," she said. "To make diners part of the experience by highlighting the agricultural ambience of the place."

"That was always part of the draw for me. Growing up in the city, just visiting a farm was cool. Eating in a farmhouse kitchen made everything taste better. Not that your grandmother isn't a great cook. But the country ambience in her kitchen added as much as the fresh herbs and spices she used in the food."

"I know. It's like I can't think of Italy without thinking of eating spaghetti in my mother's kitchen."

"I'm glad you brought that up," Lucas said. "Because I've been thinking that going with recycled stuff wouldn't just be cheaper, but it works with your eco-green theme of sustainable food."

"Okay." She reached across the console and squeezed his thigh. Not in a sexual way, but because he had her so excited about the prospect. "Although, quite honestly, I wouldn't have believed it possible, we're totally on the same page and you now have me officially excited. I really do want to discuss this with you before we talk with your dad's former partner, but if you don't mind, I need a few hours to make some business calls and talk with my agent. I have a seed of an idea on how to make the cooking school irresistible to the Cooking Network executives."

"No problem," he said as he pulled up in front of the farmhouse. "As it turns out, the stockbroker-turned–wood guy is coming to town today and wanted to walk through the cannery with me this afternoon, anyway."

"Terrific. Maybe we can talk with him about reclaimed wood while he's in town. How about I give you a call when I'm done and we can meet there?"

"Works for me."

Her smile lit up her face as she grabbed his hair and pulled him toward her.

It was a damn-the-torpedoes, full-steam-ahead kiss that jolted through him like a cruise missile. He heard the roar. It could've been gunfire or thunder or the Pacific surf in full tsunami mode.

Whatever, it had him grabbing to hold her there, but then she'd pulled out of his reach and was out the car door before his brain caught up with the rest of him.

"I guess that means I'm forgiven?"

She gave a half laugh. "Let's just say I'm working on it." And when he was considering following her up to that porch and returning the favor by kissing her blind and deaf, she shut the car door. "And," she said through the open passenger's window, "you just happen to be getting a lot closer to redemption."

41

Although she'd been raised Methodist, Phoebe wasn't sure she believed in God or the concepts of heaven and hell anymore. But one thing she was certain of: If there actually was a heaven, it would look like Blue Heron farm.

She drew in a breath at the rolling acres of meadows, plowed brown fields, and green pastures nestled among willow trees and ponds.

"Oh," she breathed, as Ethan Concannon's truck drove through the paradise. "It's not at all what I was picturing." As much as she'd loved growing up in Arizona mountain country, her family ranch had looked nothing like this.

"I like it," he said. "It's peaceful, after . . ."

His voice dropped off. She was afraid to ask, but since he'd already mentioned being a widower, she decided that it wouldn't really be prying. "After your wife died?"

"No. The ironic thing is, she was still alive when we put the money down on it. But she and our little boy, Max, were killed in a car accident before we could get moved up here from Oregon. Max was a year old when I got home from Down Range. I talked to him on the computer from Afghanistan, but it wasn't the same thing. He'd just begun to feel comfortable around me, when a guy in an SUV took a curve too fast and hit them head-on."

"Oh." Tears burned at the back of her lids. She pressed

her hand against her stomach, unable to imagine the pain he must have suffered. "That's terrible. I'm so sorry."

"So was I. I'd been gone a lot of our marriage." His voice was rough, as if he didn't use it a lot. "Two deployments in Iraq, then two more in Afghanistan. Sometimes I think it's amazing she managed to get pregnant in the first place, since we spent so many years apart, but I guess we made up for lost time whenever I was home."

He flushed a bit at that and gave her a sideways glance. "Sorry. That was definitely too much information."

"Maybe," she allowed. "But it's nice that you were able to keep your marriage together during what must have been difficult times."

"They were hell. I came home pretty messed up, but we'd both grown up on farms. Me in Oregon; Mia—that was my wife's name—in Idaho. So, since farming was what I knew, and working for my dad and brothers definitely wasn't good for family harmony, and since I wasn't the same kid who'd joined the Marines after I graduated with a degree in agricultural sciences from Oregon State, getting our own place seemed the sensible thing to do. . . . My parents weren't real happy about me enlisting."

"They probably worried about you getting wounded. Or even killed."

"I think that was part of it. Mom cried when I told her. Dad was mostly pissed off because I was the first Concannon in the family to go to college, which, although he never was one for handing out compliments, apparently he considered it a really big deal. So he hated the idea of me throwing my life away."

"I can understand that."

Hadn't her own parents felt much the same way? They'd also tried to coax her into going back to school after her marriage. But in the beginning, she thought Peter's urging against the idea was because he wanted to be able to spend more time with her. It wasn't until much later that she realized he wanted to keep her from meeting anyone else.

"So could I," he said. "But it was just something I wanted to do. Plus, my older brother made it clear that he resented me even getting a degree. So, when I went home after I got out of the military, taking with me the new environmental ideas I'd learned about farming in school, we mixed about as well as gasoline and a flame thrower."

She gave him a sideways glance and wondered if she'd made a mistake coming out to this remote farm with a man she didn't even know. Even if Sofia had vouched for him.

"You don't seem like a man who'd lose his temper."

"I'm not. As a rule. Unless someone hurts a child or a woman. Or," he added, "an animal. Which I realize probably sounds ironic, coming from someone who raises livestock for market—"

"I grew up on a ranch," she reminded him.

"Well, then, you know slaughter's never pretty. Even when it's done humanely. But I will say that it's the only bad day any of Blue Heron's animals will ever have."

"What do you raise?"

"Vegetables, which you already know. As for livestock, I've settled on cattle, hogs, and chickens. The chickens as much for the eggs as for eating.

"I was really leaning toward sheep, but as much as Mia liked the idea of learning to weave from their wool, and we weren't going to keep them penned, she couldn't get past the idea of baby lambs gamboling over the hillsides. So, although there's a strong market for lamb, I ditched that plan."

And hadn't picked it back up again, even though his wife was no longer around to resist.

"Mia was a lucky woman," she said.

"I was the lucky one," he said simply as he pulled up in front of a grassy pasture. "These are our free-rangers." He pointed out the flocks of brown birds. "I had to go to France for a breed that can take cool nights and warm days. They're slower growing—twelve weeks instead of five or six—but they're strong enough to live outdoors, the way chickens are meant to. They eat grass—we move them around so they'll always have fresh pastureland. They have perches to sleep on at night, and dust to bathe in.

"Not only do they taste a lot better than ones who are fed chicken chow, but all that running around gives them larger thighs, which make for really good eating and have gotten more and more popular with home and professional cooks. They're also more expensive, so we also have more ordinary free-range chickens."

He pointed in the distance, where she saw a row of tidy henhouses. "They're encouraged to peck for their own food outside, which is why we leave the doors open, unlike a lot of so-called organic farms that only open a tiny window an hour a day. But if they want to go inside and roost, especially for nesting, that works, too. They're vegetarian fed from feed that's strictly organic. The hogs, too."

"That's why you pick up whatever leftover parts of the vegetables we don't use," she said.

"Yep. The ultimate farm to table, then back to the farm, then back to the table as bacon." He rocked back on his heels in obvious satisfaction with what he'd created. Which was so different from Peter, who'd certainly enjoyed the wealth and privilege his family's business provided but had never seemed interested in contributing that much to its growth.

"You must be really proud," she said.

"The farm's not where I'd like it to be yet, but more and more the monthly bottom line is showing positive numbers. I've gotten together with some other local organic farmers and we've formed a cooperative. We even have a guy in Skohomish, Washington, who makes artist paintbrushes. He was getting all his hog bristles from China, but the quality's gone down, so we've established a market for those, too."

"You've really thought this through."

"Yeah, I have. My next project is to build an anaerobic digester that'll produce methane and generate enough electricity to run the entire farm from manure and other waste projects. I made the plans for it while I was in school. I always figured I'd build something to leave to my son and future generations."

"I don't want to diminish your loss in any way," she said carefully, not because she worried about angering him, but because she didn't want to add to his personal pain. "But you're still a young man."

"True." He rubbed his jaw as he looked out over the rolling green meadows and fertile fields and the home he'd built for the family who'd been so cruelly taken from him. "I've been pouring all my energies into this place, but"—he shrugged—"my mom keeps telling me that there's more to life than work."

"Well"—despite the seriousness of the topic, Phoebe smiled a bit—"you know what they say about mothers always knowing best."

"I've heard that theory." He looked down at her. "Do you think it's true? That a person can have more than one soul mate in a single lifetime?"

"I don't know," she answered honestly. Then thought about his situation. "But I do believe in that butterfly effect—that the smallest thing can change the universe. So it only seems natural that our lives are always in flux."

And didn't she know a great deal about that lately?

"And that sometimes, because of something seemingly unrelated, good things really can happen to good people."

And if there was ever any man who deserved something good in his life, it was Ethan Concannon.

Their gazes met. And held.

He had lovely eyes. The color of a clear blue mountain lake. But warmer.

"Maybe," he suggested slowly, thoughtfully, "something good is already happening. To both of us."

To hear her own secret thoughts stated aloud caused confused emotions to swell up in her, so unsettling and unbearably strong, all she could do was stare up at him.

Then he broke the spell.

"Cows need milking," he said, returning the conversation back to mundane farm talk. "We sell the milk to Clover Hill Farm, which uses it to make cheeses that literally melt in your mouth." He laced his long, dark fingers with hers and began walking back toward the truck. "Guess you never milked a cow growing up on a beef ranch."

"You'd guess wrong."

As relaxed as she was, being outside with the scent of freshly mown grass and bees buzzing over the clover, Phoebe was becoming more comfortable talking back to him. One thing living in a dangerous marriage had taught her was to sense moods. And intentions. Ethan Concannon wasn't the type of man who'd ever hit a woman.

"Our Herefords usually only gave enough for their calves," she said. "But the Angus gave great milk with a deliciously high butterfat."

"Well, then," he said, "although we're automated here, what would you say to a friendly milking competition?"

He was flirting with her. And although even a week ago, that would've had her trembling in her new sneakers, Phoebe discovered she was actually enjoying it. Enough that although she'd never developed any skills herself, she dared test him.

She flexed the fingers of the hand he wasn't still holding. "I'd say you'd better have your game on, Farmer Boy."

42

"I have a couple of problems," Kara said as she came out onto the porch with a plate of nachos, a glass of iced tea, and a Corona on an enameled tray. She'd even put the wedge of lime in the neck of the bottle.

"One is that you're wearing too many clothes," Sax said, taking the beer she held out to him.

"Ha ha." She looked down at the oversized sweatshirt, jeans, and thick wool striped socks that reminded him of a colorful caterpillar. "I think we've got a storm coming in. The temperature's dropped a good ten degrees in the last hour."

"Spring on the Oregon coast," he said. "If you don't like the weather, just wait ten minutes."

"That's pretty much the weather all year round."

She sat down beside him and pulled a chip from the mountain of nachos. That was one of the many things Sax really liked about Kara. Unlike a lot of women he'd dated over the years, she ate like a real person and not an anorexic rabbit.

"So," he said, squeezing the lime into the bottle. "Are these professional or personal problems?"

"A little bit of both." She bit into the cheese-drenched chip and looked out over the water, which was growing steelier by the minute. She was probably right about the storm. "There's one that isn't really a problem yet. But it could be. You know how Shelter Bay is a sister city to that town in Ireland?"

"Sure. Castlelough. We were in middle school when they linked up and all the boys had to learn to sing 'Danny Boy' for the Castlelough mayor's visit."

"I'd forgotten that part."

"Probably because your voice wasn't changing. That song's damn tough to sing on a good day. When you're trying to keep from croaking it, the torture tends to stick in your mind."

"Poor baby." She patted his cheek. "Well, Castlelough just happens to be the hometown of Mary Joyce."

"The movie star?"

"Yeah." She took another bite of chip. "And screenwriter. Apparently, although she based those selkie movies of hers mostly on her hometown, she also sprinkled in bits of this one. Like our whales—and lighthouse."

"She's been here?"

"For a visit with her family when she was a teenager. Her sister's husband is Quinn Gallagher."

"The horror novelist?"

"That would be him. And it's reassuring to know that I'm not the only one not up on my celebrity news. The woman from the studio acted as if I've been living in a cave somewhere the past three years not to have known that."

"You've been a bit busy."

"True. But not so busy that I haven't heard about those crazy fans who show up at her movie openings. Which is why I'm less than thrilled the studio's thinking of holding the premiere here."

"Here?" Sax scooped up a chip. "In Shelter Bay?"

"That's what they're considering. I told them that we don't have nearly the police force to handle security for a huge crowd, and they assured me the fans wouldn't prove a problem, because if they do decide to open here in Shelter

Bay, they're not going to release the location until the day of the premiere."

"Like no one's going to leak it?"

"That's what I said." She sighed. "However, since nothing's been settled, I'll jump off that bridge when I come to it.

"Meanwhile, I have another problem that's more personal. Which is why it's got to stay just between us."

"You've got it."

"There's a new resident at Haven House."

"And?"

"And I ran into her the other day at Take the Cake. She was a mess."

"Makes sense, since that place isn't exactly a day spa."

"True. But here's the thing. It makes sense she'd be nervous, because any woman Zelda takes in has suffered abuse. But I got the feeling what was really freaking her out was my uniform."

The funny thing was, most women would look more masculine in the stiff khaki with the shiny badge and heavy black leather gun belt. Sax had always found the contrast between the uniform and the hot female wearing it sexy. Plus, there was always something to be said for a woman who carried her own handcuffs. Especially when that woman just happened to be living with you.

"Maybe the guy she's running away from is a cop."

"I thought of that. I asked Zelda for any information that might give me a heads-up, in case it was a cop who might come looking for her, but except for saying 'No, it's not,' she was closemouthed."

"No surprise there."

He put his arm around her shoulder as they sat there, as was their custom whenever they both had free time together. Trey was having dinner at Sax's parents'. He and Bernard, Sax's grandfather, had a checkers tournament going. Although the score seesawed back and forth from week to week, when they'd dropped him off tonight, Trey was claiming a two-game lead.

"And I guess, since it'd be hard to bring out the bright lights and rubber hoses to interrogate a seventy-year-old former Russian ballet dancer, who probably weighs ninety pounds soaking wet, you're just going to let her remain an uncooperative witness and keep your eyes open."

"I know you think I'm being an overly suspicious cop—"

"No. Correction: I *know* that you take that protect-and-serve thing as seriously as a heart attack. And that you want to make sure you're ready if she's in more than the usual problematic abused-woman situation."

"You've always known me so well."

Sax laughed. "*Chère*, any man who'd claim to know a woman well is either a liar or a fool. I'm not the first and would prefer not to think of myself as the second. However, living with a cop has taught me that the job's a lot like being a SEAL. And that a failure to plan is a plan for failure."

"That's precisely what I plan to do." She took a sip of tea. "Plan for the worst and hope for the best. I was also hoping you'd let me know if anyone new comes into Bon Temps looking for a woman."

"You bet I will."

"There's something else."

"Hmmm?" He had begun nibbling on her neck. Sax figured they had a good two hours to themselves and had every intention of making the most of them.

"This."

She dug into the pocket of her sweats and pulled out the white plastic strip and held it out to him. It took Sax a minute to recognize what it was. Another moment to focus on the blue plus sign.

"We're pregnant?" Hot damn. Could his life get any better?

"I have an appointment tomorrow, but if you can believe a ninety-nine-point-nine-percent correct test rate, I'd say you're going to be a father."

"I already am." Trey, the child Kara had had with his old high school buddy, couldn't be more his son if he'd carried Sax's blood in his veins. "But wow." He just stared at the strip. Then looked up at this woman he'd loved for far more years than she'd ever known. "I realize I'm going to risk sounding chauvinistic here—"

"Well, there would be a first." Her grin belied her teasing words.

"But this is, hands down, the best present anyone's ever given me."

Her eyes misted up. That was one of the things that Sax loved about her. From the lace she wore beneath her sweats and khakis to her love of sappy movies, and how easily emotional she was, despite her law-and-order mentality, his sexy sheriff was a constantly intriguing study in contrasts.

"You've no idea how much I wanted to run to Bon Temps and tell you as soon as I found out."

"I would've closed the doors and come home to celebrate." He frowned as a thought occurred to him. "I guess we probably better not—"

"Stop right there." She covered his mouth with her fingertip. "Do you have any idea how many hormones are running amok through my body right now? The only reason I didn't come running into Bon Temps to announce it right away was that I'd probably have jumped you right on the spot and have forced poor Kyle to arrest us for public indecency."

Kyle was one of her deputies. He'd been green as spring grass when he'd started on the force, but had, she'd reported, been growing into a good cop.

"Plus—" She leaned forward and touched her mouth to his. Teasing. Tempting. Tantalizing. "I blew an entire week's pay at Oh So Fancy after lunch today. Do you have any idea what I'm wearing beneath this world's unsexiest outfit?"

"Not a clue." But since he'd never yet been disappointed, Sax was hopeful. "I don't suppose you'd give me a hint."

She laughed. Gave him a long deep kiss. "Nope." Then picked up her tea glass. "It's for me to know." She was half-way to the porch door when she tossed him a sexy glance over her shoulder. "And you to find out."

"A treasure hunt," he said, getting up and following her into the house. "My second-favorite thing."

"What's your favorite thing?"

He picked her up by the waist, lifting her off her feet to swing her around and plant a long, hot kiss on her. Then with a laugh, he carried her into the house.

"You're about to find out."

43

Madeline was not surprised when Pepper wasn't exactly thrilled with her opening gambit.

"You want me to tell them what?"

"That I want to drop *Comfort Cooking*."

"Do you have any idea what revenue that brings in?"

"Not as much as *Dinner at Home*."

One thing she'd learned at the Culinary Institute was to keep track of the dollars. Actually, Sofia, who'd kept her immigrant frugality even as she and Madeline's grandfather traveled the world, had taught her that if you watched the pennies, the dollars would take care of themselves. Something Maxime had definitely not learned. *Yet,* she admitted, *why should he? When he can keep marrying his very own ATMs.*

"I'm also pretty much duplicating what I do on *Comfort Cooking* with the second show. I'm willing to keep *Dinner at Home*, because it's a topic that's really important to me. Not only are families spending too much time in the drive-through lane of some fast-food chain, they go home and eat out of boxes and bags while watching TV. Everyone's so rushed these days, dinner is the one time of day that families can take a breather to get together and talk. And feel like real families, instead of just a group of individuals who happen to sleep beneath the same roof."

Hadn't Birdy said much the same thing about dinner

having become a bonding time for her daughter and grand-children?

"And I don't want to tape it in the Cooking Network staged kitchen. I want to do it here."

"Here?" Madeline hoped her agent was in the actual of-fice and not the one with the alcohol, or she'd have just spit out her martini. "Surely you don't mean in Sunnybrook Harbor?"

"Shelter Bay. And yes, that's exactly what I mean. I'm not doing these shows for ego or fame," she repeated what she'd told Pepper time and time again. Madeline disliked this new trajectory that had thrown so many chefs out of the kitchen into the klieg lights of television stardom.

"I'm doing them because I believe in them. You know my concept, which is not a gimmick, has always been family dining. So what would be more appropriate than filming the show here, in the farmhouse kitchen where I first de-cided to become a chef?"

"Hmm. I can see the marketing potential in that," Pep-per allowed. "But you already have a huge audience for *Dinner at Home*. Do you honestly believe that changing the venue will make up enough to pay for increased pro-duction costs?"

"I made a few calls. There's an award-winning guy who escaped the L.A. movie rat race by moving to Astoria. Now he's semiretired, only taking on work that interests him. He's also a major foodie."

When she named him, she heard Pepper's intake of breath. "Oh, I saw his documentary tour of Napa's wine country res-taurants," she said. "And nearly wept at that tiny bit of capel-lini nestled in a clamshell, with a single clam on top."

"It was genius," Madeline allowed, although the chef's ingenious take on linguini with clam sauce wasn't the type of robust food she preferred to prepare. "I swear I could smell the cloves, peppercorns, and star anise he'd somehow infused into the hot rock salt that shell was sitting on."

"That documentary had a concept," Pepper said carefully. "And a built-in foodie audience. *Dinner at Home*, as good a show as it is, isn't exactly groundbreaking fare."

"I know. The film guy already pointed that out." Madeline had allowed herself a moment of ego when she learned he actually occasionally watched it. "He's willing to come in way under what New York production costs are if he gets the contract for the new show."

"What new show?"

Madeline went on to explain her idea about showing the school and restaurant being built. Then filming the classes.

"I see a few problems." Which was Pepper's job. To temper Madeline's enthusiasm with the cold, hard reality of pragmatism. "The actual building of the place may draw in viewers who are already fans and interested in your new venture. Along with all those people who tune in to watch remodeling disasters, the way others go to car races to see the crashes. If it caught on, it could also build anticipation for the teaching segment. . . .

"But you said the students will be from some women's shelter? Aren't some running away from abusive spouses?"

"We'll either blur their faces—"

"I always find that so distracting."

"Okay. We won't use them in the filmed segments. Because we'll have other students."

"And how, exactly, will you get enough students to film thirteen episodes? Even if the network would sign on to the project?"

"We get a lot of tourists who come for the scenery, and this part of the coast is starting to get some great chefs that draw foodies in. But we'll also go trolling for students and viewers in a much larger pool by having celebrity chefs as guest instructors."

She rattled off a list of well-known fellow sustainable-food advocates who'd already agreed to appear if she managed to get approval.

"Okay." She could hear Pepper's huge rush of relieved breath. "Now you have me excited."

"There's one thing more."

"Will I like it?"

"Trust me—you'll love it. We'll take a certain number of the shows, and this is something for you and the network execs to work out, on the road. And teach an episode at these other chef's restaurants. Many of which already include dinners at their own farms."

"Don't go counting organic chicks before they're hatched," Pepper warned. "But I think you've got yourself a winner."

"Thanks. Meanwhile, whatever happens with your talks, I'll be staying here. For at least the next six months."

"I can understand you needing a break," Pepper said. "After all, you've had a horrible week. But are you sure this return to pastoral living isn't just an overreaction to your marriage breaking up?"

"I considered that." Madeline never lied. Not even to herself. Especially not to herself. That was one of the things she loved about cooking. There was only black and white in the kitchen—food either tasted good or it didn't.

"And I've decided that this may well be where I belong. I realize a lot of chefs dismiss the CMC accreditation as being out of touch with today's reality, but to me, becoming a Certified Master Chef was more of a goal reached. Like climbing Everest or sailing around the world."

"So, although I didn't succeed at my original plan to open my own restaurant in Manhattan, I don't need that validation any longer. What I do need is to try to finally get some balance in my life."

She'd already begun to realize that, like too many chefs, she'd gotten caught up in the addiction of marathon hours and feeling the need to exhibit superhuman endurance. She'd become so focused on building a brand to support her husband's businesses and keep her shows on the air that she'd allowed her career to consume her, working eighty to ninety hours a week.

No wonder she didn't have any friends other than her agent. Or decent clothes that weren't bought by a stylist specifically for the show. She couldn't remember the last time she'd seen a movie, and if she did take time, say, on a plane, to read a book, it was always research about kitchen equipment, techniques, recipes. That short stroll through the town when she'd first arrived had been the first time she'd taken a walk in probably a year.

"You do sound a bit burned-out," Pepper agreed, revealing that some of the stress Madeline was feeling, all the way to the bone, had come through in her tone.

"I need balance," Madeline repeated. "I don't want to be lying all alone on my deathbed at ninety and have my last thought be that I wished I could make just one more bowl of risotto for a customer."

"You've more than sixty years before you have to worry about being ninety," Pepper soothed. "But I get your point. Which now has me worried whether you're taking on too much again with this construction and a new program and breaking in a new production team, even if the network agrees."

"I've thought about that, too. And no, because I'm going to have help. I have my grandmother and friends and . . ."

She'd started to say *Lucas*. Then realized that would open up an entirely different conversation she was not yet prepared to have with anyone. It was difficult enough having it with herself.

"And?" Pepper had not become the premier agent for celebrity chefs and cookbook authors without being very good at picking up on nuances and hearing what wasn't being said.

"I have friends here," Maddy said. "Who go back to when we were kids together. And my contractor just happens to be an old friend, too. The son of an architect who used to summer in Shelter Bay. Fortunately, he totally gets what I want to do."

"How nice for you." Her agent had sprinkled a heavy dose of wryness into that comment. "Let me make some calls. I'll get back to you. Hopefully tomorrow. And keep that cell charged and on."

"I will. And Pepper . . . thanks."

"It's my job," the agent pointed out. "But I also like to think we're friends. I'll do what I can to help you achieve that balance, so when the time comes and you reach ninety, we can be toasting how perfectly our lives turned out with martinis or whatever trendy drink a new generation of mix-ologists has come up with. Ciao, darling."

"Ciao," Madeline repeated to a line that had already turned to dead air.

She might not have located that perfect balance yet, but, something told her, as she drove down the lavender-lined lane, if it did exist, like Dorothy when she clicked the heels of her shiny red shoes together, she might possibly find it right here in Shelter Bay.

44

She'd gotten not just beneath his skin, but into Lucas' mind, he realized as he walked through the deserted cannery building with Flynn McGrath. Although the guy was supposedly worth gazillions, not only had he brought along his own hard hat, he'd also come dressed appropriately in well-worn jeans, a plaid shirt open over a black T-shirt, and work boots that had not just come out of the box, but were broken in.

Which, Lucas figured, made sense, considering that the guy might now be an artist, but also dealt in reclaimed wood. As they walked through the building together, he learned that McGrath did that job firsthand.

"Gotta see the wood to know what's inside it," he said as they climbed a rickety set of stairs that would definitely have to be replaced. "Sometimes I spot it right away. Other times, I've got to live with it a while before it speaks to me."

"My father always said the same thing about a piece of land. He never began drawing until he walked every inch of it. At different times of the day."

"Duncan Chaffee was an artist," McGrath said, as he snapped some photos of the second-floor interior brick-work.

The place still smelled vaguely of shellfish. Soon that lingering odor would be replaced by the scents of sawdust, wood, and paint, which, having spent so much time on construction sites with his dad, always reminded Lucas of home.

"We clicked the first time we met when we were both SOS board members. I wanted him to design a house for me, but he was tied up in that project he was working on in Vietnam."

Like everything else he'd done, Duncan Chaffee's work had always been personal. In that case, he'd been building a school in the highlands, where he'd served during the war. After years of Agent Orange defoliation, the area was gradually returning to normal. Duncan had hoped that his school—another of his pro bono projects—would be one more building block in the restoration of relations between the two countries.

The Save Our Salmon coalition, normally known as SOS, had been another of his father's great passions. Not just for himself as a fisherman, but because he'd believed that restoring the Pacific Northwest's wild salmon and free-flowing rivers could be a vital economic engine for local communities hit hard by the loss of timber jobs and the recession.

"The Vietnam school was the last project he did," Lucas said.

"Yeah, I know. Which is a damn shame, because, like I said, he was a freaking artistic genius. He'd already recommended someone else in his firm, Dylan Delaney, to do the work, but I decided just to wait."

"Dylan's a great architect," Lucas said.

"I'm sure he is. But, like I said, I was willing to wait for Duncan. Which I'm glad I did, because if I were living up in Seattle in a Duncan Chaffee house, I'd probably never be able to give it up and move down here to start this project."

"I appreciate you giving me a shot to bid it."

"Hell, from what your dad said about you, I figure that while you might not have the fancy degree—which, by the way, I recently read that neither did Frank Lloyd Wright—

you two shared a vision about architecture, along with a work ethic I require in anyone who works with me."

"I'm used to hard work."

"You wouldn't have made it as a SEAL if you weren't. And another thing you've got going in your favor is that we vets have to stick together." He glanced through the jagged, broken pane of glass that had once been a window. "We've got company."

As Lucas looked down at Maddy getting out of the driver's seat of that rental car, he was hit by a slap of lust. And something even stronger. An emotion so strong he wasn't sure it might not cause his heart to burst.

He was, as Sax would say, so toast.

And he so didn't care.

In fact, it felt damn good being back here in this special place. With the woman that the gods, good fortune, or just fickle fate were giving him a second chance with.

And this time he was not going to let her get away.

"Hey!" He called down to her. "Stay put. I'll be right down."

Those wild black curls tumbled down her back as she tilted her head and looked up to find the source of his voice. She spotted him, waved, and sent him a smile bright enough to light up the entire coast for a month of Sundays.

"Lucky you," McGrath said.

"She's a client," Lucas said. His dad had taught him early not to kiss and tell, which he never had. Except that one time in that bunker, when they'd all been trying to take a dying battle buddy's mind off his situation. A night Lucas would've bet serious money on that none of them would have survived.

"I'd say, given the look on your face, that she's a helluva lot more than that."

"We knew each other growing up. And yeah, we share a bit of a checkered past."

"Now, see, I've always been one of those glass-half-full

guys," the older man offered. "The way I figure it, any past, checkered or not, gives you an edge on your competition. Because you can skip past all that getting-to-know-you stuff. And work on any of the negative issues."

Lucas hadn't, until this moment, considered having any competition. Other than the Frenchman who, obviously being an idiot, had put himself out of the picture. But Maddy was bright, gorgeous, and, he remembered, had always been well liked. It would be stupid to think that he'd be the only guy in town who'd notice that she was suddenly, conveniently, available.

Which meant he was going to have to pick up his game. Patience was one thing. Stupidity another.

45

Just days ago Madeline had considered herself happily married. All right. Not happily. But she'd certainly been hoping things would turn around. Because, the same way she could salvage a cloudy consommé, she'd been certain she could repair her marriage.

Wasn't that why she'd been running like a dervish, taping those shows, demonstrating cookware all over the damn country, taking care of her husband's books because he didn't trust any accountant not to gossip about his precarious financial situation? She'd even continued to work the front of Maxime's on Columbus many nights, whenever she had any time off.

And look where that had gotten her.

Having been brought up to believe that there was nothing she couldn't accomplish, she'd refused to acknowledge what Maxime had always known. That their marriage, which he'd never sincerely wanted, had been on life support since the moment they'd exchanged vows. She had pushed him up that aisle to the altar, and then once they were husband and wife, while on some level she'd realized her mistake, she'd still kept trying to fix it.

When had she stopped allowing herself to want something for herself? To be happy? To feel, as she did now, as if her heart, which had been dormant for so long, might just float all the way up there to where Lucas was framed by that broken window.

Flynn McGrath didn't look like a stockbroker. He was, Madeline thought, as Lucas introduced them, a dead ringer for Paul Newman. Not the younger one from *Hud* or *The Long, Hot Summer*, but the forty-year-old actor who'd proven he was still one of the sexiest men on the planet playing Cool Hand Luke and Butch Cassidy.

He was tall, cowboy lean, and had blue eyes that blazed out of a deeply tanned face. But when he began talking about creating from reclaimed wood, his passion was contagious.

"You're absolutely right on the mark about using salvaged wood to fit into your restaurant theme of sustainability," he said, when Madeline told him what she'd planned to do. "It'll help establish your brand."

"Oh, please." He might be sexy, but she'd hoped never to have to hear that word again.

"You're right. The term's become a cliché, but it's a necessity in this day and age," he said. "More and more businesses, including restaurants, are using *green* as a marketing tool. Even ones who might only stick an LED lightbulb over their salad bar. Having tables from reclaimed trees would definitely not only make you stand out, it'll put you at the forefront of your field."

"And get *you* some advertising in the meantime if the show gets on TV," she said dryly. One thing life in New York and the restaurant business had taught her was that everyone had an angle.

"To tell you the truth, we've got more business than my two partners and I can handle," McGrath surprised her by saying. "If you decide you want to do business with us, we'd have to put off other spec jobs we've been saving some pieces for."

"Then why would you consider my restaurant in the first place?"

"Because you're right. Being on television wouldn't hurt. Not because we need the business, but because featuring reclaimed wood on your show would help get the word out about tree salvage. These days most end up as mulch, if they're lucky. The trees we deal with have lived long, productive lives in our own neighborhoods. They've shaded us, helped clean our air, given birds a home, provided oxygen for a planet, and just flat-out made us feel better by looking at them. They deserve to be respected. Reclamation provides that respect."

"Chefs are taught to respect the food we prepare," she said, thinking how similar their work sounded.

"There you go. We've tried to build a whole bouillabaisse of green values from using nontoxic, water-based wood finishes to offering the sawdust free to residents for mulch, and recycling all our paper and wood products.

"We also always hang bare cedar boughs from our open ceiling trusses—which is something we're going to have to work in," he told Lucas. "There's a local Native American belief that it cleanses any lingering negative energy from the lumber that enters. I figure that's just one more bit of respect."

"I like that," Madeline said. "Maybe we could incorporate it into beams in the restaurant."

"Works for me," Lucas said.

"Along with sharing values, there's another reason I'd be willing to take your job on," McGrath said.

She crossed her arms. Here came the angle. "And that reason would be?"

He flashed a bad-boy grin that was pure Newman at his best. "You'd be the prettiest client I've ever worked with."

"I merely inherited good genes," she said. "Getting back to your trees . . ."

He slanted Lucas a look. "Lady gets right down to business."

"Ms. Durand's got a timeline thing going."

"Well, that might be a bit of a problem." McGrath rubbed his jaw. "Working with wood isn't like painting with oil or pretty watercolors. It's an unforgiving medium. Being a force of nature, as it is, it can bring a lot of pitfalls with it.

"It's not just the different species. Every tree is different and it can take a while to find its soul."

Madeline suspected other people might find that idea a bit New Agey. Fortunately, she often felt the same way when it came to how to treat a particularly challenging yet irresistible fish one of her suppliers might surprise her with on any given morning.

"Clients who are drawn to salvaged wood have to be adventurers," McGrath said. "Because there's definitely an element of risk. The negative part is that it can take time. The flipside is that you get to be part of the process. But you also have to be patient and trust that we know what we're doing."

"I traveled through Europe by myself after graduating from high school," Madeline said. "Although I grew up in a small village in Umbria and here in Shelter Bay, which isn't exactly the most bustling place on the planet, I managed to make a career for myself in Manhattan. So although I might not be into extreme sports, I think you'll find me adventurous enough. As for the patience, you've got me there. It's honestly not my strong suit. So, how about we tackle the project in stages?" she suggested. "Maybe start out with something like a great bar. We'll see how we work together and go from there."

"She's not only gorgeous; she's also smart," he told Lucas.

"You don't have to convince me," Lucas said.

"You know, I'm not sure it'd make a good bar, but I've got this twenty-foot slab of red elm," McGrath said. "We milled it with a Y at the top because of way the trunk split. It'd make a great focal point on an entry wall. If you don't mind a huge gash and a burn trail from the lightning strike that killed it."

"Oh!" Madeline could just imagine it. "That would give it even more character."

"Again, a woman after my own heart. If Chaffee here hadn't already staked his claim, I might try my luck."

"I didn't say anything about any claim," Lucas interjected, holding up both hands in a plea of innocence. "Honest."

"That's true enough," the wood artisan agreed. "He didn't use those exact words. But a smart man, and I like to think I am, knows enough to stay out of the way of a SEAL on a mission."

"Former SEAL," Lucas muttered. "I saw the slab," he told Madeline, obviously as eager as she was to keep this conversation on business. "It's an amazing piece. The burn looks sort of like a bird. Maybe a heron. You can even see the tree rings on the edges."

"We call it a live edge," McGrath said. "It celebrates the topography of the tree trunk and provides visual interest. We prefer to impose as little human interference in the design as possible."

"But I wouldn't want to size it down," Madeline considered the logistics.

"Good. Because I wouldn't size it down," the other man said.

"You've got room with that second story," Lucas reminded her. "We could always raise the ceiling a bit higher and use heavy beams so it would stick with a farmhouse look and not appear too contemporary."

"I really do like that idea."

"We've also got some scrap pieces we were planning to recycle," McGrath said. "I think we could work up some barstools, if you wouldn't mind having mixed species."

"I'd love that even more." This was getting more and more exciting. And to think that she wouldn't have even known about Flynn McGrath if her grandmother hadn't hired Lucas to do her remodel.

"We're in the process of moving our stock down here from Seattle," he said. "Since we're going to do this reconstruction in sections, we thought it only made sense to use some of the older sections for storage. I should have something for you to see in the next three to five days."

"That would be perfect." She could feel herself beaming and realized how long it had been since she'd had anything to feel excited about.

"Great. Here's my card with my cell on it, which would probably be best because I'm between places right now. But I think we can work out some prices and pieces that work for both of us."

Lucas and Madeline stood side by side as he walked back to his truck, the wedge-heeled cowboy boots adding to his swagger.

"I'll bet he'd make a fortune in New York," she murmured. "Women who like to think of themselves as the height of sophistication would be falling over themselves just to show him off, and pay big bucks for his furniture in their apartments."

"Money doesn't seem to be that big a deal to him," Lucas said. "So, you think he's sexy?"

"Absolutely. But that shouldn't concern you. Since you've staked your claim."

Lucas cringed. "I honestly didn't tell him that."

"But it's true."

"I already told you I intend to marry you. So I guess, in that respect, it's true. But, it's not like you haven't already done the same to me. You're just not ready to admit it yet. . . .

"However," he said, reaching out to tuck a wayward curl behind her ear, "since you're out here, want a tour? Or would you like to get down to work? Or, you know, it's going to be a gorgeous evening. I've got Dad's boat down here at the marina. We could go for a sail."

"Why?"

"For fun. You do remember the concept, right?"

"Not really. And we're supposed to be working."

"We can work tomorrow. The sky's clearing up in time for the sunset. We'll pick up some crab and sail along the coastline, soaking up the sights."

It sounded heavenly. Also impossible.

"We have work to do."

"We'll get an early start tomorrow. Clearing your mind will be good for your creativity."

"It's admittedly appealing."

"Better than appealing. I know this hidden inlet. We could anchor there, eat some crab, drink some wine, swim naked—"

"It's spring. We'd freeze."

"Nah." His hands moved over her shoulders and down her arms. "I'll keep you plenty warm enough." His lips skimmed down her neck.

Of that she had not a single doubt. Just his touch was already beginning to make her feel hot. And needy.

"I have responsibilities."

"Screw them." The temptation rumbled in her ear. "How long has it been since your life wasn't centered around work? When was the last time you skimmed across the water on a boat as the sun set into the water?"

"I live in New York. It rises out of the sea on the East Coast."

"Then you're long overdue."

"Are you always this tenacious?"

"When I want something, absolutely."

"And you want me."

"We've already established that. Yeah. I want you more than I've ever wanted any woman in my life. More than I'll ever want any other woman. What would you say to honeymooning in Hawaii? Cole went there with Kelli and they both say it's paradise.

"Think of it, Maddy—a land of mai tais and passion fruit

and flowers so bright they almost blind you, lush green valleys, volcanoes—"

"We have volcanoes here in the Pacific Northwest."

"You're just trying to get me off topic, but it isn't going to work. Picture sand that sparkles like black diamonds, and waterfalls where we can get naked and make love in warm blue-green tropical pools—"

"Do all your fantasies include getting wet and naked?"

"Most of them," he admitted. "Which probably come from all the past years of eating sand and dust. But I do have this other one, where we're skiing in the Alps and I rescue you from an avalanche, and carry you miles through knee-deep snow until we get to this chalet—"

"Which conveniently happens to be abandoned."

"See?" That crease that was not quite a dimple winked as he grinned. "Great minds . . . So, after we stumble in, I light the logs conveniently stacked in a stone fireplace, pour us some brandy—"

"Which just happened to be sitting on the table waiting for survivors of avalanches?"

"No. That would be too much of a coincidence even for a fantasy. Didn't I mention the Saint Bernard that followed along with us?"

"I don't believe he came up."

"Clearly an oversight. But, fortunately, he showed up just in time. However, there do happen to be two snifters sitting on a table, and this big fur rug on the floor in front of the fireplace, so—"

"We get naked."

"We don't really have any choice. Because our clothes are soaked and frozen from all that ice and snow."

"Wet and naked. Admit it, Lucas Chaffee. Your fantasies are in a rut."

He laughed. "Got me there," he said agreeably. "But I do have a whole bunch of others." His grin turned into a friendly leer. "Want to hear some more?"

"Why don't you save them for some other time and show me around instead? Now that I'm here, I'd like to see what you've got planned. Then, I really do want to see your ideas for Gram's restaurant."

"I've got the sketches on my laptop. But since there's no place to sit down and spread stuff out here, we can either go back to the farm or my place. Which, to be honest, I'd really prefer."

"I'll bet. Because Gram wouldn't be around to chaperone."

"I think we're beyond the age of needing a chaperone. . . . Kara called and told me that she'd told you about that night the copter had crashed. Up in the Kush."

"She told me some of it," Madeline was a bit surprised at how quickly the topic had swung from flirtatious fun to deadly serious. "Though I suspected Sax didn't share everything."

"I strongly doubt he did," he agreed. His expression was as intense as she'd ever seen it. "You might not like the idea, at least right now, but the fact is, like it or not, you can't deny that we're involved, Maddy."

"No." If she demanded honesty from him, she owed the same in return. "I can't."

"Then I have some stuff you need to hear."

Thinking back to what Kara had told her, Madeline would have to be evil Dalmatian puppy murderer Cruella de Vil to turn down the naked need she heard in Lucas' rough, flat voice.

"You can show me around the cannery some other time," she said. "It's been sitting here empty for years. It won't be going anywhere in the next few days. Meanwhile, I'll follow you out to your place."

"Thanks." He did not look relieved. More, she thought, *resigned.*

46

"I bought some wine," Lucas said, as they walked into the cottage. "Would you like a glass?"

"Am I going to need one?"

"It might not hurt."

"Well, then, I guess I'd like a glass."

"Red or white?" He held up two bottles, both labels she knew to be outrageously expensive at wholesale price. She couldn't imagine what he'd paid for these.

"I didn't realize you were a wine buff."

"I'm not. I told Sax I wanted the good stuff and he suggested these."

He'd bought them for her, knowing she'd come back to the cottage. Then again, she suspected anyone watching them the past few days would have been able to figure out where they were headed.

"That's very thoughtful of you. And I'll take the sauvignon blanc," she decided.

She loved that he actually had to look at the label to see which was which. Again, showing that, knowing nothing about wine, he'd gone to that extra effort just for her. Working his way to redemption, which, especially after that story Kara had shared, he'd already achieved.

He opened the bottle with more skill than she might have expected, poured it into a glass his father must have originally bought, since there was a row of them on a kitchen shelf, and snagged a bottle of dark beer from the fridge for himself. Then, as if he wanted to maintain some distance between them—yet another warning that this wasn't going to be the easiest story to listen to—he put her glass and the bottle on the farm table.

"Do you want anything to eat?" he asked. He seemed uncharacteristically distracted. "I didn't think about it when I was buying the wine, but I might have some crackers."

"The wine's fine." She sat down on one of the rush-seat, ladder-back chairs at the table.

"Okay." He sat across from her. "So," he began without preamble, "you know how I said that I'd told the guys you were my one regret?"

"That would be a bit difficult to forget."

"There was this Marine. He was really young. Nineteen. He was skinny with a bunch of freckles and carrot red hair. Sax called him Opie."

"After Ron Howard. From Mayberry." She took a sip of the wine, which definitely lived up to both its price and reputation.

"Yeah. That's him. Sax pretty much nailed it when it came to how he looked. But he was one helluva shot."

"Was?" She knew where this was going.

He swiped a hand through his hair. Took a deep breath. "We fought a lot of battles that day, but one of the worst was the first one, when we were trying to evac the copter before it blew. The kid was a Marine sniper and his shooting could well be the reason Sax and I lived to tell the story.

"So, I don't know how long we were fighting. Time has a way of both speeding up and slowing down during moments like that. It doesn't matter how well you can plan a mission—and this one was a clusterfuck from the get-go—the one thing you can always count on is that the plan falls apart with the first contact with the enemy."

"I've heard about that. The fog of war."

"That's it. But *fog*'s too benign a word for it." He took a pull on the brown bottle. "Anyway, we'd taken all the bad guys out, and were starting to breathe again when the kid started screaming bloody murder.

"Turns out he'd stood up during the last volley and gotten shot below his chest plate. In the pelvis. Which is one of the worst places you can get shot, because the aorta splits low in the abdomen, forming left and right arteries."

"I didn't know that."

But *he* did. Madeline thought about how even as horrific as the situation must have been for all the men on that downed helicopter, it had fallen on Lucas' shoulders to keep the wounded—and it sounded as if there was a lot of them, along with that pilot Kara had mentioned—alive. She took a longer drink of wine.

"Not many people do," he said. "Because it's not their job. The arteries branch into the exterior and deep femoral vessels, which serve as the primary arteries for the lower part of the body."

"And that's where he was shot?"

"Yeah." He dragged his hand down his face. It was not as steady as she was used to seeing it, revealing how painful this memory must be.

"You don't have to tell me about this," she said.

"Yeah. I do." He took another deep breath. "Because it's always going to be with me. I'm not saying that it always hovers over me like some dark cloud, but it's part of who I am. Who I've become since that summer we spent together. And it's not that I'm trying to impress you, but you said we needed to get to know each other better. And so, if you figure you can take it— "

"I can." She realized it was important that she hear the entire story, as horrific as she feared it would be. Because he was right. It was part of him. Part of the man he'd become. The man she was falling in love with all over again.

"I got an IV going and kept squeezing the bag with both hands to get replacement fluids in him and try to keep him from bleeding out. I'd gone through six bags, but the wound just kept spurting like a fucking geyser.

"By now the kid had figured out what had happened. He might've been young, but this damn well wasn't his first rodeo, and he'd seen other guys die the same way. Especially since chest plates don't provide any lower-body protection against IEDs. Almost anyone else would've been crying for their mother, which happens more than you might think—"

"Whenever I get a cold, I still want my mother. Or Gram."

He nodded. Managed a half smile. "There you go. Anyway, the kid sucked it up and stayed amazingly calm. But meanwhile, I'm about to lose it because he's still spraying blood like damn fire hose, which means that the only way I've got even a prayer of a chance of saving him is clamping off the artery."

"But . . ." The thought, as she imagined the scene, was so frightening Madeline felt her blood go cold. "Wouldn't that mean—"

"I've got to go into the wound."

"With your hands?"

"Well, it wasn't as if we had a fully equipped operating room on the battlefield. The worst part was that because of the altitude and the fact that he'd lost all that blood, I didn't dare give him any morphine, because his blood pressure was so low, it would've killed him for sure.

"So, like in those old Westerns, when a guy's gotta bite a bullet while the doc works on him, some of the team held him down and kept taking turns pressing on his abdomen to keep pressure over the artery while I went spelunking through his skin, muscle, and fat. Not that he had much fat, because like most Marines, he was in great shape."

"Except for the fact he was dying."

"Well, yeah. There was that. I was still optimistic, because, hell, that's part of a medic's job description. If you allow yourself to think the worst, it just might happen, so you just keep focusing on the task at hand and figure out how to make things work."

It made her realize how different their lives had been these past years. Until Maxime's sex video had gone viral, the worst thing Madeline had had to suffer since she and Lucas had broken up had been a collapsed soufflé or curdled hollandaise.

Meanwhile, in all those years in all those war zones, this couldn't have been the first patient he'd lost. And worse than a patient, she considered. A teammate.

She took a deep gulp of the wine, then reached across the table and put her hand on his. "I want to hear the rest." Okay, that wasn't exactly true. She didn't necessarily *want* to. But knew she *needed* to. And, from the despair she heard in his voice, Madeline understood he needed to tell her. "But first I want to say one thing."

He looked down at her hand, then turned his so they were palm to palm. "What's that?"

"I need to apologize."

He looked honestly confused. "For what?"

"For thinking the worst of you all these years. I was so wrong."

"Hey." He linked their fingers together and lifted their joined hands to his lips, brushing a kiss over her knuckles. A kiss as soft as snowflakes, but as warm as the embers that she could no longer deny had continued to smolder all these years. "At least you were thinking of me." His quick grin lightened the mood.

"You really *are* an optimist."

"Roger that. At least, let's just say I'm hopeful where you're concerned. . . . So, getting back to this story of how your name came up, as bad as things were, they were about to get a lot worse. I couldn't find the artery because it had retracted back into his abdomen."

Madeline's stomach clenched. Sickness welled up and burned her throat.

"What did you do?"

"We called for an evac copter, but were told we'd have to wait."

"That's what Kara said. Which is beyond horrible."

"It wasn't what we wanted to hear, all right, but the military lives by rules of combat engagement, and the rules for this mission were clear from the start. No planes flew within thirty minutes of sunrise. So putting another bird down before nightfall was not going to happen, because as far as command was concerned the LZ—that's military speak for *landing zone*—was still hot—"

"Military speak for *dangerous*."

"Yeah. Like the entire damn mountains weren't," he muttered, pushing the heels of his hands into his eyes. As if he could block off the visions, which she suspected were permanently etched on his mind.

"And to keep things in perspective, since the entire war wasn't about us, they'd been getting intel from the high-altitude, fixed-winged bombers heading back to base that there were a lot of guys down around us who weren't looking like friendlies.

"So the commander told us to hang on the best we could—we were, after all, SEALS, and used to working in dicey situations—and they'd get to us as soon as they could."

"How lovely of them," she said dryly.

Then had a horrible thought. What if Lucas had died up there on that mountain? She suspected that, as angry as she'd been at him, the loss would have hurt for a very long time. Undoubtedly forever.

"So, what did you do?" she asked. "About the Marine? Opie?"

"We were down to our final option. Which was to cut directly into his abdomen, hunt down the slippery damn artery, and clamp it. The problem was, the more I dug around looking for it, the more blood he lost, so I decided to try a transfusion."

"You had bottles of blood with you?" Kara had told her that Lucas carried more supplies than any medic anyone knew, but what were the odds of that?

"No. This was a person-to-person deal."

"On the battlefield?"

"It's admittedly risky but yeah, it can be done. In a worst-case scenario, which this definitely was."

"But wouldn't you still need to match blood types?"

"Yeah. We got lucky."

That definitely wasn't the word she would have used.

"One of the guys was type O. Which is a universal donor."

"That's an amazing risk he took."

Lucas shrugged. "The kid might not have been a SEAL, but he was one gung-ho Marine, and as much of the team as any of us. Any guy that day would've done the same thing."

"Fighting for the other guy in the foxhole," she murmured. It had always seemed like a war movie cliché. It never would again.

"That's it. By now the kid was in so much pain, I decided to risk giving him some morphine. I finally managed to find the artery and clamp it; then I shoved some Kerlix, which is a kind of bandage, into the wound, but by then, even with the transfusion, he'd lost so much blood, his chances of surviving were slim to none.

"Quinn, the sniper I told you about, gathered up some of the ponchos from the guys we'd lost, because they didn't need them anymore."

"And Opie did." Strange how knowing his nickname made the story all the more personal.

"Yeah. By now the wind had really picked up and was blowing snow mixed with sand, so we realized we had to get the kid somewhere more protected. The Chinook would've been the best bet, but we'd already had some fires on it after we were hit in the air, so we didn't want to risk another spark setting off the fuel.

"Meanwhile, Shane, the wounded Army pilot who'd been ferrying us, didn't look all that hot, either, so we decided we had to get them into the bunker."

He lifted the beer to his lips, drank, then studied the label for a long, silent time.

Suspecting he was revisiting that horrid night, Madeline waited.

"The guys who were still mobile managed to get them into the bunker," he continued. "We covered them with the ponchos, some insulation we pulled from the copter, and pine boughs that had been shot off the trees during the battle.

"We all kept our best faces on, and although everyone in the bunker knew it was a damn lie, I assured the kid he was going to be okay. He might've been young, but he wasn't stupid. He knew he was going to die.

"So that's when he started telling us his life story. About his mom, who died of ovarian cancer when he was nine . . ."

For the first time since Lucas had started telling this story, Madeline found something she could identify with. But even then, her parents' deaths were quick. Cancer was not.

"Since his dad was an active-duty Marine, he went to live with his grandmother in Kentucky."

Something else Madeline could identify with.

"He was real proud of his dad, who was deployed as a gunnery sergeant in Desert Storm. Apparently, there'd been Cunninghams—that was the kid's last name—in the Marines since they were first founded in Philadelphia in 1775."

"That's quite a coincidence. That you all would name him Opie, and Ron Howard played Richard Cunningham in *Happy Days.*"

"There's more. The kid's name was Richard Cunningham."

That would have made her smile if the tale hadn't been so tragic.

"I had no idea the Marines went back that far, to before we were a country. "

"According to the kid, who had no reason to lie, an ancestor had fought with George Washington, and after that, through every generation, whenever America needed a U.S. Marine, anywhere in the world, a Cunningham male had always been there to answer the call. Unfortunately, according to Zach, one of the guys who met his dad later down in South Carolina, Opie ended that streak."

"Oh, that makes it even worse. Not that anything's worse than death, but . . ."

"I know what you mean. And yeah, I agree. He was from Salt Lick, Kentucky, and had a fiancée who was going to school to be a beautician. They figured she'd be able to get a job fixing hair wherever he might be stationed after they got married.

"They were going to have two kids. And a couple bluetick hounds so he could take his boys hunting with him, the way he'd gone with his dad. Shane asked what he'd do if they had girls, which seemed to come as a surprise. But he thought about it for a minute, then decided he'd have to lock them in a closet to keep guys like us away from them until they were thirty.

"Or, maybe he'd switch from the Baptists over to the Catholics and lock them away in a convent. . . . We all laughed about that idea."

He blew out a breath. Looked out the window at the wide, empty expanse of ocean.

"It's going to sound really odd, because you had to have been there to fully understand, but it was cool for a while. The night was quiet, and it made the war seem like something that was happening to someone else. It was as if we were just sitting around in a bar, shooting the bull.

"Everyone started telling their own stories. All about girls." He smiled at that, but his eyes were sad. And distant. "Zach, he was the guy with the type-O blood, talked about a girl back home in South Carolina. Sax talked about Kara. About how he'd fallen in love with her, but she'd been in love with someone else, so he'd never gotten to tell her how he felt."

"I remember, during that time, thinking it must have been hard on him," Madeline said. "Nearly everyone in town except Kara could see what had happened. At least he finally got to tell her. And they've definitely made up for lost time."

"That's for sure. I talked about you. Not because I was bragging or anything about us, you know . . ."

"Having sex like bunnies all summer."

That earned a faint smile. "Well, I didn't put it exactly like that, but yeah. I told how much I'd loved you, and how you said you'd loved me—"

"Which was the absolute truth."

"I was a cretin who didn't deserve you. And, for the record, every guy in that bunker, including Opie, told me I was an idiot."

"Even a couple days ago you wouldn't have received any argument from me about that. But things change."

And people changed. Hadn't they both? Yet the chemistry was still there. Even stronger than ever. It was something she'd never experienced before with any other man. Not even Maxime.

In the beginning, when she'd first met Lucas when she was thirteen and he was fifteen, although there weren't any sexual vibes going on, there had been an instant connection. At first she'd thought that it was only because it was her first year living there and he was a summer boy, which automatically made them somewhat outsiders.

But then, each summer when he returned, the bond had grown stronger. Until what had started out as friendship blossomed into love.

But they'd been too young and too inexperienced in the ways of working out relationships. Although he'd definitely gone about it in the wrong way, she also knew now that he'd been thinking of her when he'd sent her off to Europe.

Again, while she was being totally honest, she had to admit that if she hadn't followed through on her dream, not only would she not be the person she was today, with the career she'd established and the ability to help the other person she loved, but she might actually have come to resent him for holding her back.

"You're right about things changing," he said, breaking into her thoughts. "But here's the thing, Maddy. I understand that you're a planner. You always have been, which is why you had your entire life plotted out by your teens."

"And look how well that turned out," she murmured.

"Except for the Frenchman, you've done really well, and, yeah, you might not be exactly in the place you thought you'd be ten years ago, but you're damn close. While I've always been more of a go-with-the-flow kind of guy."

"I don't believe that. Kara told me that no medic carried more supplies than you, so you'd be ready for anything."

"That was life and death. Which is my point. Life doesn't fit neatly in all those boxes on a calendar. Or on a spreadsheet or a timetable. One minute you're getting engaged and planning on babies and bluetick hounds, and the next minute, you're dying in a bunker in some godforsaken place thousands of miles from home. Just like that." He snapped his fingers.

"We've already lost ten years." He leaned toward her. "Which weren't really a waste, because if we'd gotten married back then, it might not have lasted. But we're adults now. I've never—ever—felt the way about any other woman the way I feel about you."

"I'm the same way," she admitted. It was difficult to say, given that she'd gotten married for what she now realized were all the wrong reasons. "About you."

She polished off the rest of her wine, then stood up and held out her hand. "And I think it's time we begin making up for that lost time."

He stood up, as well. His eyes were heartbreakingly sad, but she could also see a familiar spark of lust. "I didn't tell you that story to get a pity fuck out of it."

"I'm so horribly sorry about what happened up there on that mountain. To Opie; to all of you. But believe me, Lucas, that's not the reason I want to make love with you."

Granted, his story had made her want to weep. To take him to bed and comfort him with sexual healing.

But Madeline realized that was the last thing he needed.

She'd always been a control freak. Perhaps it came from her parents falling from the sky. Perhaps from working in a male-dominated world where kitchens were like chaotic circuses needing the stability of a ringmaster to keep everything running smoothly. Or perhaps it was merely her nature.

Whatever the case, she understood that Lucas didn't need her to control this situation. To soothe his pain with gentle hands and tender touches.

What he needed was the freedom to exorcise his demons with passion.

And because she loved him, and because he'd reawakened something inside Madeline, something that had remained dormant all during her marriage, she framed his tragically handsome face between her palms.

"You want me, Lucas?" Their eyes met and there was a flash of heat like a bolt of lightning over the sea. "Then take me."

47

The challenge hovered between them, from her to him and back again. A sizzle of electric charge, like that first day he'd kissed her on the seawall so many years ago, arced between them.

Her scent floated on the rain-softened air, filling his head, flogging his senses, making coherent thought difficult.

Lucas had sworn that after all this time, after how he'd hurt her, he'd do things right. That he wouldn't allow his hunger—or hers—to rush him.

"I do want you." He traced a line down her cheek with a finger, stunned to find that his hands—the same hands that inserted IVs in the midst of raging battles—were far from steady. "So much I ache."

Unlike the other night, when he'd carried her into the bedroom, he took her hand and they walked the short distance to the bedroom.

"I'm sorry I lied, Maddy." He pushed some wild curls away from her face. "It was a stupid, fucked-up lie that I've regretted from the moment you ran out the door."

She lifted her chin. Passion had turned her eyes to gleaming pewter. "Then here's your chance to make up for it."

"Oh, I fully intend to do exactly that." He took hold of the bottom of her pretty sunshine-colored sweater. "Lift your arms."

She did, shifting to help him pull it over her head. He tossed it across the room, where it landed on the back of a chair.

Practical gray cotton framed her voluptuous breasts. Forget the Grand Canyon. Or the northern lights. Maddy's breasts were the true, natural wonders of the world.

Her nipples were the color of ripe strawberries, which brought up a fantasy of spreading chocolate on them, then licking it off. Which, in turn, had him wishing he'd thought to buy some Hershey's syrup while he'd been picking up that wine.

Next time.

His lips dipped into the cleavage framed by the cotton as he inhaled her scent.

"Lord, you are one tasty woman."

"It's the lotion." It took only the touch of his mouth on her warming flesh to make her tremble. "Gram makes it from the essential oil of peaches, vanilla, and coconut." The possessive touch of a palm to one of those amazing breasts brought her to full arousal.

"It's not peaches I'm tasting." While his mouth stayed busy with her breasts, his hands whipped the thin gold belt through the loops of her jeans and sent it flying across the room. "It's temptation." He pulled her down onto the wide bed with him and got down to business. "And sex."

The metal zipper of her jeans going down sounded unnaturally loud in the silence broken only by the surf below them, the sigh of the wind in the top of the fir trees surrounding the cottage, and their heavy breathing.

"Lucas." She arched her hips.

"Soon," he promised.

He slipped a finger beneath the elastic waistband of the cotton panties that were as utilitarian as her bra, combed a hot path through a narrow line of silky black curls, then skimmed a touch along the slick, moist folds.

She was as wet and willing as he was hot and hard, and

Lucas knew that if he lived to be a hundred, he'd never forget the way her flesh gleamed like pearls in the rain-silvered light.

She reached for him. "I want you inside me."

He wanted that, too. The problem was, he knew that within two seconds he'd go off like a rocket. And wouldn't that be a great way to convince her they belonged together?

"Soon," he repeated, slipping his fingers inside her.

First one.

Then a second.

As she lifted her hips, he slid in a third and began to move them. In. "Sometimes I thought I'd exaggerated this," she managed on a whimper. Out. "In my memory." In. "But I didn't." Out again.

She was writhing against his touch, seeking relief.

"You're still so amazingly hot." In, deeper this time. At the same time he flicked the sensitive, swollen nub with his thumb. The sound, as the orgasm ripped through her, was half cry, half scream.

"That's one."

She'd gone limp. But not for long, Lucas vowed.

"If you're expecting multiples, you're going to be sadly disappointed." Her eyes, which still blazed with hunger, suggested otherwise.

"I remember differently."

Avoiding her touch as she reached out for him again, he yanked the jeans down her legs and tossed them on the floor next to the belt.

"That was then," she said on a gasp. "When I was crazy with teenage lust."

"And this is now." They may be gray cotton, but her panties were cut high on the thigh and low on the hip. He'd been with women who always fancied up in silk and lace, but none of that fuck-me-big-boy underwear had ever turned him on as much as these. "So get ready for some serious, grown-up lust."

He ripped off his own clothes, sent them scattering, then dispensed with that last barrier between them.

Their teeth clashed as his mouth took hers. Then he moved on to feast on her hot, moist body as she, in turn, devoured his. Determined to hang on to his control, he dragged his mouth down her long, smooth legs, then back up again to nip at the tender skin between her thighs, then stroked the marks with his tongue while she clutched at the hot, tangled sheets.

His tongue dove into her while his fingers stroked. This time she keened as the climax rocked through her.

"That's two," he said against her trembling thigh.

"I don't remember you being so egotistical."

"Maybe because I didn't fully understand how lucky I was." He hadn't spent the past ten years in a Trappist monastery. But he'd never met a woman as responsive as his Maddy.

"You were always amazing." He traced slow, lazy circles in those moist ebony curls.

She rolled over, changing their positions, circling his aching erection with her fingers. "I think it's us," she said, as she explored him from root to tip. "Maybe it's that we're amazing together."

"You won't get any argument from me there." Her tongue followed the trail of sparks her fingers had made. When she went to take him in her mouth, Lucas caught hold of her hair and lifted her head. "Next time," he said, trying not to pant like the animal he was. "Because I need to be inside you."

He grabbed blindly for his jeans on the floor, but she was faster, diving over the top of him, snatching them out of his hands.

"Is this what you're looking for?" she asked as she retrieved the foil package from the front pocket.

"Madeline—"

"You never call me by my full name."

Appearing blithely unthreatened by his growl, she teasingly held it out of reach, her eyes laughing.

Tormenting him further, she tore the package open with her teeth, then, with hands that were a great deal steadier than his and that demonstrated a skill she definitely hadn't possessed at eighteen, slowly smoothed the latex over his stone-hard erection.

Then lowered herself over him. Just enough to dampen the tip with hot, slick moisture.

"This is your revenge, isn't it?" he asked between clenched teeth. "You're getting back at me for ten years ago."

"I've no idea what you're talking about." She lowered herself another millimeter. "Besides, I've always heard that revenge is a dish best served cold."

Although he wouldn't have thought it possible, he swelled further when she began rubbing against his length.

"And *cold* is definitely not a word I'd use to describe you, Lucas Chaffee."

All he'd have to do would be to press his heels on the mattress and thrust upward to end the erotic torment she was putting him through. But Lucas understood that for many complex reasons, which weren't solely about him and perhaps even partly about the damn Frenchman, the tables had turned. Maddy needed to take back the control she'd surrendered to him.

"I love you," he said. Even enough, for just this one time, to allow that cheating husband into the bed with them. "More than I'll ever be able to say. But I'll never lie to you again, Maddy. And I'll never give you any reason to be sorry for this night."

Her eyes sheened over the teasing laughter.

She met his gaze. Then nodded.

"I believe you."

Then, with anticipation sparking in the air around them, she lowered herself the rest of the way down.

The shock of hot flesh against hot flesh made Lucas shudder. From her sharp gasp, he knew he was not alone.

She began rocking against him, giving him full access to those lush breasts that had starred in a lot of his personal wet dreams over the past decade. He licked them, sucked them, rolled her berry pink, hard nipples in his mouth.

There were no words. None were needed.

Lucas knew that if he lived to be a hundred, he'd never forget the uncensored passion on her face as she rode him, her wild curls tumbling over her shoulders, her head flung back, her eyes closed.

They'd both changed a great deal during their time apart, but one thing that had not changed was the way their movements were so perfectly matched to each other's. As he rolled her over, her body moved fluidly, lifting to meet his as his hips pistoned. Deeper. Harder. Faster.

The convulsions started deep inside her, clutching, then radiating outward like a tsunami, a long, powerful crest that pushed her over the edge, taking Lucas right along with her.

When she laughed and wrapped her arms around him as he held her tight, Lucas wished they could just stay here forever. In this cottage. In this bed.

Which was, of course, impossible. So for now he'd take all that he could get and worry about tomorrow later.

But as her eyes, looking like mist shimmering beneath a late-summer sun, met his, Lucas was struck with a possessiveness that nearly rocked him to the core.

Mine.

Now all he had to do was convince her of that.

Fortunately, the SEAL motto he'd lived by for the past ten years was "Ready to lead, ready to follow; never quit."

And Lucas had no intention of quitting where Maddy was concerned.

48

For the next two hours, they did their best to make up for lost time. Finally, lying sprawled on the mattress, looking like the very hot, very satiated male he was, Lucas said, "I'm not sure, but I think that might have done it."

He ran a hand down her back, over her butt, which definitely did not have buns of steel. Madeline had worried about that, but sometime earlier, when he'd kneaded her cheeks and told her how much he loved her ass, she felt every bit as sexy as he kept telling her she was.

"For a while, anyway," he amended. "But if we don't get out of this bed, I may end up killing myself."

She pressed a kiss against his chest. Which could have easily appeared on a recruiting poster for Navy SEALs. "I couldn't think of a better way to go." She stretched, feeling stiff in places she hadn't even known she could ache. But it was a good feeling. And she'd definitely felt the burn.

The thought made her laugh.

"What?"

"I just figured out how to fund Gram's restaurant," she said.

"How's that?" He was playing with her hair, seemingly fascinated by the wild texture she was certain must look as if she'd stuck her finger in a light socket.

"Workout tapes."

He lifted his head. "You're going to make workout tapes?"

"You don't have to make it sound that ridiculous. I work out." She'd walked Winnie for Sofia just last night. Of course, unlike so many of those X-ray New York socialites Maxime had been supposedly feeding at lunch, including the thin-as-a-piece-of-spaghetti Katrin, she ate. Because what was the point of cooking if you didn't love food?

"I also happen to love food. Almost as much as sex." Just a few hours ago, that order would've been reversed. Actually, sex would have been much farther down on her list.

"I love your body just the way it is." He drew her closer so they fit chest to chest, thigh to thigh. "See, everywhere you have a curve." He skimmed a touch down the side of her breast. "I have a hollow." He kissed her, a slow, deep kiss that had her drifting back into the mist. "We've always been a perfect fit. And you're the most voluptuously hungry female I've ever known."

"I am, aren't I?" She loved that description. Nearly as much as she'd loved that mind-blowing, multiorgasmic sex that had earned it.

"The hottest, most responsive woman on the planet," he said. "But I still don't get where the workout tapes come in."

"Think about it. Do you know how much money the physical fitness business brings in?"

"Haven't a clue."

"Me, neither," she admitted. "But I'll bet most of those people walking to nowhere on treadmills and climbing endless stairs that never take them anywhere would much rather burn calories having hot sex."

"That would be my preference. As long as you're the one I'm having hot sex with. But I'm not sure the world is ready for the idea."

"Why not?"

"Because if everyone was having sex, who'd build your

restaurant? Or work in it? Or get out of bed long enough to eat in it?"

"So much for your claim of being a go-with-the-flow kind of guy. Are SEALs always so practical?"

"We think in logistics. Cause and effect."

"Says the man who doesn't think ahead to stock his refrigerator."

"Why do that? When the world is filled with people who actually like to cook?" He pressed his lips against her temple. "Like you."

"Which I might consider doing if you had anything but takeout and beer in your fridge," she said. "So given that you're claiming I killed your libido—"

"Not *killed*." He frowned at that idea, showing that despite his amazing stamina and his hard, hot body, he still possessed a typical male ego. Which she found appealing in its own way. It made him more human. Less of a superhero. "It's just recharging."

"Well, I suppose we might as well get some work done while it is. Why don't you show me your idea for the restaurant design?"

"I'm not doing the design," he said. "Because I don't know anything about how stuff is used. But I do have a cool program Dad's friend sent me that'll help me make your design work."

"Is it on your laptop?"

"Yeah."

"Great. Then we won't have to get out of bed."

He laughed at that. "Talk about being practical."

He retrieved the laptop from its case on the counter and joined her beneath the rumpled sheets.

"The first thing I was thinking," he said as he turned it on, "was that, given that you're big on being organic, you'd also want the restaurant to be LEED certified."

"I hadn't gotten that far yet in my thinking, but yes." LEED, an acronym for Leader in Energy and Environmental Design, was an internationally recognized green building certification. "Lowering our carbon footprint is a natural for the menu."

"That's what I figured. It's also good business."

"It's obviously going to cost more money." She was proud of the amount she'd negotiated, but worried if there'd be enough to purchase all the items she'd need to become LEED and green-dining certified.

"Up front, true. But it's a great marketing tool that should bring in customers and get your restaurant a lot more press coverage, which is great free advertising. Once you get people in the door, your food will turn them into repeat customers. Meanwhile, by doing something as simple as adding inexpensive, low-flow aerators to faucets, you can save sixty gallons of water per hour, resulting in a twenty-five percent decrease in water usage.

"Also, by composting, which Sofia's already doing, and recycling, you can expect to decrease your garbage-collection bills by somewhere around fifty percent."

"Okay. Now I am officially impressed with your homework."

"SEALs don't believe in doing anything halfway. And homework is a way of life. I always memorized all the medical records of any new teammates."

"All of them?"

"Well, you can't exactly stop to read through stacks of papers in the middle of a battle," he pointed out. "You know what they say about the devil being in the details. . . . Wait until you see this."

With a few clicks of the keys, he brought up a three-dimensional model of the building as he saw it, and using the items in the software program's library, began moving the hot and cold lines and dishwashers and pasta cookers, and all the other things she'd need around the floor, with a mere click of the mouse.

The program was wonderful and he was clever at using

it, helping her create a kitchen that would be both energy efficient and staff friendly—and would include Energy Star appliances, light sensors, and an electronically controlled double-door steamer that would make potatoes fluffier and fresher and use less power than boiling them in huge pots of water.

But Madeline was envisioning the excitement and sensuality of voices shouting out "Fire"; hard, shining surfaces; big machines; wooden spoons; a dream wall of pots; fish searing in sauté pans over flame; the sweet fragrance of brown stocks kept at a simmer; the aroma of spices being roasted; mushrooms crackling in hot oil; and rolls of white towels making crescent swipes around the edges of beautifully plated dishes.

"I thought I was good at multitasking," Lucas said, as he added state-of-the-art antimicrobial shelving to the walk-in cooler to help prevent mold, which was always a problem with moisture. "But you're answering every question I ask about how you want the place set up, yet at the same time you look a million miles away."

"I'm envisioning it all," she said. "It's going to be perfect." Even as she said it, she remembered something. "I take that back. Thomas Keller, an amazing self-taught chef in Napa Valley, says that since there's no such thing as a perfect food, only the idea of it, the real purpose of striving toward perfection is to make people happy. That is what cooking is all about."

"So that's what you want to do? Make people happy?"

"Absolutely."

"Then marry me." She should have seen it coming, but in still imagining the restaurant she was starting to think of as hers, she'd missed the warning signs.

"I can't."

"Why not?"

"There are too many reasons to count. The first being that I'm still technically married."

"Sofia said you sent the papers back. You'll be a free woman in just a couple days."

"That's not the point. The other reason is that I already made one mistake, Lucas. I'm not going to rush into anything."

"I can understand that reasoning. But I do have one question."

"Why do I think I'm not going to like it?"

"Don't worry. It's an easy one. How long did you know the Frenchman before you married him?"

"A year." It had taken her that long to wear Maxime down. Which should've told her something.

"And how long did your parents know each other?"

She saw where he was going with this. "You said one question," she reminded him.

"Humor me."

She knew that if she didn't tell him, he'd merely ask her grandmother, who would. "Six weeks," she muttered.

"I didn't quite hear that."

"Six weeks. Okay?"

"And your grandparents?"

"Less time than that."

"I rest my case. I also have a suggestion."

"What?"

"Come away with me."

"Like, elope?"

"Well, I wouldn't object to that, except I think there are some people in our lives who might. I was thinking of going to Portland for a couple days."

"Why?"

"For fun." He played with the silver seashell earring, one of the pair she'd bought at the Dancing Deer. "You have heard of the concept, right? Where you put aside work and worries and problems and decisions, let your hair down, and just play."

"You just want to get away from prying eyes and have sex."

"The eyes don't bother me. It's not as if they're all going to be pressed against the cottage windows, watching us.

"As for the sex, I wouldn't turn it down. But the apartment I inherited from my dad has three bedrooms. Where you sleep is up to you."

She knew where she wanted to sleep. But was it where she *should* sleep? Was she jumping straight from the sauté pan into the fire?

Then again, didn't she deserve a fling? After all she'd been through?

"You know," he said. "The city has a lot of antiques stores. Since play for play's sake seems to be a problem for you, we could scout out some things for the restaurant."

"That is hugely appealing."

And practical. And Madeline had always thought of herself as an eminently practical woman. Hadn't Maxime always said that? Though he'd often made it sound more like a flaw rather than an attribute.

"But why do I suspect that spending a weekend antiquing isn't anywhere on the top ten things on your bucket list?"

"That would be true. Until I add you to the mix. Then it's right up there on the top." He gave her a friendly leer. "Okay. Maybe third from the top. After marriage. And the sex stuff."

"You really are impossible."

"I prefer to think of it as tenacious. Our timing was off the first time around, Maddy. If you think we're going too fast, we can slow down. Set our own pace. Whatever you want."

"What do you want?"

"To be with you. Any way I can get you. And if that means following you around in every antiques store in Oregon, I'm up for that. Meanwhile, because we do have to eat, what do you say to taking a shower—"

"Together?"

"Saving water is good for the planet. Then afterward we can go into town and have dinner at Bon Temps."

She laughed. "I give up. And since I can't remember the last time I had legitimate Cajun food, you've got yourself a deal."

49

Unlike the rest of Shelter Bay, which seemed much the same as always, Bon Temps had undergone a lot of changes. But two things remained exactly as Madeline remembered them: the delicious aromas drifting out of the kitchen and the feeling of welcome as soon as she walked in.

"I love what you've done with the place," she told Sax, who seated her and Lucas at a four-top next to the window, which offered a dazzling view of the harbor.

"Thanks." He put his hands in the back pockets of his jeans and looked around the restaurant and dance hall with obvious pride. "The change in décor was Trey's idea. We were picking out paint, and he decided Cajun red fit. After we went with that, the kid also came up with the Mardi Gras theme."

"It works. It just feels like a party as soon as you walk in."

"That's the point. What can I get you to drink?"

Madeline ordered a white wine, while Lucas opted for one of a surprising selection of microbrewed beers. Which was another change. She doubted there were that many restaurants in New York that could offer so many small labels.

Throwing out any idea of water conservation, they'd spent a long, spectacularly hot time in Lucas' shower, which had them arriving after most of the dinner crowd had left, allowing Sax to take them up on their invitation to sit down at the table with them while they worked their way through an order of fried Cajun shrimp.

"These are delicious," she said. "I love the way you mixed the panko bread crumbs in with the cornmeal for the breading."

"I'm not a fancy chef like you," he said. "But these days, even a lot of people who come here are looking for something lighter and healthier. The panko gives a lighter, crispier crunch because it doesn't soak up the oil."

"But it still picks up the flavor of the seasonings, cornmeal, and oil. Good decision." It crossed Madeline's mind that if she kept eating the way she had since arriving in Shelter Bay, she was definitely going to end up the size of one of Shelter Bay's resident whales.

"Gram and I are setting up a cooking school and restaurant at the farm," she told Sax. "Which may end up becoming a new program."

"So Kara told me."

"Would you be willing to teach this? And maybe a couple of your other dishes?"

"Maybe you'd better taste them first."

"You already have me convinced. So if the gumbo's as good as I expect from the aromas coming from the kitchen, would you be interested? You'd be paid."

He rubbed his chin. "I wouldn't mind teaching. But I'm no TV actor."

"Trust me. You get used to the camera. And if the network picks up the show, I'll help walk you through it," Madeline assured him. "It also fits with my theme. Cajun might be a lot hotter than the Greek and Italian food in my background, but for a lot of people, it's comfort food. You could spread the word and get more people cooking it."

"I think Emeril's pretty well got that covered," he said.

"You're better."

He glanced over at Lucas. "And I thought Kara was stubborn."

"Maddy's always had a mind of her own." Lucas scooped a handful of the shrimp from the white bowl. "And I wouldn't want her any other way."

"Yeah. That's how I feel about Kara."

"I already mentioned it to her at lunch," Madeline said, "but I'm glad to have a chance to tell you that while I'm sad about Jared's death, it's lovely to see you two together. You were always such close friends. Especially that year after Jared joined the Marines."

A shadow moved over Sax's face. It came and went so quickly that had she not been paying attention, she would've missed it.

"Is something wrong?" she asked carefully.

"Nah." He shook his head. Then raked a hand through his dark hair. "Hell, you guys are friends and it's not as if it's going to stay a secret forever." He paused another, longer beat. Blew out a breath, then said, "Kara's pregnant."

"Good going," Lucas said, punching Sax on the upper arm.

There was more. Although she'd never been to war, as these two men had, Madeline had a fairly good idea what it must feel like to cross a minefield as she gingerly asked, "Are we happy about that?"

"Oh, hell, yes. I love Trey as if he were my own son, but yeah, we'd both like a big family, so this is beyond cool. Except for one thing."

"Which would be?" Madeline was a little uncomfortable talking about Kara behind her back, but Sax had brought up the subject.

"She's refusing to get married."

"What?" That was a surprise. "She adores you. That was so obvious at lunch when she was talking about how you and Trey have bonded, and how wonderful your lives are together, and how she's looking forward to growing old together. I can't believe she doesn't want to get married."

"Oh, she's not refusing to get married, period," Sax said.

"She just doesn't want to be pregnant when she walks down the aisle."

"But she's gorgeous," Lucas said. "And I'm no expert on pregnancy, but doesn't it take a while for a woman to show?"

"Yeah. She's got plenty of time on that. In fact, she looks just the same as always except that her breasts have gotten flat-out amazing. . . . Hell." He dragged a hand down his face. "I'd really appreciate it if you wouldn't tell her I said that."

"You've got it," Lucas said.

"I didn't hear a thing," Madeline agreed. "Let me guess." Being a woman, and remembering when Kara left town to go to California to marry Jared Conway, she suspected she understood the other woman's reasoning. "She was pregnant the first time she got married. She doesn't want to repeat that experience."

"It's not the same thing at all, dammit," Sax complained, confirming her guess. "Jared was getting deployed. It only made sense for them to get married before he left. But I'm not going anywhere."

"Still, you represent a new start. A new life. It's not surprising she'd want to do things differently this time."

"Maybe. Then there's her mom."

"I thought she'd gotten to like you." Madeline remembered that not being the case back when Kara's mother had disapproved of everything about Sax Douchett. Especially the part about Kara and him being such close friends.

"Yeah. I finally won her over. But here's the thing: The night of Cole and Kelli's rehearsal dinner here at Bon Temps, Kara suggested to her that the two of them have a double wedding."

"That's sweet."

"Yeah. I guess. But with the whole world seeming to be imploding or exploding or just going to hell in a handbasket, Faith and John have been kept busy with their medical-relief work. So they haven't taken any time off to come back home. Kara's set a couple tentative dates, then some other crisis pops up, and off they go.

"Kara figures since she and Faith mended fences, after missing Trey's birth, her mom will want to be here for her when her second grandchild's born. So that's the main reason why she wants to wait until after the baby's born."

"It's only nine months away."

"More like eight. But, dammit, it seems I've already been waiting a lifetime. Plus, I've been telling her what you and I learned," he said to Lucas. "You're only given so much time, and you never know when it's going to end, so you can't afford to waste a minute.

"I don't see any reason why we can't just get hitched now. With all our friends. Then if she wants the big wedding with all the bells and whistles and rice throwing, we can do it again when her mom finally makes it back to town."

"That sounds reasonable," Lucas said.

"Doesn't it?" Sax agreed. "But you ever try to argue with a pregnant woman?"

"No," Lucas said.

"It'd be easier taking on an entire horde of Taliban."

"Give her time," Madeline suggested. "She could always change her mind."

"Yeah." Sax looked a bit more optimistic. "That's what I'm hoping. Meanwhile, I keep reminding myself that the only easy day—"

"Was yesterday," Madeline and Lucas said with him.

The mood lifted, they were still laughing when Sax took their dinner order back to the kitchen.

50

Madeline had known Duncan Chaffee was internationally admired. But nothing could have prepared her for the penthouse apartment on the top floor of the glass-and-steel tower overlooking the Columbia River.

"Wow," she murmured as the private elevator opened directly into a foyer nearly the size of the Chaffees' Shelter Bay cottage. She stared at the valuable works of art, seemingly having been collected on Lucas' father's travels around the world, scattered carelessly over tabletops some unseen housekeeper kept polished to a mirror sheen.

Museum-framed blueprints, hung side by side with modern art, adorned the wall.

Lucas stuck his hands in the back pockets of his jeans and glanced around. "I guess it's a little impressive at first sight."

"A lot more than impressive." Her heels clicked on the black marble floor as she crossed the room to study a sketch that had captured her attention, drawn in what she guessed to be colored pencils.

Done in mostly greens and creams, it showed a house and wall created of simple geometric figures. The leaves and grass were fragmented and the tree's branches were both curves and sharp angles. Although she'd never been a fan of the Cubism Maxime's decorator had forced on them, this was compelling.

She leaned forward to read the signature. "Picasso?"

"It's an early working sketch of his painting *House in a Garden*," Lucas said. "He did it in the early 1900s during his early Cubism period. The actual painting is in a museum in St. Petersburg."

"Why isn't *this* in a museum?"

Lucas shrugged. "It was a gift from a friend. That's the part Dad valued. Not what it might go for at auction."

"A gift?" Surely he didn't mean . . . "Pablo Picasso gave your father one of his sketches?"

"The guy apparently got superproductive in his later years. So much so, his villa on the Riviera was supposedly overflowing with paintings. He invited Dad there to discuss building a museum on the garden grounds. During one of the visits, Dad noticed the sketch, commented on it, suggesting that it might be interesting to use it as a model for a simpler design, one that would fit into the garden and echo the simplicity of this painting.

"The deal didn't work out because Picasso wanted something a lot grander to go along with the sprawling stone villa, but he did give Dad the sketch."

She looked closer at some black squiggly lines at the top of the sketch. "And autographed it personally to him."

"Yeah."

"Wow," she repeated. "I knew your dad was famous, but I guess I never realized you were so, well . . ."

"Rich?" Lucas filled in for her.

Now realizing the wealth that the items in this single room could well represent, Maddy nodded as she stood at the window and looked down at the river. Every time she thought she had a handle on this man, she'd discover something new about him.

As if sensing her confusion, Lucas came up behind her, wrapped his arms around her waist, pulled her against him, and rested his chin on the top of her head.

"Dad was rich, Maddy. I'm just a guy who was, until a few days ago, out of work."

"I had no idea unemployment paid so well," she said dryly.

"Honest, I had no idea how much money he had until I met with his lawyers," he said. "My first thought was that I could just give you the money for your restaurant, but I didn't think you'd take it without thinking it came with strings."

"I wouldn't think you'd use it as leverage. But I wouldn't have taken it." She considered that another moment. "Although I might let you invest in it."

Which was the way most restaurants were funded. Even with all the money she'd brought into the business, Maxime had several wealthy investors. All of whom expected a return on their investments, which was bound to be easier now that he had those beer bucks.

"Count me in." He turned her in his arms. "I'm trying to figure out how to give most of it away." His lips plucked enticingly at hers. "But I can't think of anyone I'd rather invest in."

Her lips tingled beneath his. "You're just trying to seduce me."

"Guilty." He began nuzzling her neck. "Is it working?"

The heat radiating from his body was beginning to make her head swim. Although the day outside the window was gray, the tenderness of his mouth was sending streams of warm, liquid sunshine through her veins.

"I think so." She moved her hips tantalizingly against his hard male loins, spreading the golden warmth. "But perhaps you ought to really kiss me. So I can know for sure."

"Why don't we put off the rest of the tour and go straight to the master bedroom?"

"How far is it?"

"About a mile down the hall."

"You can show me later." She tugged his shirt from his jeans and ripped it open, sending buttons flying. "Because I don't think I can wait that long to have you inside me."

The came together like wildfire, falling to an Oriental rug on the floor.

Clothes were scattered as if by gale-force winds; Madeline's sweater landed on a chair across the room, and Lucas' jeans landed on an ebony table, followed seconds later by hers.

"It's never been this way with anyone else," she said as she straddled him. The very idea filled her with wonder. And awe. "I know it sounds like a cliché, but I've never wanted any man as much as I've always wanted you. Since that first time."

"It's never been the same for me, either, Maddy." His roughened hands ran down her back, cupping her bottom, pressing her even tighter against him. "And now I know why. Because you were always in my mind."

"Okay." She leaned forward, her breasts skimming against his chest as she pressed a hot, wet kiss against his mouth. "Consider me seduced." Then his chin. "And now let me return the favor."

She slid down his body, teasing a trail of kisses down his torso, her tongue dampening his dark nipples before going still lower.

He bucked as she blew a soft, warm breath against his stomach. Then lower still.

"You're so hard." Her fingers curled around his aroused length. She ran her tongue over him. "And hot."

Control shattered as the fires burn hotter and higher, until a burst of blazing ecstasy consumed them both.

They were sprawled on the floor in a tangle of arms and legs, their bodies slick with perspiration. There were no words for what Madeline was feeling. No way to describe an emotion that was so much more satisfying, more all encompassing than mere contentment.

"I think I'm regressing," he said when his breathing settled enough to talk again.

She snuggled against him. "I feel absolutely decadent."

He ran his hand down her side. "Decadent and delectable. But even in my horny, hormone-driven youth, I never made love on a rug."

"Ah, but we made love lots of times on a blanket." She rolled over onto her stomach and gave him a saucy smile. "We'll have to do that again. When we get back home."

"Home," he agreed.

The word was sounding more and more right every time she heard it. Thought it. Putting that idea aside for now, she brushed a lock of damp, sun-streaked hair off his forehead.

"I must have regressed, too." Because she adored his taste, she touched her lips to his. "Because I want you again."

"You're not alone there." She felt his smile against her mouth. "But this time we're doing it in a bed. Because I don't think I have any more skin to leave on this rug."

Lifting her effortlessly into his arms, he strode purposefully down a long hallway lined with art that she suspected cost more than her grandmother's entire farm.

"Oh, my God!" She laughed when he dropped her unceremoniously onto the mattress. "I never would've imagined your father having a waterbed!"

"He had back surgery a few years ago. Nothing all that serious, but the doctors prescribed if for him when he got out of the hospital. Since it was comfortable, he kept it."

"Oh, we should really write a thank-you note to that doctor," she said as he joined her on the mattress, causing waves to undulate beneath them.

The sun began to break through the gloom outside the penthouse windows. Lost in each other, neither Lucas nor Madeline noticed.

51

Portland consisted of a series of neighborhoods, each with its own feel. The neighborhood where Lucas took Madeline shopping had a laid-back, small-town feel that reminded her a great deal of Shelter Bay.

Local grocery stores, she was pleased to see, offered many organic products. There were also coffee roasters, galleries, and a community center with an old-fashioned bulletin board where people had posted notices of concerts, gallery showings, apartments for rent, a found dog and a lost cat.

Walking hand in hand down tree-lined streets where there seemed to be more bicycles parked than cars, where people sat at small tables chatting and drinking coffee and eating ice cream, invoked a good-old-days feeling highlighted by an old-fashioned movie marquee that could have shown up in *Back to the Future*. Although Madeline couldn't remember the last time she'd even watched a DVD of a movie, let alone gone to the theater, even she recognized the poster of Mary Joyce, a stunningly beautiful Irish actress who'd garnered a huge international following of fans due to her sexy portrayal of a selkie queen.

"Oh, lunch!" she said, pointing toward a white taqueria food truck.

"You're kidding."

She looked up at him. "What—you think I'm too fancy

for 'real people' food? It you really watched my programs, you'd see that's what I cook."

"But not in a food truck."

"Food's all about taste. Not the size of the kitchen the food's cooked in. And I adore food trucks." She dragged him by the hand over to the window and ordered a veggie burrito, while Lucas opted for the chicken mole burrito.

"See," she said, as they sat at one of the tables and shared bites of each other's wrapped burritos. "It's great." The veggies were obviously fresh, cooked perfectly so they were still crisp. And only four dollars. "And your mole is amazing."

"You're not going to get any argument there," he said, licking the red sauce she'd gotten on her fingers while scooping the salsa roja out of the tiny container.

When he began sucking on her fingers in a way that caused a now-familiar warmth to gather between her legs, she stood up to keep from leaping on him right then and there.

"We still haven't found anything for the restaurant," she said, trying to drag her mind out of the bedroom and back to their other reason for having come to the city.

They'd stopped at a few shops on the drive to Portland, but nothing had shouted out "Buy me!" The problem, she was discovering, was that most true antiques were French or English. Finding something American that wasn't a re-production was proving a challenge.

They strolled down Antique Alley, looking in all the windows, when a weathered farm table caught her eye.

"That's it," she said. "The bar."

The table, made for a large farm family, had a pine top with a distressed finish that reminded her of the smaller one in her grandmother's kitchen, and sturdy maple legs.

"It's a dining table," Lucas pointed out. "It's not high enough for a bar."

"Surely Flynn can do something about that. Maybe add

some reclaimed wood to the base of the legs. Or replace them."

"You'd be destroying the integrity of the antique."

"I'm not intending to sell it for a profit. I want it." It was the exact piece she'd been looking for. It had character and fit in the dining room she'd envisioned. "Let's go in and check it out."

It took all her self-control to curb her enthusiasm enough to ignore the table as she browsed through the cluttered store.

"This is nice." She ran her fingers over a bronze lamp with a colorful glass shade depicting acorns around the edge.

"It's from the Arts and Craft era," the saleswoman, who'd been trailing her since she and Lucas first entered the shop, offered. "Tiffany."

Madeline checked out the inflated price tag. "Actual Tiffany?"

"Well, Tiffany inspired," the woman admitted.

"It's lovely," Madeline said. Which was true. "But not quite what I'm looking for."

She continued wandering through the cluttered shop, pausing to inspect a Depression-era glass platter, a Wedgwood box, a Chippendale chest.

"You have a lovely shop," she told the woman.

"Thank you. We pride ourselves on maintaining an eclectic inventory."

"Well, you've succeeded." She ran her fingers over an ebony nude she suspected Maxime's designer would've loved to put in the Riverside apartment. "Unfortunately, I'm afraid you don't have what I'm looking for."

"Our merchandise continually changes," the woman said. "If you could perhaps tell me what you're looking for . . ."

"The problem is, I'm not really sure," Madeline said with an apologetic smile. "I'm afraid it's one of those situations where I'll know it when I see it."

Undaunted, the clerk, who turned out to be the owner, brought various items to Madeline's attention: a nineteenth-century bronze French chandelier, a pair of silver Art Nouveau candlesticks in a lily-and-lotus pattern, a richly embossed Sheffield Victorian teapot, even a scrolled wrought-iron balcony railing from New Orleans, which was alleged to come from the French Quarter building where Tennessee Williams had once lived and that inspired him to write *A Streetcar Named Desire.*

Madeline praised but sadly shook her head at each offering.

Meanwhile, Lucas pointed out various items—a vintage ship in a bottle, a German beer stein from the 1800s, and a massive moose head, which the owner assured Madeline was not actually "stuffed," but rather, a taxidermist had stretched the moose hide on a form to preserve it indefinitely.

All of which—especially the poor moose staring at her with those unblinking glass eyes—were even less appealing than the earlier offers.

"This is nice," Lucas said finally, stopping at the table.

"It is," Madeline agreed noncommittally. She looked at the tag. "Though a bit pricey. Especially if you compare it to that one we saw in the Pearl District this morning."

A time when they'd actually been rolling around on the waterbed, but the store's owner didn't need to know that.

"Oh, dear," the woman said, glancing at the discreet price tag herself. "I'm afraid there's been a mistake. This table was supposed to go on sale today. But my clerk"—she glanced over at a woman selling a frosted-glass perfume bottle to a customer—"must have overlooked it."

Five minutes later, they'd arranged for the table to be delivered to Lavender Hill Farm.

"I can't believe you got her down to that price," Madeline said, practically jumping up and down in the passenger's seat of the Jeep. "And when you asked her to throw in that matching bench, I was sure you'd blown the deal."

"You needed a bench inside by the hostess stand. Since the bar's going to be a few feet away, it was a logical choice. And she wanted to make a sale."

"You were still amazing."

"You weren't so bad yourself, sweetheart." He ruffled her hair; then, when they stopped for a red light, leaned across the console and kissed her. "I'd say we make one helluva team."

She beamed. "I'd say you're right."

The rest of the two-day holiday passed as if it had wings. They bought more antiques that would be perfect for the new restaurant (including some weathered iron lanterns she decided to have wired as chandeliers); walked along the Riverfront; ate crab cakes that, while she honestly didn't believe lived up to her own, were still very good; drove out to a winery for a tasting, and talked. And talked.

Madeline told him about when she worked in Provence and, in her nervousness at being constantly screamed at by a chef with a horrible temper, had mistaken salt for sugar and ruined an entire batch of fig tarts. A mistake that had gotten her immediately fired.

Lucas told her about when he'd played high school football and been knocked to the ground by a huge linebacker who'd rung his bell. He'd managed to get up, but during the next play, Lucas, still confused, had run the wrong way and would've scored a touchdown for their opponents if one of his own teammates hadn't managed to tackle him inches short of the goal line.

"I never lived that down," he said, laughing at the memory. "And after I was diagnosed with a concussion after the game, Dad benched me. Permanently."

"From what I've been reading about football and brain injuries, he did the right thing," she said.

"Probably. But it sure didn't end up being my last one."

Given what he'd been doing the past ten years, she guessed that was true. She also knew they'd probably have to talk more about their years apart. But during this special, stolen time together, she just wanted to concentrate on being together.

Although she would have preferred to have him all to herself, knowing that Lucas must still be suffering the loss of his family, they accepted a dinner invitation from his architect godfather and godmother at their hillside home, with stunning views of the city lights. Fortunately, the soaring glass, steel, and concrete mansion was much warmer inside, as was the reception they received.

Not only did the couple welcome her as a longtime friend, but the wife seemed thrilled to receive a signed cookbook, and, over braised chicken legs served with garlic mashed potatoes and sautéed green beans from Maddy's cookbook, they spent an enjoyable evening talking cooking and ideas for the design of the kitchen, all of which, considering Dylan Delany's own starkly modern exterior, surprisingly fit in perfectly with the farm.

The night had dawned clear, so they walked along the river again, joining the other couples who were out enjoying the spring evening.

Then they went back to the penthouse and made love. All night long.

Maddy's last thought, as she slipped into sleep, was while perfection might not be possible, her time with Lucas in Portland had come really, really close.

52

"There's something I need to tell you," Lucas said as they drove back to the coast.

"Oh?" She glanced over at him, surprised by the seriousness of his tone.

"I don't want to marry you for your money."

Coming out of left field as it had, the statement made her laugh. "I wouldn't think so. Considering you're probably the wealthiest man I know."

"That's not my money. Not really." In fact, if he thought about it too much, which he tried not to, the idea had him feeling guilty about coming into such a windfall when he hadn't done anything to earn it. "Which is why I'm working on ways to give most of it away. The deal is, I didn't even know about my inheritance when I decided I wanted us to get back together."

"Believe me, the thought never entered my mind."

"You never once compared me to the Frenchman?"

"Of course."

"See?" The guy, while a douche bag, was not only famous, he was also ambitious. Lucas' entire life for the past decade had been defined by being a SEAL. While everyone had advised him to take some time off to transition back into a civilian society, he'd discovered that not having a goal every morning left him feeling rudderless, which, in turn, brought back some of the PTSD issues he'd done his best to ignore.

"And you always came out way ahead," she said. "In fact, you make Maxime look even worse by comparison."

"When we were first together that summer, I had no clue about what I was going to do with my life. When Dad died, I found myself pretty much in the same place."

"But now you're building the school, remodeling the cannery. It's not as if you're drifting. In fact, from the little bit Kara told me about your life these past years, it seems that taking time to drift with the flow wouldn't be a bad idea."

"I tried that for a few days and didn't like it. But I'm not the same person I was back then, Maddy."

"Neither am I." She shrugged. "We've both had life-changing experiences. But when we're together, it feels the same."

"For me, too. But there are things you need to know. Things I brought home from the war."

She turned as much toward him as the seat belt would allow. "Okay. But if you think you can scare me away, it's not going to happen."

She might not have agreed to a lifetime commitment. But he was getting to her. Which made what he had to say easier.

"I'm not as whacked-out as Scout was when she came home, but I do have some issues. I have nightmares."

"Name me one person who doesn't. My recurring stress one is having to cater a State dinner, getting lost on the way to the White House, realizing I left my shopping list back in New York, and not being to remember a single thing I'd planned to prepare. And then, when I finally get there, I'm naked.

"I realize that's not nearly as serious as the ones you usually have, which are undoubtedly from having actually experienced nightmare situations, but I just wanted to point out that although I'm sorry you have to suffer them, they're not going into any negative column on whatever list you seem to think I'm compiling."

She seemed honestly unconcerned. But since he had every intention of kissing her on the seawall on their fiftieth anniversary, Lucas decided to continue.

"I always sit with my back against the wall in a restaurant. And check out where the emergency exit is when I go in."

"I noticed Kara did the same thing at the Sea Mist, which took some juggling of chairs. I suspect it's common among cops and soldiers. Even SEALs."

"I don't trust people as easily as I used to."

"Neither do I." Which made sense, he decided. "Do you trust me?"

"Absolutely."

"Well, then." Her smile made his heart feel as if it might go airborne at any minute. "I don't see that we have any problem."

Then marry me, dammit.

Not wanting to dampen what had been such a perfect getaway, Lucas reluctantly decided since he'd apparently jumped that hurdle, this wasn't the time to push.

"Apparently not," he said easily.

53

Too impatient to sit around and wait for Lucas to be able to start work on the restaurant, Madeline began juggling her time between working on the building plans with Lucas and volunteering at Haven House. It did not escape her attention that as unsatisfying as her own marriage had been, it could have turned out much, much worse.

She'd begun teaching the basics and found that more than one resident, but especially Phoebe, had a talent for cooking. She also discovered that another of the women, who couldn't fry an egg, made the lightest, fluffiest doughnuts Madeline had ever tasted. Not only did she seriously consider offering her the job of pastry chef in the new restaurant, but she also began thinking that one of the cannery shops, when Lucas and McGrath got the building finished, could be a great outlet for baked goods.

Or perhaps they could even open up a food booth, serving simple, easy-to-eat items like she and Lucas had bought at the taqueria truck in Portland.

It was good to be excited again. And she had so much to be excited about. Her divorce papers had arrived. Although the Cooking Network hadn't embraced her idea of filming the building of the cooking school, suggesting it was better suited for channels featuring construction, on the same day she officially became a free woman, Pepper had called to inform her that they'd totally embraced her idea of a show based on the classes in the cooking school. She also, surprisingly, supported Madeline giving up the ChefSteel endorsement.

To celebrate, Madeline paid a visit to Take the Cake, where she ran into Kara sitting at a table, eating a lemon coconut cupcake. A German chocolate cupcake sat on a plate in front of her.

"My excuse," she said, when Madeline returned to join her with an island pineapple cupcake, "is that I'm eating for two these days."

"So I heard. Congratulations!" Madeline took a bite of the cupcake, which reminded her of what Lucas had said about making love to her in Hawaii. She was still, admittedly, gun-shy when it came to marriage, but a vacation trip sounded like a fabulous idea. Maybe she'd suggest it to him tonight.

"I wanted to wait until I got through the first trimester to share the news," Kara said. "But I know Sax is frustrated with me, so I understand him dumping on you and Lucas."

"We're friends." Madeline licked a bit of frosting off her thumb and remembered, in vivid detail, the quickening in her body when Lucas had licked the salsa roja off her fingers. How was it, she asked herself, that everything reminded her of him?

Because, a little voice in her head answered, *you're in love with him.*

Which she was. Truly. Madly. Deeply.

"And, having lost my mother young, I can totally understand that you want to share your wedding day with yours."

"I know it sounds overly sentimental—"

"If you can't be sentimental about a wedding, what can you be sentimental about?"

"True. But I'm a cop."

"You're a woman first," Madeline said. "I used to define myself as a chef. That was all I wanted. Well, except for that summer here in Shelter Bay. When I wanted to be Lucas' wife."

"You were both young."

"So were you when you married Jared."

"Which led to some ups and downs we probably would've gone through even if he hadn't been in the Marines. But that was then." She took a sip of tea and grimaced. "I really miss coffee."

"You're not allowed to have any?" What Madeline knew about pregnancy could be written on the head of a pin and still leave room for a thousand dancing angels.

"Although there weren't any coffee police when I was pregnant with Trey, Sax read that caffeine isn't healthy for the baby, so he's cut me back to a mug a day. The rest of the time I'm stuck with drinking this herbal stuff."

Madeline had to bite her lip to keep from laughing at Kara's obvious frustration. "Let me ask Gram. She can probably mix up some blends you might enjoy."

"One can only hope." Kara sighed, put the cup down, and bit into the German chocolate cupcake.

"You know," Madeline said carefully, "the farm's garden looks gorgeous in early summer. And there's that gazebo that would make a lovely wedding venue."

"I thought you understood my problem."

"I do. But I don't think you're giving your mom enough credit."

"Mom put her entire life on hold for Dad and me. She left a practice she loved, a vibrant city she enjoyed, to settle down here in Shelter Bay because she and Dad believed it was a safe, nurturing place to raise a family. Which, I tend to agree with, and it's why I'm here. But now it's her turn. And I don't want to mess that up. Every time I've come up with a date I think might work, some other great world event happens, so there you go."

"That's not fair," Madeline said. "To you. Or Sax." She reached for her coffee, then seeing Kara's gaze move to it, changed her mind. "Or your mom. She missed your first marriage because you eloped. She missed Trey's birth—"

"Which was solely her choice, because she didn't approve of me getting pregnant while I was still in high school and running off to marry Jared."

"We all make mistakes. Give her a chance to make up for hers. And to share this special time with you."

Kara looked out at the harbor, where a bright red boat was chugging out to take tourists whale watching. Then back at Madeline. "I was class valedictorian."

"I remember."

"Though you were no slouch yourself when it came to grades. But when did you get so much smarter than me?"

Madeline laughed. "Blame it on your hormones and pregnancy brain fog."

"Believe me, I intend to play that card every chance I get for the next eight months." She downed the rest of the tea. "I guess I'd better go apologize to Sax."

"It won't be that hard, since you'll be making him a very happy man."

Kara's wide smile lit up her eyes. Gone was the unhappy, pregnant cop. In her place was a woman bent on seduction. "The man has no idea how happy I'm about to make him."

54

"Where are we going?" Madeline asked as Lucas drove away from the farm. Although she was spending most nights at the cottage, she still hadn't felt ready to move in. Because living together was so close to getting married, she was afraid once she took that step, the next would lead to the altar.

What would be wrong with that? the argumentative voice inside her head that had been getting louder and louder asked.

I'm not ready.

So what are you waiting for?

The sad fact was that she couldn't answer that question. Other than to fall back on the same old one: *I need more time.*

Don't wait too long, the voice warned. *Guys like him don't stay available forever.*

"I know!"

"You know?" He glanced over at her. "Damn. And here I thought I'd planned the perfect surprise."

She was glad for the darkening twilight that kept him from seeing the color flood into her face. "I'm sorry. I wasn't talking about you. I was arguing with myself."

"Who won?"

"I don't know." She sighed. "What kind of surprise?"

Madeline had never enjoyed surprises. They often meant

bad things. Like the teary-eyed nun calling her out of class to Mother Superior's office, where she'd been informed that her parents' plane had crashed. The phone call from Sofia telling that her grandfather had been diagnosed with cancer. Then that later one, letting her know he'd lost the battle. And, of course, the most recent: Maxime's YouTube surprise.

He reached across the space between them and ran his hand down her jeans-clad thigh. He'd told her to dress casually, which suggested it had to do with the outdoors. Logically, she'd told herself, the beach. Maybe they were going to relive their younger days, build a fire, and roast s'mores. The idea of him licking melted chocolate off her fingers—and other parts of her body—caused her hormones to spike.

Sure enough, he pulled up in front of a picnic table she remembered Sax's grandfather having built decades ago. When they'd been kids, they'd hung out here a lot.

"You bought dinner."

"From the Crab Shack," he agreed.

He and Charity's jarhead had gotten far enough in their male bonding that Gabe had assured him that the Dungeness crabs roasted in the shell in butter were the ultimate in seduction dinners. Since he didn't want to know any more about his sister's love life, he hadn't asked for details, but Lucas had always had a good imagination.

"I've been meaning to try his roasted crab," she said. "Charity said it's not to be believed."

Two votes for the buttery crab. Lucas was on a roll.

He'd put the food in a cooler that had both hot and cold insulated sections. A bottle of champagne and two glasses were wrapped in a blanket in his pack. Along with a boom box.

"Are you sure I can't carry anything?"

"I'm a SEAL," he reminded her. "Besides, this is your night to celebrate."

"It was amazing," she said. "Having the divorce come through the same day the network called."

"Maybe," he suggested, as they strolled down the damp sand, side by side, while the tide went out and the moon rose and the lighthouse flashed its bright yellow beam, "we can make it a hat trick."

"That's from sports, right?" Except for soccer, which would have been impossible to ignore while living in Europe, Madeline didn't know much about sports.

"Yeah. It's when a player scores three times in a single game. Here we are."

"Our cave," she said as he stopped in an all-too-familiar place. "I walked past it one morning but couldn't bear to go in."

"I've felt the same way. Which is why I figured it's time to make some new memories."

He took out the blanket and laid it on the sand, along with candles in metal and glass hurricane containers. As soon as he lit them, the walls and ceiling of the cave lit up as if they were made of diamonds. Even knowing that the brilliant chips glittering from the walls were actually quartz, garnet, and fool's gold didn't make the effect any less special.

"It still takes my breath away," she said.

"*You* take my breath away." He stood up from the candle lighting and kissed her. A slow, sweet mingling of lips.

"I promised you dinner," he said, as the kiss and their bodies heated up. "But first . . ."

He got out the boom box. Along with a green box that held a bottle of champagne beautifully embossed with white flowers, and a pair of long-stemmed flutes.

He poured the champagne, handed her a glass, and lifted his in a toast.

"To you. And your freedom."

His smile warmed the cockles of Maddy's heart. "To us."

"Us," he agreed. "Together."

They'd no sooner drunk the toast than he hit a button on the CD player and Heath Ledger's voice began singing. It was the song the actor had sung in *10 Things I Hate about You* to apologize for breaking his girlfriend's heart. The ultimate redemption song from her favorite movie back when she and Lucas were first dating.

"May I have this dance?"

Maddy floated into his arms.

"You're too good to be true," he sang along with the actor, continuing to sing as they swayed while the walls glittered and the sea sighed and a full white moon rose higher in a deep purple night sky.

"I love you, baby." His voice was deep and husky as he echoed the lyrics about needing her to trust him, to warm the lonely nights, and to please stay.

By the time they got to the last *Let me love you, baby,* ending, there was no way on God's green earth she was going to say anything but "Yes. Yes. And Yes!"

As good as they'd been together that first summer, as amazing as their lovemaking had been in Portland, this time was even better.

It was truly as if they'd been created for each other. They fit perfectly. And not just their bodies, but their minds and their hearts.

And when they lay together on the blanket, the candles casting warm light on his gorgeous male body, Maddy—because that's who she'd blissfully become again, having thrown off the workaholic Madeline—thought, *Score!*

55

Maddy was still floating on air as she pulled up in front of Haven House the next morning. As much as she'd wanted to stay in bed with Lucas—they'd moved to his cottage when the night had grown too cool for even them to stay warm—a promise was a promise. And the women living at the shelter had been lied to enough times that she wasn't about to let them down.

She'd brought along her own chef's knives, which had belonged to her parents. Along with several of Sofia's. It was going to be an easy, short lesson covering knife skills.

"Why do we need to know knife skills?" she asked the women who'd gathered in the kitchen.

"So we don't cut off a finger?" one of her students suggested, earning a laugh from a few of the others.

Madeline had known instructors who would have assigned a student to stock duty for such "insubordination," but she'd always thought people should enjoy cooking. And besides, hearing a formerly abused woman being able to make a joke showed what a difference Zelda and the house were making in their lives.

"Basically, it's because we want uniform cooking time," she said. "A large piece of carrot is going to take longer to cook than a smaller one. So if you're sautéing different sizes, your smaller cuts might end up perfectly cooked, but your larger ones underdone. Or, if your larger ones are perfect, your smaller ones will be overcooked. Possibly even burned. Which we don't want.

"And then there's appearance. Unless you're in culinary school, no one's going to take out a ruler and measure your cuts. But uniform pieces just look better on the plate. And whether you're talking about a Big Mac or poached salmon, people first eat with their eyes.

"And, finally, it's about pride and respect. Skilled knife work shows that you take pride in your work. That you respect the food you're preparing. And you respect the people you're cooking for. Not taking shortcuts is telling them that they're worth that extra trouble to get things right."

She could tell from the exchanged glances and nods that pride and respect were important concepts to this group. And no wonder.

She took out some yellow onions she'd asked Ethan Concannon to deliver for her and began with the basic large dice, working her way through the medium, then finally the small. Their concentration was more intense than many of the students she'd worked with at the CIA.

Which had her worrying about why they were working so hard for perfection. It was as if they were seriously afraid of making a mistake.

"Remember," she said casually as she pulled russet potatoes from another bin, "cooking's supposed to be fun. While consistency of cuts is good, even more important is the joy you put into your food. Because, believe me, people can taste it."

She'd felt them beginning to loosen up as they mastered the julienne and allumette, or matchstick cuts. "We'll be having ourselves some French fries today," she said as the potato slices piled up on the counter.

"Okay. Now this next one, chiffonade, is fun. It'll give you really pretty fine strips." She took out basil leaves Sofia had sent along, had them stack the green leaves, then roll each stack into a short bundle.

"The problem with a lot of leaves like mint and basil is they've got this fibrous center stem." The concentration level was still high, but they'd begun to talk among themselves, and she could tell they were enjoying learning something new. Which, she hoped, would help build their self-confidence.

"Okay. Now, carefully cut across the end of the bundles. First on one side up to the stem. Then the other side." She demonstrated, knife blade flashing in the sun streaming through the kitchen window. "Move your blade backward as you cut, so you won't bruise your leaves. Then, voilà." She unrolled two perfectly cut ribbon strips.

She was just about to suggest they try it themselves when the door suddenly swung open.

And a man, holding an ashen-faced Zelda around the neck, pushed his way into the kitchen.

Eyes as cold as ice swept the room, landing on Phoebe, who went as pale as white rice and grabbed hold of the counter, as to keep herself from crumbling to the tile floor.

"Hello, Stephanie, darling," he said in a pleasant voice that was a direct contrast to the murder in his eyes. "I've come to take you home."

56

Amazingly, no one screamed. No one fainted. The kitchen, which only a moment ago had been filled with happy chatter, became as silent as a tomb. Apparently, he'd warned Zelda not to say anything, because although her eyes were as wide as the Spode saucers on the open shelf, she remained silent, as well.

"Excuse me, but I must ask you to leave," Maddy said, using the I'm-the-boss-here tone she might with a careless saucier. "You're interrupting the class."

"I'll leave," he agreed. "With my wife."

"I'm sorry." Maddy's fingers tightened around the handle of her knife. "But I'm not going to let you take her."

"She's my property. And I'm not leaving without her," he said reasonably.

There was only one of him. And many of them. But the ugly gun he was holding in his free hand gave him the power in this situation.

"I'll go," Phoebe said, slowly untying the blue chef's apron Maddy had bought all the women the first day of lessons. The color represented apprentices in French restaurants, but Thomas Keller had all his chefs wear them during prep work at his French Laundry in Napa Valley, to remind them all that every chef should always be learning.

"No." Zelda found her voice. "You can't put yourself back in that situation, dear."

"Shut up," he told the elderly woman. "Here's what we'll do," he said again with a calmness that Maddy found more chilling than the loudest shout. "I'll shoot each one of you. Beginning with this skinny old one."

He shoved Zelda to the floor and stood over her, pointing the barrel of the gun at her leg. Her still-strong dancer's leg.

"I'll continue until my wife leaves with me."

"What's to prevent someone from calling the police while you're shooting me?" Zelda asked.

"Simple." If a rattlesnake could smile, it would look exactly like this man. "This is a high-capacity Glock magazine. It holds thirty-three shells." His gaze swept the room. "Which is enough to shoot every one of you bitches more than once."

"Please, Peter." Phoebe's voice trembled. "Don't hurt anyone."

"Oh, I intended to hurt someone," he said. For the first time, Madeline caught a hint of monster in his voice. Directed at his wife. "And we both know who that's going to be. You've been a very bad girl, Steph. And you know what happens to bad girls."

"I know. And I also know that I deserve whatever punishment you decide." Her head low, shoulders slumped, she began to make her way around the kitchen island, looking much more the emotionally traumatized woman she'd been when she'd first arrived at Haven House.

But appearances, as so often happen, proved deceiving. As she reached her husband, she suddenly threw the apron over his head.

"What the hell?" His surprised shout was muffled by the apron Phoebe was still holding on to for dear life.

At the same time, one of the other women picked up a heavy iron skillet and slammed it against the back of his head.

Which was when he dropped the gun.

He and Maddy dove for it at the same time, but he was at a disadvantage because he was still fighting Phoebe, who was trying to keep the apron over his head while the other women began raining pots and pans down on him. When none of them knocked him unconscious, they began kicking him while he was crawling on the floor, still fighting for the gun.

"No knives!" Maddy shouted a warning. She understood why many of the women in the room would want to kill this man who'd destroyed the peace of their shelter. But the last thing she wanted was for any of them to end up in prison.

Just as a small sauté pan ricocheted off her shoulder, she managed to get her hands on the gun. And although she'd never held a weapon in her life and her hands were shaking from fear and adrenaline, she stood up and pointed it down at him.

"Someone call nine-one-one," she said, her voice as unsteady as her hands. "And you," she looked down at the man who didn't seem nearly as threatening now that he was cowering on the floor with his hands over his head. "Don't move."

One of the women ran over to Zelda and reached down to help her get back on her feet. Which she did, but not before placing a well-aimed kick between his legs, which caused him to curl up in a fetal position and scream.

No one said a word as they stood there, breathing heavily from their short, intense battle, watching him.

Then one, a young blonde whose accent had given away Southern roots, began to clap. Which was followed by another. And a third.

When Kara, who'd made it to the house in less than three minutes, burst into the kitchen, her own weapon drawn and ready, she found Maddy holding a Glock on a guy who definitely looked worse for wear, and an entire room of women applauding.

"God." She holstered her gun and took the one Maddy offered. "Sometimes I really, really love my job."

57

"I still can't believe I almost lost you." Amazingly, Lucas was trembling as much as Maddy had been when she'd been holding that gun on Phoebe's husband.

"Wasn't going to happen," she said, nestling against him as they waited on the blue wooden bench outside the police station for her to make her statement. The station was so small and there were so many witnesses to the attempted kidnapping that not all the women could fit inside at the same time. "We had woman power going for us."

"Yeah." He lifted her hand and pressed his lips to the inside of her wrist. "The only problem is, you forgot to wear your Wonder Woman magic bracelets today."

She laughed at that. Basked in his strength. His love. "You should have seen those women," she said. "They were tigresses."

"Fighting to protect one of their own." He moved on to kissing her fingertips one at a time. "I know the feeling."

He would, of course. The same way he'd known how easily life could be snuffed out in an instant. Something she'd discovered for herself today. Which is why she'd decided that they'd waited long enough.

"There's something I need to say—"

"And I want to hear it. But first I want you to hear me out."

"All right."

"My heart stopped when you called to tell me what happened," he said, placing his free hand over his chest, as if to prove his point. "It didn't skip. It didn't jump. I swear, it flat-out stopped. And in that drawn-out second before it began beating again, I realized that if anything had happened to you, I would've wanted it to stay stopped. . . .

"And here's the deal. I understand your need to be cautious. To not make the same mistake you did with the Frenchman. But I'm not your mistake, Maddy. I'm your forever-after love. The same way you're mine.

"So, rather than spend the next ten years arguing about when you're going to just give in and agree to spend the rest of our lives together, I have a challenge for you."

"A challenge?" This was definitely not what she'd been expecting. Hadn't she already had enough challenges for one day?

"More like a throw-down."

"A throw-down," she echoed.

"Yeah. Like that guy does on TV. You know, where he goes and tries to outcook some other cook."

"*Throwdown with Bobby Flay*," she said, realizing the popular show he was talking about. "You, who eats Pop-Tarts and doesn't even know how to operate a can opener, are challenging me to a throw-down?"

"That's about it," he agreed. "If you win—"

"Which I will." She could outcook this man blindfolded and with one hand tied behind her back.

"Don't be so sure. You are, sweetheart, looking at one motivated SEAL on a mission, and one of the things we have drilled into us in BUD/S training is that failure is not an option. However, if, by any chance, you win, I'll shut up and wait for you to realize what you're missing out on.

"But if I win, we get married. You can pick the place, but you've got a week after the throw-down to do whatever wedding planning you need to do, because that's as long as

I'm willing to wait to claim my prize." He flashed her a wicked grin. "Which would be you, Chef Maddy."

"You do realize that's an outrageously chauvinistic statement."

"You do realize that right now, I don't really give a flying fuck."

Madeline could tell by the set of his jaw, by the F word, which he seldom used, and by the determination in his dark eyes, that he was just as serious as he'd ever been in battle. But the irony of their once again mismatched timing made her laugh. She'd been about to tell him, if he hadn't interrupted her, that she wanted to marry him as soon as possible.

"Bring it on," she said.

58

Maddy might be a professionally trained chef who'd cooked in European kitchens. She might be a celebrity with cookbooks and TV shows and legions of fans.

But she was not a SEAL.

Which was why Lucas had not a single doubt that he'd accomplish his mission.

He started with Bon Temps.

"Skip the beer," he said when Sax pulled a bottle out of the cooler as he walked in the door.

"Want something else?"

"Yeah. I want you to teach me to cook."

Lucas wasn't all that surprised when Sax laughed.

"I'm serious," Lucas said. "I need to know how to cook. And not just cook. But I need to outcook Maddy in a throw-down."

Sax rubbed a cheek stubbled with a late-afternoon beard. "How long do we have?"

"Three days."

"You're shitting me."

"I'm as serious as a heart attack."

"Remember that night we dragged Shane up the mountain, half-dead, into Pakistan?" Sax asked.

"Like I'd forget that," Lucas said impatiently. "Why bring it up now?"

"Because teaching you to cook better than Maddy is going to make that look like a Sunday stroll in the park."

Lucas set his jaw. "Then let's quit wasting time and get started. Give me a grocery list, because I have to go out to Concannon's farm. No way am I going to lose points for not going organic."

"Okay." Sax thought for a moment. "She'll be expecting you to go Cajun, 'cause she knows I'd be the first person you'd come to."

"That would be my guess."

"She'd also probably expect you to use some sort of seafood, since that's all the stuff from here you've got in the cottage fridge."

"Maybe because it's what I always order."

"So she'll be preparing her strategy around that. The thing to do is throw her a curveball. Do exactly the opposite of what she's expecting. Which is what we SEALs do best."

"Roger that."

"We'll go ahead with with Cajun, but switch out the fish for stuffed pork chops. Concannon's got great pork. You can serve it with some dirty rice, and, I'd say, just maybe you stand half a chance of not embarrassing yourself by getting your ass kicked too bad."

He scribbled down the shopping list.

Lucas snatched it from his hand. "I'll be back."

"Well," Sax said, as he turned the sign to CLOSED after Lucas marched out the door like a guy going into battle, which he sort of was. "This could prove interesting."

His next stop was to Lavender Hill Farm. Fortunately, Maddy, who'd decided to stay at the farm during the throwdown preparations—undoubtedly to keep her menu a secret—had already left for Concannon's. He only hoped she didn't take all the guy's pork chops. Although he tried to get Sofia to give him a hint as to what his opponent was planning to prepare, either the older woman didn't know, or was trying to stay neutral.

"I need a soup," he said. "Something that'll go with a hot Cajun dish."

"What color is your dish going to be?"

Lucas gave her a blank look. Color? Now he had to think about that? "I didn't ask Sax. Maybe pork-colored?"

She shook her head. "I'll say a little prayer to St. Jude for you," she offered. "He's the patron saint of impossible causes."

"Thanks. But I just need a soup recipe."

"There's nothing prettier than a spring pea soup," she offered. "It's not very difficult, peas go with anything, and you can cool down the heat of the Cajun pork with a bit of crème fraîche or yogurt and crouton garnish."

"Make it yogurt," he said. "I don't even know what that other stuff is."

"Yogurt it is," she agreed. "Ethan's peas probably won't be ready to pick yet, but you're fortunate. I have some in my greenhouse."

He reached across the counter, where she was writing down the recipe for him, framed her weathered face in his hands, and kissed her. Right on the lips.

"Well," she said, blushing just a bit. "Apparently, it's true. That the way to a man's heart *is* through his stomach."

"You've had mine since the spaghetti and meatballs you fed me when I was a kid," he said. "And I would've come to you for the main course, but I figured this is enemy territory. Maddy could cook Italian in her sleep. So I've got to come up with a surprise strategy."

"Well, I should be neutral," she said. "But in case it'll help your confidence, I put ten dollars on you in the town pool."

That was fast. Though he wasn't surprised. News had always spread like wildfire through Shelter Bay. Partially due to the owner of the market, who'd probably been burning up telephone wires all over town.

"Sofia De Luca," he said, "if I weren't going to marry your granddaughter, you'd definitely be my first choice."

He kissed her again, this time on the cheek, and headed off to the farm.

"I've been wondering if you were going to show up," Sedona Sullivan told Lucas as he walked into Take the Cake and introduced himself the next morning. "I'm honored to be included. I suppose you want to know how to make cupcakes?"

"Too easy," he said. Then cringed. "I didn't mean *baking* them was too easy. Because you've obviously got it down to an art. But I want something Maddy's not expecting. Something that'll knock the judges' socks off."

"Well, that's quite a challenge."

"That's why I've come to you. You're a risk taker. You gave up that cushy, big-money CPA career to open a cupcake shop in a small coastal town. Not many people would do that. But you did, and you made it work. So, give me something outside the box. Because I intend to win this."

"Well, then, we'll have to see that you do," she said. "How do you feel about setting something on fire?"

Hoo-yah! "It's one of the things SEALs do best."

"Okay. We'll go for bananas flambé over vanilla bean ice cream. It's easy peasy. And a showstopper."

"That's what I need." He grinned. "I owe you."

"Hey, I'm only doing my patriotic duty. Besides, you falling back in love with Maddy saved me from suffering through Charity's embarrassing set-up barbecue."

Damn. He hadn't realized she even knew about that. "It wasn't anything personal," he assured her.

"I didn't take it that way. I'm probably a bit more New Agey than some people, having grown up on a commune, but I'm a total believer in fate. When I'm supposed to meet Mr. Right, it'll happen."

She was one of the prettiest women Lucas had ever seen. Not glamorous-movie-star pretty. More girl next door. And the best thing was that she was every bit as nice as Charity and Sax had both told him she was. "He's going to be one lucky guy."

Her smile was wide and filled with laughter. "You know it."

59

The day of the throw-down dawned bright and sunny, which was fortunate, because it allowed what appeared to be half the town to show up at Lavender Hill Farm to watch the event held on the back lawn.

Chairs from a rental shop in Depoe Bay had been brought in for spectators and a table draped in purple linen set up for the judges—Anne Taylor, chef of the Sea Mist; Jill Stevens, a cookbook author who'd driven up from Newport; and Dan Kenyon, a chef who'd won accolades at his Portland restaurant and who'd recently opened up a place overlooking the mouth of the Columbia River in Astoria.

Although Maddy had refused to let her producer at the Cooking Network tape the show—she didn't want to embarrass Lucas on national television—she had called and asked her to choose the panel, to assure everyone that the voting would be fair.

Adding icing to the metaphorical cake, Pepper surprised her by arriving at the farm earlier that morning, a visit she'd apparently arranged behind Maddy's back with Sofia.

"How long are you intending to stay?" Maddy asked.

"I was planning to leave right after I made sure you weren't making a mistake. But after meeting your way-hot Navy SEAL, I can understand why you don't want to return to New York."

"Lucas is special. And definitely one of a kind." He was also, amazingly, wonderfully, hers.

"Well, any woman could tell that. But it's the way he looks at you when he thinks no one's looking that won me over. Well done, Madeline." Her glance skimmed over the gathered crowd. "I also had a brief chat with that sexy Paul Newman look-alike."

"Flynn McGrath."

"That's him. I've never been much for stockbrokers, since you can't throw a rock anywhere in Manhattan without hitting one, and an affair with an artist is a bit of a cliché, but there is definitely something to be said for a man who works with his hands."

"His wood work is fabulous."

"So he told me, with an appealing, studly swagger." Her gaze found the subject of their conversation. As their eyes met, Maddy could almost hear the sizzle. "You know, it's been a very long time since I took any time off. Now that the contract for your new program is wrapped up, we've gotten you out of the pots-and-pans business and turned down the airline-food deal, and my hunky astronaut has signed on to be the new Bachelor, it's not that I have any pressing business to attend to. So I may just extend my visit a few days."

Basking in the glow of a love that she'd thought had been lost forever, and wanting everyone to be as happy as she was right now, Maddy smiled at the idea of her high-powered agent and a man who'd given up the fast track to create stunning wooden art.

Varying from the concept of the popular television program, both Maddy and Lucas were responsible for a three-course menu they'd been allowed to choose themselves. Maddy knew that Sofia had helped Lucas with his soup, so wasn't at all surprised he'd gone with a spring pea. The color, the ease, and the taste, which would suit just about any dish, made it a wise choice and something he probably could pull off well.

If he didn't scorch it on the gas burners that had been set up in the middle of the yard.

The stuffed pork chops were a surprise. Especially since they weren't on the Bon Temps menu. But she couldn't imagine even someone who knew what he was doing being able to beat her braised chicken legs with garlic and onion on mashed potatoes. Although it wasn't a difficult dish—which is undoubtedly why Lucas' godfather's wife had been able to prepare it so well for their dinner in Portland—being able to achieve such flavor with so few ingredients was part of what made it so special.

Although she knew it was a bit cliché, she'd chosen a raspberry crème brûlée, and had to laugh when she saw that both of them were using flame for their final course. Though, naturally, Lucas, being a SEAL, was going to set his entire pan on fire, rather than use a torch to delicately brown the sugar atop the custard.

Since it wasn't like the television throw-down, with the entire event appearing as if it took place within thirty minutes, with time out for commercials, Sax's parents, former musicians who'd performed at Bon Temps for years, had agreed to entertain the crowd during the cooking. Sax had also rounded up some Irish step dancers and fiddlers from Corvallis who performed at Bon Temps during his weekly Celtic nights.

Everyone showed up looking as if they were prepared for a good time.

Everyone except the man who'd issued the throw-down challenge in the first place. Lucas' stone face and flinty eyes were that of a man going into battle.

Lucas had to give Maddy points for the damn tortilla soup. Hell, even he'd rather eat Mexican than peas. It also was a lot more complicated than the recipe Sofia had given him.

But he did manage to blend the soup without having it blow off the blender's lid, the way it had the first time he'd tried it under the older woman's supervision. Although he wasn't one for nuances, it tasted great and even he could see it was pretty.

He actually thought he might have her a bit on the pork chops. He never would have thought of stuffing a pork chop. Especially with ground pork, which seemed redundant, but when he'd made it with Sax, somehow, mixed with the cayenne, garlic, pepper, paprika, and green onions, it worked. Really, really well.

A bonus was that while she was braising her chicken legs, which, admittedly, smelled insane, he was able to grill the chops. He might not be able to cook, but, hey, what guy hadn't thrown a burger or steak on a grill?

Her fancy custard with the top she'd turned all crunchy with that blowtorch looked like something that you might find in one of the Frenchman's chichi restaurants. But Lucas knew he had the crowd on his side when they applauded after he tossed that cognac into his pan and the flames exploded, making him glad he'd decided to leave Scout at Charity's for the day.

And then it was time.

The judges did not appear to be taking this nearly as lightly as the spectators. Their expressions, as they tasted their way through the courses, remained as sober as . . . well, judges.

As he'd expected, Maddy's tortilla soup won the first round for complexity and blending of flavors. But they said all good things about his, and even complimented him on the toasted butter crouton on top with the yogurt, which he figured said a lot for a guy who, although knowing his way around a can opener, had never known a kitchen mandoline existed until Maddy had pulled one out like a gunfighter pulling a Colt revolver out of her holster at high noon.

At first he was worried when the two women judges nearly had an orgasm over Maddy's damn chicken legs. It was chicken, for Pete's sake. How could it beat a grilled pork chop?

They praised his ingenuity in the stuffing, said lots of fancy culinary stuff about heat and texture and the marriage of flavors in the filling and the pepper rub. Which wasn't the kind of marriage he was going for here, but he figured it was all good.

They all agreed that the glaze created by the barbecue sauce during the last fifteen minutes of grilling was pretty. And they praised the dirty rice. Then—hoo-yah!—gave that round to him.

Sax flashed him a thumbs-up. Even Maddy smiled at him and asked for the recipe, proving herself a graceful loser.

They were down to the final round.

This time Lucas' dish was first. Although they did praise his showmanship, which was, after all, the freaking point, and said the hot bananas over the vanilla ice cream were delicious, the cookbook author worried about the calorie count from all the butter and brown sugar.

It's dessert, he wanted to tell her. *A special treat. Not something you eat every damn day.*

But he smiled and thanked her for her comments, as both Sofia and Sedona had instructed him to do.

As the crème brûlée in its pretty white dish was set in front of the judges, the yard became unnaturally quiet. It was, Lucas thought, as if every single person there were holding his or her breath.

They were not alone.

He remembered the ceremony when he'd received his SEAL pin. His father had flown down to San Diego, and Lucas had to keep reminding himself, as he'd stood proudly at attention, not to lock his knees or he'd pass out.

That was the last time, until now, that he'd been afraid of

losing consciousness without having had something come crashing down on his helmet, which occasionally had happened in his former line of work.

All three judges cracked the caramelized top and dug in. Then exchanged puzzled glances.

Which, in turn, had all the spectators looking at one another, curious about what was obviously perplexing the judges. The guy from Astoria dug deeper and took another taste of the creamy custard. Then put his head together with the other two while they conferred.

And everyone at Lavender Hill Farm waited.

Finally, the chef from the Sea Mist, who'd seemed the nicest of the trio, asked Maddy, "Did you taste the custard before you flamed the topping?"

"No," Maddy admitted. "Time was running out, and I've made this dish so many times before. . . ."

"You should have," the cookbook author, whose face had wrinkled up like a prune at her first taste, chided. If she'd been a guy, Lucas would've wanted to punch her for the tone she used with Maddy.

"Definitely," the chef from Astoria said. "Then you wouldn't have made that mistake."

"Mistake?" Maddy appeared surprised by the suggestion.

"Perhaps you'd better take a taste yourself," the Sea Mist chef suggested. Asking for a fresh spoon, she held the dish out to Maddy, who approached the judges' table and took a bite. And immediately shook her head. "I can't believe it."

"You mistook salt for sugar," Astoria Guy said.

"Something we've all done," Anne Taylor, the kinder, local chef, soothed.

Damn. He hadn't wanted to win by default. Not by Maddy making what even he figured was a pretty boneheaded mistake. Especially since she'd told him she'd already done the same thing before.

Suspicion stirred.

He shot her a sharp look, but she only returned an innocent one in return.

The crowd went wild as the cookbook author announced him as the winner. Everyone was shaking his hand and patting him on the back and telling him they knew he could do it. *Yeah, right.* The last he'd heard, the odds had been ninety-eight percent in Maddy's favor.

But he didn't care about the judges, whom he did somehow manage to thank. He didn't care about the betting that had been going on. Or all the people wanting to congratulate him. He thanked Sax, exchanging a guy hug, then moved on to Sofia and Sedona.

Then made his way through the crowd, which parted, to Maddy.

His Maddy.

"Congratulations," she said.

"I had a lot of help." More than he'd counted on. He held out a hand. "Now let's go home."

"We do have a wedding to plan," she agreed.

Much, much later, as they lay amid the tangled sheets on the bed—with Scout, whom they'd picked up on the way to the cottage, snoring from the other room—Lucas looked down into that lovely face he'd never been able to put out of his mind and said, "You threw that dessert round. Didn't you?"

Her answering smile lit up her eyes and her entire face. No one had ever looked at him with such a wealth of love, making him feel like the richest guy on the planet. "If you knew more about the culinary world, you'd know a good chef never gives away all her secrets."

"You made that mistake on the French tarts," he reminded her. "And even got fired for it. You'd never screw it up again. So just admit it. You threw the throw-down."

"Why don't you ask me again?" She laughed as she lifted her lips to his. "On our fiftieth anniversary?"

Read on for a peek at the next book in the
Shelter Bay series,

MOONSHELL BEACH

Belying the song lyrics about it never raining in California, a dark gray sky was weeping onto the black Suburban's windshield as Marine Captain J. T. Douchett drove through rain-slicked streets to carry out his mission. A mission he'd been catapulted into a year ago. A mission without weapons, which, given that every Marine was a rifleman, was not one he'd prepared for at Officer Candidates School, the War College, or even during years of combat.

The rain was appropriate, he thought wearily as he pulled into the parking lot of a Denny's restaurant. As tough as this assignment was, it always seemed a lot worse when a benevolent sun was shining and birds were singing.

The drizzle reminded him of home. Back in Shelter Bay, his father and brother Cole would've already gone out on their fishing boat. Maybe his grandfather, who often missed his days at sea, would have gone with them. The small coastal town would be coming to life—shopkeepers down on Harborview Drive would be opening their doors and lowering their bright awnings; beachcombers would be walking at the edge of the surf, gathering shells and agates; locals would be sitting around tables at the Grateful Bread, enjoying French toast and gossip while tourists lined up at the pier to go whale watching.

Memories of his hometown not only comforted him, they reminded him of his family, which drove home the significance of this mission for which he definitely never, in a million years, would have volunteered.

But the first thing J.T. had learned at OCS was that every Marine was part of a larger picture. And the tradition of "Leave no Marine behind" was a sacred promise that went beyond the battlefield.

He and his passenger, a staff sergeant who, despite years of marching cadences still had the slightly bowed legs of a man who'd grown up riding horses in Abilene, retrieved their garment bags from the backseat. They entered the restaurant, walking past the tables to the men's room, where they changed from their civilian clothes into high-necked dark blue jackets, dark blue pants with a blood-red stripe down the outside of each leg, and shoes spit-polished to a mirror gloss.

Although he could feel every eye in the place on them, J.T. put on a focused but distant stare and glanced neither left nor right as he walked straight back to the Suburban. Neither man spoke. There was no need. They'd been through this before. And it never got any easier, so why talk about it?

After being waved through Camp Pendleton's main gate, passing a golf course, a McDonald's, a Taco Bell, and a veterinarian's clinic on the way to his destination, it occurred to J.T. how appearances could be deceiving.

The tree-lined streets he drove through, set on hillsides behind a lake shadowed by fog, with their manicured lawns and children's play park, portrayed a sense of tranquility. It could, he thought as he turned onto Marine Drive, be any one of a million suburban neighborhoods scattered across the country.

What made his destination different from most was that these tile-roofed, beige stucco houses were home to warriors. Another reason he was grateful for the rain. On a sunny day, more people would be outside, and the sight of the black SUV carrying two Marines wearing dress blues would set off alarms that would spread like wildfire.

J.T. leaned forward, trying to read the house numbers through the slanting rain. He could have used the GPS, but found the computerized female voice a distraction in situations like these.

The house was located at the end of a cul-de-sac. A white Ford Escape with a child's car seat in the back was parked in the driveway. A bumper sticker on the small SUV read MY HEART BELONGS TO A U.S. MARINE.

Exchanging a look with the sergeant, J.T. pulled on his white cotton gloves and climbed out of the Suburban. The heels of his shiny shoes clicked on the concrete sidewalk.

A pot of red geraniums on the small covered porch added a bright spot to the gray day. A blue star flag, signifying a deployed family member, hung in the side window.

J.T. took a deep breath. He knew the sergeant standing beside him would be saying a prayer. Wishing he still possessed such faith, J.T. found his own peace by envisioning himself back home. The remembered tang of Douglas fir trees and brisk, salt-tinged sea air cleared his head.

Although he'd rather be back in Afghanistan, facing a horde of Taliban than be standing at this front door on this rainy California day, J.T. squared his shoulders and braced himself as he reached out a gloved hand to ring the bell and shatter yet another woman's heart.

Shelter Bay, Oregon
Nine months later

It wasn't the same. J.T. wondered why he even thought it could be. Shelter Bay hadn't changed. But *he* had.

Giving up on sleep, he crawled out of the rack at dawn and ran out of town to the coast, boots pounding the empty streets, across the bridge, and along the hard-packed sand at the ocean's edge. He didn't run for physical fitness, or to achieve any elusive runner's high. The truth was, he was out in the morning fog, as he'd been every day since returning home, trying to wipe out the memories that ran like an unending video loop in his head. Even as he feared they'd always be with him, J.T. continued to run. And run. And run.

Arriving back in town, he passed the blue and white welcome sign, announcing that the sleepy Oregon coastal town he once couldn't wait to escape was not only the Pacific Northwest's whale watching capital, but home to Navy Cross recipient Sax Douchett.

Knowing how his former SEAL brother hated that hero tag, J.T. suspected that Sax cringed every time he was forced to drive past the sign.

Another sign he ran past was yet more proof that while *J.T.* may have changed during the dozen-plus years he'd been away, not much else had. The Rotary Club continued to meet on Tuesdays at the Sea Mist restaurant, the historical society on the first Thursday of every month at the museum, and summer concerts were still held on Sunday afternoons at Evergreen Park.

Although the calendar might say summer, a cool, misty rain blowing in from the Pacific had followed him, dampening his hair and brown T-shirt as he ran along Harborview Drive.

Again, everything looked nearly the same as it had when he'd left town in search of adventure. It was high tourist season, and although it was still early and wet, people were out in full force, crowding the sidewalks as they shopped in quaint little galleries and souvenir shops, standing shoulder to shoulder at the seawall taking photos of the sea lions lounging on the docks, and watching with binoculars for the resident whales that made Shelter Bay their home.

A fat orange cat lounged in the window of Tidal Wave Books next to a stack of Gabriel St. James' new photo book. The former jarhead (not that there was really any such thing as a *former* Marine), was J.T.'s brother Cole's best friend. While in Shelter Bay for Cole's wedding— which J.T., who'd been in Afghanistan at the time, had missed—St. James had fallen in love with a local veterinarian and stayed here.

When he went inside to buy a copy of the book, the friendly store owner chatted away as she rang up the sale. But although he could see her lips moving, J.T. couldn't hear a word she said over the roaring that was like surf in his ears as another memory flashed through his mind.

When a pregnant wife had asked to spend the night before her husband's funeral next to the flag-draped casket, J.T. had sneaked her into the funeral home. Not wanting her to have to sleep on the hard tile floor, he'd gone to Walmart for an air mattress, pillow, and sheets. Until he'd stood in the aisle, he'd never realized sheets came in so many damn colors. Since women liked flowers, he'd grabbed the ones with roses, which she'd seemed to appreciate.

Marine notification officers stayed with families for as long as was needed, which meant visiting the woman at the hospital after she'd given birth. While showing off the baby boy who'd never know his father, she'd confessed that her dead husband sometimes still visited her at night and they'd make love.

When he'd been ten years old, his family had taken a vacation road trip that had included a visit to Little Big Horn Battlefield National Monument. Having felt the lingering warrior spirits, J.T. wasn't about to discount her story of the ghostly visits. In fact, as he accepted the white bag with the blue wave and store name on it, he wondered if perhaps he was turning into a ghost himself. If the bookstore owner reached out to touch him, would her hand go right through his body?

Since that memory made him thirsty, on the way back to Bon Temps, his brother Sax's Cajun restaurant, where he'd been staying in the office, J.T. dropped into the VFW hall. The heads of various game animals still hung on knotty pine walls while a snarling grizzly continued to stand over a jukebox that offered up mostly country.

While Trace Adkin's rumbling baritone sang about a soldier who'd died and met up with his grandfather, who was also buried at Arlington National Cemetery, J.T. put the bookstore bag on the peanut shell–covered floor and took a stool. "I'll have a Bud."

The bartender, who'd shot the bear during R & R after participating in Operation Just Cause in Panama, lifted a brow. "Little early, isn't it?"

"Since when did Navy frogmen become the beer police?"

"Just saying . . ." The former SEAL twisted off the cap and put the bottle on the ancient bar, which had been carved with initials and symbols of various units going back to World War II.

"Well, don't."

The ice-cold beer went down smooth and took the edge off the hangover that had continued to linger during his run. After polishing it off, he tossed some bills on the counter, picked up the book, and left. He did not say good-bye. Neither did the SEAL.

Maybe he'd turned as invisible as he felt.

Or maybe not.

"Where the hell have you been?" his brother Sax demanded when J.T. walked in the door at Bon Temps and found both his brothers waiting for him.

He tossed the bag onto a table. "And that's any of your business why?"

"Because you're our baby brother," Cole, the eldest, said.

"I haven't been a *baby* for a helluva long time. And where I go and what I do isn't any of your damn business." He went behind the bar and pulled a bottle of Full Sail IPA out of the cooler.

"That's what you think." Sax snatched the bottle away before he could open it. "Everyone's been walking on eggshells around you, waiting for you to settle back in. But it's been six weeks of your drinking up my profits, and you're still spooking everyone in town—"

"Not to mention worrying Mom and Dad sick," Cole broke in.

J.T. thrust out his jaw when he wanted to lower his head in shame at that unwelcome news. "Low blow, bro." He rubbed his stubbled face, trying to remember how long it had been since he'd shaved.

Sax heaved a long, weary sigh. Raked his hands through his hair. "Look, we both know it's not easy."

"I had nightmares," Cole volunteered. "Once I even grabbed Kelli by the throat while we were sleeping. Scared her nearly to death."

"And I had ghosts," Sax said. "Not just memories, but real ones who talked to me and followed me around for a while. Which, by the way, no one but Kara, Cole, and now you know about, and I'd like to keep it that way. But, like I said, we understand. So if you've got PTSD issues, we're here to help you get help. Before things get worse."

"Thanks. But I don't have PTSD." He'd read all the symptoms and none of them had said anything about becoming a ghost himself. "And I don't need any stupid intervention."

He was just exhausted. And weighted down with a deep-to-the-bone sadness he couldn't shake off.

When he tried to snatch the bottle back, Sax moved it out of reach.

Frustrated by this entire situation, J.T. lunged.

Sax dodged, threw down the beer and connected with a strong left hook to the chin that caused bells to ring inside J.T.'s throbbing head. Which didn't stop him from jumping on Sax.

"Trust a damn SEAL frogman not to fight fair," he said as he took another blow that had him staggering. As his knees buckled, he dragged Sax down to the floor, where they rolled, fists flying, elbows swinging.

Cursing like the Marine he was, Cole grabbed J.T. by the shirt and jerked him to his feet. "That's enough."

"The hell it is." At least he wasn't feeling dead anymore. Every atom in J.T.'s body was in battle alert mode. "He never would've gotten that first hit in if he hadn't cheated and if I'd been totally sober."

"Oh, we can take care of that problem," Cole said. He grabbed J.T. under the arms. "You take the kid's legs," he told Sax. "A swim should sober him up quick enough."

He'd definitely lost his edge. There'd been a time when it would've taken a helluva lot more than two guys to pick him off his feet.

J.T. cursed and kicked as they carried him out the door and unceremoniously threw him into the bay, which was cold enough to have his balls going up into his throat.

He had just sputtered to the surface, determined to take them both on, when he saw Sax's fiancée standing on the dock.

"I thought you boys would've outgrown this stupidity by now," she said.

"He started it," both Sax and J.T. said at the same time.

She looked up at the drizzling sky as if seeking patience.

"Pitiful," she muttered. "You'd think three grown men, one of whom is about to become a father"—she shot a hard look at Sax—"would have better things to do than get into brawls. Want to give me one reason why I shouldn't run you all in for disturbing the peace?"

"We were only trying to sober the kid up," Sax said, sounding, J.T. thought, uncharacteristically chastened.

"That's another thing." She turned to J.T. "You've been drunk for six weeks."

"Not drunk ... merely not entirely sober," he said, amending his statement when she gave the cop stare he imagined she used on perps when trying to get them to confess. Which, in this town, where nothing exciting ever happened, probably involved teenagers bashing mailboxes or spraying grafitti on the water tower. He boosted himself out of the water and onto the dock. "And I haven't been driving."

"I know. I've received reports. You're starting to scare tourists, the way you're constantly running around in those combat boots."

"I couldn't run if I were that drunk." Though standing upright on the floating, bobbing dock wasn't as easy as it should have been.

She shook her head. "You know the trouble with you, J. T. Douchett?"

"No." But he had no doubt the former Shelter Bay High School valedictorian was about to tell him.

"You need something worthwhile to do with your time." Her tone suggested she didn't consider running and drinking worthwhile pursuits. "And fortunately for all of us, the solution just came to me."

"What?"

"You may not have read the flyers tacked up all around town, but Shelter Bay's holding its first film festival. And none other than Mary Joyce is going to be the guest of honor."

"Good for Shelter Bay. And who's Mary Joyce?"

"Jeez," Sax said. "What planet did the Marines assign you to for the past three years?"

"I've been a bit occupied."

"She's only the hottest actress in Hollywood," Cole said.

"She's an Irish movie star who plays the queen of the selkies in a blockbuster series," Kara added.

"And a selkie is?"

"A seal woman," Sax said, his tone thick with disgust at having such an apparently boneheaded brother. "You know, like a mermaid."

"But hotter," Cole said.

"I'll refrain from telling your wife that you keep coming back to that," Kara said dryly. "Anyway," she said to J.T., "she's also acquired a crazy following of fans who dress up like selkies and reenact scenes. I'm assured they're harmless, but since my department doesn't have the manpower to handle additional security, I'm deputizing you to act as her bodyguard and keep them at bay with that hard, mean stare they teach all you Marines in basic training."

"No way."

"Way." She folded her arms across the front of her starched khaki shirt. "Trust me, J.T.—you may have been a big bad Marine, but do you really want to mess with a hormonal, pregnant sheriff who's armed and carries her own handcuffs?"

"Plus, there's the fact that if you upset my woman, *I'll* have to shoot you," Sax warned on something close to a growl. Although J.T. didn't believe for a minute his brother would follow through on the threat, he thought back again on that pregnant woman he'd bought the sheets for and felt his resolve crumbling.

"Well," she asked. "Do I hear a volunteer?"

Damn. He'd had drill instructors who weren't as tough as Sheriff Kara Conway. Knowing when he was outnumbered, J.T. managed, just barely, to stand at attention. Then snapped a salute. "Aye, aye, ma'am."